D1752834

Chaos Destiny
Sacrifice for peace or live a life in chaos

Mussie Haile

Copyright © Mussie Haile 2021
1.Edition, digital edition published 2021

Self-published through -
Print on demand: Ingramspark, Amazon
Mussie Haile, Ohmstr. 52, 60486 Frankfurt am Main

ISBN Paperback 978-3-949553-00-4
ISBN Hardcover 978-3-949553-01-1
ISBN e-Book   978-3-949553-02-8

A catalogue copy of this book is available from the German National Library. Details are available online under http://dnb.d-nb.de.

Mussie Haile asserts the moral right to be identified as the author of this work.

Map by Rob Donovan
Cover by Pantelis Politakos
Interior Book Design by Ksenia Siziakova, Kevin Peake
Editing John Gund, Ian O Reilly

This book is a work of fiction, and any resemblance to people or institutions, whether living, deceased or otherwise still shambling is entirely coincidental.

All rights reserved. No part of this book may be reproduced in any form by any electronic or mechanical means, including information storage and retrieval systems (except for the us of brief quotations in a book review), if you would like permission to use material from the book please contact mussiehaile83@gmail.com.

Contents

CHAPTER ONE The Forest Clearing	11
CHAPTER TWO The Town of Kleas	23
CHAPTER THREE Preparation for the Hunt	32
CHAPTER FOUR The Middle Kingdom	36
CHAPTER FIVE The Woods of Ciroc	80
CHAPTER SIX In Times Past	105
CHAPTER SEVEN The Elves of Ciroc	122
CHAPTER EIGHT Alive Again	129
CHAPTER NINE Fears and Regrets	155
CHAPTER TEN The Battle For Tonar	162
CHAPTER ELEVEN	188

CHAPTER TWELVE   204
The Journey Continues

CHAPTER THIRTEEN   231
Chaos in Chaos

CHAPTER FOURTEEN   241
Consequences

CHAPTER FIFTEEN   253
Shewit, the Life of the First

CHAPTER SIXTEEN   273
It was a lie

CHAPTER SEVENTEEN 283
One Last Time

CHAPTER EIGHTEEN   291
Self-fulfilling Prophecy

Final Note   303

Imagination

It makes all the difference in a human life. It decides whether you are going to fulfill your dreams or just sit on the sidelines and wait for something to happen. If you cannot imagine what you want, you cannot create. Imagination is the most powerful tool that humans have. And yet, despite it is also the most natural of our gifts, we deny it as unimportant, lose it on the way to adulthood, or do not take it seriously at all. We always start with imagination. Then we create.

Tonar

Sinora Mountains

The Middle Kingdom

Land of the
Berseker

Technocons

Piece Island

Kleas

Ciroc Woods

PREQUEL TOAS
In the beginning, there was harmony

In the beginning, in the realm of nothing, there was only vibration. For a million infinities the universe vibrated. Each particle for himself, in harmony with all others. Until one day, one particle missed for a millisecond the beat of the vibration. Everything changed. This one particle vibrated higher to catch up and to be in harmony again. And this unbalanced moment led to many unbalanced particles that all wanted to become back in sync again. And chaos began.

Particles became bursting stars, one after another, in the pursuit to vibrate higher and higher. And still, to this day, they are only seeking balance and harmony. One of these particles, which became a star, is the Land of Toas today. The first particle that missed the beat of the vibration and brought chaos to all others. That's why, the elderly says, the world is in balance today. Toas needed to vibrate so much more and higher than all other particles, that it found its rhythm, making Toas a place of gods, magic, and many races living together. So much beauty came out of his misery, that this little particle also learned that chaos does not always do bad. Chaos is not always the end but maybe the beginning.

So, it created a test, a possibility that if the inhabitants of Toas are not careful, everything will fall into chaos, so the legend says. Therefore, every 100 years a child is born with the mark of chaos, a child-like the particles, a child of Balance and Chaos. Through their sacrifice, harmony will be restored. If not, chaos is on the way, and maybe with that, a new beginning.

CHAPTER ONE

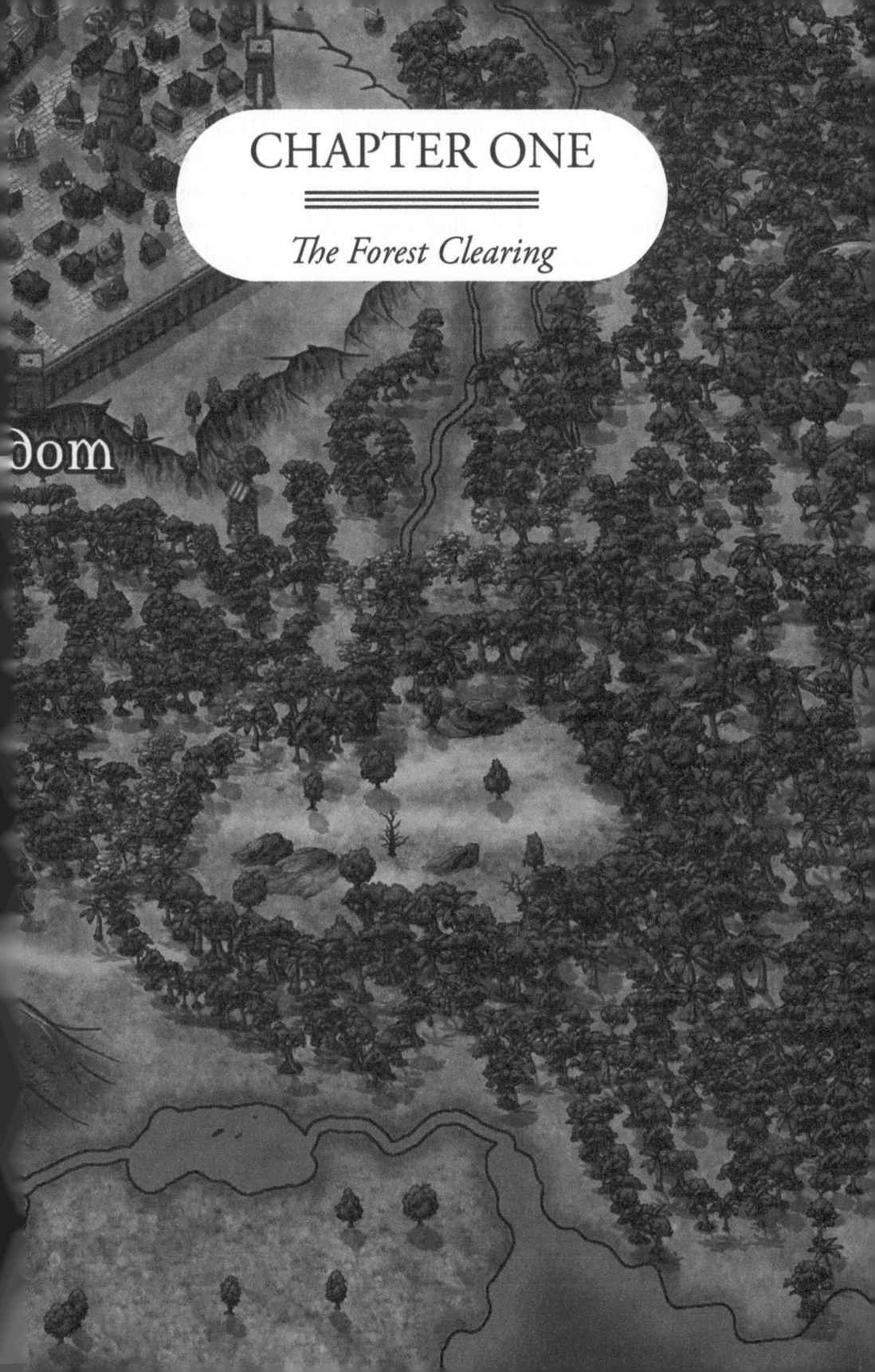

The Forest Clearing

The Forest Clearing

Sacrifice for peace or live a life in chaos? Eldana was for a second, lost in her thoughts and struggled. *Would you sacrifice yourself for the peace of the world? If you had no gain in it.* That was the question after all, they expected her to answer with yes. It was not the time to think about this. She focused back on the threat in front of her.

There were seven of them in a semicircle. Nobody moved. Swords drawn; faces grim. It seemed as if the world stood still for a breath. It was a cold, misty night. The fog surrounding them brought a chilling aura. The forest clearing seemed surreal; even animals seemed to be deliberately keeping quiet. Not a single bird was heard. The seven figures stood there as if in rigor mortis. The only indication they were alive was their breath, hot with anger.

They held their swords upside down, a display of strength and determination in Toas. They needed to show strength. Nobody stood above the law. The gods of Toas had set the rules. And those who broke the rules would be punished.

The seven figures were clad in robes – not ordinary robes – each mantle was decorated with a different pattern. Each pattern was a sign of the elements of this world.

Their gazes were drawn to their target at the center of the forest clearing. There she stood, facing the seven warriors. Her life was about to change forever. Eldana's brown hair shone. She had a sword in her hand, long and lethal, with the sign of the King of Toas inscribed on its hilt. She was wearing similar clothes, decorated like the robes of the seven warriors. On hers, only the symbol of light was present. Her taut body was that of a fighter. Her mind was sharp and focused on every move around her. She was ready to fight against all seven. She was a princess and a goddess, a servant of the crescent moon, a traitor; doomed to die. Around her stood her teachers, ready to punish her for treason.

The forest clearing shimmered with a lustrous beauty and wonder. It felt odd to make such a beautiful place a battleground.

But the place was not always beautiful. Once, the clearing had been a battlefield, one where thousands had seen their last light,

Chapter One

when all creatures fought about the reign on Toas.

Elsewhere, near the clearing and deep in the forest stood two creatures. They blended entirely with the forest around them, unnoticed, thanks to the potent protection spell.

The first; a woman armed with a bow. The first arrow was notched, aimed at the closest enemy of Eldana. This archer was a magician. Siem, from the house of the Middle Kingdom. She belonged to Kajewll, the last magician class trained according to the old rules of magic. She knew all forms of magic, even the forbidden ones, and had mastery over the element particular to elves: fire. Next to her, a man. His head bowed, calmly focusing on Eldana. He was a Berserker with a battle-axe in his right hand. They were both dressed in robes, also with symbol of light on their back. Waiting for the slightest movement on the battlefield, they were real friends of Eldana. His name was Hermon, and he had the gift of exerting an uncontrollable, enormous power in battle. A curse he received from his father – Biniamin – the King of the Berserkers ruling over the mountains of Sinora.

"Do you know why we're here, Eldana?" asked Sinto, the unofficial leader of the group of seven.

"Yes," Eldana answered.

"Then surrender yourself to the Council so that we can complete the prophecy. Do you understand this?"

"Yes," Eldana agreed with a whisper.

"Very well, I will come to you now and take the weapon from you." Sinto made the first kind gesture towards Eldana.

When he took his first step, Eldana lifted the sword slightly into the air and pointed it in Sinto's direction. There was a twitch of disbelief in the faces of the warriors.

"Stop," ordered Eldana. Her tone was harsh. Sinto stared at her in disbelief, same as the other warriors, but still stopped on her command. The warriors were able to pull themselves together, but now they hummed softly, a sign of focus. They were getting ready to fight.

"Don't fool around, child! We only want to help you," said

Sinto, in a slightly alarmed voice.

He raised his hand and gave the other warriors the signal to stop humming. They stopped immediately but kept the grim look on their faces. Eldana stretched her hand forward and whispered three short words to herself. In response, a gust of wind swept through the clearing and transformed into a wall of energy bursting from her outstretched hands. A protective shield now covered the surrounded woman.

But magic was exhausting. Eldana could not believe what had happened in such a short time. The last 10 hours had taken its toll. She had to run through the night, the tunnel of the castle, and the nearby woods, yet was still not safe. Nobody had controlled her chambers, and no guards had been close to her when she had made her escape. How did they find her so fast?

Eldana flicked her hair and dismissed the thought, before digging her boots into the ground, as much for balance as for defiance. She recited the old verses of battle magic, whispering them slowly and quietly at first, then faster and faster as she focused. She knew the verses inside out, thanks to her time with her teachers. Those same teachers surrounded her with just one goal, to bring her home even though that would mean killing her. A tear rolled down her face as she looked in the direction of Sinto and quoted the centuries-old verses. She realized how important this moment in her life was; she was ready to fight to death against the man who was once like a father to her.

Very long ago, Sinto and Eldana had laughed together. He was the first warrior of the Middle Kingdom to train Eldana.

It had not been an easy task, a being of Balance and Chaos was not born every day. The saying went, the more powerful that sacrificed being, the more beautiful the next hundred years would be. Therefore, seven warriors trained this being in becoming the most powerful of all in everything that was there to know.

His first task for her was to learn how to conjure an energy wall.

"Ironic," Eldana muttered as she stood before the Seven. The magic that these people had taught her might just save her life

Chapter One

now. She was a little girl when she had first encountered it and had stumbled into her energy wall several times. She made all the mistakes anyone could make, first conjuring only small energy bubbles, a smaller version of a full protective shield. Sinto could hardly stay composed during training, always in fits of laughter. This memory of him, which once brought tears of mirth to her eyes, only hurt Eldana now. It was as if her entire history was playing out in front of her.

"This will save your life one day!" Sinto had once said with a severe undertone several times in the years of training.

Back then, she looked at him, eyes blazing; it was unclear why he had always been so serious. Although it upset her, she did what he asked anyway. And finally, after months of training, she had created her first protective shield in the form of an energy wall. It was her favourite memory.

Eldana remembered him lifting a stick from the ground and hitting her on the cheek. It was just too quick for her to avoid it. She had been less annoyed by the pain than by his irrational behaviour. He had swung again and again. Her anger multiplied; no one would hit her like that. Sinto was just about to hit her again, but this time she built up an energy wall of protection. It almost failed, but it was enough to counter the strike of the stick. Eldana remembered looking at him with rage. He had smiled then, but today he did not.

Eldana's protective shield blazed around her. Her eyes were still wet with tears. She had regained her composure. She was tiny compared to the warriors around her, yet there was no trace of doubt or fear in her. She was as determined as them.

"It is time," she spoke, and her voice was commanding. All of the warriors gripped their swords tighter. She muttered the magic verses again. She stopped one last time for a second and breathed deeply. All the warriors hummed, this time loud and clear. There was no longer any doubt about where this situation was headed. The Seven turned their swords and slowly approached Eldana. The louder the humming, the brighter their swords shone. It was inevitable what had to follow now...

"This is madness. Eldana is our daughter!" Sinto just shook his head and whispered, but his words drowned in the humming. He was angry that he had lost control of the situation. The warriors' weapons were brightly lit, infused with the power of Toas. Sinto stood in front of everyone and lowered his eyes once more, shaking his head. As the leader of the warriors, his task was clear. He could not show any weakness.

"Kill her," he said in a clear, loud voice to the warriors.

For a second, Eldana was shaking to the bones. *Was this real?* She forced herself to remain calm. *Sinto is like your father, an enemy now,* she thought. It felt strange. She needed to die, yes, in a proper ritual, not like this. Her thoughts were racing; her soul would be lost in darkness instead of bringing peace to Toas if they succeeded, at least this was what she thought...

Inside, she was numbed by the words of Sinto, but on the outside, she knew what to do. She moved to the left, and the ground beneath her burned. The verses that she listed before could now be heard in the air, getting louder. The spell worked and was becoming stronger with every second. By the moonlight that still hung in the pre-dawn air, her power would increase, just as she had once been told that her power was always linked to the moon. Its power unfolded a unique energy wave in her, mentally and physically.

Two of the warriors leapt into the air and attacked Eldana, their swords clashing against her protective shield. There was a spark, and the shield threw them back against their fellow warriors. They attacked again, bringing down their swords harder on the shield, and got the same result. Such blows from a warrior would have killed any normal being. The energy wall stood firm in the wake of the first attacks. The second wave came immediately. The warriors jumped, all of them now, thrusting and slashing. After each attack, they struck faster and harder, but the energy wall withstood it all.

Eldana staggered from the exhaustion. She struggled to hold

Chapter One

the wall, and they saw the effort it cost her. The voices of the verses were still in the air. Hermon and Siem watched her, worry etching deep lines across their faces.

"*Werhi haily*," Eldana called out, and, as if in response, the moon suddenly shone brighter and illuminated the entire clearing.

The wind blew the trees around her as the earth under their feet moved, just lightly. Dark clouds formed in the sky. The warriors still jumped towards her, round after round. Eldana raised her hand and waited for the next one to attack her. The moment his sword hit the wall, Eldana initiated a strike from the air; a lightning bolt streaked through the sky and hit the warrior. He fell to the ground in front of her. The earth burned like hot lava where she stood, all the elements were now in motion and thunder rumbled through the sky. Another warrior jumped forward and pulled him back. They all looked at the wounded warrior, horrified with the severity of his injuries.

It was the first time in such a long time that a warrior of the Middle Kingdom had been wounded. Through the sacrifices of the goddesses, there had been no violence for decades. The Middle Kingdom was known for their magic and fighting prowess, something that set them apart from the other human kingdom, Tonar, who had just a handful of magicians. It was clear that the seven had underestimated Eldana tremendously.

"Watch out, warriors of the Middle Kingdom!" Sinto cried out. "The moonlight gives her incredible powers."

The warriors nodded and prepared for the next attack, grim but determined. But there was another emotion on their faces too, rage. This was supposed to be easy. The voices in the air brought Eldana into a trance-like state; she became faster. The runes on her coat glowed. Eldana now fought with unrestrained power. The waves of attacks started again, fiercer, and harder than before. But despite all her skills, Eldana knew that this game would not last much longer.

The warriors smashed against the wall relentlessly, but it always

The Forest Clearing

bounced them back. Eldana threw down another bolt of lightning onto one of the warriors, but he was prepared now. He held his sword out to block the attack and felt only half the force of the lightning.

Sinto was horrified; her powers were many times greater than he had expected. They were not able to break through her wall. She had always been a special goddess. But this? No. All of the goddesses had been special every hundred years, but Eldana had something that the others did not. The fire burned in her more than in all the others put together!

A thought grew in him that terrified him. *What if she defeats us?* He tried to shake it off quickly but could not. Their defeat would mean he would no longer be the respected teacher he was. A loud scream snapped him out of his dreams.

The wall disappeared and Eldana shouted, "Now!"

The warriors paused for a second, puzzled. And moving from behind Eldana, her two friends who had stood in the darkness now stepped into the light.

"I guess it's our turn now. Are you ready to do some damage, Hermon?" Siem looked at him out of the corner of her eye while still focusing on the closest of Eldana's enemies.

"Well, you know I'd love to avoid it, but I'm making an exception here!" he said. Siem looked a little confused but forgot about it quickly.

"Run, my brother. Help your sister; she needs you." Hermon's face changed from a smile to anger, and the Berserker ritual began. He cried out; it was a sad, loud, painful cry. His bones snapped, his body expanded, and he started bleeding in lots of places on his back, legs, and arms. The sure signs of a Berserker. In a sick reversal, the pain invigorated him. It transformed him. Hermon leapt forward to battle.

The warriors recognized that sound. They stopped again and could not believe their eyes as the Berserker raced towards them. The battle had turned.

Chapter One

"Calm down!" Sinto cried out, standing amidst his warriors. "Use Protection Spells!" he said, knowing that the people known as the Berserkers were nearly invincible in their rage mode. Even if they expended all their magic, there was no guarantee that the Berserker would die.

But the seven warriors stumbled back, looking at Sinto, angry and horrified.

"It's all your fault, Sinto, how could you let us walk into a trap like this?" shouted Tabeli.

"Blaming doesn't help now. Concentrate, Tabeli!" Sinto replied.

"Don't you tell me what to do. One of us will die and it's your fault. Your love for her makes you blind!" Tabeli looked angry.

Eldana overheard the conversation. Sinto glared at her, Tabeli followed his gaze and met Eldana's. He spat on the ground.

Hermon was close to the fight now. His body kept growing, in a single leap, he had crossed over to the clearing.

Siem readied her bow and spoke the words of her tribes, words from long ago when life was still full of magical creatures. The arrow glowed, and the runes appeared on the wood. As she let go, the arrow burned through the air, leaving a trail of fire behind it.

The warriors braced themselves. Sinto's eyes widened as Siem chanted with a smile.

"I call upon the power beneath. Come to me, souls of the night, insatiable in the dark, bind your magic to my demon arrows. Come to me, visit the living one last time...bring harm to whom you touch. Let my foes taste my power. I am Siem, Daughter of the first hour!"

Sinto saw the arrows racing through the forest air and called out. "Demon arrows! Protect yourself!"

But the arrows flew faster and faster. Before hitting the first warrior, the runes on the arrow illuminated strongly. The warrior managed to block the blow with his sword at the last second, but the impact was violent. With a gasp, Sinto cast a protective spell to support his warrior, but the effect was still intense as everyone was thrown backwards through the mud. The warrior laid on the ground, shaken, but still alive.

The Forest Clearing

"Through the runes, the souls of the ancient spirits come into the arrows," Tabeli said slowly. He was talking to himself as if he were both in awe and shock, while helping the fallen warrior to his feet.

"A wizard usually says that a field of war like this one is a jackpot for demon arrows. The soil contains the souls of thousands of people; it helps to awaken the power of the arrow. We've fallen into a trap!" Tabeli shook his head furiously, glaring at Sinto. Two others fought doggedly against Hermon; only their speed allowed them to avoid the deadly attacks of the Berserker. In his magical state, one could not easily kill a Berserker; their injuries healed too quickly. Every blow just bounced off his powerful body. The only thing they could do was avoid his attacks. While everyone was still distracted by Hermon, Eldana took her chance and ran towards the forest. She tried to get away, but she was weakened from the fight. Suddenly, three of the warriors jumped to block her way to the woods and quickly launched their attack on her.

Siem turned to see Eldana stumbling under the furious attacks of the warriors. She readied two more arrows and fired them at the warriors around Eldana. The attacks were still fierce but expected. Eldana parried the sword thrusts as much as she could while she casted another spell. The mark on her coat and her eyes glowed with an eldritch light, as a wave of fire welled from the earth and raced towards the warriors from behind. It was sudden, but the warriors were skilled and cautious. All of them jumped aside, but one. The warrior burned and scream in horror. His comrades rushed to help him but had to fight off the arrows at the same time. Eldana took the opportunity and fled towards the forest. Before she reached the edge, Sinto suddenly appeared before her. His strikes were harder than the others, much harder, but she parried them with her own blade, feeling each blow she blocked make her weaker.

"Enough! It does not have to end like this. Stop this, Eldana!" said Sinto as he pulled back. Eldana stood in front of him in a fighting stance, breathing heavy as she watched him.

Chapter One

"Let me find another way. I've already found it; you just have to give me time, that's all," she panted.

Sinto was annoyed by her try to change his mind. "Silence! We have laws, and we have kept them for a thousand years. You won't change anything," he growled, enraged.

Sinto swung his sword at Eldana, but she dodged it, bending low. At that moment, Hermon leapt to her side, grabbed her and jumped over Sinto only to run towards the edge of the forest.

"I could have done this alone!" Eldana struggled against her captor. She had hoped that there was a hint of understanding in Sinto. After all, he was a father figure to her. Hermon should not have interrupted that moment she thought could have been a turning point.

"That's not the gratitude I expected. You have been surrounded by enemies and weakened, my magical state is only staying for so long and Siem's demon arrows losing the element of surprise and Sinto just swung his sword at you," Hermon tried explaining her what seemed to him as pure logic, but he could see the anger in her eyes. He kept quiet and just jumped further.

He arrived at the edge of the forest and grabbed Siem, who shot off another arrow. Quickly and with full force, he jumped into the woods, high and deep enough that none of the warriors could follow them, Siem's invisibility spell did the rest. They were gone. Disappeared into the darkness of the forest.

All the warriors relaxed, and some dropped their weapons after seeing the three disappeared into the woods. The fight took a toll on the warriors. They all gathered around Sinto, waiting for instructions. He spoke softly when everyone arrived.

"I'm sorry, my brothers. It seems we're not just dealing with the Eldana that we know any more. She's got help, renegades protecting her. Together, they are stronger and faster... but we have more experience and training!" Sinto looked over at a younger warrior who came limping towards them. He tried to give them confidence with his words.

"We haven't been in combat for a long time, and none of us

expected such violence. We must prepare ourselves better in the future."

Tabeli walked beside him, visibly shaken by what he had just seen. "As much as I value you as our leader, my brother, she means a lot to you and we may have to go much harder than we've ever had to. Can you handle that?" Tabeli looked desperately at Sinto with the warmth of a good friend and placed his hand on his shoulder. Sinto looked away from Tabeli and paused for a few seconds.

" I can handle it. No one is above the law," said Sinto, his eyes wandering over the forest.

Tabeli gazed at him and nodded. Behind them glowed the forest clearing in the pre-dawn moonlight, scorched earth and holes everywhere from the fight. It was all so different from the calm it had been moments ago. But no one was concerned. All they thought of were the three who had escaped them. For them, the battle was not over; it had only just begun.

CHAPTER TWO

The Town of Kleas

The Town Of Kleas

It was midnight when the three companions made it to the small town with the name of Kleas. It was surrounded by a stone wall and protected by a large moat. Rich towns in Toas usually had at least one mage guard per tower. Here there was only one old guard who floated just above the entrance for the entire City.

Confused by this weird instance, Siem tried to explain it to herself. "What's the point of that? The mage guards usually float in circles to protect the entire city, what if we choose to access from behind? Also, why is there just one? He is never able to guard the entire city alone." Siem was truly perplexed; she probably knew best about the guardians amongst the three.

"Well, maybe he's bored, I mean he can't spend his life floating around in circles, can he?" Hermon laughed about his own revelation.

"Chosen by the Dakar, these are dead magicians who did not want to die immediately and would rather protect others for another century. There is a huge waiting list to become a guardian magician, and in our circles that's a great honor, so stop blabbering about it being stupid, Hermon!" Siem said in annoyance to her companion, who was now back in the normal confines of his body. It did not seem like he had just gone berserk not long ago.

"Well, now the lady seems to know what she's saying."

Siem made a little lightning bolt appear in her hand. "Keep it up," she said, looking at him threateningly.

Siem and Hermon kept arguing about the mage guardian's logic and why Hermon choose being annoying; Eldana stayed seated on the ground under a tree and did not look up or follow their conversation. Siem noticed the silence after a while and walked towards her, serious again.

"What is it?"

Eldana looked up, tired. "They wanted to kill me."

Siem looked irritated, and Hermon approached with a stern look on his face. All the goofiness had vanished from his expression.

Chapter Two

"Of course, they want to kill you. They believe in the prophecy," Hermon reminded her.

"Yes, but without ritual. Don't you understand?" Eldana's voice broke. "They wanted to kill me *without* the ritual. That means that I would not enter the light and save the world, but would be trapped between the two worlds, forever!" She could not hold back her tears.

Hermon and Siem looked concerned and stood by her side. There was no awkwardness or secrets between the three of them. After a while, Siem broke the silence.

"Night is coming soon and we are not safe yet. We have to go inside the town and hide."

Siem had always been the one to keep everyone else in check. She knew that her friend was upset, but there were more pressing concerns. Eldana and Hermon nodded and moved without exchanging another word about this topic.

"What shall we do about the mage guardian?" Hermon asked. "These guys are always stronger than you think." His gaze wandered to Siem, although there was no official leader of their group, it was always her who had to make a decision.

"I'll distract it, and you take Eldana into the city." She looked at Hermon and said nothing more. He moved towards Eldana and grabbed her by the arm. She was weak. The fight and the loss of home had depleted her. That made her vulnerable, whether she cared to admit it or not. They walked together towards the gate, with Siem remaining a little further away. She casted a cloaking spell with the soft murmurs of her voice.

Thus cloaked, Eldana and Hermon then strolled ahead. Nobody but Siem could see them. Hermon sometimes nervously looked to the top to see if the guard was making any unusual moves. Nothing happened. He was not sure what to expect but no cloak was perfect and it could break any time. As if on command, a short lightning bolt crashed right in front of Hermon and Eldana. They both immediately prepared for a fight.

Siem cursed from a distance but quickly got hold of herself.

The mage guardian uttered a few short words and tilted his head down.

"Who dares to deceive Benok the Great, guardian of the town of Kleas, with simple cloaking spells?"

The guardian mage hung in the air, his black robe flowing with the wind. His hair was snow-white and flowing along with his robe. He mumbled magical verses that hall through the air and light rings appeared around the city that seemed to be there all along. From where Siem was, she could only imagine what would had happened when Eldana and Hermon touched them.

She had misunderstood the situation. There was only one mage guardian at the gate, not because this place was poor but because he was as strong as ten mage guardians put together. Hermon turned around and cursed in the direction of Siem. She ran towards them faster than she had ever run, knowing what could happen next. A mage guardian knew no mercy, his only mission was to protect the town.

Siem screamed to draw attention to herself, but the mage was just focused on Eldana and Hermon. Hermon was already changing into a Berserker; but Eldana was still tired from the previous fight and therefore moved slowly. The more of the power of magic moved through the body of one, the more the person is affected. Eldana's physical body and mind were severely weakened. Siem flashed through all possible spells in her mind as she ran. One of them was called *Tawoub* - the earthquake to swallow them from the earth and a shroud of earth to protect them from the mage's attacks.

Siem was about to cast the spell, the symbol on her coat glowed and magic flowed through her, at the same time the ground below Eldana and Hermon mirrored drift sand. The guardian mage seemed to sense the plans of Siem, and suddenly moved his attention towards her.

"Good, focus on me!" Siem mumbled to herself, abandoning *Tawoub* and instead pulled one of her demon arrows out of her quiver while running. She was ready to shoot in seconds. As she

Chapter Two

mumbled the words that would channel the souls of her ancestors into the arrow, with the arrow aimed at the mage, she was only able to shoot at the guardian, he floated to the right and let the arrow drop into the lightning surrounding the town where it just vanished. The mage's attack followed immediately. A volley of lightning circles came towards her after he raised his hand just slightly. But Siem had learned to deal with strikes like this in the past and was relieved that she knew what to do. She did a roll, jumped into the air and floated at the same height as the guardian mage. She uttered just one word.

"*Midri!*" A wave of sand gathered from the ground and spun around in the air, circling, and forming a wall. The energy circles crashed against the wall of sand and disbursed into the air… but the shock of the airwave pulled her lightly out the air. The power was immense for what was just a little flick of the hand. Siem knew this was not a fight she would win. But that was not the goal; she had to protect Eldana and Hermon.

Siem steadied herself and was about to shoot the arrow just as the mage raised his hand once again. But at that moment, Eldana lifted her hand to the mage instead. He saw the movement and looked down at Eldana.

"I am a traveller seeking shelter. My powers are fading, and I have been betrayed by my dearest. The magician that you are fighting wanted to smuggle me into your beautiful town to sleep and have good rest before we travel on. We can pay, and we are ready to give the shelter of our choice double of what they are asking for!" Eldana said in a soft tone.

The guard stopped his attacks. Where the eyes of a human should have been, two opaque, emotionless pebbles stared back at her. A couple of seconds passed. Siem floated back to earth. Hermon just held his breath. They did not understand what was happening. Hermon was slowly returning back to his normal self, sensing that the danger no longer existed.

The stare felt endless, but it must have been only a few minutes. Then the gate opened and the light surrounding the town disappeared, without another word from the mage. It was a long wooden gate that made the earth tremor a little as it moved. The guard raised his head again and stared straight ahead. Eldana also seemed to wake up from her trance and said, "Thank you, guard," before walking forward. Hermon looked puzzled but followed without another word.

Siem was still confused. She did not understand why the mage had so suddenly stopped attacking her. The demon arrow was still on the bow. She put it back and walked slowly towards the gate. As Siem passed the guard, she heard a soft, gentle voice from far away.

"You have a lot to learn my child, you will have to protect Eldana to death, and your powers must become stronger than the strongest magician ever. This will be your destiny."

She paused and looked up, but the guard did not pay any attention to her. She knew it came from him. They were both children of the Middle Kingdom; only he had fallen in the battle of the first hour. It was a battle between magicians and old elves who thought themselves gods. "Why me?" she whispered, more to herself than to him, then went on without waiting for an answer.

Once inside, she met with Eldana and Hermon again. Siem wanted to ask so many questions. How did Eldana know how to deal with a mage guard? Hermon beat her to it in a rather unconventional way.

"Wow, Eldana, what was that?" He still looked red from his exertion. Hermon was stronger than many Berserkers, who would have taken longer to regain their strength, but he walked along with his friends, albeit slowly. "How do you do that, just ask a mage guard if you can get in? Just like that?" Eldana looked at him and smiled impishly.

"You have to be friendly sometimes," she said sweetly.

"Yes," he agreed, "but it's still very crazy."

Eldana laughed but did not go into further explanation. They looked around at the streets of Kleas, which turned out to be much broader than either of them had thought; almost a city!

Chapter Two

Only then did they become aware of its beauty. In fact, the walls of Kleas did no justice to the wonders they saw inside. The streets were full of energy and flying creatures from all over the world with incredible powers. It was full of magic. There were shops filled with magically enhanced toys and gadgets. Along the streets were blue, green, red, and purple flowers; the delicate scents filled the air. The houses were rounded with curved domes and painted with bright colors. Even the sky was a different shade of beautiful light blue inside this place. From the outside, Kleas had looked old and boring; therefore, not many people were drawn to it. Perhaps it was a spell, crafted to make it look that way. The people of Kleas believed in peace. They also believed that envy was the reason for conflict, hence the reason they went through pain to hide the beauty of their city.

"If you use such a powerful hiding spell to keep all this beauty hidden, you need very powerful magic," Siem observed. Eldana and Hermon nodded reverently. It was like a different world. The buildings all looked new. Even the water barrels were clean. Trees stood by the sides of the roads, waving their branches, animated with more life and sentience than any regular forest tree. They wandered for half an hour through the town in a state of awe.

But after a while of wondering and marvelling, it was time to find a place to stay. They eventually found a charming tavern that looked inviting.

On entering, a bell rang at the door, and a shimmer of dust fell on the three. They felt positive energy all around. "A positivity spell," said Siem, and three laughed in pure delight.

"Amazing how great I feel," Eldana said, as she blew the dust from her robes. Hermon was laughing too, and it filled the whole hall with joy. "I haven't felt so good in a long time!"

"It's mostly used on children's birthdays to keep them in a good mood - no sudden squabbling and crying over presents! Sometimes it's even used for funerals, but that's only in some cultures," Siem said. Hermon and Eldana were thrown into fits of laughter as though Siem had said the funniest thing. The tavern was still empty, only the bartender looked at them and smiled warmly. He probably belonged to the human species.

"Greetings to you at the Tavern of the Wholesome Laughter," he said. "My name is Techle; I am the bartender and the owner of this laughing parlor. Come in and enjoy a cold beer, and don't worry about the laughter spell. It should wear off soon."

He didn't need to say it twice. The three had all been hungry and thirsty because of the journey and the fight with the warriors. They ordered a mountain of food, from healthy to greasy to sweet, everything was on offer here. Hermon got a whole field of leaves for himself, while Eldana only had some mushrooms. Siem didn't care; she wanted to have everything. Magic costs a lot of energy, so she was especially drained.

They feasted, laughed about past humorous memories, and drank for hours. Although they knew it was due to the positivity spell, it was nice to feel such joy for once, and, before they went into their rooms, they spoke briefly with the owner of the tavern.

"Thank you for a delicious meal. It was an honor," said Eldana.

"Always a pleasure," replied Techle. "Just next time, please do not come to my tavern as fugitives. We are not fighters, you know. I am a simple tavern owner and probably won't be able to protect you when the warriors show up, if they manage to get past the guardian mage. I can keep you hidden, but don't ask me to fight."

Astonishment spread over their faces. "You know about us? How can this be? We haven't told anyone!" Hermon looked outraged.

"You don't have to, my child. You are here in Klea's walls. As you now know, this is a magical city. That means everyone knows everything. Outside, the city is protected by a strong protection spell, but there are none inside the walls. On the inside, we live in peace. There are no secrets here because there is no need for them. We are all-knowing in order to be all-helpful."

It was strange moving about with their hearts on their faces, but that was the city of Kleas, the city where minds were bared and those that were impure were sent away.

Chapter Two

Eldana replied first. "Thank you," she said sincerely, but Techle shook his head.

"Don't thank me. Thank the city. We've lived safely for more than a thousand years!"

Eldana lowered her head and took the man's hand. "Thank you, my friend, you've helped us very much." Techle did not say another word but merely nodded.

When the innkeeper had left them, they went upstairs into their rooms. It was a pleasure for them to receive such hospitality. They all fell asleep calmly and with little worry. Techle had not promised too much. The spell gave them a feeling of security, even if only for a few hours.

CHAPTER THREE

Preparation for the Hunt

Chapter Three

Even though the fight had drained them all, what was left of the seven warriors was ready to be on the hunt again. It was just what they needed. The warriors had not left their homes for a while. The average citizen of the Middle Kingdom was responsible and respectable. None would dare use any forbidden battle magic spells. The only excitement that these seven had was the training of the next chosen one that would bring peace to Toas. In this case, Eldana. She had always brought excitement to their lives, now more than ever. A being of Balance and Chaos is born only every hundred years. The duty of the seven were passed down from generation to generation, some generations never had the honor to train a BC, so Eldana had been trained by each one of them with diligence. Seeing that vanish was painful.

Eldana was much stronger than they thought, and it had been a long time since they had used battle magic. Sinto would help the others unlock the power that the warriors held within themselves. To defeat Eldana, they would need every ounce of power they could gather.

Sinto spoke the word of power, as the warriors paired for training. "*Ha ley na ne.*"

"The warrior of water, you will fight against the fire-breathing dragon," Sinto said. His eyes roamed amongst the seven. They watched him, apprehensive.

"Remember the art of fighting," he said. "You are warriors, not only teachers. We need to remember our skills!"

Sinto sensed that everyone was excited. A lot of energy was in the air, very unusual, much more than before. They were eager; ready. He wondered where this came from. It seemed as if new energy was forming from their hate of the would-be goddess Eldana. They felt betrayed. There was Adonay, the bald-headed warrior had let Eldana drink from his own bowl the very day she arrived. While Sinto had no emotion for Eldana at that time, Adonay was the one who had always given her a silent shoulder to cry on. Then there was white haired Berhun. He had admired Eldana from afar, but he was disappointed now with her actions. Their feeling of betrayal created something that many did not know, the desire to fight again, to win...and then also the desire to *kill*.

Sinto knew what this meant. The warriors were on the way to becoming barbarians, barbarians who knew that there was no return. The hatred gave them strength and they needed it to continue to fight. Two warriors were fighting so loudly that they all heard it, and not just for fun, but for blood. Sinto came along and yelled,

"What's wrong with you? This is just training!"

Both turned and the glow in their eyes was one he had not seen in a long time. It was the old warrior's glow that shone in their eyes. But both stopped with some reluctance, and Sinto could see that they didn't want to stop there.

"We are sorry, Sinto," said one with apparent difficulty. "It was just nice to get back to doing what we were meant to do. It makes me feel stronger and more powerful than anything else."

Sinto knew where the energy came from. Tabeli stood there and laughed joyfully.

"Finally, fire." He sighed and looked at the two again. "As long as you don't kill each other, go on, Sinto should be happy with that?"

He looked at Sinto with a smile and knew that he had to help him. Sinto belonged to a time when honor was worth a lot. In those times, everything was different, people didn't fight each other like barbarians. Even the enemies had respect for each other. This young generation of warriors had never experienced this. It was difficult for them to understand what it meant to fight. Some had never fought before. Their senses were overwhelmed by the power.

While the warriors trained, Tabeli and Sinto went to check on other preparations for the hunt. They came upon two other warriors that were readying their weapons. One of them took a stone and spoke softly the words of magic. The stone started to glow and changed color from green, to red, to blue. The warrior threw the stone into a bush, there it imploded and took everything with-

Chapter Three

in a radius of three meters with it. Sinto made a bewildered face.

"Interesting new way to use magic," he said. "But is it enough to stop a berserker?"

Tabeli and the warrior looked at each other, puzzled. Tabeli decided to answer for them both. "Not yet, but soon," and added with a slightly sceptical undertone, "Don't you believe it?"

Sinto looked at him with tired eyes. "Oh Tabeli, we both know that we have been out of proper fighting for far too long to stand against the only son of the Berserker King, so it won't be easy."

The two warriors who had been working on the weapons looked at each other, insecure. Sinto noticed their glances and said, "As long as we have two fearless warriors like these, we'll be fine." He laughed and slapped one of them on the shoulder. Tabeli noticed the tension and grabbed Sinto by the arm to lead him away.

"More men," he said in a strained tone.

"For the king," the answer came back promptly. Sinto's look revealed that he was incredibly grateful for the rescue. Tabeli only shook his head. He returned Sinto's gaze with one that said - be quiet!

So they went on through the night and inspected the warriors. The flames of duty burned within them. Even though they had mixed feelings about Eldana, they knew that their duty had to be fulfilled. Weapons were forged and artifacts were fitted with magic. They were ready. The preparations for the Great Hunt were nearly complete. In the morning, they would set off. The only one who could not sleep that night was Sinto. As much as he was happy for his men, he thought about Eldana and how much he missed the little young lady who was so unable to take care of herself. He had been with her every step of the way, refusing to let weakness creep into her body. She was a being of Balance and Chaos, and he had made sure she knew that weakness was unacceptable. Maybe he was a bit too hard on her, but it was because he cared for her. She was like his daughter and now, sadly, he knew that he had to kill her too soon.

Tonar

CHAPTER FOUR
The Middle Kingdom

The Middle Kingdom

Chapter Four

Eldana had gotten up early. After they left the town of Kleas, there was no other big city nearby to hide in. Eldana decided to walk back into the center of danger. They wandered the forest and through the night back into the Middle Kingdom.

Hermon was absolutely baffled by this. "You just left the Middle Kingdom, Eldana!" He tried to find logic in it. "Why would you want to go back here? After just doing all that running away and fighting, you're just going to walk right back into the center of danger? That makes no sense."

"Let me explain it to you." Eldana sat on the ground with her legs crossed and a flower she just found. She played with it while she explained.

"If you try to change something, you need to go where you can change something." She looked at him "The warriors would never believe that we would come back to the Middle Kingdom, they are hunting us now. But to change something, we need to do it where it hurts."

Hermon bit his lip, before his protest was heard. "All right, if you know how to end this and think this is the only way, let's go back."

Eldana nodded. "I do." Siem just smiled but did not add anything.

During the day, they hiked. At night, they hid in the forest. They took turns keeping watch. Hermon was still asleep. Eldana was to replace Siem.

"You're up already?" Siem asked Eldana.

"I couldn't sleep any more. I feel the warriors are getting closer. I can feel their aura. Not quite the same as in the clearing but stronger than in Kleas...Maybe we should have made a bigger round trying to avoid them."

Siem looked in the direction they came from. "I don't think they have left yet."

Siem looked back at Eldana and started to worry. "I feel your strength as well, stronger every day but far from what it needs to be. I would carry you to the end of the world if I had to, but you will need your full power to beat them all."

Eldana looked baffled. "I think I did a pretty good job the last time. Don't you think?" Her serious tone could not be overheard.

"Yeah, you did. But if Hermon and I hadn't been there, how long could you have kept that shield up? Would you have defeated all seven? I'm going to assume that wouldn't have been the case."

Siem had led many before, but she was used to leading armies of mages, not such a small group like this. She realized that perhaps her words had been discouraging, so she added, "You are one of the strongest warriors I know. No one has ever been able to fight the seven warriors of the Middle Kingdom for even a minute, let alone surprise them all together." Eldana took the compliment and nodded eagerly. "But when you meet these warriors in the future, you must be stronger, better."

Eldana understood the point. There was still much training ahead of her. At that moment, Hermon awoke and yawned heartily. Just as he did so, a morning toot escaped him that made him stop immediately. Siem and Eldana laughed themselves to the ground.

"All right, enough laughing, let's move on," said Hermon, looking at Siem expectantly and with the hope that this would be forgotten in a second. She gathered her things, still giggling to herself over the farting Hermon. He took the whole basket on his back and set off. The women followed him.

"How long do you think it will take us to reach the city in the Middle Kingdom?" she asked.

"I don't know, but we have at least one more day. We should be there soon."

After another day of wandering further through the forest, they saw the first villages close to the Middle Kingdom. They were sparse and scattered at first. For Hermon it was normal, but not for Eldana, who had always been kept isolated from other people by Sinto. Nevertheless, she was doing well. She knew that attacks from the warriors in the Middle Kingdom should not happen so easily here. Siem was angry that she was constantly woken from

Chapter Four

her sleep in the basket on Hermon's back by the loud noises surrounding her. "Silence!" she screamed from inside before snuggling back into the soft straw. Eldana and Hermon laughed at this desperate attempt to finally have peace.

It was by chance they had become such tight friends, especially as they were all brought up so differently. Siem had come in contact with Eldana and Hermon fighting at a stream when she went to fetch some water as a child. Sinto would use any possibility to make Eldana train, he would instruct her to carry two buckets of water with magic floating above her shoulders and not set them down until she had climbed back all the way to the camp. Hermon was just there to drink and was disturbing the training. They fought over who could take water first and Sinto was enjoying it, thinking this could lead to another training moment. Siem, who was just working to become a sorcerer, passed by to cultivate her skills to control water. She saw them fight, separated them quickly and made them reconcile. Amazingly, they had listened to her. Siem was as different from them as she could be, with her pointed ears and delicate features. She was very beautiful. Every evening, Eldana would go to the stream with her buckets and she would see Siem training there. She knew how to use her bow and would entertain Eldana by shooting at animals in the nearby wood. Soon, Hermon joined them. Many times, Eldana came back late from the stream, and always got shouted at by Sinto because of it.

"Siem, we are here," Eldana said, smiling as she looked over the magnificent structure of the gate. Two dragons were carved into the emblem on the wooden bridge. Both had a crown pointing to the center where the King resided in his castle. There were guardian magicians here as well, not just one, but three of them at each tower within the wall They could feel the powerful magic in the air. A capital as great as this could not skimp on protection. This ensured they'd be safe from armies, but the common man could still sneak in. With a city as big as this, there were always people coming and going, as whomever paid the right price got in. There was another mechanism to protect the city though, the magic mirrors, which reflected the innermost thoughts of the people that passed by. Those with nefarious intentions were removed from the city. There were placed at the beginning of the entrance.

Siem, tired and dishevelled, peeked out of her basket. She had only been able to sleep a few hours that night. They had been travelling for two days now.

"Finally, Hermon let me go-" Before she could finish the sentence Hermon had thrown the basket on the ground. "Thanks," Siem said angrily. But she didn't add anything more, aware that her mood was not the best. Eldana only looked at her sympathetically. She had spent several nights in this basket and knew the feeling.

"What do we do now? Hermon asked.

"We go in," Eldana replied curtly and took the first steps towards the gate.

"Woah, woah, wait a minute, I think your energy is great, but let's go over the plan again. I think I forgot it." Hermon looked at them both.

"Tell us what you remember." Both looked at him questioningly.

"So...we are going in...to convince the King to stop persecuting you. Then we must find the most powerful mage, Lord Taboon, to help us change the system. We also need allies, so we need to talk to the Guild of Free Warriors. And we must do this quietly without drawing attention to ourselves, so the warriors of the Middle Kingdom don't find us and lynch us on the spot."

"Forgotten something?" Siem asked and smiled sweetly.

"What?" Hermon spoke.

"How do we make sure we're not discovered?"

Hermon raised his finger. "Ahh exactly... We are a family. I am the papa, you are the mama, and Eldana is our child. Right?" Hermon wasn't sure, so he looked around for confirmation but neither of them was giving anything away. Both just stared at him. Then after what felt like an eternity, Siem said, "I think it was right, what do you think Eldana?"

Chapter Four

Eldana tried to suppress her laughter but couldn't. "I think so too." Both laughed out loud.

They entered the gate to the city and went through without any problems. They paid the toll and split up. Hermon went to the Free Warriors Guild, Siem to the magicians, and Eldana to the King.

"Be back outside the gate in three hours. No detours. No long discussions. Find out what we need to know and come back," Siem instructed.

All three had transformed themselves with change spells, which were a pretty common spell in the Middle Kingdom. People often used them to appear more beautiful in the hopes of enticing suitors. There were even posters plastered all throughout the city. *'A better you today, these words are all you have to say!'* they said. No one would think it odd to see.

The Middle Kingdom

The Guild of the Free Warriors

The first to reach their destination was Hermon. The guild of the Free Warriors was only a little way from the entrance gate, after all, near to the city entrance to offer their services to those seeking trade and adventure.

Unfortunately, in the peaceable Middle Kingdom there just wasn't that many who sought out a dangerous life. The Guild of the Free Warriors was a small building; there just wasn't that many Free Warriors. When Hermon entered, he was immediately greeted by a magic being guarding the door. "How can I help you, stranger?" it asked. The servitor-being had the shape of a human but only when it needed to did it develop the sense organs. It was speaking, so the mouth was created, then disappeared again into the mass. Hermon always thought these creatures were weird but said nothing.

"I'm looking for supporters for our cause," he said in an overly loud voice.

"What cause?" the thing asked.

Hermon came closer. "We want to change the cycle of the 100 years. I am a friend of Eldana who…" Before he could finish the sentence, the magic being created hands, and put them over Hermon's mouth. At the same moment, it created a mouth that moved close to his ear.

"You live dangerously. Hermon, son of the Berserker King". Hermon retreated away from the hands and mouth. He had never mentioned his name and did not look like any Berserker. The change spell was supposed to make him unrecognizable.

"We should talk inside. It's too dangerous out here," said the thing as it shifted once more, moving aside to let Hermon in. He went in, still stunned, cautious and on guard.

Once inside, he saw the barman first, looking bored from the lack of guests. There were many small curiosities scattered around the room; little circles of light that hovered in the air; magical lamps. There were also tables, full of runes and signs that were

Chapter Four

constantly changing; and chairs that creaked as one approached. Everything was in motion, except for the few people in the room. They were cloaked in silence, dark hoods covering their faces. Hermon took all that in and felt at home. Here sat free men and women, able to do what they wanted. They were mercenaries that sold themselves to the highest bidder. They were able to protect themselves and hold their own against any army, and as such they focused on themselves, not carrying anyone else's burdens. Hermon was the son of the Berserker King. His burdens followed him everywhere. He admired the freedom these warriors enjoyed, even though they were looked upon by every kingdom as dishonest men. He could even see himself here one day.

The magic servitor created a hand, pointing into a corner where one of the guests was sitting. "That is where we will speak," it said. Hermon hesitated to take orders from a being so strange. "All right," he said gruffly, following the creature's hand signal. The chairs creaked and turned as he walked past.

When he arrived, the being bowed to the person in the corner. "This is the son of the Berserker King. He seeks allies to break the cycle of balance and chaos," it introduced softly. It then turned to Hermon.

"Hermon, this is D'rmas, warrior of Qeltifom." Hermon didn't know quite how to act so he nodded briefly. D'rmas nodded back. D'rmas was a tall bald man with an overgrown beard. The golden ring that looped through his nostrils glittered when light hit it.

He waved his hood away and looked Hermon in the face. "Sit down." The warriors of Qeltifom had a special quirk about them. They were not bound to just one class of power but could use two. They mastered the magic arts but also the sword. They were incredibly valuable as allies but also unpredictable. You never really know if they will use you for their own purpose. They lived solely by reputation. Once they campaigned for a cause, they would fight to the last breath to end it, and they were quick. They were said to be as fast as the warriors of this City of the Middle Kingdom, who were incredibly fast.

"Tell me about your journey, Hermon," the stranger started the conversation, his eyes dark as night. His hands and ears were a little longer than usual, making him look gangly.

"We seek assistance in the fight against the house of the King. Every 100 years, a warrior-princess, for the good of the world, is sacrificed to the gods, Camin and Lowus. These sacrifices are to maintain the balance of this world. Otherwise, there will be chaos once again! Her sacrifice would give more power to the warriors to keep the creeping evil in the heart of creation at bay. She is chaos alive, and balance at death, or that is how it was supposed to be. But Eldana, the current princess to be sacrificed, resists because she has found a way to maintain the balance permanently. This would mean that there need never again be any concern about chaos." Hermon paused to see if his opponent was taken by his story or had already lost concentration. He couldn't interpret the look.

"Why are you involved?" D'rmas asked. "You are a man with a strength that many not dare to dream about. You are of royal blood and could live a life as a king. Instead, you are helping a leper who has no idea what she is getting herself into."

What D'rmas said was true. But not for Hermon. There were many reasons why he was trying to help her. Eldana had been the first to treat him without fear. All others saw only the king's son in him. Perhaps, Hermon considered, he trusted her because he saw in the princess a kindred soul. She was a princess after all, and faced the same control and expectations as he had. Indeed, Eldana would have continued to be a princess if the mark of chaos had not been discovered on her body, and she was thrust into a life that she had never asked for. Then there was the fact that she was a warrior too; Eldana and Hermon had spilt blood on the same battlefields. There was a kinship in strife that no other who had not endured such hardship could understand. But in the end, even after all of those reasons, Hermon looked up and just said, "Because she needs help."

D'rmas now leaned back in his creaking chair. "So, you want

Chapter Four

me to help *you* because *she* needs help? Is that all?" The older warrior looked at Hermon scornfully.

"You have no reason why I should help, do you? You think I should help because it's the right thing to do? What do you take me for? Do you think I got all my skills for nothing?" asked D'rmas.

Hermon nodded, controlling his temper. Warriors of the free Guild were supposed to be noble, to step in when the balance of nature was threatened. "I figured…"

"So you haven't thought for a second about what I want for my services?" D'rmas insisted.

Hermon could feel his anger starting to rise. Who was this guy that would allow an innocent woman to be slaughtered? There was more at stake here than just Eldana, though. Hermon couldn't let his feelings get in the way, but his inner Berserker was starting to break free, and blood spilled from his finger, which he tried to hide, but it too late. He couldn't get too angry!

D'rmas watched all this, bemused, before he stood up. "Well, I think I should go."

Hermon looked stunned. "Why are you leaving now? Is that it?" He glared at the creature that had brought him to D'rmas. It created shoulders that it used to shrug. It had no idea what was going on.

"Offer me something I can't refuse," D'rmas created a little ball of fire. "How about a little fight?"

Hermon thought he heard wrong. "What do you mean? You want to fight me? Are you crazy?" D'rmas lauged, giving Hermon a challenging look.

"Berserker son, you have come to enlist me. You bring nothing but your dignity and the duty to do right. Why should I care?"

Hermon could only look puzzled. No one had ever fought him just for 'fun'. Usually, others always ran from Hermon. They don't stop. They shook with fear! The power of the Berserkers was known throughout the land. Unless they had the same power themselves, there was hardly anyone who would go to that trouble willingly.

"You would go down in history as D'rmas the Great, who changed chaos forever. Is that worthless?" Hermon stood up and confronted D'rmas. He wasn't angry. He was curious. Why would anyone risk their life to fight him?

"I'm not interested in glory. I'm interested in the perfect fight. I'm tired of wandering this world and not meeting a worthy opponent. Show me that you are one and I'll join you," D'rmas paused and looked Hermon in the eyes.

It was rare to meet someone who drew fascination from fighting. But he understood. Challenges like these were normal among the Berserkers. Tournaments would often be held as part of a long-standing tradition. Part ritual, part staging, but still demonstrations of power and a crucial part of the culture, but the goal was not to die in the end. Hermon had to play by his rules if he wanted to take this fighter with him. He would have to be careful not to kill him. He needed him. All the other free warriors had stood by the windows of the tavern and watched with interest. The magical servitor had been right to put Hermon and D'rmas together. All other warriors were weaker. D'rmas, however, had the strength and will of many and seemed to be the leader of the whole.

D'rmas drew his sword. He cast a spell that turned his arm to stone and made his helmet appear. The crest on the helmet began to glow.

"Will you do me the honor, Berserker prince?"

"Yes." Hermon nodded. "But this is not a fight to the death." D'rmas head lowered, he was ready to fight. "Every blow counts. Servitor, play the referee!" The creature immediately hovered into the air to their side.

"The winner is the one with the first three hits, both magical and physical." D'rmas smiled and nodded.

They moved to the back of the Guild house, where there was a courtyard out back, with a circle was drawn on the ground. Neither of the fighters could leave this circle until the fight was over. What Hermon underestimated was the speed with which D'rmas

Chapter Four

struck. Before Hermon could even make a punch, D'rmas was right before him and struck him with his stone fist in the center of the chest.

Whether it was the unbelievable speed or the stone arm, the punch brought with it a force of incredible strength. Hermon flew across the courtyard and crashed into the stone wall. Slowly, D'rmas pulled himself back into his combat stance.

"One-nil, I'd say." The free warriors had followed them and were snickered. They liked that, a fight like the old days. Hermon, his head still resting against the stone wall, turned slowly around and glared at D'rmas. This was about demonstrating strength, not killing. He had to keep telling himself that. Hermon's eyes turned a deep red. His body grew and bled. A deep scream of pain emanated from him, a pain he missed yet hated so much. The magical servitor quickly created a spell that made the courtyard soundproof. Passers-by outside the guild, who had heard a part of the scream looked around curiously, but the sound had been smothered just as quickly as it had arrived and they went on, chalking the noise up to fanciful imaginations.

D'rmas concentrated. He knew it was getting serious. Hermon eyes firing daggers, his transformation was complete. Hermon restrained from attacking. *Not yet,* he thought. His rage was too great. He needed time to fully be in control. D'rmas shouted a spell of belligerence, much like the Berserkers did when they magically summoned their true nature. D'rmas charged towards him to strike a second time with his stone fist. He commanded the sword to ignite, and it became as hot as lava.

"Two-nil now," D'rmas boasted as he struck the Berserker across the back. Despite the force and speed he'd used, it lacked the same effect as his first strike. This time, Hermon was prepared. His rage was so extreme he would have ripped D'rmas head off, but he held back. With a kick, he could have sent D'rmas to the ground! Hermon launched himself at D'rmas with a barrage of blows but D'rmas was quick. He dodged every blow effortlessly and vaulted back a safe distance from Hermon to gloat from there.

"I expected more from you, Berserker son," said D'rmas as he hurled himself at his opponent again. Hermon reared back and protected his body with his mighty arms. None of the blows hurt him, no matter how fast D'rmas was. Even his fire sword barely made a scratch on Hermon. Without any pain or sign of distress from Hermon, these blows could not count in the challenge.

D'rmas reared back, threw the sword in the air, and said two words that turned it into a frighteningly giant axe. Hermon stared at the display of power and chuckled. He had seen better from Siem and Eldana and was unimpressed. D'rmas swung the axe and Hermon feinted to the side. The rock behind him was cut in half. D'rmas decided to try another strategy this time. He stood in front of Hermon and transformed into a miniature version of himself. The momentary shock Hermon experienced was all he needed. D'rmas rolled under Hermon's legs and stood behind him in an instant. Before Hermon could react, he returned to normal size and struck with a hard punch. D'rmas reared back and rejoiced loudly.

"Three-nil." He seemed to know exactly what was needed to spice up the fight and he delivered. "You lose, Berserker! I would have thought better of you!"

Hermon panted, and nodded, but Hermon's eyes red and his rage barely contained as he said, "How about one more? Why don't you prove, beyond all doubt, that you really are the better fighter?"

"Four-nil would not be bad," D'rmas gloated, and agreed.

Hermon had seen and heard enough. Now it was time to end this charade. This time Hermon launched the attack. This somewhat daring move unnerved D'rmas. In a flash, D'rmas stone arm had turned into a shield. Hermon struck with the full force of his fury and the shield broke. The blow hit D'rmas in the face and had him violently flying halfway through the barracks, but before he touched the ground, he saw a huge shadow above him. Hermon appeared again and this time. he kicked him in the side. D'rmas suddenly flew into the crowd of the other fighters and was

Chapter Four

caught by them. Hermon stood there and grinned with a proud tilt of his head.

"Three-one," Hermon growled, as the Qeltifom warrior struggled and wobbled to his feet.

D'rmas was beyond insulted. He had truly believed he would best the Berserker completely, and the blows he sustained bruised not only his body but his spirit. He was a fine warrior that hated to be dishonoured. He did not intend for the Berserker to have the final laugh. He intended to win. He bowed his head and muttered some words, summoning his strength to create a huge shield around him, a gigantic bubble of energy that looked impenetrable.

The free warriors were astonished. The power one had to muster to create such a shield was overwhelming. It required even more to destroy it. They doubted even the Berserker had such power. D'rmas saw with satisfaction that everyone else was terrified. The shield around him rumbled and glimmered with power.

Hermon was not impressed. Most of them had never and were probably not ready to see what came next. He vaulted off, speaking the Berserkers' tongue - "*Seberu,* Berserker!" The power of the Berserkers came from the depths of Taos like any other magical ability, but the power that Hermon accessed now had not been seen in this world for centuries, only the oldest clans of the Berserkers knew how to access the deepest powers of Toas. The blood that ran down his body turned black, as did Hermon's eyes. It would leave him completely drained for some time after the fight, but Hermon did not care. D'rmas wavered for an instant, shocked by this display of forgotten magic.

The ground of the courtyard tremored, rumbled – and split in two! People screamed as the force of Hermon's power unsettled everything, rocking the walls of the Guild house, and sending the spectators stumbling. D'rmas most of all felt the full force of it as his magnificent shield broke and he was struck in the chest. He fell to the ground and trembled. The fight was over. Hermon had won. After a few minutes, Hermon wore his human form, and stood over the struggling D'rmas, who looked up at him.

"What was that, Hermon? I have never felt such power." D'rmas asked as Hermon fell beside him, feeling faint.

"Something I am reluctant to show, a force from the depths of Toas so powerful I can barely control it myself." Hermon breathed heavily and sweat glistened his brow. They said every time a Berserker went berserk, his life span was reduced.

D'rmas nodded. "Thank you, Hermon. Here's to our future battles." He signalled to the magic servitor who conjured a cup of ale in their hands. D'rmas took a swig and gave Hermon a contented smile. "We can leave as soon as my healing spells put me back together again!"

Hermon smiled triumphantly. He had convinced him. "So be it. Welcome, Brother D'rmas."

Chapter Four

Mikko & Lord Taboon

Siem was careful. She knew that if she were caught, she would be threatened with immediate death. Here was the center of all evil, everything ruled by the minds of selfish beings who had given in to hubris and darkness. The change spell helped her look different, but she still had a hard time acting normal. Siem was the most responsible of the three companions, she was constantly worried about the other two. It annoyed her that neither of them thought about how dire the consequences would be if they were caught!

"We're going to be fine," she muttered under her breath, reassuring herself not for the first time that day. She looked down and shook her head, lost in thought. The fact that Hermon had problems controlling his temper and Eldana was incredibly stubborn did nothing to allay her fears. She had more than enough reason to be worried. As she muttered exasperated curses under her breath and walked towards the magic citadel, she noticed that someone was following her. She felt the same life energy for a while, which was very unusual in such a huge and crowded place like this. Usually, you only feel the same energy but fleetingly because someone is constantly walking past you. But this energy was constantly behind her and always with the same intensity.

Fear washed over her like a wave. Had she been discovered? Was there anyone here who knew she was in town? She had to come up with a solution and fast. She subtly glanced back but saw nothing unusual.

Moving a little further, she saw a street on one side. Siem didn't care that she had no idea where it led. Instinct had her walking briskly into the dark alley. The passage was narrow, and the walls were decorated with magical signs. At a small restaurant in the wider street behind her, food was just delivered to customers who were loudly rejoicing about it. Foe powder and gnome cake were served, a delicacy in the capital. The customers were practically drooling. But Siem concentrated on her stalker, not the food...

She noticed the energy drifting away as she moved into the alley. Relieved and a little careless at the same time, she laughed to herself. Siem realized how silly and paranoid she was being. That could have been a dear old grandmother walking the same way she did! Maybe she should take time to enjoy the sights and sounds like the locals were. She reached the end of the alley and felt the fear rise in her again. It was as though all the problems of the past years had hit her all at once. She almost broke into tears but stopped herself upon realizing that the street was crowded with a lot of people. Siem might be frightened, but that didn't mean she couldn't have some dignity. The energy that had haunted her was back and it was clear that these waves of emotion were no coincidence.

She buried her fear and dug out her power. She cast four spells at once to protect her. An energy wall was built. Her hands caught fire and were surrounded by floating magic circles as her entire body took on a shade of dark red. While Siem prepared for battle, the sound ebbed away in the restaurant behind her turned. Where just a moment ago everyone was laughing and the mood was light, the people from the restaurant now watched with as much curiosity as fear at the scene unfolding at the end of the alleyway. Even if magic was a common way of life in the city of the Middle Kingdom, "battle magic" was not welcome and very rare. Only a small part of the population was allowed to use this magic, let alone master it.

The guests were astonished when Siem rose in a ball of fire, looking like a phoenix rising from the ashes. She took one last deep breath. She had to be quick and precise, not too many people should see what was going on. After all, she was on the run from the King's Guard! She jumped out of the alley and immediately turned to the wall of the house where she felt the energy radiate from the most.

She did not think. She saw a shadow on the wall and a body. Immediately, she shot two fireballs in that direction. The shadow jumped away immediately and shouted *"Mikkkooooo!"* She did

Chapter Four

not understand what this being wanted. She had to make sure she had the advantage, especially now in this precarious position. This had to be done quickly and quietly. There was too much at stake...

She shot three more fireballs against the creature, but it was quick. Her fireballs hit the wall behind it which was already scorched from her first attack. The creature was fast and windy. None of the fireballs hit its body, even though they had been incredibly fast. At the last second, it jumped away every time. Siem kept shooting and it kept screaming *"Miiikkooooo"* with every shot. Siem noticed that she couldn't hit it and stopped for a second. The creature just stood in front of her. It didn't attack either. It just stood there, staring. Siem was irritated. She stopped the fire and changed back, drifting to the floor and regaining her normal hues and colour once again.

The being just looked at her and smiled. Siem had not noticed that before. It smiled. It hadn't attacked. It didn't want to kill anyone.

"Who are you? And why are you following me?" she looked right at him. It was a "he" she presumed.

"So now you ask Mikko Mikko? *After* you fire?" The figure didn't seem outraged. Although his question was challenging, he seemed more amused and from the way he spoke.

"Yes, Mikko Mikko, now *I* ask, and *you* answer. Why are you following me?"

There was no aggression, just curiosity from the figure. She could see it in his eyes. The longer she watched him, the safer she felt. There was no sense of aggression, just curiosity. He took a step towards her. He stood tall with black hair and wearing a robe billowing in the air. He stared at her with a confident smile while his brown eyes assessed her. She was irritated but that wasn't new. The warriors of the Middle Kingdom could all move so quickly, she reminded herself.

"Siem..." He said softly and kneeled to lower his head. "Guardian of the one who turns against all." That wasn't a question, it was a statement. He knew who she was. It seemed their consciousness had been marked into the minds of many. But Siem did not know by whom.

Siem did not want to attract more attention. Too many beings had already been spectators of this show. "Please stand up," She begged. He looked up again at her.

"Why are you following me?" She pressed again.

"I heard about your story, Siem. It is similar to mine. I too was expelled from the School of Mages. My name is Mikko. I am at your service."

Siem was a little baffled. Suddenly, she heard a voice behind her, one that was at once too loud to ignore and yet too quiet to understand. But the word she understood was like a fist in the eye. "Traitor!" Siem turned and realized just at that moment that a group had formed around her. A large cluster of beings, some of them their spectators. The one who was in charge was an old lady. She looked at Siem with big eyes. "I recognize her from the warrior images sent out by the Seven. " She said, adding, "Whoever captures her will be greatly rewarded."

Siem had forgotten to use the change spell after she had transformed back from the fire phoenix and now it looked like she would pay dearly for it. Step by step, these new attackers came closer and closed the circle around her. Siem did not want to hurt anyone. But she took two steps back and ignited her hands with fire again just so that no one would get a stupid idea...

"If we catch them together, we can share the reward," said the old lady. You could hear the greed in her voice. The horde of people advanced on Siem. She felt like a wild animal driven into a corner with no possible escape.

"Don't you dare!" Siem warned, her hands and eyes bright red. They whispered around her. "Demon...fire witch."

Siem turned around to Mikko, still standing in the same place as before. She had nearly forgotten him. He looked at her but didn't smile anymore. He glowed. " Mikko at your service," came out of him.

"Then do something!" She yelled at him. He nodded and stood

Chapter Four

in front of her. He whispered words of magic. Every word was imbued with power. Her heart stopped for a second when she heard what he said. It was dark magic. Every word triggered an avalanche of whirring runes around her. What took her minutes, he did with just a single word. The voices in the air that Mikko had released overshadowed every other sound. She didn't know what was happening. All around her, the creatures began to scream, but the runes swallowed the sound. The humans started to run, but they could barely move, trapped as they were by the rune power.

They moved slowly, very slowly. And even though their mouths were wide open and screams should be heard, it was silent. Only the three rune words were in the air. Siem looked down on herself and noticed that she was not taken by the spell. She could move freely. She looked at Mikko, "You froze her?"

Mikko nodded "Every second seems like a whole day to them. They will be a little busy, but not for long."

"What do you suggest we do now?" She asked. He had saved her and seemed to know a lot about magic.

"I'm taking you somewhere safe."

Siem nodded. Even if she could escape here, she needed allies in this city.

"Mikkooooo, Mikkooooo," He cried the same way he had before. He suddenly threw her in the air and jumped after her. The entire thing happened so fast that she knew if she were a mere spectator it would only seem like a blur before her eyes. She couldn't tell if she was flying two meters through the air or two thousand. It was as though time was not playing a significant role anymore. She was everywhere at once. She only saw the face of Mikko flash before her briefly. His mastery of time was impressive and not to mention, insanely powerful.

They landed again. It felt like a dream. She knew that she had been in another part of the city recently, but she could no longer say exactly where she was.

"My mind is clouded," she said. He smiled at her observation as he put her down then took a few steps away.

"Everything happens so fast you lose the feeling of time and space, and you can't distinguish between a dream and reality." He explained.

Siem nodded and listened intently. He knew his stuff, that was for sure, and she would be foolish to not learn a few things from him. Fortunately, Siem wasn't foolish.

She noticed her surroundings now and frowned. Mikko's magic had brought her to the outside of the Mage Guild buildings. A single White lighter Mage was set up there. It was very unusual for a building to have a White lighter Mage – who were very powerful guardians.

The building itself looked very unimpressive. Brown walls with black runes of marble surrounded the building. The roof had four different chimneys. Each one spewed out smoke the same color of the chimney, red, yellow, blue, and brown. They were the colors of the Magic School. The smoke swirled around the guardian mage like some sort of protective shield. Two dragons woven by magic hung in the air. It was entrance week for the magic students. Accordingly, many magicians were outside with their children. The novices wandered together through the square in front of the building. For Siem, it was a beautiful and breath-taking sight. Here she had spent the first years of her education. This was her home, at least it used to be. Elves, beings of balance and chaos, Berserkers, and other human mages that crafted magic here.

"I am always amazed at how beautiful the surroundings are." His tone was sarcastic and almost bitter.

Even though she despised the magicians for their weakness, she loved this place. "Tell me your story, Mikko."

"My story?" he repeated thoughtfully. "It's not that simple." Siem's gaze told him she expected more. Siem smiled encouragingly. She hadn't done that in a while.

"You won't like my story," He warned after a few seconds of silence. Siem heaved a sigh. "I don't think I'm supposed to, but at least I'm sure I'll understand."

Mikko nodded. "I am a magician novice. I was trained by Lord

Chapter Four

Taboon."

Siem lifted her head. She had expected anything but this. He was the apprentice of the one magician that she had come here to oppose.

"Is that so?" She said sarcastically. "Is that why you're helping me? Know your enemy better than you know your friend?" She was ready to use her defensive magic. The trust they'd just amassed began to fade in her eyes. She turned her hands in his direction and forgot for a second that the same person had just helped her. Mikko saw and raised his hands in his defense. "I could have attacked you much earlier, but I didn't. Don't you think I'm being kind to you?"

"Who knows? Why should I trust you?"

He looked at her and nodded. "I am at your service. Believe me or not, I had to leave because I had my own ideas about justice and our 'mutual friend' wasn't too happy about that."

"You mean Lord Taboon?" Siem clarified, for the strange Mage to nod, once.

"And what are your ideas of justice?" asked Siem thoughtfully.

"Well," Mikko smiled. "First of all, I don't kill anyone. I don't need to manipulate anyone to reach my goal and I always tell the truth."

Siem nodded. "That won't get you very far in a world like this."

"The truth is the magicians in these great halls think I am a charlatan. I have defeated most of them back in the Great Hall and quickly."

She believed him, every word he said. She felt at one with him. He was a rebel in the true sense of the word. Siem hadn't felt connected to someone like she did with him in a long time. Every second she thought about it made everything seem crazier. Siem, a powerful magician, was struggling with her emotions. Damn it! The internal struggle was visible on her face. Siem looked as torn and confused as she felt.

"What am I gonna do with you?" She blurted out. "First you save my life, then you tell me that you are playing for the wrong team and now you look at me with those big googly eyes."

Siem let her defences fall completely, magical and emotional. She knew that her trust for him was unusually quick, but she cared about him for some reason and that made her nervous. He hid nothing from her, and that was very rare. He had laid himself bare before her. Yet it seemed to her that she didn't know him at all.

"Okay, so what do you want from me?" Siem asked. She relaxed her posture and looked at him, waiting for a clear answer. He looked puzzled by this direct question but immediately gave her an answer.

"I want to help you. This is about us walking in there and facing Lord Taboon together, two mages against one." After a while, he spoke again. "You will change this world, Siem. Your name is already on everyone's lips, and I think it is good that someone like you can make it this far."

"Someone like me?" She wondered aloud. She looked at him and could barely suppress the urge to laugh.

"Well, you're a woman and a woman doesn't usually do that," Mikko said, somewhat apologetically.

Siem rolled her eyes and couldn't bother pretending to be shocked by the misogyny of it all. He felt awkward and kept stuttering in a haste to justify his words. The last thing he wanted was to offend her.

"Well, you are with a princess, a princess who probably didn't volunteer... but you are standing right here trying to change the world beside her. You should be dead. You should have been forgotten because of what you have done and because you are a woman, yet you are not. You pose a threat to all those who stand against you."

He tried again when she met his words with a blank stare. "I want to stand up to these powerful sorcerers and change the system... with you, a beautiful, powerful, and amazing woman."

Siem smiled then. She realized that there was much more at stake here than she had initially thought.

Chapter Four

Mikko continued, "I am powerful but not a natural leader. I do things alone. You, on the other hand, have come so far with little help and without a man at your side." She tried her best not to roll her eyes again.

"I am not alone but yes, the first steps were hard, and after that, the help I received was not much, so I am proud and happy that I have come this far. I will fulfil my duty as a guardian and save Eldana from certain death."

"That's what I meant," said Mikko. "You're a leader. You do whatever it takes to pursue and fight for what you believe in no matter the risk, and I find that incredible. That's why I'm here. I've been hiding for the last few years, ashamed to be myself. I feel the light is not strong enough to protect me. But with you, the light in my heart glows again and I am ready to fight with you. I feel, somehow, that we may even have a chance to win…"

Siem was a little embarrassed at the attention they got from his loud declaration. People who passed by stared intensely at them.

"Well then, Mikko," Siem began. "You now belong to the new circle of the Protectors of Eldana. We are happy to have you with us."

The magician laughed out loud. His smile was brighter than the sun in its full glory. She also laughed. She turned and looked at the building.

"Thanks again for bringing me here. I will go in and demand Lord Taboon's help and stop this terrible hunt."

The color in Mikko's face drained instantly as he gave a horrified gasp.

"That's what you wanted to come here, to appeal to Lord Taboon?"

Before he could finish his sentence, Siem was already on her way into the building. Mikko was puzzled but ran after Siem and grabbed her by the arm, speaking the runes of time and speed. Through the magic, it could have been difficult to fool the mage guard, but Mikko knew his way around and was fast and shrewd. The mage guard sensed a slight source of power but in a magic school that was normal. It didn't matter.

They emerged inside the school much faster than expected; two merest flickers of light and air that went unnoticed. The two ended up near the door to Lord Taboon's chamber. It was located in a side corridor, cut off from the main hallway, and with many magical inscriptions on the walls. Siem held her fingers to her lips as she stepped forward, and peeped into Lord Taboon's office with a spell. Siem and Mikko carefully walked in after knocking and immediately heard whistling. The office of Lord Taboon looked exactly as one would imagine the office of a leading magician. Thousands of books were placed on impressively tall antique bookshelves. Everywhere, there were mystic signs and crystals for different purposes. Lord Taboon was just about to put away a scroll when he heard the knock on the door. He assumed it was one of the students looking for help again. He tried to appear friendly when he approached since he had been told far too often that he seemed quite scary and aggressive.

"Come in," He said in a lovely tone with his best smile. A young woman and a man stood there in front of him. They looked quite nasty, but that was normal for Lord Taboon. Everyone looked nasty to him.

"How can I help you, students?" He stated.

Siem was the first to speak. She felt her heart flutter for a moment, but her nerves were tempered by the memories of their recent chase. "We are not students," she said steadily. She looked their nemesis in the eye.

"We are friends of Eldana and demand you to stop hunting her."

Lord Taboon's smile disappeared. He looked at the young her for a few seconds before continuing. "So you must be Siem."

They had not met before, but the seven must have spread the news that Eldana is not alone after the battle on the forest clearing.

"I've heard a lot about you, that you were this naive wasn't one of them. "Siem didn't give him the pleasure of being unsettled.

Chapter Four

She had known her plan was a long shot, but she had come prepared, and she wasn't alone either.

"Tell me, child," Lord Taboon said, "Do you understand what is at stake?" He took a step closer. Mikko looked nervously behind them at the door, then at the several large windows that went from the ceiling to the floor, but they all were on Lord Taboon's side.

"I know what's at stake, and it has nothing to do with Eldana's life or anyone else's, we need to defeat evil, "Siem said angrily, desperately. She suddenly realized how futile this plan had been. It wasn't that Lord Taboon couldn't listen to reason; it was that he had chosen not to. He was obsessed with maintaining the old ideals.

"But child,. Lord Taboon came one step closer to her. "We don't have to defeat evil. We just have to keep the balance, that's all."

Siem took a step back. Mikko already grabbed on to her and was ready to jump. Maybe, she had made a mistake coming here. She had heard the man was a man of reason.

"No, that's not going to happen," she said.

Lord Taboon's hands changed color to a blazing blue. "Yes, my child," said Lord Taboon, as he began to speak to the runes. Mikko cried out and grabbed Siem, trying to jump out of the window, but suddenly Lord Taboon was standing in front of them.

Mikko screamed his name and attempted to jump with Siem through a portal. It was not as relaxing or as exhilarating as the last time. It hurt this time. When they came out of the warp they were still in the air. Mikko's spell had worked, but through the glimmering light of the magic warp tunnel, they could still see Lord Taboon at the end. Siem landed hard and rolled, as did Mikko, too, as they saw Lord Taboon's fading image summon his warriors to his side.

"She is here. Find her," Lord Taboon shouted, before he finally disappeared from their view.

When Siem regained consciousness, she found herself laying in a dark room. She got up immediately and saw Mikko laying nearby. She rushed to him.

"Are you okay?" She asked.

He turned around and got up. "Well, that wasn't my best work." He teased, making Siem laugh despite their situation. "But next time you try to attack the strongest mage in our kingdom, please let me know!"

Siem nodded with a smile on her face "I'll be happy to do that and trust me there will be a next time. Tell me where you took us."

He pointed his finger outside. "See for yourself."

Siem went to the window and peeked through the thick curtains. There was a mighty gate with guards outside. "The city gate, perfect!" She mumbled to herself and Mikko smiled. Siem needed more time to recover. The jump had taken a toll on her. She was not yet back to her full strength. She kept watching the entrance gate while Mikko picked himself up again. This unexpected, violent flight had cost him greatly. Siem did not seem to notice. Her mind was somewhere else. She hoped that Eldana was safe and had better luck with her mission than they had with theirs.

Chapter Four

Eldana and the King

Eldana hated it in the king's chambers. She had snuck past the guards outside without anyone seeing her, leaning into the shadows, and becoming one with them. Inside the palace, things were different; there were no guards.

The hubris of the King was clear in every cornice, stone, and tapestry. This place was old-fashioned, inflexible, the whole ambiance that came with the place gagged any imagination; all meaningless opulence and glorification of dead people who did not deserve the right.

One of the reasons she hated it was that time here appeared to stand still. There was no change. She didn't want to be part of a machine that followed rituals without understanding them. That's exactly why she was here. She needed to convince the King. She also knew there was a possibility she would suffer an instant and cruel death, especially if she failed. She was not afraid of death though.

Eldana was alone, with a hood pulled over her head. Her mind wandered briefly down memory lane. Everything seemed to be an irony. Why make her train so hard only to sacrifice her?

Maybe the gods are greedy, she thought. Maybe they wanted what power she had to offer at its fullest manifestation. There were no guards or staff. Eldana knew why. There were mirrors all over the walls that kept the palace in order. Each mirror had the power to read intentions and communicate with its observer.

When Eldana looked into one of the mirrors, she saw stories of her childhood., questions from her master and friends, which she answered as naturally as a dream. But it was no dream, some catchers recorded everything and then passed it on. It all felt like a dream...but Eldana knew that it wasn't.

Her mind was being probed.

This allowed the King to know everything about everyone. The king was a man whom Eldana barely knew. She scarcely remembered him from when she was a child. Emotionless, he sat on the throne like a statue. Eldana tried to avoid the mirrors, but it was not easy. Every time she came closer to one she felt the pull to look into it and dream.

Eldana wandered through the halls along the path that had been paved especially for her. She eventually found some larger mirrors decorated with different colors and ornaments that she could not ignore. Eldana felt that the pull from the larger mirrors was even stronger. It drove her crazy not to look into them.

At that moment, she was inside the king's suite of rooms. But the magic of the King had fashioned this section of the palace into the likeness of catacombs, with many different corridors and heavy doors with magical symbols.

A set of stone stairs led down to a small pool. It was crazy, the things the king had crammed into this part of the palace using magic. She had just passed the last mirrors, so she thought she was safe. This was the first time that she had walked that far into the king's castle, and she didn't know what to expect. The pool had a bluish color and was transparent. For a second, she started to feel dizzy, but it quickly passed.

The far end of the pool became a big waterfall. Many of her friends were waiting at the bottom and yelling, "Jump! Jump! Jump!" They all laughed and rejoiced. Siem and Hermon were there. They waved at her and she waved back. Everything was filled with happiness. Eldana jumped in, and after a few seconds, she was deep inside the pool. Eldana then swam back up and could hear the roar of laughter.

She swam to the edge of the pool, under the waterfall where everyone was standing. Siem helped her out. She looked at her from top to bottom and yelled, "You look like a wet dog!" which caused a roaring from all friends. Eldana waved it away.

"What are you doing here?" Siem asked as she pointed up at the edge of the waterfall. Eldana looked confused and pointed her finger upwards to the point where she jumped from. It was obvious what she was doing here. She just wanted to jump into the water and come to Siem.

Chapter Four

"What are you doing here? Asked Siem again.

The smile on her face started to fade. Eldana wanted to answer but could not remember why she was here. It had been so clear before. Then it came back to her in one fell swoop.

"I am Eldana, and I must see the king, to ask him to stop trying to keep the balance. I must ask him to stop." Eldana answered.

The smile on Siem's face fell, and her figure faded away slowly. Eldana had a pounding headache. She became nauseous. She had given herself away. The people in the pool weren't real. It was all the mirror's trick. The spell was strong, but it was wearing off after Eldana gave herself away. She had been deceived. She had no time to lose. She had to leave. She began to run, speaking the protective magic she had perfected so well, but it went wrong. The shield shimmered and disappeared. The figures from the pool were chasing after her.

The second that Eldana had started running, the whole room changed. The mirrors were everywhere, closing in on her, appearing to grow in size. *Had there ever really been a catacomb? A waterfall? A pool?*

With a sudden whoosh of air and one of the large mirrors flew towards her, slowing only at the last minute to block her path-

She struck the mirror, and it broke. Every time one of these mirrors fell to the ground, the others adapted. After the third strike, no mirror broke immediately after one hit but only after two. After the sixth, it took three hits to take a mirror down. Eldana could not keep up this number game forever. She broke through them one by one even as the mirrors became stronger collectively. With each time that they changed, they became faster and better. Eldana was used to fighting but this was pushing her limits.

The fights were relentless. Where did they all come from? The mirrors had become so strong that it was no longer possible to move forward. As she tried to manoeuvre them by outrunning the first couple of mirrors, they came in closer and closer, leaving her with nowhere to run to. There were too many of them. Suddenly, the mirrors stopped, and she had heard a loud rumble.

The rumbling came up again, this time louder and stronger than before. Those who had just stood in front of her now moved a few meters away. She had room to breathe again. Still, the princess's heart raced.

There was a third rumble. This time she heard a voice from far away. And that voice said her name;

"Eldana."

How long has it been since a king called someone personally, rather than have their courtiers or advisers announce their arrival? She couldn't even remember.

There was a time when she would have been happy at being personally called by the King. Who would not rejoice after hearing the voice of the ruler of kingdoms, the closest to the gods by his position? He was feared and respected by all. At school, the benevolence of the king and his protection for the realm was imprinted on the minds of children. On all coins, it was the king's face that smiled from it. At harvest, after the gods, it was him that everyone paid homage to.

"Eldana." The voice rumbled out loud once again.

"Eldana, why won't you listen?" The voice asked. Resentment grew in her at the sound of that voice.

"Because it's wrong." She replied calmly.

"Do you deny the meaning of keeping evil away?" The voice replied instantly. In the last words, there was great astonishment. The rumbling echoes around the voice grew louder and longer.

"Are you evil yourself?" The mirrors that had once pulled back, trembled again and came closer.

Eldana was not frightened. She didn't care. "That's rubbish! It's all wrong, the chaos mark, the legend it is all just fear!" She shouted. The rumbling stopped again. The mirrors stopped moving.

"Tell me about it, child." The voice came again, but this time in a kinder tone. It was light and even inviting.

Eldana knew what this was all about. She had been on the run too long not to realize this trick. She was being stalled, plain and simple, so she could be caught. The King was not able to under-

Chapter Four

stand her.

Now the question was, how did she deal with it? She answered first. "Well, I figured out a way to stop all this, no more good, no more evil. The struggle ends."

But her answer was met only by a reflective silence. Eldana looked around. There were far too many mirrors to attack all of them.

"You dare to question the balance?" the king spoke.

Chills were running down her spine at the threat in the King's voice. But yeah, she *did* dare.

But how the hell was she going to explain that to someone who claimed that this balance was his creation in the first place, even everyone knew he is not? All the peoples of Taos had agreed on this one thing. They all knew the cost and yet they went down this road sacrificing away. He was too deep in it to understand. She had hoped for so much more.

Eldana had to get out of here. She thought through all the spells she mastered but none of them made her go faster. She needed to create a diversion to get out. "Yes, I do." She didn't think twice before she shot a bolt of lightning into the ceiling.

With a crash, blocks of stone fell from the ceiling, smashing most of the mirrors nearby, but not all.

Eldana began to run. She was inches away from the door. The few mirrors that had not been hit began to transform. They grew larger and larger, closing in on her. There was no way out. Eldana ran in a zigzag and made it past one mirror. She tried hard to not look at it. Once caught, she would be gone. She ran past the second and saw a light towards the exit. There was only one mirror between her and freedom.

Eldana ran as fast as she could and fired a lightning bolt. The final mirror burst and she was free.

She had done it! She was outside but knew she couldn't stop running. Any hope that she might have had for winning the King was gone now. They would not stop hunting her. They would not listen to her.

She had almost reached the gate, but exhaustion was spreading through her body. When would it all end? Maybe she should just give in and let it be over with!

She became overwhelmed with weakness. Nothing made sense anymore. Her whole plan was in shambles. She felt she was getting sick and the world was spinning. She stumbled through the city, heading for the outer gates – and almost got there! - when she fell. She had lost her balance for only a second and yet this was enough to throw her to the ground. Eldana could not hold on any longer. She staggered for several meters and tried to hold on to something, but that was not possible. Passers-by looked at her with confusion yet carried on with their routines. A lady from the market screamed as Eldana reached into her basket. She knocked her hand away and left hurriedly. No one would help Eldana.

After a few more meters, she fell to the ground. No one came to help. She only heard the roar of the crowd, scattered conversations of many different people. Then there was just static. The King's magic mirrors had been far more powerful than she had given him credit for, and the toll that they exacted was terrible. She was hallucinating. She could hear all of her friends screaming. She thought she felt hands clasping her. In her hallucination, she was carried across a field of flowers by friends that she loved. They were all especially friendly and had no reason to be angry. She would just die now, she thought, and heard exotic new names and saw people she had never intended to meet. But they were all in the flower field together. All the problems of the past few weeks had faded away…

But something was wrong. The voices became clearer, like it was all real. They screamed her name from the flower field, but she could not move.

Slowly, she became curious. Was this death? She heard her name very softly but growing louder steadily. Suddenly, there was a huge wave of water, a wave that disturbed and completely soaked them all. What was happening? Eldana was confused as she tried to keep the water away. A second wave hit her in the face. She didn't

Chapter Four

know what was happening to her. The voices became louder and now she could understand who it was. Siem was screaming her name, about to throw more water on her. The whole dream world around her collapsed. She was not dead. She was with Siem in a hiding place with lots of different people.

"Are you back?" Siem looked suspicious with the bucket of water in her hand, leaning it towards a confused Eldana.

Eldana blinked and ran a hand over her face.

"What happened?" she asked. Hermon quickly rushed to her side and held her up.

"I don't know. You tell me." Siem said. "Hermon found you on the ground, some streets away from the king's palace. He said you were muttering incoherently, and somehow you had blended with the ground. He almost did not see you. Then he brought you here."

Eldana looked around to discover that she was in some kind of room with stone walls and fairly large shutterless windows. People were talking among themselves.

"A-All of that? That had been a dream?" Eldana said, for Siem to only shrug as she looked at her with big, worried eyes.

Not all of it, Eldana thought to herself. Not the palace itself. Not the voice of the King. But the King must have cast some sort of curse or enchantment upon her as she had escaped, or perhaps it was an aftereffect of the magic mirrors? She didn't know, but she was thankful that somehow Hermon had sensed her.

"Where are we? And who are these people?" the princess asked.

"Well, to answer the where part of your question, we're under a bridge," Mikko replied.

Eldana gave him a curious look. "Who are you?"

Mikko looked at Siem, signalling her with his eyes to do the honor of an introduction. Siem rolled her eyes.

"Eldana, this is Mikko. He began stalking me almost as soon as we split up. And I caught him."

"Hey," Mikko objected. "You forget the part where I saved your sorry hide. Twice."

"Uuuuh", Hermon exclaimed, widening his eyes in excitement. "You saved Siem? Twice?" he asked.

"I'm guessing she's not one to be at the receiving end of a saving hand, yeah?" Mikko asked with a smirk.

Hermon chuckled. "You got that part right," he said.

"One more word from you two, and one of you is flying out these windows," Siem cautioned.

Mikko smiled but didn't say anything more. "It's such a pleasure to meet you, Eldana," Mikko said. "Siem hasn't told me much about you. But from the little she's told me, and the things that I know about you, I dare say you're one of a kind."

"The pleasure's mine, Mikko," Eldana said.

"How long are we going to stay here?" Eldana asked. "We should try to find an inn or something. I could use a decent sleep after my ordeal."

"The thing is..." Mikko started, "I think we all experienced ordeals of our own, Eldana. And we kind of..."

"By we, you mean yourself and Siem, yes?" Hermon interrupted.

"Yes, myself and Siem," Mikko corrected. "We kind of racked up some trouble, and Lord Taboon's goons are searching the entire city for you."

Eldana sighed.

"Honestly," Mikko said, "if I had known that Lord Taboon was the person you wanted to meet, I would have stopped you."

"We just have to stay here for now till everything blows over," Siem said, to which the others agreed, and Mikko offered to go find them all something to eat.

"Fine fellow, isn't he?" Hermon asked after Mikko had gone.

Siem pouted and shook her head as she contemplated.

"I don't know much about him yet. But at the moment, I think he is." She replied.

"Whatever the case, he's, well, better than my guy," Hermon stated.

"Your guy?" Eldana asked.

Chapter Four

"Yes," Hermon replied. "My journey to the Guild of Free Warriors was successful."

"I didn't think it was going to be," Eldana stated.

"Same thing I told him. I mean, the free warriors value their freedom, their ability to choose for themselves; albeit a choice affected by the amount one was willing to pay them for their services!"

"You didn't promise him anything we don't have, did you?" Eldana asked.

"No. His pay's going to come after we're successful." Hermon replied. "Plus D'rmas is different."

The plan was to find an alternative means to keep the balance instead of sacrificing innocent people. So far, what the three friends had were their guts telling them there was another way. No one had ever tried to find out, but all three of them were certain of that. To do that, they would require protection, and that was where D'rmas came in.

"That's his name?" Eldana inquired.

"Mhmm," Hermon affirmed. "He actually requested a duel. Between the two of us."

"What?" Eldana asked in shock.

"I was shocked too," Siem said. "I know his kind. Their magical ability makes them more advantaged and stronger than most, but against a berserker, especially one like Hermon, that's still madness."

"I did tell him that," Hermon stated. "However, he's got his quirks too. He's fast, as fast as the soldiers of the Middle Kingdom. The goal was to strike the most out of a cumulative goal of three strikes. He'd gotten three strikes when I evened the playing field after I asked for a dessert. I called on the ancient powers of my clan."

"That's dangerous, Hermon," Eldana said. "Imagine what could have happened if you'd lost control. You could hurt people you know."

"I'm glad I didn't. At least, we've got him among our crew.

We're one step closer to fulfilling our mission."

Eldana was still drained from her experience at the King's palace. She sighed and laid down on her back. "I need to rest." She said. "D'rmas went to survey the routes out of the city. We can visit an inn when he returns and has told us it's safe to. Until then, you'll have to manage here."

Then Hermon sat up from beside Eldana and moved towards Siem. "We're still going to need supplies," Hermon told Siem.

"Yes, I know that," Siem replied. "But for now, we've got to keep our heads low, and make do with what Mikko provides."

"I know I've asked before," Hermon said, "but this Mikko guy, you trust him?"

He gave Siem a questioning look.

"Do you trust D'rmas?" She retorted.

"D'rmas is different, and you know that," Hermon said. "He's a Free Warrior, not some Guild magician. We can count on our contract with D'rmas. He has his reputation to protect and maintain."

Siem was still pensive.

"You know we can work some spells to get him to reveal his true intentions," Hermon suggested.

Siem's eyes flicked towards Hermon. That was all Hermon needed to be apprised of the absurdity of his suggestion. "We're too tired to work a spell of such magnitude," Siem said. "And even if we were to combine our strengths, Mikko is no low-grade magician. I've seen his feats firsthand. He'll know we're trying to enchant him the second we start."

"I guess we'll have to let time decide for us, then," Hermon said.

Siem nodded. Her eyes then moved to where Eldana lay. She looks like one who's fought a hundred battles in a very short time, she thought. Siem wished she could help her friend in a greater capacity, perhaps lift the burden she presently carried from her shoulders, but she couldn't. This was Eldana's destiny. She was a being of balance and chaos, one that had gone rogue. Siem was

Chapter Four

sure that they were all playing the parts destiny had assigned them. She just wished sometimes that it wasn't so difficult.

It was almost dusk when D'rmas returned. Mikko had returned some hours before. The golden ring that looped through D'rmas' nostrils caught the light of the flame floating above the quartet.

"Finally, he is here," Hermon stated.

Eldana looked up at him, but her face didn't reveal any emotions.

"How're things like out there, friend?" Mikko asked.

"They've died down a little," D'rmas replied. His voice was deep and crackly. "The guards have upped their security. And the goons of the man you two angered still roam about." He looked at Siem, and Mikko.

Hermon sucked air through his teeth. "Siem has not the flair for diplomacy at all." Hermon joked. Not one of them laughed.

"We need to get out of here," D'rmas said. "We've got to go somewhere with more publicity, like an inn or something."

"An inn? Wouldn't we be discovered in public? We should be in hiding, keep our heads low." Hermon argued.

"True, my friend. We'll keep our heads low, just not here. Lord Taboon is masterful in the use of magic. He'll use it to ferret out the places that could easily be hiding spots. In a public place, we have the cover of a crowd. It's easier for us to escape if an attack is made."

"We should be on our way then," Eldana said.

D'rmas looked at Eldana. The last time he had seen her, she was in a state of delirium.

"I'm afraid we haven't been properly introduced," D'rmas said. He walked forward a bit. "D'rmas, formerly of the Qeltifom clan, now a member of the Guild of Free Warriors."

Eldana offered a small smile. "I'm Eldana." She said.

D'rmas grunted, then nodded.

"Let's move," Siem said, getting to her feet.

The streets were still teeming with people, so the group merged themselves with the crowd. As they walked, Siem and Mikko used magic to keep track of the energies of the passing crowd in the hopes that they would be able to detect anyone who was coming too close.

"Do we have any particular inn in mind?" Mikko asked after a while.

"No, but…" D'rmas began to say when Eldana cut him off.

"Yes, we do," she said.

Siem and Hermon knew what Eldana was going to say before she said it.

"The Tavern of Wholesome Laughter." She said. "It's not in the capital, but in the town of Kleas…"

"That's still close to the capital," D'rmas observed.

"Yes," Eldana said. "But we know its owner Techle. His tavern can guarantee our safety, at the very least, for a couple of nights."

Hermon sighed. "I could use his positivity spell, right now."

"He uses spells on his customers?" D'rmas asked. There was a hint of confusion in his voice.

"Relax," Hermon said. "I did say it was a positivity spell. There's nothing to be worried about."

Mikko moved closer to Hermon and whispered into his ear. "The warriors of the Free Guard don't like being surprised. That this one is ready to brave the prospect says a lot."

Hermon looked at D'rmas. He found himself wondering what kind of man lay behind the fierce warrior, and if he was capable of establishing a working, amicable relationship with people. *We'll soon find out,* Hermon thought.

It took them another day to travel back to Kleas. With the help of Mikko's ability to use magic to speed up their journey, things got a lot faster. This time, at the gates of Kleas, they did not use any spell to hide and the guard, without hesitation, opened the gates. It seemed that once you arrived in Kleas before, you would always have a place.

A soft golden light spilled out the windows into the streets of Techle's tavern when the group got closer. At the door, they could hear the sound of gentle music coming from a flute.

Chapter Four

Siem pushed the door, dinging the bell hanging at the doorpost. The air was filled with the happiness magic that they experienced the last time they had been there. Immediately, Siem felt a refreshing wave of strength and vivid optimism. They all felt it as they walked in. Even D'rmas face had a soft glow to it.

The people in the tavern were either too engrossed in the flute's music or conversing in their little groups, to look at the new people enter the room. Techle was behind the wooden counter, wearing the same hospitable smile he'd worn when Eldana, Siem, and Hermon had come to him earlier.

"I see you've increased your ranks," he said, taking the group in. His eyes lingered on Mikko for a moment, but then he smiled and asked, "What brings you back here?"

Siem smiled. "Your excellent service of course, plus we're in dire need of somewhere to rest for the night." "It's not just that," Hermon said. He let his eyes scan the small crowd in the tavern. "When we left, you said you could keep us safe?"

Techle didn't say a word. He only let his lips spread wider, an indication that he was eager to listen.

"Well, we need that help."

"Hmm…" Techle said. "Follow me."

"Holly!" He called.

A young lady with blonde hair walked towards him.

"Our guests here need special service. You'll handle things around here while I take them out back." The young lady nodded and smiled as she went straight to the bell at the end of the bar and started to ring it with full swing.

"Oi fellas, Holly is back," she announced loudly. Half of the guests grunted with some form of happiness. Techle looked bewildered at Holly, but she just smiled.

"Shall we?" Techle asked as he pulled off his apron and handed it over the counter.

He turned and walked towards a door set in a dark alcove. The door was small, so it required the group to walk in single file and led to a wider corridor. The moment Techle walked in, torches hanging on the wall whooshed as they came alive with flame.

"This place is a magical wonder," Mikko observed, his eyes coated with awe.

"Indeed," D'rmas affirmed. "It's not the owners working magic here. The place itself is riddled with magic, magic coats the entire town of Kleas!"

"I get the feeling that if we had come in here without an invitation, we would never make it through," Mikko said.

"You've spoken true," Techle said. "Anyone who tries to enter without a guide would never leave this corridor. They would walk, and walk, and will never see the end."

"Spooky," Hermon said.

Techle got to a double door at the end of the corridor and pushed it in. The doors swung noiselessly inwards to reveal a small lobby with wooden floorboards. The double doors closed of their own accord once the entire group was in.

Eldana took a look at the door and spotted the little runes carved along its posts. She looked around the walls and also found carvings of runes a bit bigger than the ones carved on the doorpost. "The magic of the house caters to your needs," Techle declared. "All you need is to make your request, or inquiry and attach the word 'mezah' to it. Like so: I need a tankard of mead, mezah."

A dark silver tankard materialized out of thin air and moved into Techle's grasp.

Mikko's face was suffused with disbelief. As if sensing his thoughts, Techle handed him the tankard. Mikko noticed the tankard was full, brought it to his nose, and discovered that its content smelled very well like mead. He put the tankard to his lips and sipped. Then Mikko's eyes flew open in astonishment.

"By my hand, this is mead, real mead." He exclaimed and burst into laughter.

The rest of the group had smiles plastered on their faces, too. Techle gave a humble bow. "I can usher you to your rooms, but everything is pretty straightforward. You go in through that door there," he pointed further to the left.

Chapter Four

Hermon could spot other doors through the doorway.

"And have your pick of rooms," Techle continued. "In case you're confused, you know what to do."

"The house can issue us suitable rooms too?" Hermon asked wide-eyed.

"Of course, Hermon," Techle said. "This house can do almost anything within the confines of good. Don't ask me what little it can't do. I trust you all can handle yourselves from here?"

Techle, getting a satisfactory reply from the group, nodded and turned to leave when Eldana called out to him.

"Yes, Eldana?" He said as he turned.

Eldana, Siem, and Hermon left D'rmas and Mikko - who were requesting dishes from the house and bursting into laughter whenever their request materialized from the air -- and moved closer to Techle.

"We were wondering if you could do something extra for us," Eldana said, looking up to Techle.

"The house is entirely at your service," Techle said.

"We cannot stay in Kleas long, Techle. People are looking for me, and we have something crucial we must do. We would be happy if we could get supplies that would aid us in our journey."

"What are we looking at here?" Techle asked.

"Horses, food, and water," Hermon supplied. Techle seemed to lapse into contemplation for a moment. "I'll see what I can do." He said.

"Thank you," Siem said. "We are in your debt."

Techle smiled and said, "The Tavern of Wholesome Laughter does not keep track of debts. How else can you ensure laughter and total happiness? Rest well. I'll be back in the early hours of the morning."

"That there is an excellent fellow," Hermon said.

"I concur." Siem agreed.

"I should have a soothing bath, a nice meal, and rest," Eldana said.

"Same here," Siem replied.

"Please, can I stay with you girls?" Hermon pleaded. "I fear that D'rmas and Mikko may try to drag me into one of their manly exuberances."

Eldana and Siem laughed.

"Aren't you a man?" Siem asked. "Learn to deal with it."

"Come on." Hermon pleaded.

Siem and Eldana began to move towards the door that led to their rooms.

"Sorry Hermon," Eldana called back to him. "You're all alone for tonight."

She and Siem burst out into another spell of laughter before they walked out of the lobby.

Hermon combed his fingers through his hair and puffed air from his mouth. "What a night." He said to himself.

Just then, Mikko walked into the lobby.

"Hey, Hermon." He called.

"O, come on... Not now." Hermon complained under his breath.

"Have you tasted the ale here? By my hand, there's no comparison in the whole world. D'rmas has already proven to be a cold fellow when it comes to drinking. Don't say no too."

"A tankard wouldn't be bad, I guess," Hermon said.

"Splendid," Mikko exclaimed.

Back at the ladies' chambers, as Eldana stepped out of the bath she swore she felt like she was a new being. It was like the water in the bath sipped out any trace of weakness in her, unclogging her body, leaving it refreshingly free and light.

She got into her underwear, a light white cloth that was both shirt and shorts seamed together at the waist, then got into bed next to Siem.

"Well?" Siem asked as she turned to face Eldana.

Eldana had a brilliant grin plastered on her face.

"It was wonderful," Eldana said. Her voice was full of excitement. "I feel like I can take on anything right now."

"Yeah," Siem said. "That's exactly the kind of optimism we

need at the moment. The last few days have been trying. And the more we move through difficult odds, the more insurmountable our task becomes."

"Yeah," Eldana agreed. "Hope is a fickle thing. I'm glad I can feel it again though."

"Same here."

Eldana and Siem talked a little, reminiscing of times when all was happy and easy, before Eldana's initiation, before her life was required for the balance of chaos ritual.

With time, the night grew silent as sleep stretched its kleptomaniac tentacles, sending the people of the city into nightmares, pleasant dreams, or no dreams at all. Eldana was swept up in a nightmare. In it, the air was dark, pale, and dank. She felt something constrict around her throat, cutting off air from her lungs.

"You're ours, girl." She heard voices declare. *"No matter how far you run, you will eventually give us what is ours!"*

CHAPTER FIVE

The Woods of Ciroc

Kleas

Ciroc Woods

Chapter Five

The cock had crowed its first when Siem's eyes flew open. Turning her head to where Eldana lay, she found her struggling within bed covers.

"Eldana," Siem called as she grasped Eldana by the shoulders and attempted to shake her awake. Siem shook harder, and Eldana opened her eyes with a start. She gasped and sat up. She watched her friend heave and pant for breath.

After a while, when Eldana had regained her breath Siem asked, "Another one?"

Eldana nodded.

"We made a deadly mistake. We forgot to put a protection spell over our minds before falling asleep," Siem said.

"We could not help it," Eldana replied. "We were all spent."

"You would be dead by now, if not for the magic in this place," Siem observed.

Eldana sighed. "I think it is time to move."

Eldana conjured a ball of flame with her mind and let it float in the middle of the room. The room was flooded with bright yellow light, and as its features came into illumination, Eldana noticed some things that were not there the night before.

"Woah," she pointed towards the two brown rucksacks made with leather hide huddled together at the far end of the wall.

Eldana and Siem swung their legs out of bed and stepped out. Tentatively, Siem reached out and cast a search spell.

"*Reiena*," the magician whispered, before visibly relaxing. "There's nothing capable of danger in them," she reported.

Eldana grabbed one of the rucksacks and opened it. Then smiled as her eyes took in its contents.

"We're set for the perils in our journey!"

Siem cocked her brows inquisitively.

"Supplies, there's a dagger, dried biscuits, dried meat, spices, salt, a can, and a robe, which probably has some spell over it..."

Siem smiled. "Indeed. The universe finds opportunities in our present difficulties to smile at us."

Eldana closed the rucksack and dropped it beside the second

one. "We ought to start getting ready," she told Siem.

The girls made sure to have a bath, not solely for the sake of cleanliness, but for the magically induced, refreshing feeling they got afterward.

"What a way to start the day," Eldana said when she was done.

Soon they were fully dressed. Eldana had her hair packed and tied in a bun. She wore her rune-covered robe and her sword was strapped to her back. Siem had a quiver full of arrows strapped to her back, her retractable bow in a pouch on her belt, and an ornate dagger, which she kept hidden in her boots.

The cock had crowed the second time when there was a knock on their door.

"Hermon?" Siem called.

"Unfortunately, not," a familiar voice replied.

"Techle?" Eldana asked.

"Greetings," Techle replied. "Can I come in?"

"Oh, sure," Eldana said, moving towards the door.

She unlatched the door, then opened it to reveal a smiling Techle.

"I trust you had a pleasant rest?" Techle asked, walking into the room.

"More pleasant than we've had in several days," Siem replied.

"Good," He looked around the room and spotted the rucksacks. "I see you've found the supplies you requested."

"Yes. Blessings on you." Eldana replied.

"It is not much," Techle said "But it has the rudimentary things that you will need on your journey."

"Are the others ready?" Siem asked.

"I suppose so," Techle replied. "This place is tailored to meet the specific needs of its guests. If you need to be awake by the first light of dawn, you will be.

"Now," Techle's face turned serious, "I don't know the details about your journey, but I feel it's a very serious one. There are horses outside, fine and strong breeds. They'll take you wherever you want to go. I'll advise that you keep your senses keen. Not all

Chapter Five

is as it seems in this world."

"Thank you, Techle," Eldana said. "How can I ever repay you?"

Techle smiled. "Like I said the tavern does not accrue debts. Just be safe."

Eldana and Siem nodded. They each picked up a rucksack, and giving Techle one final farewell glance, nodded to indicate their readiness. Techle replied with a nod of his own, and a line of light began to burn on the wall until a door frame was formed. Then the section of the wall cut out by the frame of light grew translucent until there was nothing there but the dark blue of dawn.

Eldana and Siem exchanged looks. Then they walked through the doorway and into the silent morning.

The morning was cold. The visible puffs of breath coming out from the nostrils of the horses were testament enough. There was a trio of men, sitting in a small circle, close to where the horses stood. The cloaks they had on rendered them unobtrusive, but they did more than that.

"Isn't this marvellous?" one of them asked.

"What is, Mikko?" Hermon asked.

"These cloaks," Mikko replied. "I mean, it is so cold out here, yet I feel nothing."

"You know, the weakling is right. I do not feel a thing, not even a bite of cold," D'rmas said.

"Hey," Mikko warned. "I've told you to quit calling me a weakling."

D'rmas laughed tauntingly. He had begun calling Mikko a weakling since the magician had drunk himself into a stupor last night and lost an arm wrestle to D'rmas.

"Hermon, please remind your dear friend here that losing an arm wrestle when you are heavily drunk does not make you a weakling," Mikko said.

A small smile appeared on Hermon's face. "I do not know

about this, Mikko. I just want to be left out of this, whatever it is," he said. Hermon was sure that Mikko would not see the last of D'rmas taunts unless he were to oblige the warrior to a duel.

After a span of silence, Mikko conjured a ball of flame and let it float in their middle.

"What's that for?" Hermon asked.

"I do not know," Mikko replied. "We cannot just sit here, waiting in the dark."

"Of course we can, and we will," D'rmas stated. "Your magic ball will attract the attention of unfriendlies, if it has not already."

"Fine," Mikko said. With a snap of his fingers, the light went out. "How much more time do you reckon the girls are going to take?"

"They're women, let them be," D'rmas admonished. "They take time putting on clothes and sitting before mirrors."

"Trust me," Hermon told D'rmas. "Those women are not the kind for that, at least not with the task at hand."

"The task at hand..." D'rmas parroted, his voice low and his face thoughtful. "So, what's the plan?"

"What?" Hermon questioned.

"I mean the plan after here. When we get out of Kleas, what next?"

"Erm, you want the truth?" Hermon asked.

"Why else are we here?" Mikko questioned.

"The truth is we do not know where to go next. But we do know where the end is. What we need is a route to the end, so we will keep going until we find it."

"Wow," Mikko laughed. "I had no idea you three went into this without coming up with a solid plan!"

"There was no time for any," Hermon replied.

"So we'll be walking out in the open, while the world is gradually descending into chaos, very good," Mikko said.

"If I did not know better," D'rmas said, "I would say you were scared."

"You know, maybe, I should give you the fight you're asking

Chapter Five

for," Mikko said, his voice tainted with fury. "Don't think your ability to channel two classes of magic makes you impervious. You have no idea who I am."

D'rmas chuckled. And the three fell silent once more. It was not long before they heard the sound of sizzling in the air. Hermon was the first to see the line of light slicing through the air, forming a door frame.

"They are here," he said. They had come here, some moments ago, through the same portal. The men stood as Eldana and Siem walked out of the portal with rucksacks on their backs.

"Ah, they got theirs too," Mikko said, patting his own rucksack.

Techle stepped out into the open as Eldana and Siem walked out. He watched them join the group, and then they turned towards him. D'rmas was the first to speak. He cleared his throat. "Thank you, friend," he told Techle. "For your immense hospitality, I say thank you. We cannot thank you enough. I hope our paths cross again."

Techle smiled and nodded, before Mikko said his thanks, and so did Hermon, and the women.

"As some of you may have guessed, the house decided to save you the hurdle of crossing the gates successfully," Techle said. "You are a few miles away from the city's southern gate. Your journey, wherever it may lead, will not be an easy one." He hoped his kindness and his willingness to discard tradition would not throw the world into endless chaos.

D'rmas smiled.

Finally got your challenge, Hermon thought.

"I do not know what fate holds for you all," Techle continued. "But all of you have destinies, paths set out for you that you must follow. Be safe, my friends. The world is going into a state of disarray. Evil has already entered the hearts of men and clans are rising against clans. Do not get trapped in it. Most importantly, be successful."

"We will keep that in mind," Siem replied.

Techle gave them a word of blessing, one with roots in the ancient magic of those who had walked the land several millennia ago.

"*Mo sa el,*" Techle said.

"*Mo sa el,*" they all replied.

He gave them one last farewell smile before he stepped back into the portal.

"That there is a fine gentleman," Mikko said.

"Indeed," D'rmas replied, his eyes still fixed to the spot Techle was standing in moments ago. "And a nice house too."

The comment roused a measure of small laughter among the men. Hermon could not help letting out a mild chuckle.

As Eldana approached the horses, she whispered magic words of illumination. "*Merai,*"

Immediately, the air around the horses softened into a mild silver glow, revealing the creatures. Eldana felt a stab of sadness and nostalgia at the use of the spell. It was a trick Sinto had taught her back then when things were all good between them. Now Sinto was leading a group of warrior magicians to kill her. Eldana tried to swipe thoughts of him away. Now that Sinto's intentions were clear, if she ever faced him again in battle, it would be with cold, rigid emotions and the self-sustaining desire to see his head fell off his neck rather than hers.

The horses were impressive, beasts of thick, refined musculature and noble carriage. They stomped their feet and snorted as the group drew closer.

"Easy," Eldana cooed. "Easy." She stretched forth her hands in a calming gesture while she stepped closer.

"Wow, she's good." Mikko commended.

"Yeah, she should be," Hermon said. "She practically grew up around horses."

"If it were me, I would not take the time to bring them into submission. A simple control spell should do the trick," Mikko said.

"Not Eldana," Hermon replied. "She is averse to binding animals without their will."

Chapter Five

"A good story," D'rmas chipped in. "But horses are horses."

"Not to Eldana," Hermon said. "She prefers them when they are companions. The assurance of their loyalty is certain that way."

D'rmas grunted.

Eldana placed her hand on the head of the first horse to her right, a maroon mare with patches of white and a luxurious mane. She looked up at it and smiled. "Hello," she said. "I'm Eldana. I'm going to call you Betsy."

Betsy pushed her head closer to Eldana's palm.

"I've found mine already." She called out to the company.

For the rest of the group, picking a horse was a thing of little circumstance now that they had all been calmed. Siem picked a black steed that she named Harold. Hermon and the rest of the men did not bother assigning names to theirs. As soon as they were all settled, they spurred the horses into a trot, and soon they moved into the woods.

The woods of Ciroc, as the people in the city center called it, was a massive expanse of thick, giant trees. The ground was always carpeted with dead leaves – even when the trees were not deciduous – and shrubs – which burst with life, even when the trees stole much of the sunlight. It was normal for people to wind up lost when they ventured into it without a clear destination in mind.

Eldana and her group of five found traveling through the Ciroc woods an apt manoeuvre from the amount of attention they would attract if they followed the major roads.

Lord Taboon and his goons would still be in search of Eldana, so would Sinto, and the king of Middle. Plus, the whole of Toas had gone out of hand. If they got themselves embroiled in a skirmish between towns, they would not be able to fulfil their mission before chaos swallowed the entire land.

The first few hours of their journey into the forest was done in silence. Siem and Eldana rode in front. Hermon rode alone a little behind them. D'rmas and Mikko brought up the rear. The hooves of their horses made a shuffling sound across the mat of leaves, and shrubs. The only evidence that the sun had risen was the few streaks of sunlight that pierced through the thick canopy of trees. At one time, they came upon a black jaguar, nestled in the low branches of a curving tree. The magic cloaks Techle had provided them prevented them from unwarranted attacks. So, the jaguar stared at them inconsequentially until they passed under it, away from its sight.

Along the way, Mikko stopped to relieve himself.

"What?" Mikko asked when D'rmas stared at him endlessly. "Is it a crime to take a piss now?"

D'rmas simply looked away.

Mikko walked away from his horse and further left into the company of trees in his search for privacy. "A man has got to do his thing without an audience." He joked, before walking off.

Hermon took the temporary stop to meet up with his friends. He kicked his horse, and it came up to Eldana and Siem.

"How are you holding up?" he asked.

"Fine," Eldana replied.

"You?" Siem asked.

"Fine," Hermon replied. "Our passage through the woods has seen no obstacle or incident since we started."

Siem turned to see if Mikko was on his way back. He was not. But before she brought her face back, she caught D'rmas with a scowl on his face.

"Speak for yourself," she told Hermon and pushed her head forward, gesturing towards D'rmas' position.

"What is wrong with your friend?" Eldana asked Hermon.

"O come on, Eldana, not you too," Hermon moaned. "He is not my friend. Besides his occupation, his clan, and his name, I don't know anything else about him."

Siem chuckled.

"Okay," Eldana said. "But what is wrong with him?"

"I do not know," Hermon replied with a little off-handedness. "I guess he is just bored. D'rmas is a man who is in love with the heat of action. I should know. I almost killed him because of that love. The morning has been uneventful so far, no challenge, nothing."

"I imagine the silence must be depressing for him," Eldana said.

"Well, he should get himself together," Siem said. "It will not be long before he gets what he is asking for."

"And Hermon?" Eldana called.

"Yeah?" He replied.

"That thing you said about not being D'rmas' friend?"

"Yeah, what about it?" Hermon asked.

"I think you should start thinking about knowing him better," Eldana advised.

"No, no, no," Hermon said, shaking his head vehemently.

"What?" Eldana asked with a touch of incredulity. "Why?"

"Because I do not have to," Hermon replied. "What's there to gain anyway? His way of life and mine are kingdoms, years apart!"

"Eldana is right, Hermon," Siem supplied.

Hermon groaned.

"What we are doing is too important to depend only on contracts. It will need loyalty, the kind that stems from friendship and trust. We need to build that among the entire group if we are to succeed. There is only so much just the three of us can do. Mikko's apprenticeship under Lord Taboon makes him an unusually strong magician, and so is D'rmas. We need their strength!"

"Fine," Hermon said, rolling his eyes.

Just then they heard the sound of footsteps coming up to them. They turned to find D'rmas walking up to them on his horse. His left hand held the straps of Mikko's horse, bringing it along with him.

"He's not yet back," D'rmas said in a deadpan voice.

The four of them exchanged stares for a time until Eldana broke it.

"How much time do you reckon he has taken?" she asked everyone.

"I would say four hundred and eighty heartbeats," D'rmas supplied.

"Is that not more than enough time to empty your bladder?"

Siem asked, staring at Hermon.

"Why are you looking at me?" Hermon questioned, surprisingly.

"You are a guy," Siem replied.

"Yes. And so is D'rmas."

Eldana rolled her eyes and Siem sighed.

"Yes," D'rmas replied, cutting off the span of silence. "That is more than enough for a man to take a piss, even if his bladder were full to the point of bursting."

"Could he have run away?" Eldana asked.

"I do not know. Why would he escape?" Siem asked.

"I would not place escaping past Mikko," D'rmas said. "The level of silence and utter boredom in this place scared him until he almost pissed his pants. He could not help but imagine how scary the real action must be."

"Thank you, D'rmas," Siem said. "We appreciate your sarcasm, really."

He grunted.

"Do any of us still remember the exact path he took into the forest?" Eldana asked. "He might be in danger. Maybe a wild animal has him or something. This forest is not without threat!"

"He still had his cloak on him," D'rmas said. "That should have protected him from any premeditated attack."

"What if the attack is not premeditated?" Hermon asked.

"Excuse me?" Eldana replied, incomprehension written plain on her face.

"I am saying that the attack, if this is what it is, could be premeditated on Mikko's part." Hermon rephrased.

"Mikko cannot be that stupid," Siem stated.

"While we sit here on horses debating if he is in danger," Eldana said, "he could be slipping beyond our salvation."

They climbed down their horses and turned to the dark woods all around, half-guessing the route that Mikko had taken. Before they ventured, D'rmas whispered a short spell. Immediately, the air began to stir around them. It gathered momentum with every passing breath, and then it formed a wall ensconcing the horses in. They would graze and walk about for as far as the air wall allowed and still be there when the party got back.

The party moved in an unordered formation, shouting Mikko's name as they went. The forest bounced back the echo of their shouts and there was no response, yet they continued anyway.

"Here," Hermon called suddenly.

Everyone turned. He was to their far left, standing in front of a rough-barked tree. "It is wet," he said, inclining his head towards the bloom of wetness at the foot of the tree.

"This is where Mikko did his thing," D'rmas said, casting his eyes about the surrounding area.

"Could he have taken off?" Eldana inquired.

"Mikko!" Hermon called.

Just then, they heard the snap of a branch. They turned towards the source of the sound, their hands reaching for their weapons. Siem had notched an arrow already. They heard a branch snap again, and this time they were sure of the sound's direction. Their hearts beat in anticipation as they waited.

Without warning, a robust deer walked out to them from the cover of trees.

"Pheew," Hermon sighed.

Eldana and Siem had relief burnished clearly on their faces. D'rmas just grunted.

Without warning, there was a tight twang as Siem let her arrow loose. The deer fell to the ground with an arrow sticking out of its heart.

"What did you do that for?" Hermon cried with disbelief.

"One, it got me all worked up for nothing. And two, it is meat. The dried stuff we have in our bags probably will last longer than anything we try to find here. It will be wise of us to assume that there will come a time when the woods will offer nothing in the way of food. Best we stock up and eat now."

"Ah, I like her," D'rmas told Hermon.

"We still have to find, Mikko, don't we?" Eldana asked.

"Yes, of course," Siem replied. "Hermon you will stay behind and prepare the venison, while the rest of us continue the search."

"Is that not dangerous?" Hermon asked. "Me, alone in this forest?"

"Don't be such a whiner, Hermon," Eldana berated. "You are not alone in the forest. We will be here too, just in a different location. We cannot all stay behind. We do not have time to spare. Mikko is still out there, come on!"

Hermon tilted his head and pressed his lips tightly together. "I owe Mikko a punch," he said.

"Ah, on that I agree with you," D'rmas said. "He will get more than that from me."

Hermon drew a dagger from its sheath hanging on his belt. He sharpened the dagger on a whetstone before he knelt beside the dead deer. Eldana, Siem, and D'rmas left Hermon and the sound of shredding flesh behind, venturing deeper into the forest.

"How I wish we had a seer," Siem said, after almost an hour of shouting Mikko's name in the forest and coming back with nothing. "Locating Mikko would be like this." She snapped her finger.

"None of you know how to work seer magic?" D'rmas asked. His tone held the mild inflection of surprise.

"Do you?" Eldana asked.

"No," D'rmas replied. "That is beyond the standard magic of my clan. I just assumed that you two would know how to handle it."

"No," Siem replied. "Seer magic is not my best suit either. I tried it during my training, fell sick for almost a week. I did not try it again."

"What do you do then, when you want the services of a seer?" Dramas asked.

"I get a seer. Or I use other mediums. Though they are nowhere as effective as the seers, they serve their purpose."

D'rmas was about to bring Eldana to answer his question when she called out.

"Hey guys, why does this look familiar?"

Chapter Five

D'rmas and Siem stopped in their tracks and walked towards where Eldana was standing with her head slightly bowed, looking over something on the ground.

Siem's eyes bulged with recognition. There, lying on the floor in careless abandon, was Miko's magic cloak Siem lifted it with the tip of her arrow and inspected it. She found nothing on it that would shed more light on how it had come off its wearer.

"We are sure this belongs to Mikko, right?" Eldana asked.

"No Eldana, the evidence is too overwhelming to think this as a coincidence," Siem said.

"Indeed," D'rmas agreed.

The three of them fanned out into the forest, calling Mikko's name at the very top of their voices. But they got nothing in response.

"*Merai midri.*" D'rmas said, stretching a splayed palm towards the forest ground. Immediately, bright imprints of footsteps glowed from among the leaves. First, it was a single pair. They moved around in a circle, but a circle without a definite circumference.

Then Eldana gasped. "Look." She pointed; her eyes lit with alarm.

More footsteps began to appear coming towards the single pair. Whoever it was that owned the multiple footsteps, turned back to where they came from when they had gotten close to the person with the single pair of footsteps. When they disappeared, the single pair was no longer there. They were gone, like they had never existed.

"Are you guys thinking what I am thinking?" Siem asked.

D'rmas and Eldana responded simultaneously. But their replies could not be more different.

"That Mikko was a spy and this was the rendezvous?" D'rmas said.

Eldana on the other hand said, "That he may have been abducted."

However, as soon as she was done speaking, both her and Siem cast D'rmas a stare.

"What?" D'rmas asked. "That too is a suitable explanation!"

After a while, he said, "Whatever we choose to believe, one thing is clear. If we decide that the individual footsteps that have just been revealed belong to Mikko, then he was alone, and when more people came towards him, he left with them. Whether it was by coercion, or by his will."

"What do we do?" Eldana asked. "We cannot just surrender him to the uncertainties of his fate."

"Going after those footsteps would be foolish," Siem said. "Without foreknowledge of who the people Mikko's with are, we will be sitting ducks."

D'rmas grunted his approval.

"I have heard of a seer near these parts," D'rmas said. "But going to them would mean deviating from our current path. They live at the skirts of the forest, closest to Kleas." D'rmas must have noticed the looks of uneasiness Siem and Eldana passed among themselves because he asked, "Is anything the problem?"

"No, nothing," Siem replied. "You could have told us you knew a seer before now, though!"

Eldana wished there was some other way. She thought of casting a communication spell, wherein they could speak with the seer through a medium of communication – a bowl of water, or a mirror. However, whilst the communication spell would go through to the seer, they would still need to give her something of Mikko's she could use to access visions about his whereabouts. That was the only way to operate because the seer did not know Mikko. Thus, the purpose of the communication spell was defeated. If they were going to get back Mikko, they would have to leave their path.

"Fine," Siem said, finally. "We should at least get back to Hermon, and tell him what is going on!"

They were still deliberating among themselves when suddenly D'rmas picked up the sound of whistling in the air and commanded the others to hit the floor. Sure enough, a dozen arrows

Chapter Five

hit the trees with a thud. Without D'rmas warning, the arrows would have hit all of them.

"Ambush!" D'rmas was yelling.

Eldana quickly conjured a sphere of air over them as another hail of arrows flew in. The arrows bounced harmlessly off the surface of the shield.

"Do you think they are the ones who took Mikko?" Siem shouted.

"I cannot say for sure. We established that there were no signs of struggle when Mikko went along with whatever group had shown up here."

"But if they all pointed arrows on him, that would be more than enough incentive to make anyone do anything peacefully."

"I agree," Eldana said. "But what I do not know is why they are not giving us a chance to come in peacefully if they are the same ones.." She said as another volley of arrows snapped and splintered on the shield above them. They shuffled deeper into the woods warily.

D'rmas looked at the two of them but said nothing. He had his ideas, his own theories. If Mikko went in with these people without a struggle, and the same set of people were not giving them any of that chance, it only meant that his suspicions regarding Mikko had been right all along. Whether he was right or not, one fact remained: right now they were being shot at by people they could not see. Fortunately, all he needed was a way to make their attackers come into visibility.

"We cannot just lie here and keep waiting for their quivers to empty. It might be a very long time." D'rmas told Eldana and Siem angrily.

"D'rmas is right," Siem told Eldana. "I want to get a piece of these bastards myself!"

One of Eldana's arms was still maintaining the shield over them. "I have an idea," she told both of them. "But you have to have your weapons on the ready."

"What are you planning?" D'rmas asked.

Eldana looked from one to the other. "We cannot attack while we are still under this shield. So, in the second it takes them to restock their arrows, I am going to let down the shield and try to still the air, you know, to freeze any arrows they fire at us completely. Once I have done that, we try to flush them out of the forest."

"Leave that bit to me," Siem said. "That is more like my area of specialty…"

Eldana nodded. "Remember guys," she said. "After the shield is lifted, you will be vulnerable…"

D'rmas chuckled. "I am not sure I have turned into an amateur overnight, have I?"

Eldana looked ahead towards the edge of the densely packed trees and hissed a breath through her teeth. This was the time. It was now or never.

With her arm still maintaining the shield, she got to her feet, waited…

The first hail of arrows came, slender and pointed, rushing towards them with a singleness of purpose. Eldana waited, taking one breath to prepare herself. The moment they hit the shield, Eldana let the shield go, and made a speedy step forward. Then she thrust her fingers into the air. She connected to the air around her, as a being of balance and chaos, she did not always need spells for this. She felt the air like a slight tingly sensation in her veins, and then she willed her intention into it…

At that moment, the unseen attackers let their arrows fly. Siem and D'rmas saw them come towards them. Defenseless against such a deluge of arrows, it looked to them for a moment, that the arrows would pierce through their bodies indiscriminately. But then the most amazing thing happened.

The arrows slowed in the air. At first, she had to blink to tell herself that she was not having hallucinations or anything of the sort. In truth, she was not, when she had opened her eyes, the arrows had frozen in mid-air.

"Siem, now!" Eldana yelled, turning back to look at her.

Chapter Five

It's my turn now, Siem told herself.

She closed her eyes, and when she opened them the area had grown taut. Her hair danced in the air like crazed snakes. Eldana had felt this before. Since she had known Siem, she had always known that her friend shared an uncanny connection to the spirits of the forest. No sane mage, no matter how great would try to battle Siem in the forest. Not alone anyway. Ordinarily, Siem was an impressively strong magician, but in the forest her power became mystical.

"*Kitab mezah!*" Siem muttered, whispering the spell with which she called upon the ancestors of the forests.

Without hesitation, they answered. Siem felt their ephemeral presence all around her, ready to give her guidance; ready to do her bidding.

"Ancestors of the forest," she said, "disclose those who have decided to remain in the shadow of your midst. Let the hidden attackers be brought into the open."

With a howl, the wind whipped around them violently. D'rmas saw the forest trees shake violently like they were fighting amongst themselves. Then the first of the attackers flew out. A stout male dressed in shroud-like clothing. The dressing made D'rmas bare his teeth in a visceral growl. He brought forth his sword, and stooped, ready for action. The dressing was a signature one. One he recognized all too well because his clan and these were sworn enemies.

Eldana noticed the sudden shift in D'rmas' stance.

"What is the matter?" she asked him.

"Sandoc," he seethed. They were one of the most violent tribes who believed in upholding the tradition, no matter what.

One by one, sometimes in clusters, the Sandoc would either run out of the cluster of trees or fly out. The ancestors of the forest were agitated. But whether they ran out or were thrown out, the Sandoc clung to their training, still standing, their weapons drawn, and poised for an attack. The Sandoc had formed a dense circle around the three of them. Siem, Eldana, and D'rmas drew close to each other, forming a tighter knot of defense against the attacking Sandocs.

"How did they find us?" Eldana asked.

"I intend to ask," D'rmas growled, hoisting his sword higher.

"What of Hermon?" Eldana asked. "I hope none of them went for him."

"I am not certain of that," D'rmas replied. "But even if they did. They would realize, too late of course, that that was the greatest mistake of their lives. They would rather face us than a berserker in full form."

"Of course," Siem agreed. "We are about to teach them that."

The stout man who had been thrown out earlier stepped forward. His carriage and the confidence in his scarred face suggested that he was the leader of the group.

"Listen and listen carefully," he said without any preliminaries, "We are the Sandoc and we are here on a mission. We will show no mercy in the execution of that which is our mission. We expect no resistance, but if we get…"

"Do you usually talk this much before a fight?" Siem asked, her anger visible.

The Sandoc leader stared back at Siem, his expression a little indifferent. Then he turned and looked at D'rmas.

"We have one of the Qeltifom clan here with them, tell me, you are more knowledgeable of our culture, do you accept for us to carry out our mission unchallenged?"

Rather than answer his question, D'rmas asked him one of his own:

"How did you find us?"

The man sneered. "The Sandoc have their ways. Are you impressed, free warrior? Or frightened."

"You wish I was," D'rmas laughed. 'Why are you here?"

"To take the being of Balance and Chaos and the Siem into our possession and have them delivered safely."

"And me?"

"Our orders are to kill you. You do not feature in the plan."

Chapter Five

D'rmas smiled and nodded. "How classic," he said. "Well, I must warn you, one of the Sandoc clan, that we are not afraid. And have no plans of going anywhere with you. Nor do I have any plans of being put to death by you or any member of your clan."

The Sandoc leader looked at Eldana and Siem.

"Does the free warrior speak your mind?" he asked. "You two do not have to go down the path of violence. You have the choice of coming with us freely and willingly to avoid injury."

"Look at us closely," Eldana said. "What do you think we are saying?"

The man stared at them, and they stared back with a steely resolve.

"Fine," the man said finally. "Let it be known that in line with our custom, we had given them the chance for easiness."

"You did not have a problem with giving chances when you fired hail after hail of arrows at us," Siem said. "Hiding like cowards in the trees."

The Sandoc leader stepped back to the circle of his clan, and then the two parties stared murderously at each other. The Sandoc, in their larger numbers, at the three in the middle. And Siem, Eldana, and D'rmas stared fearlessly back. They could never be more certain in themselves. Then the first Sandoc ran swiftly towards Siem. The soldier was so fleet that it looked like his feet barely touched the ground. He ran towards her with his sword raised in the air. Without thinking, Siem nocked an arrow and sent it towards the soldier. The soldier rolled on the ground, dodging, but she had expected it, and so had nocked a second arrow just as soon as the first was leaving. She fired the second, which got the soldier straight in the heart, as he was coming up from his role.

As if that was the cue, the remaining group hugging the edge of the trees rushed in to join the fray.

"*Kitab mezah!*" Siem cried out.

Again, there was a rush of air. Her arrow glowed, and it speared through the air, its tip glowing brightly until the entire shaft was covered in bright light. The arrow hit a formation of the Sandoc resulting in an explosive blast that scattered a section of them into the air like twigs. Before Siem could nock another arrow of such magical ability, the Sandoc were already upon them.

D'rmas launched into the fight, swinging his sword, parrying, blocking, weaving in and out of strokes, and drawing blood. He danced, and it was a dance unique to the free warriors. But the Sandoc had one of their own dances and made for tough opponents.

Nearby, Eldana also had her hands full. But she was the being of Balance and Chaos, and she commanded a greater share of the warriors. She fought, unfazed by the numbers she was facing. She fought with a melee of sword strokes and magic. She would duck under blows aimed at her head, and reach out with her foot almost immediately, tripping her attacker, then slam into him with a condensed form of air, and then delivered a killing blow with her sword. The fight raged on, with more and more of the Sandoc dropping to the floor. Siem and Eldana fought like demons, their combo of magic and blades never failing them.

The leader of the Sandoc rounded on D'rmas. He lunged towards the free warrior with his sword, but D'rmas was quick and parried the stroke. As they moved, their eyes stayed on each other trying to ascertain weak points on their stance – points where it was more likely for each to strike blood.

Like a rehearsal, the two of them danced. Striking, parrying, and striking again. The Sandoc slashed at D'rmas, aiming for his throat, but D'rmas was not born just the day before. Though the Sandoc was fast, D'rmas had seen his move even before he made it. Quickly, like the strike of a viper, D'rmas raised his sword vertically, intercepting the Sandoc's strike. In the same second, he went under the Sandoc's sword and slashed the Sandoc across the thigh.

The leader turned to face D'rmas, apparently unfazed by the cut D'rmas had just given him. But for the line of blood at the edge of D'rmas blade, there was no indication that the leader had been hit.

Instead, the Sandoc chief just smiled.

Chapter Five

"I would not expect any less from you," he told D'rmas.

"This is not a point you concede," D'rmas corrected. "Whether you like it or not, I've drawn your blood."

"Fair. But let us see who lies dead at the end of this!"

The man was still speaking when he dashed at D'rmas. He made to strike at D'rmas right side but feinted to the left. D'rmas saw the move but was unable to react in time. The Sandoc's blow nicked him on his ribs.

The Sandoc gave a bloodthirsty smile. An indication that he was not done yet. D'rmas was furious. The Sandoc had not wounded him deeply, but the cut still hurt. It was then that he remembered what was said about the strike of a Sandoc blade: "One little strike could hurt like the sting of a thousand scorpions."

"You feel it, eh?" the Sandoc asked him.

D'rmas gave him a furious glare.

Enough of this! D'rmas thought.

He dashed towards the Sandoc, striking so fast that soon all that could be seen were two men and chaos of metal strokes and sparks between them. Noticing that the Sandoc's attention was on parrying and blocking his strikes, D'rmas stooped low and stretched his legs, upsetting the Sandoc's balance. The Sandoc swayed, but the momentary lapse was enough for D'rmas to land a blow on the Sandoc's head. The Sandoc chief staggered backward. D'rmas launched a few strikes, which the Sandoc blocked. But this time, his parries were weak and disconnected, still trying to regain control of himself.

D'rmas did not give him a chance. He kept striking, one heavy blow after the other. The Sandoc would stretch out his sword and parry each huge blow, but it was taking its toll. As he reached out to parry yet another blow, D'rmas reached out with his feet, kicking out the blade from the Sandoc's grasp. D'rmas whirled, extending his sword in the process. The move had been so quick that for a time the result of the strike was not visible. The leader of the Sandoc knelt on the ground, confusion stirring in his eyes. He turned and looked at the environment, littered with the bodies of his people. Then he looked to see Eldana and Siem coming up to join D'rmas. He had failed his ancestors.

But surely it is not my fault, he thought. The magician did not tell me how strong they were when he sent me?

Just then a line of blood grew on his neck, and then it grew till blood spurted out of his neck. D'rmas, Eldana, and Siem watched him struggle to breathe with a look of indifference on their faces. The Sandoc chief fell dead.

The fight was over, and those Sandoc who had not fallen fled into the woods. The three companions had just turned to leave when Eldana heard the sound of singing. She halted abruptly. Siem turned, a confused look on her face.

"What is the matter?' she asked as she fixated on Eldana.

"Do you hear it?" Eldana asked.

"Hear what?" D'rmas inquired.

He stepped closer to where Eldana stood and listened keenly.

It was the voice of a single person, singing in a language she could not understand. The unknown singer's voice was high-pitched, yet, Eldana found the song serene, with a powerful soothing effect.

"Hmm," D'rmas said, a smile growing on his face. "I can hear it too."

"Singing." Siem supplied, a grin on her face.

The volume of the singing increased and was soon accompanied by a rich rendition of unseen flutes. The louder the music got, the stiffer the atmosphere grew. It was like the natural air was being sucked, and in its place, the aura of the music spread, swallowing the mind of any ear within its reach.

Eldana, Siem, and D'rmas had smirks on their faces, as they swayed and turned stupefyingly. Their eyes no longer held any personality, just vacancy and excitement.

They were too ensnared in the song's enchantment, they did not notice the people that began to walk out of the surrounding trees.

They were a group of tall, elegant people, with amazingly bearing and luxurious hair. At the lead was a woman, whose eyes were a shimmering honey-brown. She looked at the trio dancing around, trapped in her enchantment, and with a quick finger gesture commanded that the trio of Eldana, Siem, and D'rmas be captured.

A small group of bare-chested men with fine bows and arrows slung across their shoulders stepped out of the larger group and walked towards the troika. None of the companions resisted when they were being dragged away. Their minds were still deep in the enchantment.

Hermon's hands were covered in glossy red blood.

The deer had been full of life. Removing its entrails was easy. Skinning it had been the difficult part, but Hermon had pulled through. All was quiet around him as he proceeded to cut the deer into strips that would be easier to prepare, and smoke.

As he worked, his mind kept whipping up images of Eldana and Siem. He had been friends with them for a long time now. He had seen much by them, done much by them, and so had they by him. He could not help but worry about the amount of time that had elapsed since they had gone in search of Mikko.

What if something has happened to them? He asked himself. *Something dangerous.*

Sometimes, when such thoughts came to him, he tried to immerse himself fully in his work, but he usually never succeeded.

He had cut and gathered foliage from the surrounding forest and arranged them into a large platter, on which he arranged the strips of meat, seasoning them with salt. He was about to light a fire to begin smoking when he heard it.

He brought his head up and sharpened his hearing. Hermon had thought he had heard a voice. Several heartbeats passed, and he did not hear a thing. So, he waived his concern aside and turned back to the meat.

Then he heard it again.

This time it was clearer; the gentle voice of a woman, singing in a language he could not understand. Hermon's fingers let go of the dagger he was using to process the venison, as he felt a soothing flush of cool bliss inside him. The feeling spread throughout his whole body, exerting overwhelming dominance, until the look on his eyes drained out, and was replaced with a vacant expression. His face held a wide grin, as he got to his feet, and began to sway like one who was being a marionette.

As Hermon danced, there was nothing else on his mind save the intoxicating tune. People marched out of the cover of trees and surrounded him. But Hermon was too far gone to notice them.

CHAPTER SIX

In Times Past

A much younger Eldana ran down the stairs, her hair flying free in all directions. She giggled, and the sound bounced off the walls. She had sped down a flight of stairs, when an older woman came around the corner, just behind her.

"Eldana!" The older woman called, an anxious look on her face. "Come back here."

"No." Eldana's gleeful voice floated back to her in response.

Eldana giggled and ran off.

"O, what am I going to do with this child?" Her pursuer complained. She held up the skirt of her dress, and hurriedly descended the stairs after Eldana. As Eldana came off the last stairs, and into a huge room, she bumped into somebody and fell hard on her haunches.

The fall hurt just enough to bring tears to Eldana's eyes. Some parts of her hair had fallen across her face, so she parted it, tucking each part behind her ears. Then she looked up to find a man looking down at her.

"Did I hurt you?" he asked.

His voice was deep and had a reassuring quality to it.

Eldana shook her head in the negative, and he smiled.

"What is a princess like you doing running about the palace?" The man asked.

Eldana smiled sheepishly. "Nothing?"

"Ah. You should take extra care when running about." The man advised.

Just then, Eldana's attendant maid, the older woman who had been chasing her, stepped off the stairs and happened on the duo. "I'm sorry, sir." She apologized to the man when he took a glance at her.

"No, need to be." He replied. "I take it you are here for this little adventuress."

"Indeed." The woman replied, stretching out an open palm towards Eldana. "Come, Eldana, we must be off."

Eldana sighed and placed her tiny hand into her maid's palm. The man smiled at her, and she smiled in return.

Chapter Six

A few steps up the stairs, Eldana turned and asked, "What is your name?"

The man smiled. "You will know that soon enough."

Just then, one of the guards walked up to him.

"The king will see you now." The guard told him.

It would be almost a month before Eldana saw him again. Though it was under very different circumstances.

Eldana had gotten into a rage, and as a result, had released a blast of raw energy that smacked her maids into the wall, and upset object in the room. Fortunately, the maids walked away with but a few scratches and swellings, nothing grave. The king had heard that she was getting more erratic with the use of her powers and had decided that it was time she began her training.

Magical training in the palace was conducted in a large room with a row of massive columns at each side of the hall's longer rectangular lengths, with a glass-domed ceiling. On a few occasions, training that involved working with nature was conducted in a special glade not too far from here.

Eldana walked into the room with unsure steps. Being in this hall was different from her usual routine, and she allowed her eyes to roam this grand place. She was small, in her early teens. She had stopped in the middle of the hall and was admiring the skylight when she heard a voice from behind her.

"What do we have here?"

Eldana turned, and then her eyes widened in shock. "You!"

Standing before her was the man she had met some time ago by the stairs. He still smiled that comforting and reassuring smile.

"Surprised to see me?" he asked.

"I was told to come here for my training." She said.

"Indeed. I can help you out with so many things, Eldana. You are destined for very great things. And you have been given tremendous power by the world itself, to fulfil that destiny."

The man looked at the uncertainty on Eldana's face. "Does that scare you?" he asked her.

"A bit. I guess." Eldana replied.

"You do not have to be scared. I'll take you through it, all the way, till you have grown and matured enough to master your powers easily and become what you were made to be. Do you think you can do that?"

Eldana nodded.

"Good." The man said, straightening his stance.

"The first thing you are going to learn today is an elementary protection spell. A good protection spell can be the difference between a long life and certain death. So, you are going to learn how to create a protection bubble using the element of air. I am told you have been able to control the elements since your infancy?"

"So I am told," Eldana replied.

"Good." The man replied. "This will be easy then."

As he opened his mouth to begin giving instructions, Eldana interrupted:

"You did not tell me your name last time, and I still do not know it now."

The man smiled.

"My name is Sinto, I am going to be one of your teachers. I have taught people like you in the past, and I am honoured to train you as well. With time, I hope that I can help you realize your full potential."

Eldana smiled.

"Thank you, Sinto." She said.

Sinto's lips spread into a big smile.

"Now, you are already familiar with the elements, although you mostly access them in a state of chaos, and as such cannot use them to do things that involve finesse. I'll be teaching you the control and inner peace required to take these elements and knit them together like yarn."

Eldana giggled.

"You will find as we go on, that you will not have times for laughter anymore, Eldana. As a young child, you received the mark of chaos and with that, responsibility is given. You have been chosen under so many other children. You need to under-

Chapter Six

stand the gravity of it. From now on, Training is your only focus. All you have to do is to learn." Sinto's face revealed no expression.

They lay in a row, like stacks of hay, under the cover of the brush. There were about ten of them in number, three adults and seven youngsters. Each of them had eyes fixed forward.

"Now," one of the men said.

The group inched forward until they reached a berm.

The man who gave the order for them to move had his black hair woven into two large pleats that ran down to the back of his neck. His full black beard was also in two pleats and ringed with miniature gold discs. He stretched his head over the berm and caught sight of exactly what they had come here for.

A family of Warugs. The only thing they had in common with goats was their physique. They had sharp carnivorous teeth, claws instead of hooves, and serrated horns. They usually moved in families of six – the male, a larger female, and their typical offspring of five. They constituted one of the most ferocious beasts to walk the land of the Berserkers, and only a few sought it out as a challenge. Those who succeeded were revered among their tribe.

The leader of this expedition, Biniamin, had chosen the Walrug as his challenge and had come home with the head of the female, who usually had more bite than any in the family. It had been a long time ago, but he still flushed with the feelings he had felt that night as he was carried the grisly trophy shoulder high. That victory had betrothed him the most beautiful girl in the clan. Now it was his son's turn, and he prayed that he would bring to his house even greater glory. He prayed because he had seeds of doubt in his heart as regards his son's capacity to operate to the full glory of his bloodline. His son was too care-free, too soft at heart. He possessed none of the rigidity and rigor that had flowed from generation to generation. Biniamin would often stay up at night, gazing into the stars, and question what he had done wrong to deserve such a slight.

Biniamins' bloodline was one of the strongest of the Berserkers, and as such constituted the royal family. There were five berserker families in the royal clan. Biniamins' ancestors had ruled over the entire clan for as long as any berserker had histories for. But there was a provision, in their lore, for the chance of kingship to be challenged by any member of the five royal families; the Zelalus bloodline, the ones whose women were as strong as their men. The Whogatas bloodline, the family that chose leaders by brute strength. The Habtus bloodline, the ones that loved to keep to themselves. And the Yohano bloodline, the fastest runners. So far, such challenges had been deemed unnecessary because the current bloodline had proved its mettle. Every generation.

Driven by his fear that the kingship of his bloodline would be challenged in his son's lifetime, Biniamin had called his son into his private chamber, on the very eve of the ritual. A young Hermon walked in, aware that later that night he would have to choose a challenge for tomorrow, but totally in the dark as to the severe reprimand he was about to receive.

Hermon who had just joked about the Walrug challenge with his friends was stunned when his father asked him to choose precisely the Walrug challenge. It took him a while to regain his voice, and when he did it was lacking in vitality.

"But father", he said, "I did not envisage this."

"Life, Hermon, does not throw at you what you envisage. This you will soon learn as you grow older."

"Father is there not some other way?" he asked.

"You have to prove your mettle to the clan, assure them that you will be a substantial king."

"But isn't there..."

"Silence!" Biniamin roared, cutting Hermon off.

He grabbed his son's head between his large palms and dragged him forward.

Hermon trembled as his father seethed.

"You will not bring disgrace to our family name! You will sit

Chapter Six

on that throne! Return from the hunt a failure, and you can find yourself another home!"

Biniamin let go of Hermon's head and the boy staggered. Hermon left his father's chamber shivering.

The following day, when it was time to pick a challenge, Hermon did not bother to pick from the pool of lots the rest of the children had picked from. He thrust his chest forward, wore a stern face, and with a stentorian voice declared his intention to hunt the Walrug. His mother placed her hand over her mouth to keep from screaming. But her eyes glowered with fear. Fear for her son. The boy could face great danger and go berserk, exhaust himself after. and while he lay weak, recovering, he could be hurt. Besides, going berserk would be the beginning of the shortening of his lifespan. Biniamin had smiled proudly. And soon, the boys from the rest of the royal family indicated their interest in hunting the Walrug.

Now, at the cusp of launching an attack on the Walrug family, Biniamin could not help but wonder if he had just led his only son to die.

Hermon's arms ached. He had been keeping his muscles taut for a while now. He was frightened that if he let his arm relax, his trembling hands would betray the fear that ran wild inside him. When had he ever taken another life? Yet, here he was required to not just take a life, but to take the life of something that would be very eager to take his.

He watched his father look over the berm for the umpteenth time, before beckoning the rest of the group forward, and very slowly, they inched towards the berm on their bellies.

Hermon cast his eyes over, and caught sight of the Walrug, his heart pealed like thunder, and he felt a chill across his back. He had seen images of the Walrugs in the clan's archives. His father even had the head of the one he had killed during his time, hanging on the wall in his private chamber. But seeing them alive and healthy was jarring.

He could spot the father of the family, smaller in size than the mother. However, it was the cluster of children that grasped Hermon's attention. They were little, tender looking, and innocent; starkly in opposition to the ferocious look of their parents.

Biniamin appraised all the boys and whispered to them to attack his signal. When the signal came, as expected, the Walrugs were surprised.

A shrill ululation rent the air, and the boys ran forward, exactly as they had been taught to do. As they sped closer to the confused Walrugs, they split into groups to deal with the mother and father. Hermon, unable to let the innocent children become a sport, decided to herd them away from the slaughter. That was when it happened.

Biniamins' eyes shot wide open in horror. What he was seeing was not impossible, but uncommon, and very rarely reported. His heart sank in despair, as it dawned on him that he may lose his son. He had made sure that the family of Walrugs to be attacked was alone. It never crossed his mind that there would be more of them in such proximity.

Biniamin let out a scream, trying to draw Hermon's attention to two grown female Walrugs charging at him from out of the surrounding brush.

The other children had their hands full with prospective kills to notice the predicament Hermon was in. It was the tremors Hermon felt on the ground that alerted him that something was up. He turned, and rolled to the side, just in time to avoid being impaled on a Walrug horn Hermon landed in a crouch and watched guardedly as the two new Walrugs circled him, baring their glossy needle-like teeth. He heard shouting, and recognized the voice as belonging to his father. Hermon was sure that his father would be coming to save him. All he had to do was stay beyond the reach of either of the Walrugs till then. He cast a glance towards the rest of the children. They were making difficult progress trying to kill the Walrugs. He was all alone. One of the Walrugs charged from his left, intending to run him through with its horns. Hermon ran towards it, before leaping, somersaulting, over it, and rolling as

Chapter Six

he landed. Immediately, he began to run towards a tree, with the intent of climbing it and staying out of reach. He had not made it far, when he felt a massive and painful impact on his feet, knocking him off the ground. As he fell, he remembered something his father had told him once:

"Never engage a Walrug in a race. They run like the wind."

Biniamin, and the group of men with him, had vaulted off the berm and began running to cushion the rapidly unravelling massacre when he saw his son try to run. He had enough time to think: *No Hermon!* before he saw his son go down. Both Walrugs swooped in on him immediately.

Hermon held the horns of one of the Walrugs keeping it from tearing at his face or throat. But he could not do anything for the second one that was tearing at his legs with its teeth. Hermon could feel his strength begin to wane. Pain engulfed him like flames…

Suddenly, like there was an explosion in his head, his vision went black.

The sound of the guttural cry was what struck Biniamin and the other men. They all felt it, the release and connection to magic so deeply rooted and ancient among the Berserkers. It was magic only the fewest could ever tap into. And they could only do that after a lengthy routine of meditation and practice. But there, right before them was proof that it could be tapped through some other way.

Biniamin watched as the Walrug over Hermon, was rent into two longitudinal halves. Hermon stood to his feet, only that he was not just Hermon. He had gone fully berserk. He was huger now, thicker limbed, with elongated claw-like nails, and short tusks where his incisors had been. His eyes were wells of a glossy blackness. He roared, and the sound blew through the entire place like a wind of horror. The Walrugs intimidated into submission by the daunting countenance, and posture of the berserker, ran into the cover of the surrounding brush, whining,

The berserker turned towards the young boys in the square and began to move towards them when it collapsed to the ground. Gradually, as the group drew near, the berserker morphed back into Hermon. He was out cold. There were scratches, and bloody cuts all over his body; effects of his transformation. But they would soon heal thanks to his magic.

Later, when Hermon came to, he was intimated of his ability, and the immense responsibility he now had to bear where his clan was concerned. The ability to go fully berserk was a curse that had been placed on the five royal families by an unknown god. On each full transformation he made, his lifespan would take a huge dip. His clan was blessed with an unusually longer life than the other races. As a Berserker, throughout his lifetime he would lose about half of his lifespan turning. He could even die before his parents.

"But that is the sacrifice you are required to make," Biniamin told him. "For the good of our people…. I am proud of you, Hermon," he told Hermon after a while.

Hermon dared not let his father know of what he was thinking. He did not want any part of a responsibility that made him lay his life down, unwillingly, for his people.

The School of Magic was one of the most prominent edifices in Toas. Its scholars and cesspool of knowledge aside, the structure alone was enough to make eyes twinkle with wonder. Its architecture was a remarkable blend of human art and magical finesse. The school invited attention from all over Toas, both for those interested in learning magic and for those without. And among many other archaic traditions that the School of Magic maintained was that it was only open for boys.

The bells tolled this morning as the young apprentices, dressed in gray robes and round purple necklines, walked out of their quarters, tomes in hand, in a fashion that was casual and orderly.

The learning center itself was a behemoth tower made of stone, windows of glass, and suffused with prehensile magic to prevent its destruction, either by the weather or a more forthright physical attack. It stood alone in the quadrangle, linked to the rest of the building by bridges.

There were floors inside the learning center organized according to levels of magic. The higher one got in their grasp of magic, the higher they went in the building. Not very many had made it all the way to the top. To do that would require decades worth of time. Few came close to a hundred years old.

Students who took rudimentary classes would branch out from the numerous throngs streaming into the building, and go through a huge black double door, a little beyond the entranceway, and into a large hall with desks spaced equidistantly.

Today, the basic students had a new addition. A girl sitting in the second row. Her presence in the hall roused whispers. The whispers became a buzz when it was confirmed that the new abecedarian was indeed a girl.

When the teacher, a mage who had seen nearly a century and a half, began to teach, one of the students thrust his hand into the air.

"Yes?" The mage asked tiredly.

"I'm sure there must have been some sort of mistake," the boy said as he stood to his feet, "but there is someone in this lesson who is not supposed to be here, or in the entire building for that matter."

"Yes?" The mage said, indicating for him to progress.

"There is a girl in the hall, sir." The boy said finally, pointing to where she sat, reclining into her chair's backrest.

The mage stepped forward. With his eyes, he combed through the entire lot and then spoke.

"Most of you are very well familiar with the severe ban on women folk as it concerns the learning of magic."

A good number of the students murmured their assent.

"Well," the mage continued, "the various kingdoms in Toas, have decided that such a ban be lifted." What he did not tell the boys was that the potential for magic had been discovered in far too many girls even stronger than in any boys that it could no longer be just a hidden. Looking at the girl now, he said:

"Why don't you stand to your feet and give your fellow student a little introduction. Your name alone is enough for now."

The girl stood to her feet and faced the entire populace, unabashed.

"My name is Si-Siem," she said. Her voice carried through to the very last person at the furthest end of the hall. She turned towards the mage, gave a short bow, then took her seat.

The mage smiled.

"Now everyone", he said, "Si-Siem here is the first woman to officially learn magic in our school. She will be addressed by the title of Si attached to her name."

Now an even larger number of boys murmured until one of them spoke again "How is she already a Si, you need to be a Be first?" an astonished boy asked from the crowd. Si was the abbreviation of a novice magician where Be was the one for beginners to advanced magic. Most of Toas magicians only reached Be, if they got so far to receive a title at all.

"O, yes. Si-Siem is a special kid." The mage said. He seemed to be enjoying the reaction among the apprentices' faces. With a small chuckle he looked first to Siem and turned back to start the lesson. But not before he gave them a last reminder.

"Most of you have grown thinking you have a monopoly on strength and accomplishment in magic. The women are going to give you a hard run for that claim."

The following week, Siem got into a fight with one of the boys in the class and used a levitation spell on him. The boy, along with a company of three others, had waited beside the doorway for her. And when she walked in, bushwhacked her. They had hit the books she clutched in her hands away.

Most astonishing of what Siem had done, was not that she stood up to the bullies, but the magic she had instinctively used. The levitation spell was not taught to students. The knowledge of such a spell was reserved for two levels above her present company.

It was clear that she was a prodigy. Mages clamored to have her in their classes.

It was another decade until another girl joined the school. It was not so difficult for her and Siem to form some sort of bond between themselves.

More women joined the school onwards. Siem formed a guild for the new cohort of female mages. They looked after each other, they defended themselves.

And then, Siem was forced to leave the School of Magic.

"You have broken the rules binding your contract with this place," the head mage told her. "You have a lead role in this place, more so among the female mages of whom you are the first. Your actions are reprehensible..."

The other mages in the council looked at Siem severely, as they pronounced her crime. "Dabbling into dark magic. What were you thinking Siem?"

Siem did not try to plead, or cry, or let any crack appear in her steely demeanor. She watched the council with cold eyes, and when they delivered their verdict, walked out without looking back. Knowledge is power, she had learned. So, she became knowledgeable in everything. Even in the knowledge that they thought was dangerous. She knew it will help her someday.

═══

Eldana sat cross-legged, eyes closed, hands drooping by her side. She sat within a circle of lit candles, darkness pressing hard against the circumference of light, like a thirsty demon.

"You must take very deep breaths," her teacher had said. "Each breath is a step that calms your mind, aids you in emptying every thought, so you can easily access that which you already have but don't know."

Her teacher had a clean-shaven head and a striking jaw, from the city of Tonar. Mosa was his name, one of the seven, and in concord with the agreement regarding the training of the child of Balance and Chaos, he was the one selected from the human race to train the being of Balance and Chaos. He was going to teach her not just the tradition of humans, but also how to use her psychic powers.

Mosa was calm, and fun to be around sometimes, but Eldana still preferred to be taught by Sinto. But in this, she had very little choice.

"You have much to contribute to the entire land of Toas. And the gods would have you be trained by every race in Toas. I am not abandoning you, Eldana. Just giving other people their rights to raise you."

"Why is this so important?" Eldana had asked, a pout on her face.

"It is right that you be intimate with the ways and traditions of all the races, Eldana. You are the chosen one, given to the gods to restore balance for another hundred years. There is no bigger glory than that. As the stronger you are, as more beautiful the next hundred years will be for my children, and their children." He smiled at her.

"What about me?" Eldana looked at him with a serious look.
"What about you?" Mosa's face resembled a huge question mark. "You will be with the gods. Luck is on your side!" He nearly danced in anticipation for this event, just being happy for Eldana.

She could not tell if she was the only one seeing the irony of everyone having a great life and her being dead or how they called it "with the gods". This stupid mark was just on the wrong person, she thought. But she knew he was not the right person to talk about this.

Eldana reluctantly agreed to keep going with the lesson.

After a few historical lessons on the human race, an instructional guide through their society and practices, and theoretical drills on psychic magic, Mosa decided that it was time Eldana to do actual training.

So, here she was, quiet and still for the past five minutes, try-

Chapter Six

ing to calm her body, and empty her mind of every thought. She pulled up every instruction Mosa had given her about psychic magic, in detail. He had told her that some people, use a mental visualization of them lifting the desired object with their hands, he suggested a few more ways people used their psychic powers but insisted that there was no specific way of exercising the power.

"That is why meditation is important." He had told her. "It gives you the chance to know yourself better. Only then, can you find unique ways to do certain things."

"So, there is no guarantee meditation is going to work for me? Eldana had asked him.

"No." Mosa had replied. "But it will help you find what will."

Eldana began to get frustrated. She had emptied her mind, and yet she was still not feeling anything. Mosa had laid a metal rod in front of her. That was what she was going to be lifting with her mind.

"How would I know when I lift it?" she asked.

"You will know." Mosa had replied. "You'll feel a strain in your mind."

Eldana was yet to feel anything of the sort. She was about to rise to her feet, and storm away when she remembered something that Sinto had said to her.

It was on one of those early days when she had failed to steer the air into forming a wall of energy. Eldana was sitting, hopeless, on the floor.

"You are a child of Toas, Eldana." Sinto had told her. "You do well to remember that."

"You say these things to make me feel better for my inadequacies." Eldana had moaned.

Sinto chuckled. Then he gripped Eldana's shoulders warmly.

"No, I am not, Eldana. I tell you the truth and nothing but the truth. That is my job, remember?"

Eldana was quiet.

"Listen. You are a child of this world. It belongs to you just as much as you belong to it. When you doubt yourself, reach into

Toas for help."

Now, about to put her psychic powers to use, Eldana found Sinto's advise refreshingly useful. She smiled and thanked Sinto silently. She made a mental note to prove herself to the old man.

Bringing herself back to the task at hand, Eldana plucked out her thoughts, one after the other, until her mind was empty, fresh, and rich for growth. Slowly, she began to reach towards the earth as Sinto had taught her. Through her yearning to be one with the earth. She felt her mind-stretching, making contact with everything around her, and becoming one with it. And then suddenly, she felt a spark in her mind.

"Dear God Camin!" Eldana heard someone exclaim the holy name, and her eyes flew open.

She found herself looking down at Mosa and Mosa looking up at her. She was floating in the air, along with the metal rod, and the ring of candlelight.

Mosa had never seen someone display this level of psychic power with such ease, especially one who was a first-timer. Some people lifted boulders with their minds, and things as heavy as entire houses, or full-grown elephants. But that took years of exercise to strengthen the mind. The mind was like the body in some ways and needed to go through similar exercises. Multi-tasking was even more difficult. To lift different objects at once or do something like what Eldana did – lift them while maintaining a particular arrangement – required decades of training. But here was a beginner doing these things. And there were no signs yet of haemorrhaging from stressing the mind. The story of the being of Balance and Chaos and their immense power was one that had entertained the ears of every person in Toas since childbirth. The mark of chaos was powerful. Not very many got to personally encounter one, or to see them use their powers. But here he was.

"How?" he asked no one in particular, his eyes still fixed on Eldana.

Eldana smiled and lifted Mosa very slowly with her mind until he was level with her in the air.

Chapter Six

"Have I pleased my teacher?" she asked.
Mosa stuttered as he searched for words to put in his mouth.

CHAPTER SEVEN

The Elves of Ciroc

Ciroc Woods

Chapter Seven

Not very many creatures in Toas knew of the times before the new gods – Camin and Lowus. The times before Camin and Lowus were rife with unbridled chaos. It was like the world was turning against itself like a snake and tearing itself apart. The elves were witness to these times, and so were the orcs. They were creations of gods who had withered away for some unknown reason, leaving their creations, and the world they had created to fend for itself. In this chaos, created by the new and the old gods, magic ran like wildfire through the land, manifesting without cause or provocation, and making alterations in different places.

When the world settled under the reign of Camin and Lowus, ancient gods whose pre-existence was unknown, the humans and a lot of other races rose. And so too, did their kingdoms, cities, and towns. The majority of the elfsoc – a name ascribed to the elves by humans – settled in Kleas, and indulged their immortality, watching the world move with very little involvement.

Now, that the end of the hundred-year cycle was due and the being of Balance and Chaos was still alive, the world was unravelling again and returning to its state before Camin and Lowus. Chaos was coming back. A rash of killings had begun in Kleas and the Middle Kingdom. The elves, indifferent to the plight of others but theirs, lived in the woods, where they could look after their own affairs. They had survived chaos before. Surely, they could do it again?

They made a part of the Ciroc, rarely travelled upon by anything asides animals, their home.

The elves were led by Fraweyni, Child of the First, Daughter of Tessa. She was the sole child of the very first elf, Tessa, who grew tired of the world two millennia ago, and micronized herself to become part of the stars. She was a beacon of strength, wisdom, and power to her people, and she led them like they were an extension of herself.

Once they had secured their place in the forest, she had sentries stationed at the outskirts of the space they had cut out for themselves. The sentries morphed into trees and alerted others through a special signal whenever intruders stepped within their boundaries. Unwilling to let any of her people die in a skirmish, Fraweyni would, with an attachment of guards, let out her voice – which was so soulful, magical, and powerful that it could bring the stars to brightness in some days – and sometimes the minds of intruders.

Earlier today, she had been alerted to the presence of a magician within her boundaries. He was alone, the sentries had told her. But magicians were dangerous, and even though this one was outnumbered, he could still cause a fair amount of harm. So, she sang, and as expected, had ensnared him.

She got bothered, however, when moments later, the sentries reported that there were three more magicians within their boundaries, who looked to be searching for something or someone.

"They must be friends of the magician we captured." She said.

But why were all three here? She asked herself.

A magician strolling this deep into the Ciroc, she could call a mistake. But three more was something else.

Could they be looking for a way to launch an attack on us? She asked herself.

The best course of action, for her, would be to have them killed immediately. But she was seeing more than an accidental invasion here, and so had to interrogate them. She had lived so long in the world to be drawn to hasty conclusions. At eight hundred years, she had taken after the wisdom of her mother, Tessa.

"Meko", she called one of her lieutenants, a slender elf with long dark hair. "Take some elves with you, and find out from which direction these magicians came from."

Not long after, Fraweyni had captured the three magicians, Meko reported that there was another one, a young man, processing meat a few distances away from where the other three were found.

With all of them captured, Fraweyni proceeded to probe their minds for information about their identity, and of course, the rea-

Chapter Seven

son why they had ventured so deep into the Ciroc, instead of joining their respective kingdoms in preparing for war. Fraweyni had them sedated with the fragrance of the petals of a Linthaea – a magical flower with the ability to render creature's unconscious while keeping their minds alive, but numb.

Fraweyni had the tribe's most skilled telepath, Kochob, probe their docile minds.

It had taken hours to get into Eldana's head, because of the kind of magical energy radiating inside her. Kochob painstakingly procured a memory of her from childhood, meeting with a Sinto who was going to be her teacher.

"What is it?" Fraweyni asked when Kochob disentangled his mind from Eldana's with a gasp.

"This one." He said. "She's one of them. The princesses of the King."

"A being of Balance and Chaos?" Fraweyni asked.

Kochob nodded.

"Hmmm..." Fraweyni mused. "A being of Balance and Chaos who is still alive while the world crumbles into chaos. It seems like she grew a mind of her own!"

"How is that?" Meko asked. "I thought beings of Balance and Chaos were supposed to be sacrificed before they knew enough to question the purpose of their sacrifice?"

"Something about this one is different," Kochob said. "I just do not know what it is. There is also some kind of sorrow, numb. She hurts," he said, his face long and serious.

Kochob was still recovering from the amount of energy he had expended in boring into Eldana's mind. These beings had been set up by the human king as an equilibrium between the good and the evil constantly wrestling for the hearts of men. Finding magic meant humans could live as long as they wanted, even as long as the elves, but because most of their minds were not prepared for it they strayed into evil ways, and allowed the evil that hovered around their minds to make vessels of them. The human race was not the only race susceptible to this evil, so the sacrifice every 100 years of a princess, chosen among the king's many children by the gods, was not only for the good of the human race but for the whole world as well.

"You sure you are up for this?" Fraweyni asked him.

"Yes. I just need a little rest." He replied.

Moments later, Kochob sat at Hermon's head, with his eyes closed, as he peered into Hermon's memories. He found one memory that revealed his identity. An incident in his childhood where he keyed into rare ancestral magic and faced two fierce beasts alone.

It was dusk when Fraweyni checked up on Kochob again. Showers of light, from the globes the elves had sung into existence, illumined the woods within which they dwelt, and giving it a soft pastoral quality. Fraweyni was decked in an ankle-length flowing gown with a laurel of blooming flowers resting on her head.

Light glowed from within Kochob's tent making the tent translucent. Fraweyni parted the tent opening, and almost bumped into Kochob himself.

"My lady." He apologized and bowed slightly. "I was just on my way to you."

"And in such a hurry," Fraweyni said. "I can only imagine what would have happened if we had not caught ourselves in time. How are you faring?"

Kochob sighed and moved into the tent. Fraweyni followed him.

"The identities and relationship of these three are really interesting." He said. "The three of them," the elf pointed at the unconscious bodies of Eldana, Siem, and Hermon, "are trying to re-invent themselves. Yet, still, help the being of Balance and Chaos restore balance in some other way."

Kochob pointed at Hermon. "This one is called Hermon. He is a berserker. One of the five. Son of Biniamin."

Chapter Seven

"*The Biniamin?*" Fraweyni asked. Her eyes reflected a little light of interest now.

"Yes," Kochob replied. "He transformed into full berserker at a young age, during a coming-of-age ritual gone wrong. He was told he had to keep making the transformations for the protection of his clan. He fled to get rid of the curse."

"What about this one?" Fraweyni asked, pointing at Siem.

"Her name is Siem or Siem, and she is obviously of elven blood, although her family is unknown."

Fraweyni's eyes shot wide open. *Unknown family?* she thought. "Are you sure?" she asked.

Kochob nodded in affirmation. "It was her mother." He said. "Her mother was an elf."

"Do you know who she is?"

"Sadly, no. She never met her, and the father only divulged her mother's identity years later."

"If her father told her that, there is every tendency that he was lying. I mean, he is a human. Mortality is such an impediment to those of them without magic. They rarely get their facts right." Fraweyni objected.

"I am not sure he was telling a lie."

Fraweyni looked at Kochob.

"The level of magic I saw her perform," he continued, "was of elven strength. No human could achieve that."

Fraweyni's face grew pensive.

"There is something else," Kochob said.

"What?"

"She was a Si from day one in the School of Magic. And was also, up until her expulsion, the mind behind the notorious Women Guild in the School of Magic."

"Ah," Fraweyni's eyes brightened. "A woman of mettle."

"She was the last of the *Kajewil*. The last students to be taught magic according to the rules of the old magic."

"An oddly interesting troika indeed," Fraweyni observed. "What about the other two?" she asked.

Kochob looked at Mikko, and D'rmas.

"One is a free warrior of the Qeltifom clan, and the other is a mage novice, apprenticed under the notorious Lord Taboon. But rebelled and decided to help the company."

A cloud of silence perfused the atmosphere as soon as Kochob was done speaking. Fraweyni's gaze was unfocused as she retreated within the walls of her mind.

"What shall we do with them? This is the weirdest mix of characters that I have ever seen in my life." Kochob asked after a while.

"Leave them for now," Fraweyni said. She would just watch them and see what they were up to.

She turned, and walked out of the tent, into bright lights and serenading music. Her mind was racing. Something was very different about this group and whether this was a good or bad sign was still hidden in the stars.

Reader   Report

The elves were witness to the times before Camin and Lowus, as were the orcs. They were rife with unbridled chaos. These two were creations of gods who had left their creations and the world to fend for itself. In this chaos, created by the new and the old gods, magic manifested without cause or provocation, and making alterations in different places. When the world settled under the reign of Camin and Lowus, the humans and a lot of other races rose along with their kingdoms, cities, and towns. The majority of the elfsoc – a name ascribed to the elves by humans – settled in Kleas and watched the world move with very little involvement. They were indifferent to the plight of others and lived in the woods, where they could look after their own affairs. Because the end of the hundred-year cycle is due and the being of Balance and Chaos was still alive, Chaos is coming back. A rash of killings had begun in Kleas and the Middle Kingdom.

CHAPTER EIGHT

Alive Again

Ciroc Woods

Siem opened her eyes, and for a moment could not remember anything but her name. Slowly, everything began to come back. She took a good look at her surroundings.

She was in a tent that rose high into the sky, pointed like elfin ears, and slender. There was a cluster of belongings at the far end. A table, bags, a chair, and a few other household things. They were not much, but they were enough for simple living.

Mikko! Siem sat up quickly.

The last thing she remembered was going into the woods with Eldana and D'rmas in search of him. Then she remembered Hermon, who they had left behind, and felt a pang of worry. He would be all alone, without a clue as to what happened to them. Siem herself had no clue, and so decided to catch up with the time she had missed.

Just then, the flap over the tent parted, and a head peeked in. Siem was about to summon a gust of wind to blast the person away when she stopped. Eldana was smiling back at her from the tent's entrance.

"Eldana?" Siem asked.

"Yes, sleepyhead," Eldana taunted as she came in. "Who do you think it was?"

Siem swallowed and looked around again.

"What is this?" she asked, using her eyes to gesture at the tent. "Where are we? What happened to the others?"

"Woah, easy mother hen," Eldana said, and laughed.

Siem took one look at Eldana, and let her rising anxiety abate. She figured that Eldana would not be smiling or jesting if everything was not okay.

"Is everyone okay?" Siem finally asked.

Eldana looked at her and said:

"Yes."

"Where are we, Eldana?"

"We are among the elfsoc." Eldana replied.

"The elfsoc?" Siem questioned with surprise. "Are we in Kleas?"

"Nope," Eldana answered. "We are still in Ciroc."

Chapter Eight

"What are the elfsoc doing in Ciroc?"

"I asked the same question when I got to know where I was," Eldana replied.

"Turns out," she said after a while, "that they were the ones who took Mikko."

"So, he is safe?" Siem asked.

Eldana studied Siem and nodded in the positive.

"You have a thing for him," Eldana said.

"Hm?"

"Mikko," Eldana insisted, "You like him."

"No, I do not." Siem refuted, her eyes flaring, color coming to her cheek, and she immediately looked away.

Eldana made to speak, but Siem cut her off.

"If you are going to pry to see if there is a sliver of affection in me for Mikko, stop." She said.

"I was going to ask if you were ready to come out," Eldana said.

Siem sighed. "Fine."

Siem walked out of the tent, and into a glade. It was small, like a courtyard in the forest. Siem spotted elves going about their normal lives. The sight of them reminded Siem what beautiful creatures elves were - tall, and gallant, with looks that could rarely be rivalled by any other race in Toas.

"Where exactly are we going to?" Siem asked Eldana, as they headed into the trees.

"Their queen has been wanting to see you." Eldana supplied.

"What for?"

"I have absolutely no idea. Perhaps to interrogate you?"

"Interrogate me?"

Siem scoffed.

"I have got a barrel full of questions right now." She said. "Like, why am I here?"

"Well, that one I can answer for you," Eldana replied. "We are here because we invaded the elves' boundaries."

"That's preposterous," Siem said.

"Do not tell them that to their face, or they will send you back to sleep!" Eldana joked.

The pair walked into another clearing much like the one they had come from, only larger. There were groups of elves training with swords, long staves, bows, and other assorted more delicate weapons. Siem thought she saw someone familiar going at an elf with a sword. She narrowed her eyes in scrutiny. The person was laughing and dancing with his steps, jumping about like a graceful butterfly.

"Is that not D'rmas?" she asked.

"It is," Eldana replied.

Siem watched D'rmas weave in and out of the elf's sword strokes, and deliver an equally lethal combo of his own, which the elf deflected or dodged.

"Impressive, right?" Eldana asked.

"Totally," Siem replied. "Won't they hack themselves to bits with the way they go at each other?"

"My thoughts exactly. But Merhawi says that the blades of the swords are made blunt by magic. So strokes would hurt, but not maim or injure."

"Hmmm..."

"Well, D'rmas finally gets something that is not boring."

They walked between the trees again and left the training ground behind. Bits of sunlight fell in tiny shafts, giving the forest a little taste of the daylight, it was missing. Siem saw a few squirrels jump from tree to tree, and birds flit through branches while chirping non-stop at themselves. A gentle breeze cruised through, ruffling leaves from the lowest branches. Everything was serene. Safe. Natural.

"I can see why the elves would want to leave Kleas and retire here," Siem observed.

"It's unsullied by the chaos that's unravelling outside." Eldana supplied.

They got to a place where the trees formed an arched entranceway.

"Wow," Siem said with awe written clearly on her face. "I had

Chapter Eight

forgotten what excellent manipulators of nature the elves are."

"Welcome," a voice said.

Eldana and Siem looked up abruptly and spotted another elf.

This one looked young, but so did most of the elves. Siem knew the elf had probably seen more millennia worth of time than most things in the world. The only indication of age the elves had were their eyes. Their eyes glowed with the amount of knowledge and experience they garnered through their immortal lifetimes. The eyes of the oldest among them radiated with fullness, meaning, and age.

Eldana and Siem came to a halt as the elf approached.

"Hi." They greeted.

The elf nodded and introduced herself. "I am Meko. One of Fraweyni's lieutenants."

Siem was about to speak, but Meko cut her off.

"There is no need for that. Fraweyni demanded that she see you as soon as you were awake."

Siem was annoyed at being interrupted.

"What did you think I was going to say?" Siem asked.

"Introduce yourself. Am I wrong?" Meko asked cocking her brow inquisitively.

Siem quietened. She was boiling inside, but she hid it well.

"Now, if you are ready," Meko said, cocking her brow, and gesturing for the both of them to follow her.

"Lead the way," Siem said.

Meko turned and went into the arched pathway.

As they walked into the pathway, a little behind Meko, they were hit by the soft fragrance of fresh flowers. Their hearts beat slower, their countenances grew lighter. The pathway broke into a small glade, with a grove in the middle. The grove was hollow in between walls of vegetation. Flowers budded and bloomed everywhere.

"In there," Meko said, pointing into the entrance to the grove.

Eldana and Siem began to go in when Meko stopped them.

"She will see you first." She said, starting at Siem. "You, Eldana will wait out here with me."

Siem looked at Eldana in a questioning manner, but Eldana nodded.

Siem nodded and sighed. "Here goes." She said, walking into the grove.

Fraweyni lounged on a hammock made from vines. Her eyes flicked towards the entrance when she noticed some movement. With her mind, Fraweyni unwove the vines and controlled them to let her down slowly.

"Welcome, Siem," Fraweyni said, a slight smile on her face.

Under Fraweyni's gaze, Siem felt a compelling urge to prostrate. The elf was beautiful. More beautiful than anything she had ever seen. Her eyes were like little radiant balls of gold, her features slim and perfect. Her hair was woven into a ponytail, which she let curve out to the front of her shoulder. Her smile was scintillating.

And then Siem knew. This was the elf's true form. The elves hid their true forms from the rest of the world, choosing to morph themselves into other shapes instead. And it was for good reason. With this level of beauty in the constant display, men, the humans especially would run mad with lust and desire. And though, an attack on the elves was often considered nothing but foolhardy, the Toas had seen enough to know that nothing stopped the humans – besides an impressive display of determination and strength – when they set their minds to covet something.

Siem's words had been snuffed out, together with her breath.

Fraweyni gave a knowing smile. She was pleased whenever her beauty was able to produce reactions like Siem's before her.

"I trust you are feeling yourself?" the Elf Queen asked Siem.

She shook her head, bringing herself together.

"Yes, I am." She replied. "There is only the problem of a missing time I cannot account for."

Fraweyni smiled. "Why don't you take a seat."

With the flick of her fingers, branches grew rapidly from the surrounding trees, and petals from the flowers above fell – a lot of

Chapter Eight

them in a flurry until they formed a cushion on the seat.

Siem smiled. "You all seem perfectly comfortable here, in the Ciroc," she observed.

"Well, the elves are creatures of nature after all. And though we have had to put up with the rest of the world, since the reign of Camin and Lowus, the recent outbursts of chaos have led us to seek better homes, ones we can easily defend for ourselves. We believe things will only get worse."

Siem nodded.

"But you can change that, can't you?" Fraweyni asked. "You, Eldana, Hermon, and the rest of your group."

Siem looked at Fraweyni, trying to discern if she could trust her. Fraweyni stared back. Siem decided that she would have to trust, their love for privacy, their tendency of non-involvement, and their pride as a race.

"We are trying to," she replied slowly.

"It is nice to see a group of people trying to create a path for themselves other than that which the gods have selected for them. It is a wonderful attempt, but one that is often fraught with tragedy."

"We entertain the possibility of that in our hearts. However, nothing can ever be done if there is no hope or optimism."

"Hmmm" Fraweyni mused. "Optimism."

"Tell me about your childhood, Siem," Fraweyni said suddenly.

Siem was a bit taken aback by the sudden change of events. She did not know what the elf was aiming at, but she did know that she was supposed to display a level of courtesy. She was their guest after all. Siem started small, from the first memories of her childhood, in a small town in Tonar, and her father, whose face she could scarcely remember.

"What about your mother?" Fraweyni asked suddenly, cutting Siem's story short.

"What?" Siem asked, a look of surprise and suspicion crawling into her face.

"What about your mother. Any memory of her?" Fraweyni

asked.

"No," Siem replied warily. "I have no recollection of her. My father told me she died before I was born. Any reason why you are asking these questions?"

Fraweyni primmed her lips.

"Your mother was or is clearly an elf," she said.

"Yes. I remember my father telling me that on a few occasions."

But I always wondered why any elf would leave her child behind. The elves are too proud a people to do that. They prize family."

"Well, I would not say what your mother did what was right, if indeed she left you, and is still alive, but I can say I understand her a bit."

"Yeah?"

"Yes. You see, my people frown at relations between them and humans, not to mention, falling in love with them as your mother did." Fraweyni waited for Siem's response, which came back hot and quick.

"Yeah? Well, I guess that is why the world is the way it is. Chaotic, You and your people do not involve yourselves in anything, and so you all have to rely on the life of one girl to ensure the world exists in balance and order. But why should I care? The elves are dignified immortals. Their minds and magic are strong enough to protect themselves, and as long as they stay safe, will survive the chaos, while the rest of the world goes up in flames."

Fraweyni watched Siem effuse with anger until she stopped.

"Come with me." She told her when she was done fuming.

Fraweyni got up and walked out of the grove. Siem followed closely behind. They walked out and found Eldana sitting at the massive roots of an oak tree, with her back against its trunk. She was throwing rocks absentmindedly at the tree opposite her. Meko was a little to her side, singing to a flying squirrel that had fallen off the tree and broken an arm.

Eldana got to her feet. Fraweyni attracted by her sudden motion, looked her way.

Chapter Eight

"Ah, Eldana." She said with an apologetic smile. "I had been under the impression that my talk with Siem would be swift, and then I would see you immediately. There is something I need to show her, and while you are free to retire, and wait till I call upon you."

Eldana puffed air out of her mouth in a bored expression.

"I have been doing nothing anyways, other than watch Meko there sing to a squirrel."

Fraweyni laughed, and Eldana and Siem looked at her with surprise and then smiled. Fraweyni's laughter was melodious. Like a chronicle of happier times, and happier things.

"Meko did you hear what Eldana said? You are bad for the company. You should improve on that."

Meko who had just finished singing to the squirrel set it on the root of a nearby tree and watched it scamper up and into the safety of the branches of the tree.

Eldana stepped into pace with Siem, as Fraweyni led their little procession.

"The elves are an annoying bunch," Siem muttered to her.

Eldana smiled. "You see," she said, "they are not all beauty."

"Oh, I concur," Siem breathed.

Fraweyni led them to a huge tree, with a trunk the size of three trees, and with very thick branches. The Queen got close to the tree and stopped.

"I am sure none of you are familiar with The Purge," she said.

"What purge?" Siem responded.

"I thought as much," Fraweyni replied wearily. "We did not want that appearing on history books. You see, millennia ago, in the times of old magic, the elves lived openly. Even tried to contribute the little we could into the affairs of Toas. But we were not like the others, the humans, or the rest of the magicians. We and the orcs had existed long before you all came along. And so, whether we liked it or not, we had a god-like impression wherever we went. We do not know if it was fear, or envy, or both, but the elves were unsuspectingly set on. These are the number of my people who never joined the stars."

As she spoke, etchings began to appear on the tree. They grew gradually, from nothing till they glowed like embers in full emphasis.

Eldana was wide-eyed with shock.

"Are these...?" she started to ask.

"Names. Yes." Meko supplied.

Siem was perplexed. The etchings were everywhere on the tree, from the trunk even to its branches.

"These are all the killings that instigated our move into the Ciroc," Fraweyni said.

The sorrow in her voice was so evident, it pulled at both of their hearts.

"So many lay on the ground, their blood rich with their life. I had to hear their soundless cries, feel their regret that they would never join their kin in the stars. We buried all of the fallen elves here, all who had fallen by some horrible magic, and all their bodies birthed this tree, a monument and a testament that they once existed. They are trapped in the lightless place, in limbo. They are lost and cannot shine. The number of bodies we put in the ground still weigh our hearts down to this day."

The silence stretched as they stood at the foot of the tree, with its body glowering with etchings until Fraweyni broke it.

"Perhaps you can see why we do not involve ourselves in the affairs of the world. It is the only way we survive. We left Kleas because some of us began to be killed. Without cause, without provocation."

Siem felt a pang of remorse for how she had addressed Fraweyni earlier. But that was the beginning of the chaos. No one could control it, it just started slowly within everyone.

Fraweyni turned and gazed at both.

"I do not care if you understand why we must not involve ourselves." She told them. "This is not meant to garner pity for ourselves. You know enough already, to know that the elves detest pity. I just want you to know that we are not the picture of self-involvement, piety, selfishness, and lack of empathy that world has painted."

Fraweyni smiled, and her face brightened. It was almost like the sorrow that had been on her face moments ago was never there. The etchings on the tree began to disappear, until the bark was just normal brown, and webbed with cracks of age.

"I think I will speak to you both. We do not have all the time, I am afraid," the Queen said.

"Meko?" She called.

Meko appeared in a moment, and her expression grew grave when she saw the great tree behind them.

"O, please dry those eyes, my child," Fraweyni said.

"Yes, mother," Meko said, wiping her sleeves across her eyes.

"Kochob says he needs your help." She told Meko. "He says he is at the training ground."

Meko nodded and left.

"Meko's brother was among the count of the slain in Kleas before we fled," Fraweyni said when Meko was gone. "I do not know how they were able to discern our true nature. We had disguised ourselves as humans."

"The slayers must have had magicians among them." Eldana supplied.

"That is what we think," Fraweyni replied. "Poor girl. I do not know if she will ever trust your kind again."

Eldana and Siem's hearts were filled with sympathy for Meko.

"We should seat," Fraweyni suggested.

She flicked her fingers, and vines sprouted from the ground and wove into sturdy chairs. Fraweyni sat and gazed at Eldana and Siem.

"You were right when you mentioned that the Ciroc is an apt home for us. Indeed, it is. This place was our home once, till we migrated into the city, and had to live in constant disguise. Now we are free. And we intend to defend this place. We were not expecting to be discovered any time soon. So, imagine our surprise when one of your friends was spotted by our sentries wandering within our borders."

Siem wanted to tell Fraweyni that Mikko was not wandering. He had been found within their borders because he sought to empty his bladder. But she kept her cool.

"We could have easily killed him." Fraweyni continued.

"That is the penalty for violating your borders?" Eldana asked incredulously.

Fraweyni smiled coldly. "When you have suffered losses as we have, nothing is too drastic to ensure your safety," she said. "Anyways, I decided not to. We did not know what he was doing so deep in the Ciroc, and if he was alone. If he was acting alone, we were safe. But some of us had fears that a team had been dispatched to locate our whereabouts. If that happened, we would have to be forced to fight. And with the coming chaos, there would be inevitable losses on both sides. It would not be a bad thing if our number remained the way it was, you know. For the sake of clarification, I had him taken, not before I dazed him of course."

"Dazed?" Siem asked.

"Yes," Fraweyni replied. "The same thing I did to you two, and the free warrior, when you came looking, and the same thing I did to Hermon. Apprehension is easier that way, especially with magicians."

"So, what next?" Siem was intrigued. "You dazed us, and had us taken in."

"Correct," Fraweyni said with a nod. Like a teacher nodding satisfactorily to the answer one of their students gave correctly to their question. "When you had been brought in, I had Kochob interrogate you."

"Interrogate?" Eldana asked, a scowl of confusion on her face. "I have no recollection of being interrogated."

"Same here." Her counterpart seconded.

"Was this done when we were still in your daze?" Eldana asked.

"No," Fraweyni replied. "It was done when you were asleep, heavily under the soporific effects of the Linthaea."

"You have that here?" Eldana asked.

Chapter Eight

To find a healthy Linthaea herb was rare. Most of the Linthaea in Toas were sickly.

"Yes," Fraweyni replied. "You will be amazed at how great they flourish around us."

"If we were asleep," Eldana started, "how were you able to interrogate us?"

"With a telepath," Fraweyni stated. "He goes by the name of Kochob. He is the best telepath among us."

"That is how you got to know about my mother," Siem said accusingly.

Fraweyni nodded.

"If you have scoured through our minds, that means you know everything about us," Eldana said.

"I am afraid that is how it seems, Eldana," Fraweyni said. "However, you should know that as a race that values privacy, your secrets, thoughts, and past are safe."

"Great. That is supposed to make me feel better." Siem said heavily.

"I cannot say that I am sorry for what has been done." Fraweyni began. "But I wish that you understand that we had to make sure of your identities, ascertain why you were this deep in the Ciroc, and determine if you were a threat to us."

"We understand," Eldana said.

Siem nodded, but it still annoyed her nonetheless. Maybe it was because Fraweyni knew so much about her, but she knew nothing about Fraweyni besides what was already in the book of races.

"So, are we..?" Siem started, her eyes on Fraweyni.

"Are you what?" Fraweyni questioned.

"A threat?"

"I think the fact that you two sit here, alive and unbound, should speak for itself."

Siem quietened and leaned into her chair.

"The elves have outlived an era of chaos before, the battle of the first hour, when all who could do magic faced those who they considered the face of the gods," Fraweyni told them. "We can do that again. That was one of the reasons we moved into Ciroc. But there is something about you three."

"Three?" Eldana questioned.

"Yourself, Siem, and Hermon, of course," Fraweyni replied.

"Oh," Eldana said.

"You are more like siblings in many ways. You are young, have seen but little of the world yet, but still have more experience than an average human in his entire life span. But more intriguing than your youth is the similar desire you harbor. The will to redefine yourselves. To not be described by the seeming ills fate has latched onto you. That is impressive. Such a level of hope and optimism you display is rarely seen. Some might even call it dreamy."

"Dreamy." Eldana scoffed.

"You are the being of Balance and Chaos," Fraweyni said gently. "The child marked by chaos. You were raised to revere Camin and Lowus, and you started to dislike the idea that you were being reared for slaughter. Somehow, you become self-aware and escape. Then the world begins to descend into chaos. Because the amount of energy that is supposed to go from you to Camin and Lowus, so they could keep chaos at bay, is still within you. The world is crumbling. Chaos is returning. People have died because of your decision. To think that all you have to do for the world to have calm and peace is to sacrifice your life, and yet you run, in search of another path. Would that not be termed as selfishness?"

Eldana grew sad, and sorrowful as Fraweyni's words settled. She knew there was truth to what Fraweyni said.

All this is my fault, she told herself. The displacements, the deaths, even Meko's brother, all my fault.

"And you forsook your destined path, for a path that none of you yet know. What better way to define a dream?"

Siem noticed Eldana begin to sink into herself, and placed a palm on her hand and squeezed comfortingly.

"You are wrong." She told Fraweyni. "Just because we do not yet see what we desire does not mean it does not exist. That is why

Chapter Eight

there are hope and optimism. Sadly, I fear the elves have lived so long they have forgotten what those feel like. Everything is systemic, planned, and factual for you now."

Fraweyni smiled indulgingly.

"Another misconception of the elves," she said. "Everyone dreams, Siem. Imagination is key. The elves are not exempt from that. Everything first starts with imagination, a dream. Even the gods who formed this world, first conceived of it as a dream." She lightly chuckled and smiled. "Don't you forget the stories of Toas and the first particle. Every child in Toas learns it, don't you?"

Both nodded.

"You see, nothing is always given, nothing is set. You can change your destiny."

"Why are you then making this look like it is all futile?" Siem asked. "Does Eldana not deserve her life? An opportunity to live? Don't we all?"

"Yes, we do. However, I think it would be lackadaisical of you to ignore the repercussions of your actions. Having them in mind fosters responsibility, sharpens focus, and makes sure that you give your all, even your life, to make your dream real."

Fraweyni gazed at the young woman sitting in front of her.

"Cheer up." She told them. "Your journey is going to be difficult, but it does not mean that what you search for cannot be found."

Eldana looked up at her like she was just hearing her for the first time.

"What?" she asked.

"You were right in thinking that there is another way. There very rarely is none. When it comes to fate, the world is full of forks, a myriad of paths branching out from one major road. But believe me when I tell you that you are not ready yet. None of you is."

"What?" Siem and Eldana questioned at the same time, gazing at Fraweyni like she did not know what she was saying.

"You are gifted magicians. All of you in your company. But if you want to reknit fate's yarn, you are going to need more than just gifts." Fraweyni said.

"That would not be the case," Siem said. "If the elves decided to get involved in things. Again."

Fraweyni grew thoughtful. "We may not involve ourselves directly." She said after a while. "Not yet. But we can indirectly."

Both traded uncertain glances.

"You see, the three of you are a source of intrigue for us. We may be able to help the world reshape itself if we help you."

Eldana's eyes brightened.

"You mean you are going to teach us?" she asked, incredulously.

"Yes, Eldana. We are going to teach you three what we know. But you are most especially. Siem here has had training as a Kajewil in the school of Magic. Whereas you ran from your teachers even before your training was complete. Too much is at stake though, the fate of the world and all that lives upon it. You will be trying to learn pieces of magic that takes decades to learn in only a few days that you will be staying with us…that is if you agree to this."

Eldana gave Siem an eager look.

"Of course, we agree."

Fraweyni nodded and smiled.

"I will arrange for you and Kochob to meet. In this fight, telepathy is something you want to gain considerable skill in," she said. "Now," she sat up from her seat, "I believe a visit to the infirmary is in store. One of your friends and one of my commanders tested their limits during training, and I fear they got the better of each other."

"I can bet you anything that it is D'rmas." Eldana said.

Siem chuckled.

"Who else would it be?" she asked rhetorically.

Fraweyni led them through the forest. As she walked, flowers bloomed. Both of them followed behind, and their eyes admiring the magic Fraweyni created effortlessly.

"Can you imagine?" Eldana whispered to Siem. "Being taught

Chapter Eight

by elves."

"Yeah," she whispered back. "I feel strongly that we are going to be successful, now. Plus staying here will give us the secrecy we desperately need at the moment. When we continue our journey, things will have worsened for sure, but we will be ready, and maybe Sinto, Lord Taboon, and the King's search for us will have died down."

The infirmary was a large white tent, decked by curtains of flowering vines. They met Meko by the entrance speaking with a male elf. They both turned and bowed their heads acknowledging Fraweyni's presence.

"How are the patients doing?" Fraweyni asked.

"They are back on their feet already," Meko replied.

"Their wounds were not too severe, I hope?"

"No, mother."

"I thought there were things in place to prevent something like this happening?"

"The blades were blunted," the elf Meko had been speaking with said, "but they can still hurt!"

"Well, whatever happened, your friend is in there. You can check up on his welfare." Fraweyni said to Siem and Eldana, before signalling for Meko to come with her. She bade Eldana and Siem farewell and instructed the male elf to help them find their way to their tents when they were done.

Siem watched them go, then turned to the male elf.

"Is Fraweyni Meko's mother?" she asked him.

The male elf looked at her, "Of course. She is our mother. She is the daughter of the first. She guides us."

"Come on, you know what I mean." Siem rolled her eyes.

The elf looked at her, then smiled. He seemed to hesitate for a short time, but he eventually gave her an answer to her question.

"Yes."

"See? That was not so hard, was it?" Siem asked the elf.

He smiled, and parting the opening to the infirmary's entrance, ushered them in.

Alive Again

Later, at night, Eldana, Siem, Hermon, Mikko, and D'rmas had been invited for a feast of sorts, which Fraweyni was personally hosting.

"How do I look?" Hermon asked, making an exaggerated twirl.

"Like a human child eager to impress?" Siem said.

"Come on." Hermon's face soured.

"I think you look good, Hermon." Eldana said after a bout of laughter.

"There," Hermon looked at Siem, "that is how things like this are done. With compliments!"

Eldana laughed again.

Hermon was in brown trousers, black boots, and wore a brown leather jacket with silver studs over an off-white shirt.

Eldana and Siem were in dresses, as Fraweyni had recommended.

"You do know we are just going out to eat with the rest of the elves, right?" Siem asked him.

"Of course," Hermon replied, a puzzled look on his face.

"Good," Siem said. "Because trust me, the elven ladies are going to give you about as much time they give a fly."

Eldana burst into laughter, as did Siem.

Hermon frowned, as he asked, "You think I do not know that?" And then; "We should be going!" He said angrily, heading towards the tent's exit without waiting to see if both followed, laughing all the more.

The feast was held in a large clearing, with the edges lined with tables and chairs that went full circle. Flowers hung from the tables like hair.

"I have no doubt the elves conjured the tables and chairs from the plants," Eldana told her friends.

"Their mastery of nature shows such power!" Hermon said. "The elves are surely the most powerful race in Toas."

"They are also the oldest," Eldana said.

Chapter Eight

"That's if you count out the orcs." Siem corrected.

"Oh, those," Hermon said.

Small globes from which light emitted were positioned in strategic places around the clearing, flooding it with so much light that were it not for its too-golden color, it would have been mistaken for sunlight. The tables were already laid with flagons, goblets, and platters of meat and fruits. As Hermon, Siem, and Eldana took their honored place at the head table, Hermon turned to both:

"You know for someone who is not worth more than the time given to a fly, I can be really valuable. What did you two do all day, asides talk with Fraweyni?"

Eldana laughed.

"Come on, Hermon. You know I did not mean that, right?" Siem asked with a broad grin. "But to answer your question, we did nothing. We idled away the whole day, doing absolutely nothing."

A smile grew on Hermon's face.

"What did you do?" came from Eldana.

"Every single platter of meat was prepared under the supervision of yours truly," Hermon said with a bow.

Eldana and Siem jokingly gave him a round of applause.

Just then, Eldana spotted D'rmas and Mikko walking towards them. "And look who finally decided to join us." She said, gesturing with her head towards the approaching pair.

Siem turned her sight towards their direction, and her heart leaped at the sight of Mikko. She had not seen him since he was taken by the elves. Seeing him now brought back the feelings she had tried to put on hold since their first meeting. His black hair, stylishly curled, accentuated his facial features, and Siem could not find his smile more dashing.

"A good evening to you all." D'rmas greeted them on getting to the table.

"Evening, D'rmas." Hermon replied. "I hear you and one of the elven commanders had a tit for tat during training."

D'rmas guffawed. "I was as sure as chaos itself, that I was not going to let another person that was not a berserker defeat me. He won the fight in the end. He is an elf after all. But I did make it extremely difficult for him. Now he knows enough to turn the other away if he ever has to face any from the Qeltifom clan."

"Good for you," Hermon said, shaking his head.

D'rmas, Hermon, and Eldana got into a discussion about the elves and their seemingly haughty attitude, leaving Mikko and Siem to themselves.

"Hello." Mikko greeted with a smile.

"Hello," Siem replied with a smile of her own. "How have you been?"

"Hmm", Mikko said, mashing his lips together, and shaking his head contemplatively. "Well, for someone who lost all awareness of himself while taking a leak, and then waking up to find himself among one of the most revered and feared races in Toas, I would say pretty well."

"Good," Siem said and looked away.

Mikko studied her. "Good?" he asked. "Just that?"

Siem looked at him, shifting a bit uncomfortably.

"You are alive. You are safe. What else do you want me to say?"

"I don't know," Mikko said, resigned. His eyes remained on her face. She stared back, unblinking before he looked away.

"This is the first time you are seeing me in days, after my, erm, abduction. And this is all you say?"

Siem folded her arms across her chest and affected indifference. "If my sense of observation is still correct, I know this is also the first time you are seeing me in days. And this is all you do? Question me?"

Mikko smiled. "Of course not. Where are my manners? It is nice meeting you. Again."

The smile on his face vanished. He stared at Siem a moment longer, before turning, and walking to the other end of the table, so he could sit beside D'rmas.

Her eyes stayed on him as he walked away until she got hold of

Chapter Eight

herself. She did not understand why she had reacted that way to him. And she chided herself for it.

You behaved like a child, she berated herself.

Siem sat, angry at herself for the things Mikko was making her feel and do. It did not take long after Mikko and Siem's mild altercation for Fraweyni to grace the table. She sat in the middle of the head table, Meko by her right, Kochob by her left, then Siem and Eldana after Kochob – in that order – and Hermon, D'rmas and Mikko after Meko.

The elves sang a short song, a kind of prelude to the feast proper, and then the eating began.

"Humans do this before eating," Fraweyni said to the hearing of everyone at the table. "Pray to the gods." She put a slice of meat into her mouth and chewed.

Her movements were light and swift; her chewing gentle.

"That was a prayer?" Hermon asked.

"Yes," Fraweyni replied. "But not a prayer to the gods, no. A prayer to nature. The elves are also, as most of your books must have told you, creatures of the song of nature. In that short song, we thanked nature for allowing us uninhibited access to its gifts. And wished that our access continued."

"Just that?" Mikko asked.

Meko looked at him.

"Forgive me." He said. "But the song sounded like it said more than what you just said."

A burst of small laughter broke across the table, with the exceptions of Meko, and Siem – who felt her heart lurch at the sound of Mikko's voice.

"Well, the language is elven, Mikko." Fraweyni replied. "And interpreting elven language word for word into your language is just not possible."

"Oh," Mikko said and went back to his plate.

As they ate, a small company of female elves walked into the center of the clearing. Gradually, music from flutes began to grow, until they were clear and sonorous.

The female elves at the center began to dance, making gracious movements with their arms and feet. The spectacle arrested the interest of everyone in the clearing. There were moments, when the flutes sang slowly, infusing the atmosphere with calm, and an attitude of veneration, and then the melody picked again, going faster, lightening the atmosphere, and returning the mood of feasting.

"What is it with the performance?" Siem asked.

"It is a story. Something like what the humans call an epic. Only in our case, it is a tragedy."

Siem looked out in puzzlement. The voice that had just replied to her did not belong to Fraweyni. Eldana shared the puzzlement and looked to where the voice had come from.

They met Meko's eyes.

"Did you say something? Eldana asked.

"The dance," she said. "It is a story about us. A sad story."

Finally, Siem thought, she speaks. "What does it say?" Siem asked of the recalcitrant elf.

Meko swallowed the bit of meat that she had been chewing. Her movements were gentle. Just like Fraweyni's.

"It tells of the emergence of the First, the spread of the elven race, our survival of chaos, and the injustice we have met in the hands of the new races, in that order."

For a while, the clink of knives on plates were the only sounds that indicated life at the table. The dance was concluded, and the dancers moved back to their tables with applause from the other tables.

"Finally," Mikko told D'rmas under the sound of the applause. "I have never heard or seen something so depressing."

D'rmas grunted and nodded his affirmation.

Half-way into the meal, Fraweyni raised a hand for silence. When the entire place had grown quiet, she lifted her goblet of wine.

"This is to our suspects-turned-guests." She said. "Mikko, D'rmas, Hermon, Siem, and Eldana. We speak our blessings to their endeavour and pray that it is achievable."

She rose the goblet higher, and many other goblets went into the air.

"There is an extra bit of news," Fraweyni said, as she dropped her goblet back to the table. "Our guests are going to be staying with us a little longer, before continuing the journey we interrupted."

Whispers broke across the tables. The elves were in doubt of the decision Fraweyni was presenting them. Fraweyni was well aware of their objections and reservations, and so let the whispers go on for a while longer. Then she lifted her hand into the air and asked for quiet.

"I know, and understand my children, your grievances." Her voice was soft, comforting, like a mother's.

Siem watched the exchange and developed a newfound respect for Fraweyni. There was something to admire in the way that she led the elves. There was no doubting the love that churned inside her.

"I have lost a father, a mother, a husband, and very recently, a son. I feel the same loss you feel for your departed brethren. What is worse, I feel twice the sense of loss you all feel, because I carry both your burden and mine. We had decided, a long time ago, shortly after the purge, never to involve ourselves in the affairs of Toas. We went into reclusion, using our abilities to shapeshift to hide us. However, we were discovered, and we lost more as a result of that. What does this say? That whether we are involved or not, chaos still finds us. Now, while I do not doubt that we can hold our own in here, I am not throwing away the possibility that chaos will find us here. I have lost enough of my children. I am not ready to lose any more. Not even one. These people," she gestured towards Eldana and her friends, "are trying to restore peace into the world. That way we can live peacefully. This is not a path that was chosen for them, but a burden that they have chosen for themselves. We must have a hand, this time, even though inconspicuously."

Eldana watched the elves sitting at the tables. She saw their countenances lighten, as Fraweyni spoke. It was like her words were dousing the flame of doubts they had in their minds.

"It is true, that humans and the rest of the races have been cruel to us. But we have lived long enough to know that there are those among them who are different. Who does not share the greed and bloodlust of their kin? Merhawi the Great, who we all sing about in our epics, was a human. We cannot let the deeds of a foolish majority tarnish the entirety of the human race."

After the feast, Siem excused herself from Eldana and Hermon's company. She had spotted Mikko leave the table with D'rmas, without so much as a glance her way. Despite herself, she had felt a spike of hurt, and decided to resolve things with him.

"Hey." She called, as she walked up to him.

Mikko turned, and seeing her approach, stopped.

"Hi." He said as she came to a halt in front of him.

"Hi, D'rmas." Siem greeted. "How did you find the feast?"

D'rmas grunted.

"I found it boring at some point. And entertaining at others." He replied.

Siem laughed. "I think we all felt that way. The elves and their ways, huh?"

D'rmas shrugged. "The elves and their ways." He parroted.

D'rmas was no child and understood that Siem was seeking time alone with Mikko, so he bade them goodnight, and told Mikko not to get lost on his way back.

"Do not pick a fight, D'rmas." He called out.

D'rmas, still walking, laughed.

Mikko watched him leave, with a smile on his face.

"Nice fellow, hm?" she asked when he faced her.

Mikko smiled. "D'rmas has his quirks." He said. "But in a nutshell, one can survive around much worse."

"Are you saying he is a bad companion?" Siem asked, her eyes widening exaggeratedly.

"Oh, of course, no," Mikko replied immediately. "I am only

Chapter Eight

saying there are lots of people he is better than."

Siem laughed. "I know what you meant. I was only trying to have a pull your leg," she said.

Mikko chuckled, as he mock-pleaded, "Please do not tell him I said something of this nature about him!"

"Of course, not. Your secret, or rather, his secret is safe with me," Siem said.

Mikko breathed a sigh of relief. "D'rmas would as soon challenge me to a fight as he would someone who sullied his warrior ego. He would think I called him a softie if he heard what I just said."

She nodded.

'What a character, hm?" Mikko chuckled.

"Aren't we all?" Siem replied.

They caught the eyes of each other for a moment, then looked away.

"Look, erm, I just wanted to apologize for how I reacted earlier," she started. "Being around a race as proud as the elves takes its toll on the mind." She lied, and blood rose to her cheeks. Her eyes were blinking rapidly.

Mikko nodded. "I understand."

"So, everything is good between us?" she gave him an inquiring look.

"Of course," Mikko said, his lips spreading into a smile. "Everything was always good between us. I just wanted to give you some space to allow whatever was going on with you to abate."

Siem felt her heart lurch at what Mikko had just said. She locked eyes with him for a couple of moments, and Mikko thought he could see a gleam in her eyes.

"Tomorrow then?" she said, putting an end to the moment of silence.

Mikko smiled and said, "Tomorrow."

As he walked back to his tent, his face was all lit with smiles. Even though his mind cautioned him to not jump to conclusions and misinterpreted what he thought the gleam in Siem's eyes met.

Alive Again

While Siem lay in bed, she tried to convince herself that the happiness she felt was only because she had mended things with Mikko, and not because they had shared some moment of connection. She was used to being alone.

CHAPTER NINE

Fears and Regrets

The Middle Kingdom

Fears And Regrets

The capital city of the Middle Kingdom was preparing for war. One look at it, and one would be inclined to think that it was a military Kingdom. Most of its citizenry had taken to staying indoors, due to concerns for safety, or the fears of being forcefully conscripted into the army. The streets were filled with squads of soldiers, in red capes emblazoned with two intertwined dragons, with crowns on their heads – the symbol of the Middle Kingdom – silver mail, and silver helmets. Sometimes, a different battalion would patrol, all outfitted with dark blue body suited armor. These were the acclaimed warriors of the Middle Kingdom, known throughout Toas, for their incredible speed, agility, and precision at killing.

King Henok, sat On his throne, made of bars of sky iron, and the femur of his prizes – people, and beasts who had met their end by his blade. His full dark gray hair was matted back, and his head ringed with a silver band studded with jewels of variegated color. He had a grim expression on his face.

Standing before him were two men in black flowing robes with runes emblazoned on them.

"How is it that none of you has the girl by now?" Henok asked.

"My King," one of the men began.

"Please, Lord Taboon." Henok interrupted. "Spare me the encomiums of royalty and go straight to the point!"

Lord Taboon, the shorter of the two with a staff in hand, made a slight bow, acknowledging the king's wishes.

"If the girl were alone, my king, she would have been caught long before now, as she has little experience outside the palace. However, she is in the company of devious characters, characters that have proven their potency for mischief in the past. I am talking about none other than Siem, and Hermon."

"Am I supposed to know who they are?" Henok asked.

Lord Taboon bit his lip. Time, and time again, it was Henok's underestimation of his foes that came around to bite him in the hind. Lord Taboon had been Henok's teacher in the magical arts while the king was young and still went by the title of prince. But

Chapter Nine

on days like today, he had to stop himself from chiding the king. Henok had a temper, and in the eye of his raging temper, the king was known to make decisions that he would regret later.

"My king," Lord Taboon said. "Those two are extremely notorious. Siem studied in the School of Magic here for five decades and had to be expelled because she dabbled into forbidden magic, without express authorization from the council. Hermon is a berserker. One of the strongest in his clan. Surely, you can understand our difficulty in obtaining the girl. Plus last time we ambushed her, she displayed powers even beyond what a being of Balance and Chaos is capable of."

"She tried to infiltrate my palace, Lord Taboon," Henok said. "And it is all because of your incapacity to do what needs to be done. Must I do everything myself? You have seen more time on earth than that girl, you have had a lot more worth of exposure to magic than she does. If you cannot handle her, one who has not even completed her training yet. Then I do not know what you can do."

"You can count on me, my…" Lord Taboon began to say when the king cut him off.

"Count on you?" Henok questioned. "For Camin's sake, I am not counting on you, Lord Taboon. You are not the only one charged with bringing the girl back and letting the necessary sacrifice be made. The whole of Toas is going up in flames. Do you know the toll it takes trying to prime the city for battle? I received news from our underground intelligence network in Technocon, that the Technocons sold some of their technology to Tonar. I can only imagine what they are planning. Now, we have to arrange a parley with the Technocons, which, trust me, is going to be very expensive! All this would not be necessary if you had done your job!"

Lord Taboon stood silently as Henok fumed.

"My king, if I may." The man standing next to Lord Taboon said. "I trained Eldana personally. And even amid this debacle, I am sure that part of her that once shared a connection to this place, and to what was required of her as a being of Balance and Chaos is still alive. I can bring her around."

"Apologies, my King," Lord Taboon interrupted, "but Sinto's soft spot for the girl is what got us into this mess in the first place. He cannot be trusted to do what needs to be done."

"Do not get ahead of yourself, Lord Taboon," Sinto cautioned. "If I remember correctly, a little bird told me that her less powerful friend, Siem, infiltrated your School and you could not stop her! I know my duty, as do you. Do not presume to say what I can and cannot be trusted to do."

Lord Taboon grew quiet.

"You were saying something," Henok said, indicating for Sinto to go on.

"Yes, my king. If I can get to her, in body, or through an intermediary source, I can try to talk her into coming back."

Lord Taboon scoffed.

Sinto ignored him and continued.

"Since we are so desperate to have her back, every means is on the table. We cannot forgo one for the other. A little niceness as tactics would not be a bad thing. I could try that out, and see how it goes."

Henok contemplated what Sinto said for a while. Lord Taboon and Sinto stood obediently before him, awaiting his decision.

"Do any of you know her current location?" the King asked.

"Unfortunately not, my king," Lord Taboon answered. "The last we had seen of her was when she tried to infiltrate the palace."

"Both of you do not even know where she currently is, how are you going to talk to her?" He said, more to himself than to the men standing before him. "Do what you have to do." Henok finally said. "Both of you. I would very much like to reign over the Middle Kingdom in a world that is not spiralling out of control, please."

Having said this, Henok dismissed them from his presence.

Chapter Nine

Outside the throne room, Lord Taboon turned to Sinto, "Your liking for that girl may very well be the death of us."

"I know my duty, Lord Taboon." Sinto told him. "I do not need you chanting that in my ears every chance you get."

Lord Taboon smiled. "Well, I am off to find her. My way. The soldiers are not giving me what I want."

"Do not do anything foolish, Lord Taboon." Sinto warned.

He knew Lord Taboon was very tricky. He was one of the few who were permitted to dabble in forbidden magic because he had whispered a lot into the King's ears. And he used that with impunity. Most times it was during training sessions with magicians and soldiers. Sinto found the act despicable every time, but there was nothing he could do. Nothing anybody could do. He had the favor of the king. Something he got from training the king since he was a child. Somehow, Sinto did not want Lord Taboon to catch Eldana. He feared the kind of things and experiences would subject her to if he caught her.

Lord Taboon walked closer to within inches of Sinto.

"And you say you are doing your job." He told Sinto, staring him in the face.

Sinto stared back, his face a mask of indifference.

Lord Taboon turned and walked out into the soldier-filled streets, and towards his quarters.

Sinto came into his chambers and plunked himself into an armchair. He sighed and closed his eyes.

It was only the night before that Camin and Lowus themselves had visited him in a vision.

"We had a deal." They had told him. "And you have failed us."

The gods, though man and woman, spoke at once, as though they were of one mind. Sinto had listened quietly.

"You were to raise the being of Balance and Chaos and prepare them for the sacrifice. That is your life goal, your only path. Keep them servile, and when we get their life force, you get to keep a little for yourself."

"And I have been doing that," Sinto said.

"She has run away," They hissed.

Sinto flinched. "I will have her back. I promise!"

"You better do." They said. "Or we might not need for you."

Sinto got up from the armchair and walked towards the huge table close to the window. There was a corked jar of cider on it, and an empty goblet sitting just beside it. He filled the goblet, drained its content, and filled it up again.

His heart bled with hurt, fear, and regret as he thought of Eldana. He regretted ever opening his heart to her childhood exuberances.

I guess at some point, the heart gets the better of you, he thought.

He had never expected to see her as more than a child of chaos and balance, who will end up a sacrifice of power to the gods – a sacrifice that would enable them to restore balance and order to the world. But throughout the years of his training her, he had indeed developed a fondness for her. In fact, he had even begun to see her as a daughter. And she saw him as a father. An image of her flashed through his mind, and he felt a pang of hurt. Her eyes had been always filled with respect and admiration for him. Always. He never showed it because he wanted her to be strong. Not once had she caught him staring at her.

But there was something else that moved Sinto more than anything else in the world, His fear of death. He wanted to live as long as possible. Regretfully, he knew that if he was not of use to the gods, he would lose the subtle increases in his life span he was getting from every successful sacrifice of a being of Balance and Chaos.

He knew what he had to do. He walked to a small chest sitting atop his bed. Unlatching it, he lifted its lid and retrieved a purple silk scarf from it. The scarf held memories, Happy memories, but also painful. It was the scarf he had bought Eldana, the day she had learned how to build an energy wall with air. The magician, he was about to meet, would be needing something of Eldana's to be able to trace her location. He folded the scarf and put it within his robe.

Chapter Nine

As he walked out of his chambers, he thought of going along with Tabeli. Tabeli had personally recommended the mage he was about to meet and knew of her whereabouts. But Tabeli posed a problem. He was well aware of Sinto's weak spot for Eldana. And if he discovered her whereabouts like he was going to if Sinto took him along, he could decide to act on his own, and bring Eldana in, through whatever means necessary.

No, Sinto thought, shaking his head. This journey, I must make alone. He told himself.

As Sinto descended the stairs towards the exit, a man peered out of the corner at him. When Sinto was well beyond the gate, the man walked out hurriedly from the corner, and towards the gate, He had a mop of brown hair, and a long scar running from the left side of his cheek. On getting to the gate, he peeked his head out and caught Sinto walking down the street. Looking around to ensure that he had not been seen, he walked out of the gate casually, with his hands on his pocket, and followed Sinto from a distance. The man remembered last night very clearly. He had been met by a member of the guard and had been instructed to keep tabs on the head of the palace guard.

And that was what he was going to do.

You are the prey now, the scarred man thought, *and I the predator.* He smiled and began to walk faster as Sinto disappeared around a corner.

CHAPTER TEN

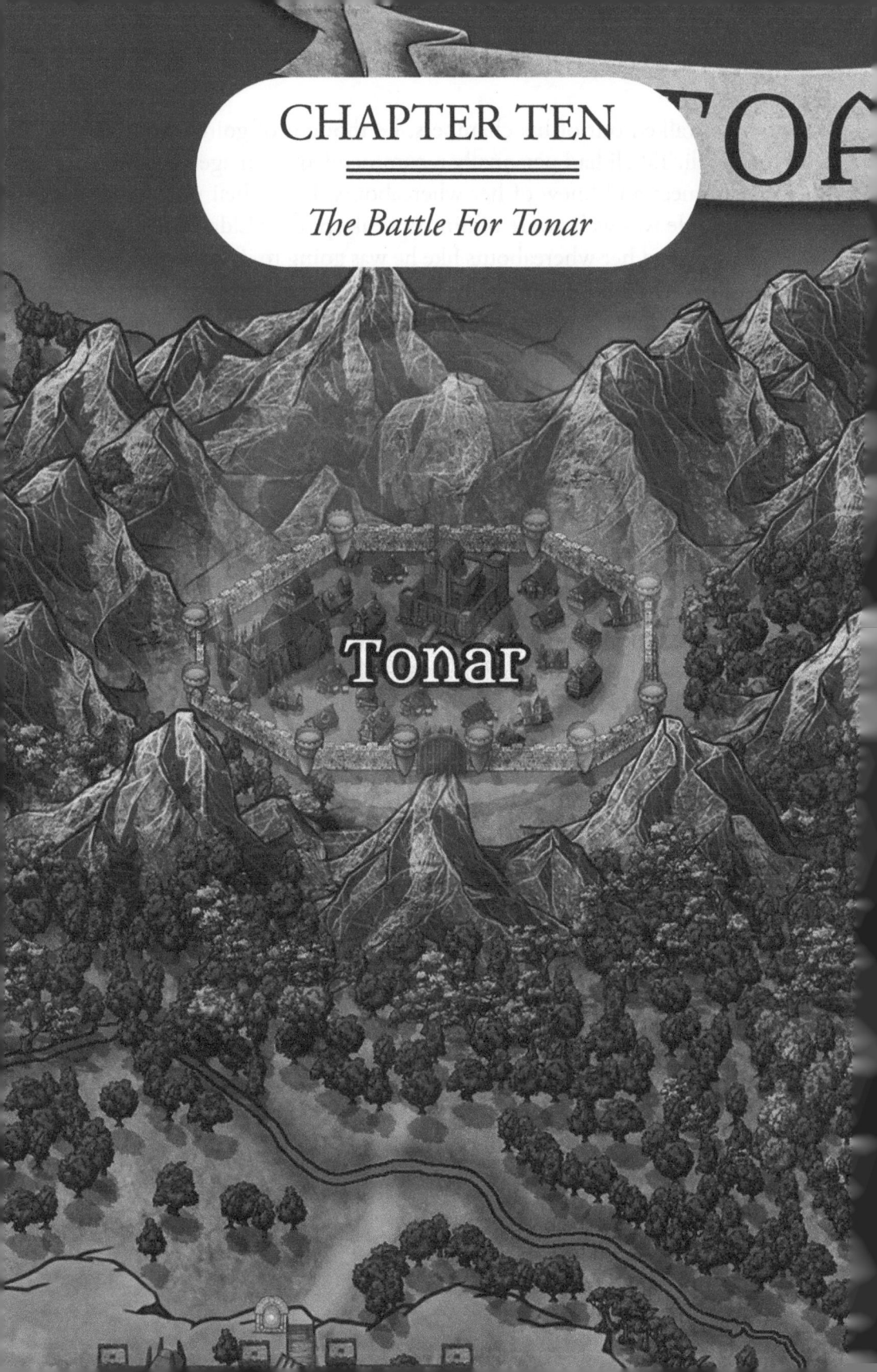

The Battle For Tonar

Tonar

Chapter Ten

Sinto and Lord Taboon stood before Henok, who was pacing like a lion in a cage. This was about the third time in one week that he had summoned them. Sinto prayed that this was not yet another request for a report on how far they had gone in capturing Eldana.

Lord Taboon, on the other hand, followed the King's every move. He had raised and trained the King and knew when something grave was bothering him. This was one of those times. Now, the King's official counsellor would have asked Henok for the reason behind his agitation, but some privileged people, like Lord Taboon and Sinto, understood that that would only be a waste of time and life. Henok's anger could be dangerous. When he was angry, he was highly erratic. In the fury of his rage, people had lost their lives as quickly as it would be to draw a breath.

"We have to attack!" Henok said suddenly.

Sinto's brows furrowed in confusion.

"Pardon me, my king. I think something must be wrong with my ears. I seemed not to have heard you well," Sinto said.

Henok stared into the distance for a while, then turned and went to sit on his throne.

"Your ears work correctly, Sinto," Henok said. "You heard what you heard."

Sinto flashed Lord Taboon a questioning look. Lord Taboon pressed his lips together and then moved a slight foot forward.

"My king," he began, "I think the confusion here is the uncertainty of who exactly we're attacking."

"My attempts at establishing wartime interactions with the Technocons failed," Henok replied.

"Pardon me, my king, but may I ask why the Technocons rejected such a lucrative partnership?" Lord Taboon asked.

"Is it not clear?" Henok said, "Tonar, has probably fed them lies about us!"

"But as a country of their own," Sinto said, "is it not appropriate that they make investigations of their own before making a decision on which party is lying or not?"

"I had asked this same question to the ambassador, and he had told me that without a doubt, he had said they told them the same thing."

"What was their reply, sire?" Lord Taboon asked.

"Well, you can imagine," Henok said, "the Technocons themselves are a very proud race. They told our ambassador that they had done more than enough investigations to make their claims salient. In their words, as part of the races in Toas, their contribution to its existence is to ensure the continuity of peace. And their way of doing that is by not aiding us with their technology. Because we have magic and an already strong army."

"And we have the money to pay for their technology," Sinto said. "This was supposed to be a trade."

"We have tried that. It did not work," Henok said. "The 'technocons' are using our possession of magic as a bias. They insinuate that we would become too strong if we added their tech to our magic."

"So they offered to give it to these magicless humans instead," Lord Taboon completed.

"That is not of concern to them," Henok replied. "I got intel from my spy network that the humans of Tonar have been preparing for battle. The Technocons are still shipping them gadgets and upgrades. I do not think there is a better time than now. If we attack Tonar now, we can prevent any further questioning of our authority over Toas."

It was an unspoken fact among them that an attack on Technocon was close to impossible, even with their magic and the Warriors of the Middle Kingdom in their possession. The technology of the Technocons was virtually magic of a creative kind. It was magic that could be compressed into portable objects, but the effects these objects had were still mammoth. These Technocon's were creatures with a head half of their body, perhaps that explained why they created such powerful tools. Most of the time, they wanted peace, so they could continue creating their little, strange type of science magic. Other times, they backed the underdog, but seldom got into conflicts themselves. The people of Tonar on the other hand, were humans, just like them, but without magic, except for very few among them. The people of the Middle were druids. It was rare to see any of them without magic.

However, Lord Taboon and Sinto were still at a loss as to why the king had requested their presence. They were not generals, and not experts on battle strategy, either. It was not clear what the king had called them out for. If it was for counsel, which they had been inclined to think was a reason initially, then Henok showed that he did not need much of it!

"I have sent out word to the generals to prepare our troops. The earlier we attack Tonar, and silence their growing presence, the better. However, a little help would be needed to combat whatever tricks they will have up their sleeves. I require your magic."

Henok's tone was clear. This was not a request or a plea. The King had given a command.

"What are we to do?" Sinto asked. He was secretly happy that Eldana's case had not been brought up. Because, once again, he would have sounded incompetent before the monarch.

"Gather your men," Henok said, staring at the both of them. "Make sure they are ready. We will leave in two weeks."

"Two weeks, my lord?" Sinto asked. He was unable to keep the shock out of his voice.

As head of the guard, he always ensured that his men were ready. That preparedness was part of the reason he had remained head of the guard for decades. But though their recent major altercation was weeks ago, with Eldana in the clearing of Kleas, they had expended so much magical energy that they needed more time to recuperate.

"Is there a problem, Sinto?" Henok asked.

"No, my king," Sinto said recollecting himself. "There is just this one minor thing."

Henok raised his brows inquisitively.

"My men are not yet ready to devote the amount of magic that you would deem satisfactory for the war effort."

"Why is that?" Henok asked.

Sinto stared at Lord Taboon. He hoped that the wily bastard would not do something that would place him in the king's anger. Because no matter how hard he had tried to evade mentioning Eldana, she still found a way to affect the king's plans.

"It is just a simple matter of recovering the strength we had lost during our altercation with Eldana and her friends at Kleas."

"Eldana, and a bunch of criminals like her, you mean to say," Lord Taboon corrected.

Sinto looked at him, lowered his head slightly, and flashed Lord Taboon a smile. It was a gesture to show the king that he was in total agreement with Lord Taboon's view. Meanwhile, in his heart, he thought:

Stupid bastard.

"I thought it has been weeks since you fought with the girl?" Henok asked.

"You are right, my king," Sinto said, "but as Lord Taboon will also confirm, the level of magic Eldana exhibits unprecedented levels. And her friends in her company too. The three of them are all very powerful."

Sinto turned to Lord Taboon, fixing him a harsh glare. Lord Taboon smiled in return. He had grasped the meaning behind Sinto's expression.

Watch as I save your hide, old friend, he thought.

"My king," Lord Taboon said, "Sinto is right. Why else do you think the girl had been able to best the royal guard, which is comprised of no ordinary mages. Sinto himself was there! And just like he said. And it was not just the girl. The Siem and Berserker are both fearsome magicians. It took them almost everything to keep from getting killed."

Sinto felt relief flood through him. Although, he took care not to reveal that.

"We, Lord Taboon and myself are in no doubt in true shape to contribute our all to the battle, but I cannot say the same for the members of the guard."

Chapter Ten

"How much time do you need?"

"A month, my king," Sinto replied.

Henok shifted in his throne.

"Sinto, we do not have a month. Attacking Tonar in two weeks is even too delayed. The goal here is to decimate them before they can amass enough power to constitute a major obstruction to our authority. We already have the Berserkers, the Elfsoc, and the Technocons to deal with. Adding Tonar to the list will reduce our authority in Toas to shambles. We have to attack, and we have to attack now."

Lord Taboon's face had grown pensive as the king talked, and Henok had noticed it.

"Lord Taboon," Henok called, pulling him out of his thoughts, "now is not the time to play cozy with your thoughts. If you are cooking something up, say it here immediately so we can deliberate on it."

"My apologies, my king," Lord Taboon said, bowing simultaneously. "There might be a way to go around Sinto's problem."

Sinto stared at Lord Taboon. Immediately, he knew he was not going to like what the magician was going to say.

"Go on," Henok said.

"There is a magic ritual that could replenish their magic, and get them ready even before the time for the attack."

"I can tell there is a caveat coming," Henok said.

"My king, he is talking about using dark magic," Sinto chipped in.

"Thank you, Sinto," Lord Taboon said, turning to acknowledge the other man, albeit sarcastically, "you took the words right out of my mouth."

Henok reclined into his thoughts for a moment. Then he asked:

"This magic ritual will have them at full strength in time for the attack on Tonar?"

"Yes, my king," Lord Taboon replied with a flourish.

Dark magic was not just a specialty with Lord Taboon. It was a hobby, something he relished practicing. And he did not hide that. He was one of the very few in Toas who practiced dark magic somewhat openly, courtesy of being Henok's favorite teacher years back and being one of his most prized counsellors now.

"My king," Sinto said, "dark magic, while seemingly stronger, is unpredictable. The members of the guard stand the risk of death or even more horrible things if even the slightest thing goes wrong with the ritual Lord Taboon is proposing."

"What could be worse than death, Sinto?" The King asked. "The future of the Middle kingdom seriously relies on us being able to spring a surprise on an entirely unsuspecting Tonar. While I respect your concern, I do have to overlook it. There is no time. You have nothing to fear. Lord Taboon is skilled in the dark arts. Nothing will go awry."

Sinto pressed his lips together. There was nothing more to be said. The king's tone was clear. He had made his decision already.

"Lord Taboon," the king called. "I expect that you will supply an army of magicians to win my war!"

Lord Taboon smiled. "Of course, my king."

Henok nodded. "Then you are both dismissed," he said. "I expect that everything will be ready in two weeks."

Sinto and Lord Taboon bowed at the same time, before turning and walking out of the throne room.

Everything was quiet and still as they made their way through the trees. Nobody spoke. There was no need for that, not yet. They moved under the cover of the dark sky, which was lightened by the hue of first light. Ordinarily, this time of the day was not ideal for troop movement, especially movements made without the aid of torches. But this was no ordinary army. These were the warriors of the Middle Kingdom. Each selected soldier that made up the mass of this army was handpicked from a young age, and trained rigorously. The only people who seemed to have a problem at moving around where the people within the walls a few miles

Chapter Ten

from the forest. The warriors of Middle Kingdom were skilled at navigating in the dark, among other things. It required extreme skill for such a deluge of forces to be able to make it through the trees without making a sound. At the front of the army was a row of horsemen. The horses moved silently, and the men swayed smoothly with the movement of the horses. The horses moved surely and steadily without making a noise with their hoofs.

One of the horsemen moved closer to the horse in the middle. "My King," the horse rider saluted, "We're almost there."

"Thank you, General Senay," Henok replied. "If we're to win this, our numbers alone aren't enough. We can do more damage if everything goes according to plan."

"I'll see to that, my lord," General Senay said. With a quick bow, he retreated from the King then turned around and went down the length of the column to consort with other generals.

About a week before the attack, the generals had sent scouts out into the forest to survey the terrain and the walls of Tonar. Tonar had suddenly assumed a strictness towards the admittance of people within her walls. Attempting to go in would subject the scouts to intense scrutiny from the guards at the gate. And the King had made it clear. He wanted this to be a surprise. If the identity of the scouts were revealed, the element of surprise was sullied. Each of the scouts had returned with about the same report:

Tonar had heightened their level of security. But apart from that and the fact that the huge walls kept a lot from going out, there did not seem to be much happening inside the city. The indication that they might be expecting an attack was nothing.

The generals kept sending scouts out to establish certainties that they could work with for plotting strategies. Then two days later, the army left the Middle and bled into the woods. The scouts had kept ahead of the general body of the army every step of the way, ensuring that the forest was clear enough for the army to move undetected. The scouts had left with a smaller group of soldiers, who would help stage the catapults and battering rams required for the assault.

Lord Taboon and Sinto moved by both sides of the king. Sinto had members of the guard walking behind him in hooded robes with runes etched into all of them. Sinto imagined when the attack would begin, how all those runes would begin to glow as they worked their magic. He wished that there would be no loss of life among his company. But he knew how futile such wishes were. There was no way they would engage in battle with Tonar and not come up with casualties of their own. He prayed that whatever augmentation Lord Taboon had them undergo during the dark recovery ritual would give them enough strength to be able to shield themselves from harm. He looked over to the other side where Lord Taboon rode.

Lord Taboon was more battle-thirsty. He looked forward to the prospect of using his dark magic tricks on human, suspecting and unsuspecting alike, magician or no magician.

Feel my wrath! the magician thought. The company he had contributed to the ranks of Henok's army rode behind him. They wore robes too that had runes inscribed all over them. But unlike Sinto's men, Lord Taboon's were practitioners of dark magic, students of his who shared his maliciousness. Before embarking on the march, he had reinforced how important it was that they stay alive no matter what.

"Your lives are what matters to the Middle Kingdom's victory," he had told them. "Not the warriors. Yours. The longer you stay alive, the greater the chances of victory, and of course, I don't need to tell you that you can't go back to whatever lives you left before becoming my students. Don't hesitate. Let all the darkness out. See this as the test of everything that I've ever taught you."

As he approached Tonar steadily, he did not doubt that they would tear through the city, and as a consequence, show the whole of Toas that the Middle Kingdom would not be trifled with. They remained the undeclared and unofficial center of power in Toas and would be treated as such.

Without warning, they broke out of the trees and into a massive clearing. General Senay held out his hand at this point and

Chapter Ten

signalled for the army to halt. The city of Tonar stood before them, several miles away, but unmistakable. Its walls shone a dull white in the darkness. Senay pulled out a spyglass from his belt and peered through it.

Exactly according to our projections, he thought, before pulling the spyglass from his eye and then handed it to Henok.

"My king," he said, "You might want to take a look."

Henok received the spyglass from the general and put it to his eye. It was dark, and he was not supposed to see the city so clearly, but the view he got was that of the entry gates firmly shut.

The spyglass was a magical instrument and provided its light, therefore, it was one of the excellent choices to bring along for surveillance. Henok directed the spyglass to the rampart. It was empty. He smiled. He had expected this.

The fools won't even know what hit them, he thought.

He had spent a few years among the regular people of his court during the years following his ascension to the throne. And he had learned during that period that the people were generally less active during the early hours of the morning. It was the sweetest and deepest hour of sleep. And so it was that Tonar seemingly slept on, sitting ducks, as the massive army surrounded them. The very best strategists in Toas could see, even before the battle started, what direction it was going to take; and a number of them were present, as they carried the ranks of generals in the Middle Kingdom's army. It was evident. They had come upon Tonar with the intent to carry out a massacre.

"My king," Senay said as he came up to where Henok at on his horse, a little distance away from the main body of the army.

"Yes, general," Henok responded.

"Everything is ready," Senay said.

Henok stared one more time on the majestic walls of Tonar and pressed his lips together.

"Good," he said. "Fire when you're ready."

Henok retreated behind the row of catapults, to where Sinto and Lord Taboons at in their horses, and he watched as General

Senay ordered the first set of projectiles primed into the catapults. Then the soldiers made way for a row of Sinto's men to come forward. Placing their hands over the projectiles they whispered:

"*Fire and fury! Fire and fury!*"

With a whoosh, the projectiles; boulders of rock cut perfectly to fit into the launch cups of the catapults – caught fire. The magicians stepped a few feet backward as a row of soldiers came forward and manned the catapults' release levers.

Senay rose his hand into the air, and for a few seconds everything went silent, the anticipation of battle hung in the air like a whisper, and then he brought it down. The soldiers pulled down the levers, and the catapults twanged as they rose into the air, flinging the projectiles towards Tonar.

Henok's face along with a considerable part of the army was illuminated by the fire on the moving projectiles. He had a pleased look on his face.

Now the ambitious Tonar must come to an end. All they'll see is my fire falling from the sky like rain! the King thought.

Lord Taboon watched with a sneer on his face as the fireballs fell over Tonar, burning with magic fire.

Come on! Lord Taboon thought as he followed their trajectory. He was aching for action. And his skills were better employed on other things than putting fire to balls of rock. And he was looking forward to unleashing those skills.

Everyone watched as the balls of fire stopped abruptly over the air of the city, and scattered as if on impact. But there was nothing there! Just sky!

Could those be the mages of Tonar? Sinto asked himself. They weren't supposed to be up by now, except maybe Tonar had taken to keeping sentries out on the lookout since Toas had begun descending into chaos. "Maybe we are the chaos." He murmured while still being confused about what just happened. Henok speaking brought him back from this idea.

"Fire again!" he told Senay. Henok himself was a bit taken aback, but he did not show it.

Chapter Ten

The general ordered another assault. As before, Sinto's men set the boulders on fire, and the soldiers hurled them into the air. Henok's eyes stayed dutifully on their trajectory until they were over Tonar, about to land into the city...

Then the same thing happened again. The balls stopped as if they had hit something and scattered. Their pieces tumbling off the air and falling to the land around the city. But there was another extra piece of detail that Henok picked up this time around. The shield blazed into visibility the moment the projectiles touched them. He had not seen this before because of the size of the explosion, but he saw it now, the way the shield shimmered and revealing the extent of its coverage. It spread over entirety of Tonar from wall to wall. Henok gazed at General Senay, and they had the same thing on their minds. This was one thing gone wrong with their plan already, and they had barely started the attack. It was not presumptuous at this point to accept that the entirety of their plan was now in shambles. Sinto and Lord Taboon drew close to the king.

"My lord," Lord Taboon said, "they have a magic shield!"

"I have eyes, Lord Taboon," Henok replied dryly.

"What we don't know is if it's the work their mages or the technology that the Technocons had shipped to them."

"I don't know the specificities either," Henok replied. "But Technocon or not, the both of them are still magic, and we have a sturdy shield over Tonar that's stopping us from reaching our…"

Just then General Senay yelled:

"Incoming! Everybody take cover!"

Henok's eyes flew to the sky, and then he saw them, little bright things like stars, speeding out from within the walls of the city towards them. Henok had not seen such things before, and it was the puzzlement and the speed at which they came that made him too slow to react.

The ground erupted in plumes of dust and chunks of stone as the little starry things hit the ground all around them. The force of the explosion knocked Henok off his horse, throwing him high into the air, and casting him to the ground.

Sinto could hear very little. It was like the entire environment was covered with a heavy blanket of wool. Everything was muffled except for the ringing sound in his ears.

What had just happened? He asked himself as he struggled to get to his feet. His arms gave and he fell back to the ground. Suddenly someone hurried to his side and grabbed him by the shoulders.

"Sinto! Sinto? Can you hear me?"

"What?" Sinto said, straining to ascertain who was calling him.

He turned and stared at the face of the person. It took him a while before he realized who it was.

"Tabeli?" he asked.

"Praise be to Camin and Lowus," Tabeli exclaimed.

"What is going on?"

"I don't have the answer to that right now," Tabeli said pulling Sinto up to his feet. "All I know is, the humans had fired explosives at us. Much like what we tried to hurl at them, but much prettier."

Sinto groaned.

"I think I may have a few broken bones," he said.

Tabeli looked at his leader. His eyes took at the end of broken bones sticking out of his arm, and the blood all over his side. While the robes they wore protected them to a certain degree from lethal magic, it did not protect them from natural reactions that the magic had kicked up. Like the impact of its explosion, and the debris.

"It's nothing that a healer can't fix," Tabeli replied.

As Sinto moved along with Tabeli, his senses began to get clearer, and he began to feel his body liven with pain.

"How bad do I look?" he gasped.

Tabeli simply stared back at him and he got the message. Sinto closed his eyes about to mutter an energy spell, but Tabeli stopped him.

"You don't have enough strength as it is. You need all you've got to be able to go through the healing process, which is going to be

Chapter Ten

very hurried so you can join us on the battlefield. Skimming off the little you have could turn out ugly."

Sinto sighed. Everywhere was enshrouded in a cloud of dust. He could hear voices of the soldiers scampering about trying to rally help for some people. It seemed that those who were at the front had it worse. It was then that Sinto remembered the King.

"What about the King?" he asked.

"Don't worry about him," Tabeli said. "He's way better off than you. Thanks to that crazy dark mage, Lord Taboon."

Sinto sighed with relief. No one could be trusted more with Henok's protection than Lord Taboon, Henok was his special responsibility.

Then from nowhere another thought dropped into his head. *If the Tonarians had been able to scatter us with their explosions, then why weren't they attacking?*

Then it hit him.

"Mages on me!" he yelled suddenly. "Take positions and make a shield spell!"

Already in the sky, more of the little stary things were flying towards them.

Mosael stood on the rampart and watched with scrutiny as the forward formation of the Middle Kingdom's army was demolished.

Fools, he thought.

As general of Tonar's armed forces, Mosael had seen to it that everything had been planned to the slightest detail, way before he had gotten wind of the Middle Kingdom's movements. He had gone up to his king and asked for the security around the city to be tightened. Toas was falling apart. Chaos was coming. The human magicians at the court where the being of Balance and Chaos was trained had sent word that the being of Balance and Chaos had escaped, plunging the entire Toas into inevitable doom. Mosael, having spent thirty years of his life defending Tonar and the throne, was determined to see Tonar through these perilous times.

The king of Tonar was old, and in ailing health, but the Prince, though considerably young, was equal to the task, and aided his father in the running of Tonar's affairs. Mosael was his godfather, and a trusted hand to the throne, so it was easy for both of them to consort with each other on how the kingdom was to be run.

While it was true that Tonar had enjoyed peace for a lengthy number of years they had not seen a major battle throughout the lifetime of the current king's father – Mosael did not subscribe to the idea of relaxing during a time of peace. He drilled the soldiers like they had an impending battle. Left for him, the battle was something that could spring upon them without warning, given their geographical location. To the north, they had the Berserkers and the Middle Kingdom to the west. Both lands were filled with people who were far more powerful, because of their magical abilities. There were a few magicians among the humans. But in a bitter exchange, they would not be able to hold their own and protect the entire kingdom at the same time. Desperate to have Tonar strong enough to resist the neighbouring kingdoms should the need arise, Mosael paid a visit to the king and his son and proposed a pact with the Technocons.

"Indeed, we're largely without magic," he said. "That fact alone makes us weak. No matter how courageous and skilled our men are in combat, we will never be able to survive a face-off with an army of magic users."

"What do you suggest?" the King croaked.

"That we have a trade treaty with the Technocons."

"Why the Technocons?" The prince had asked. "We could create an alliance with Berserkers?"

"Allying ourselves with them is not trustworthy," Mosael replied. "And it will not be an equal partnership on our side. And you know that. A trade deal with the Technocons will offer us magic of our own, and then we will be able to hold out against any foe, magic or no."

Chapter Ten

The King and the Prince did not say a word, so Mosael assumed that was his go-ahead.

"To make a trade deal, we'll have to have something to trade." The Prince said.

"We have ore," Mosael replied. "The Technocons often use ore to make their technology."

The King looked at his son. He did not need his permission; it was more a gesture. The Prince nodded back. Mosael was more trusted. He was the exit strategy when everything went crazy. "You have my blessing, then." The King informed him. Mosael nodded and walked away with fast steps.

He started the conversation immediately. Making the trade deal with the Technocons had gone relatively easy. The Technocons had the knack for tipping over in favor of people they deemed weak and almost helpless. They wanted to keep the balance. And in a place like Toas, where magic ran deep to the roots, the humans of Tonar were the weakest. But the technology was not the only thing Tonar got when they made the deal. They also got a warning to be wary of the Middle Kingdom.

About a week later, Mosael got word from his spies that they saw an unusually large movement of soldiers and weapons. It was unknown at the time if they were planning on attack on Tonar, but Mosael had geared the soldiers up for battle all the same. Until some days later when it became clear that the Middle Kingdom was planning an attack on them. But that was their undoing, and all the opportunity he needed to turn the tide in his favor. They would think they had the element of surprise, and they would try to utilize it to the fullest, unknown to them that Tonar was waiting like a lioness stalking its prey while lying low beneath the cover of grass. Technocon had outfitted Tonar with such an array of gadgets to turn the prey into a hunter in no time.

Before the attack, Mosael had had his men plant gadgets in the trees that would detect any movement and report it to a magic screen that he held in his palm. And as he had expected, the reports came. These gadgets obeyed no gods and exposed the nature of the technocons as being similar to those of the humans of Tonar who would rebel at the gods at any chance they got. He did not know how many the soldiers were – the gadgets did not reveal that. But he knew that Middle would leave no stone unturned.

He had turned to his men then, knowing that things would get ugly real fast, and ordered:

"Get the shield up!"

There were rod-like devices fixed to the ground at strategic points all around the rampart. The soldiers went about activating each of them. Upon activation, the rods emitted a low whine, and then a spear of light shot out from its tip into the air. With all the rods spitting out the light, they converged together, and then a shield began to grow from their point of convergence until the entire sky over Toas was covered. Once that was done, the shield lost its luminousness, and became invisible. From somewhere behind the fence, a low hum permeated the atmosphere, the source of the energy.

Mosael's intuition to pull up the shields had been right because not long after, a lieutenant had run to him.

"General," the lieutenant said, "They've launched the catapults, and the projectiles are covered in magic fire."

Mosael trusted the Technocons technology to do the needful, but he realized that he was not the only person here. He had an entire army under his command, and his duty, aside from commanding them, was to see to their safety. Even if they were to die, it should be for something worth their lives.

"Order the first wave to step off the rampart," he told the lieutenant.

And then the darkness of the dawn was suddenly filled with a bright red. He saw the projectiles hurtling straight towards the city. Watching them hurry towards impact, instilled a sliver of uncertainty in Mosael. He began to move back a little but was too late.

The projectiles had come too close. Then they exploded, and he cringed and shut his eyes, expecting a rain of fire and pain on his

Chapter Ten

body. And when he felt nothing, he opened his eyes just in time to see shrapnel from the explosion tumble off the shield. He smiled. This was exactly what the Technocons told him would happen. All of this at the cost of nothing except an alliance.

When the next wave of projectiles came, he stood close to the edge of the wall and watched them come. He was unafraid.

And now, a taste of your own medicine! he had thought.

He ordered his men to fire the missiles – miniature forms of cannonballs, but with much more explosive power. He had watched the first wave of missiles scatter the attacking army's impressive front, and now he was watching it scatter them again.

One thing that had dogged him all his life as a soldier was his intuition; his uncanny ability to feel things within his bones. Now his bones were telling him that now was the right moment to attack, under the cover of dust and debris that the explosions had racked up.

He called up the colonel in charge of the first battalion.

"I need you to take your troops and make a head-on charge at the army, now that they are in a state of disarray."

"Yes sir," the colonel said and walked out.

Mosael gave the order for the gates to be lifted, and watched as the first battalion, consisting of brigades of horse soldiers and footmen, charged towards the battlefield.

That's just to keep you company, he thought. Tonar welcomes you with open arms.

Thanks to Sinto's warning, the mages were able to rally around and cast a shield spell that lessened the effects of the projectiles, but some soldiers were still caught in the explosions, but not as much as the first series.

Lord Taboon had performed a teleportation spell, ferrying Henok away in mid-air. Thus, saving the king from the pain of broken bones. Now, the King was deep within the ranks of his elite squad, surrounded by the fastest, most bloodthirsty and efficient soldiers in Toas. Going for the head of the king of the Middle Kingdom now would be a capital suicide statement.

Sinto was still gritting his teeth from the pain of getting his wounds healed when he heard a chaotic yelling rise among the ranks of the soldiers. It was the first horseman running towards where he sat at a tree with the hands of a healer hovering over his arm that told him that they were in deep trouble.

"Incoming!" Senay yelled, as the first wave of Tonar soldiers went through their confused ranks and began wreaking havoc immediately.

Sinto was in too much pain to react quickly, and the horseman would have impaled him to the tree had it not been for the healer kneeling in front of him. The spear passed through the healer's throat, spilling blood on Sinto's face. Sinto used the opportunity to cast a spell.

"*Touerneya zechai!*" he yelled, flinging his arm towards the horseman.

In an instant, the horseman and the horse went up in flames, and they went barrelling through the forest, a horrific duet of neighing and screaming.

Sinto was still weak but he had enough strength to work a little magic. The magic he was about to perform was dark – but he was left with few options. He could not lie around, close to helpless, while he waited for a healer. He rolled to his side and placed his hand on the tree, as he whispered the words:

"*Ohm sab hagez,*" the huge tree shrank. Sinto's wounds healed synchronously. His strength began to replenish, until he was not just back to himself but felt stronger, at which point the entire tree died.

He got to his feet. He had only walked a few feet before he was met by Tabeli and the rest of the guard.

"We thought you would have left us by now," Tabeli said.

"Ah, trust me. It's going to take more than a horseman and a spear to steal me away."

Chapter Ten

"We're glad you're back to us," Tabeli said. "The battle is fierce. Our skills are needed, as the Warriors of the Middle Kingdom face the human soldiers who have an upper hand, courtesy of the damnable technocons technology!"

Sinto looked at the faces of his guards. This was not the first war they had been in, but Tonar had sprung them a surprise and seemed to be making the most of it. He needed to be sure that his soldiers were ready. The steely glares he received filled him with assurance just as well as it did fear. Whatever ritual Lord Taboon had taken them through to replenish their strength left them looking bereft of any human compassion or feeling.

The sound of footsteps approaching them told Sinto that he would have to save his worries for another time.

"Guards on me!" Sinto yelled.

Out on the plains before Tonar, the smell of magic burnt the air, the runes on their robes blazed, as did their swords as they engaged the incoming horsemen in battle, slicing with their swords, and killing with spells.

The battlefield was pure, unbridled, chaos. A blend of the Middle's magic, and Tonar's newly acquired technology. Mosael was not liking the way the battle was going. It seemed like the Middle Kingdom was beginning to gain the upper hand, but it was not just from their soldiers, but their magicians as well.

"Damned magicians," he cussed.

However, the battle had not reached Tonar, it was still being contained within the forest. And that was the only thing that pleased Mosael. But he knew that he could not just keep sending men out like fodder to engage the enemy in battle and stall them in the same position. He needed a powerful move. Something that, if it did not make them win, would put the army of the Middle Kingdom on the retreat. And then it hit him. He did not need a complex strategy. He already commanded the attention of the enemy on one front. All of them, due to being surprised was focusing the entirety of their energy towards repelling the attack from the front and gaining an advantage. This one-sidedness in their focus was what was going to be their downfall.

Turning, Mosael called to his right-hand colonel, who was also his daughter. She had risen to this position only by pure merit. Mosael was happy that she was every bit the soldier he was and more.

"I need you to get me the colonel in charge of the para-troops," he said.

His daughter looked at him with steely eyes, devoid of any feelings that reflected the kinship they shared, but full of duty and loyalty.

"Yes, sir," she said and walked off the rampant to deliver his summons.

Mosael looked back to the battlefield. *Use your magic all you want*, he thought. *But today you will feel the might of Tonar!*

Lord Taboon was having one of the best times he had ever had practicing dark magic in the many years he had lived. He was wreaking untold horror on the battlefield, and his students were doing the same.

A few of them *had* died though.

They were skilled, but not skilled enough to handle a swarm of soldiers. Lord Taboon was hemmed in by a circle of horsemen, who kept on firing those little stars at him. His defense shield was holding so far. The stars would speed towards him but explode in an intense cloud of fire blanketing him, and covering the horsemen from his vision. He saw one of his students work black magic on one of the horsemen, causing him to bloat until he burst in an explosion of blood, organs, and bone. But the student was too focused on killing that he did not see another horseman in his back until it was too late.

Chapter Ten

The horsemen threw a spear...

Straight through the back of his student's neck. Lord Taboon was not too bothered about one loss. Hadn't Lord Taboon given them an opportunity of a lifetime? He had told his students that death awaited them, but they would get the chance to practice their magic as they saw fit. Now, all he had to do was find a way to extricate himself from this circle. The spell he was about to chant was one of the most powerful that he had ever done, and having to do it while keeping up his shield was going to be the trickiest part.

Lord Taboon began to chant, in harsh growling sounds. They were magic words from ancient orc lore. Too powerful and dangerous to meddle with that as he sang the words in harsh sputtering growls, and the air around him began to get dry and hot as life was drawn out from it. The horses began to grow restless, and so did the soldiers. Rather than run for their lives, they charged; all of them, at once. And that was their mistake. Probably the last mistake they would ever make. With their spears poised, and the tips glowing with energy, the human soldiers drew ever so closely to Lord Taboon. The words began to drop from his mouth quickly now, and then his eyes grew red – starting from the irises and then onto the whites. But the redness did not stop there. It branched into the skin surrounding his eyes like little red veins. The soldiers were a few feet away from him when a wave of red burst out from Lord Taboon slammed into them. It caught them, like in the teeth of a trap, and they floated in the air, struggling in terror. Lord Taboon let the shield around him fade, and then he stepped into the open, staring at the circle of floating soldiers and horses as they fought against the hold of his magic. Letting out a menacing smile, he opened his mouth, and then the red wall holding them intensified in color. The soldiers and horses began to scream and thrash. They screamed even when beams of red light poured out from their eyes, nostrils, mouth, and ears, and flowed into Lord Taboon's body. Lord Taboon trembled as all the beams entered him...

But as soon as it had arrived, the beams stopped, and the red wall disappeared. The ring of horses and soldiers fell carelessly to the ground, their skeletons shattering on impact. Lord Taboon opened his eyes and smiled.

The battle raged hard. Sometimes, it looked like the Middle Kingdom were winning, and all of a sudden, the tides would turn and it would seem as though Tonar was winning. However, one thing was sure: Tonar was in no way as weak as Henok had thought them to be. The King himself was directly facing the consequences of his assumptions. Even his ring of guards was not safe. They were being barrelled by ambitious soldiers from Tonar who wanted to make a name by being the ones to kill the King of the Middle Kingdom. So far, his elite squad had proven their usefulness, slicing to pieces in the space of seconds anyone who would dare venture close enough.

General Senay was not allowed to try the attacking strategies he had prepared. From the start of the battle, the goal had become rather simple. Withstand Tonar's assault enough to not get themselves thrashed. So far, the plan seemed to be working, though it was not going too smoothly. He turned to a soldier and handed him a parchment he had just prepared.

"Take this to Sinto or Lord Taboon, any one of them you find is fine. They will likely not get the chance to read it, so my suggestion is this: that they should redistribute some of the stronger magicians to the front of the battle. We need them to begin to hit at Tonar so that they can stop reinforcements coming at us! I will order my soldiers to spread into a semi-circle so that we can hit them from all sides as well as from the front. That way we will be able to finish off the remaining soldiers so we can now make an advance. Do you understand me?"

"Yes, sir," the soldier replied.

As the soldier came out, another ran in, bringing in reports of the direction the battle was going. General Senay had soldiers like this, scouts, who would study the battle and get back to him. The constant update informed his decision on what strategy to use,

Chapter Ten

and what reinforcements to make.

"Report," he ordered the soldier.

The soldier opened his mouth, and that was all he ever did. A bolt of bright light shot out from out of nowhere and speared through him. The soldier was dead even before he fell to the ground. Smoke was coming out from the hole on his back. Senay stared nonplussed.

"What just happened?" he asked one of his colonels at the planning table.

They were still about to respond when another one hit the tent. And then another and another.

"The sky!" Senay heard someone shout from outside. And when he went outside, he saw bolts of light falling from the sky in a storm.

There was an army of flying men up there! In the sky, shooting bolts of light into the army of the Middle.

Senay saw that all of them had a contraption fixed like a backpack, except this one spat fire from its underside. As if that was not enough, it was as if the forest suddenly came alive. More men were pouring in than he had seen. And then it hit him. They were being hit from more than one angle. He felt his spirits drop. There was no doubt that the Middle Kingdom had better soldiers but Tonar had the better strategies.

In truth, Senay did not care about the magician-warriors, only his soldiers. Already the lists of the dead were growing by the second. It would be up to him to visit all of the grieving families and tell them that their kin had died in service to the kingdom and to the King, who had sent them into battle based solely on an assumption.

It would be General Senay who would hear the soul-shattering cries, the piercing wails, and would be the one to try and console them. Tonar had had the advantage of them since the start.

Tonar's newly acquired technology from the Technocons was wreaking untold havoc. The Middle Kingdom had been fighting for survival since then, and as such had focused the brunt of their attention to the front, where the heat was coming from. They could not see that Tonar had already had something even more audacious planned. Now, they were facing soldiers from all sides, and most jarring of it all, soldiers from the sky, raining arrows of white light!

"Where are those damned magicians when you need them?" Senay asked.

He saw more and more of his soldiers fall from the arrows from the sky, as they were too busy withstanding the attack from the front and the sides. They could not put up a shield as it would be too weak. The men he had here were known more for their physical strength than their magic. Senay saw all this, and he knew what he had to do. The battle here was over. Without the magicians, this would easily turn into a slaughter. He did not know where the magicians were, and he could not wait for them to come to save them. If he did, there would be nobody to save by the time they arrived. He moved into his tent, which surprisingly, was still standing amidst the hail of projectiles. He grabbed the special horn made for the retreat signal. It had been long since this horn had been sounded in battle. Indeed. the glory of the Middle Kingdom had been decimated today. He moved out of the tent, and put the horn to his lips, blew with all his might. The horn was infused with magic that allowed its sounds to travel far and wide so everyone could hear it.

"Retreat! Retreat!" the soldiers shouted among themselves as they ran back into the forest.

Mosael heard the horn, and a smile split his face – the first since the battle began. Tonar had successfully set the Middle Kingdom to their heels. But he did not plan on stopping there.

Chapter Ten

Sinto heard the sound of the horns. It was time to leave. Even for someone as strong as him, this display of force from Tonar was not what Sinto had expected at all. Using magic fire as they ran back into the forest, he felt the defeat in his bones. He knew the King would be furious at this terrible humiliation. And he also knew that he would be blamed for this.

CHAPTER ELEVEN

The Life of a Telepath

Ciroc Woods

Chapter Eleven

"There are certain things you have to keep in mind if you are to master the skill of telepathy. A focused mind, will, and consideration."

Eldana and Kochob were under the shade of a huge beech. Eldana sat on the ground, with her legs folded while Kochob leaned on the tree in front of her. Today was one week since Eldana had consigned herself to Kochob's tutelage, yet she was no closer to reading a mind than she was when she started.

"Why should you have a focused mind?" Kochob asked.

"Because, like a dagger, my mind must be sharp and precise to be able to penetrate the walls of someone else's thoughts," she replied.

After the third day with Kochob had yielded nothing, Eldana was beset by frustration. Fraweyni had requested her presence in her grove to enquire of her progress, and Eldana had told her that she did not think she was cut out for telepathy.

"Eldana," Fraweyni said with calm, "A being of Balance and Chaos can master all the forms of magic. No magic and I mean none at all, is exempt from their mastery. All you have to do is learn."

"I am trying." Eldana had cried out with exasperation. "I truly am. While I am here trying to learn new skills, all the world is eating itself up."

"I understand your frustration, but you know, this is important."

Eldana nodded and sat. "I just wish there is something I could do to, you know, to speed things up," she moaned.

"Whatever it is you need to do, you are doing it," Fraweyni told her.

Today, Kochob was taking her through exactly the same thing, just with different words.

"The will of a telepath is just as important as their focused mind. You have got to use that well, deftly, like a thrusting force, to get into another's mind. And lastly, you need consideration so that you do not destroy the victim's mind. Reading minds can be very tasking work, and very addictive too. There are only a few things as sweet as knowing the secrets of another."

Yes, Eldana thought, *I know that well enough.*

The first thing Kochob had done when he began his lessons with Eldana was to take her to the training ground. Siem had been practicing her archery, shooting arrow after arrow into the bulls-eye of the stuffed targets. Mikko was using long wooden staves to train with another elf. Eldana had spotted him and remembered what Siem had said about his speed.

Wow, he is fast, she had thought.

Kochob signalled for an elf to give Eldana a sword.

"No offense, Kochob," Eldana chuckled. "but I know enough of sword fighting. I do not think there is enough time for us to revisit this."

"This is not about your skill in sword fighting," Kochob told her.

Eldana raised the sword in her hand and cocked her brows inquisitively.

"Strike me," Kochob said.

"What?" Eldana asked, her tone rising a few notes higher in mild confusion.

"Strike me," Kochob repeated.

"But you don't have a weapon in hand!" Eldana protested. "I mean, I know you are an elf, and are fast, but so am I. I have been trained. You will only get yourself injured."

Kochob had sighed, "If you are that concerned about my well being, you can blunt the edges of the sword."

Eldana eyed Kochob, wondering what exactly he was up to. She muttered a spell over the edges of the sword. When she was done, she ran a finger over the edge of the blade. There was no blood. She nodded satisfactorily.

Seeing her nod, Kochob nodded. "Now."

Eldana looked at him. "Are you sure about this?" she asked him.

"Oh, please stop being such a wimp," Kochob cried with mock

Chapter Eleven

frustration.

There was resounding laughter from all around. Eldana turned to find that all the elves had stopped their training to watch. She spotted Siem and Miko at the fore, and they gave her an encouraging smile.

Eldana pressed her lip into a hard line and gripped the sword. It was an elven blade, long and slender with a hilt. Eldana rolled the blade in her palm and then settled into a stance facing Kochob.

She saw the look in Kochob's eyes. His gaze was anticipatory, expectant. It was almost like he was begging her to attack. There was no fear in his eyes.

Oh, you have no idea what's coming, Siem thought, and then Eldana dashed forward.

The elves were taken aback by the speed at which Eldana lunged at Kochob. This was the first time that they had seen her fight. It looked like Eldana was going to thrust the sword into Kochob's shoulders. But at the very last second, Kochob twisted his torso to the side. Eldana's thrust went through air. But she had something up her sleeve. She flicked her wrist to the left, in the hopes that she would nick Kochob across the chest, but once again, her blade passed through thin air.

Mikko's mouth was open. He had seen the fight between D'rmas and the elven commander. But this one was something more exhilarating. D'rmas and the elven commander had used speed and brute force. Here, he was seeing speed, skill, thoughtfulness, and improvisation on the spot.

Eldana moved away from Kochob, her eyes on him the entire time. He seemed to have more in him than he let out. She circled him, but he stood still. She made a feint at him when she was behind him. He did not move. She tucked her lower lip into her mouth and smiled, the glint of mischief in her eyes. Still, behind Kochob, she slashed at his neck. Kochob zinged low, evading the strike, and the second strike that followed immediately.

The elves were beginning to cheer now. Eldana was beginning to get furious. She had struck numerous times at Kochob, and not even one of them had touched him. He had evaded all of her blows effortlessly,

She noticed Kochob attempt to spread his legs a bit wider. She lurched at him before his raised leg touched the ground. She knew that now his mind was still making a decision, and he was out of balance, it would be difficult for him to evade her blow.

With lightning speed, Kochob applied pressure to the foot that was still on the ground, and turned, letting Eldana's thrust go through the air. Eldana had gone in with such speed, that she sped past Kochob when she missed him. She turned, immediately, and went into a melee of strokes. Kochob dodged all of them. Neatly.

Eldana stopped. She was heaving, but Kochob was looking calm, still maintaining his poise. Eldana gave him a look of incomprehensibility.

How's he doing this? She asked herself. It is almost like he knows every move I make before I make it...

The thought had not matured into completion, when her eyes widened, as realization dawned on her.

Kochob saw her reaction and smiled satisfactorily.

"I think this lesson is over." He told her.

"Of course, it is," Eldana said. "I could have gone on trying to hit you, and would never have. And that's because you were reading my mind. You knew all of my moves before I even made them."

"I believe I do not need theorizations to impress upon you the use of telepathy in battle. In battle there are specific magics, especially the ones that are forbidden, that can be used by certain malicious mages. Those spells when used, are impossible to counter or stave off. No shield is potent against them."

"So you are saying no matter how strong I get, there is absolutely nothing I can do to avoid the spells you are talking about?" Eldana asked.

"Yes, I believe Siem knows somethings about these kinds of spells." He said, throwing a glance across to where Siem stood.

"Crazy mind reader," Siem muttered under her breath. "Stay

Chapter Eleven

out of my mind."

Kochob, now faced Eldana, "The only way you can avoid those spells is by telepathy. You can access the mind of your opponent and discern what their next move is going to be, and then you can plan an appropriate defense or counterattack. I must warn you though, certain people are trained to resist telepaths. Your level of magic is a natural mental defense for you, but you need to work on it so that you are near impenetrable. Your friends, especially Siem and D'rmas, had mental fortifications in place. An ordinary telepath would not have been able to penetrate them. But then again, I am not ordinary."

"So, if these mages have been trained to resist telepathy, my ability as a telepath is as good as useless then," Eldana said.

"Not entirely," Kochob replied. "You see, a lot of things go into a fight, other than force, and magic. There is a skill, tactic, strategy. Some even resort to fighting dirty. Battles are essentially a fight for survival, after all. There is only too much that the mind can focus on. If you can create something else for the mind to focus on, it borrows strength from what it already focuses on, and gives it to the new object of interest. Therefore…" Kochob cocked his brows suggestively for Eldana to fill in the theory.

Eldana's eyes widened as the implication of what Kochob had just said struck her.

"Therefore," she said, "the mage's mental fortification is weakened."

Kochob nodded with satisfaction. "And then you get your opportunity to stab through their mind."

Eldana had smiled then, imagining how formidable she would be in battle. She had not known how difficult it would be to learn the skill.

Now, she was sitting, her eyes closed trying to get into the minds of the birds chirping overhead for the tenth day in a row.

"It is almost noon," Kochob said, suddenly. "I suggest you take some time off to collect yourself. We will meet again at dusk."

Eldana sighed and stood up. She had a look of dissatisfaction on her face. She bowed slightly to Kochob, and Kochob bowed in return before Eldana stalked off.

On her way to the tent that she and Siem shared, she stopped by Hermon's. He always possessed this quality that made her spirits rise whenever he was around. And at the moment, there was nothing that else she needed. She went to his tent to discover that he was not in. Eldana muttered something about friends not being there when you need them and walked off. She was not ready to retire to her tent just yet. Not with the way she was feeling. She strolled through the forest, hoping that its life would suffuse her with the feeling of betterment that she so desired. She was at a part of the forest filled with lots of singing birds when she heard someone speak beside her.

"Rough day?"

Eldana turned. There was nobody from where the voice had come from. Just a young tree. Eldana squinted. She thought she saw the tree move. Suddenly, the tree began to shrink in size, its bark growing smoother, and smoother. Some of its branches disappeared outrightly, while the ones that remained, melded into hands.

Eldana stared wide-eyed with wonder as what had once been a tree was now Meko.

"Hi." Eldana said awkwardly in surprise.

Meko nodded, acknowledging Eldana's greeting. "You look every bit like you had a rough day," Meko repeated.

Eldana sighed, coming back to herself.

"A rough day, indeed."

"You have still not been able to use telepathy?" Meko asked.

"I guess word travels fast," Eldana replied in a dejected tone.

"Just give it some time," Meko advised.

"That is all I seem to be giving it," Eldana said. "I mean one would think that a psychic would learn telepathy easily."

Meko chuckled. "Psychics read spirits, not the human mind. I understand how frustrating this can be. You know, once, I was in the same spot as you are in now."

Chapter Eleven

"Yeah?" Eldana replied, her face brightening.

"Yes," Meko agreed. "You see, telepathy is not as easy as Kochob makes it seem. But my difficulty was not strictly with telepathy," Meko said. "It was that I could not control nature."

"What?" Eldana asked with incredulity, then burst into laughter, for the elf to join in.

"You do not mean it," Eldana said.

"I am serious," Meko replied.

"But I thought, as elves, the power to manipulate nature comes to you easily, like, well, second nature."

"True," Meko replied with a smirk. "But with me it was different. Imagine how I must have felt. All my mates were growing flowers and causing them to bloom, weaving vines into furniture and whatnot, and I was still struggling to make a flower bud open!"

Eldana laughed, for Meko to join in (with some little chagrin).

"It sounds banal and ridiculous now. But it was a huge problem for me."

"I can only imagine," Eldana said. "So, what helped you?"

"I had to ease myself. Relieve me of thoughts, and whatever weight was clouding my focus," Meko said. "You know, right now, nothing will make you feel so light and free than a swim."

Eldana looked eager.

"Oh, please do point me to where I can get one. There is nothing more I need at the moment."

"There is a pond not too far from here," Meko said. "You just have to go straight through there." Meko pointed to the left of where they stood.

"I do not have to make any turns?" Eldana asked.

"No. None at all. You just move straight. The land rises from here to there though."

Eldana smiled appreciatively. "Thank you, Meko. Really."

"Do not thank me yet. Thank me when you have felt better."

Eldana smiled. "Well, I best get back to my mother. She likes to have me around." Meko said.

"I will see you later, then," Eldana said.

"Later," Meko corroborated.

Eldana watched Meko disappear into the trees and smiled.

She is so friendly, she thought. Eldana realized that the hostility that Meko had displayed earlier was just the result of distrust. At least now she saw that the company were peaceful.

Eldana turned and went through the direction Meko had pointed out. Just as Meko had said, the land began to rise. Eldana had never heard of this section of the Ciroc before. However, she had never had cause to be here in the past. The atmosphere gradually eased into one of a humid chill.

I must be getting close, Eldana thought. As she walked, she thought she heard a thunk from the woods to her left. She turned and saw nothing. Leaving no stone unturned, she reached out with her mind, feeling psychically for any objects in the region. She felt rocks, squirrels, birds, but nothing more. She brought her mind back to herself and walked on.

Soon, she began to hear the sound of crashing. The crashing grew louder as she walked closer until she came to a chasm at the bottom of which lay clear blue water. She looked to her left, and saw a river that stretched out from the horizon, and fell into the pool beneath as a waterfall.

Excellent, Eldana thought, feeling a flush of excitement.

She turned around, looking for any path that might lead down to the pool. She found one soon enough, a trail through the brush. She followed it until she broke out the trees and into a small band of sand which the pool lapped at. She stood for a moment, staring at the crystalline brightness of the water, then she pulled off her boots, and sunk her feet into the soft wet sand. Eldana exhaled from the feeling of coolness that wrapped her feet.

Smiling, she unfastened the studs on her shirt, folded it neatly, and placed it on her boots. Her trouser followed, and so did her underwear. She walked to the edge of the pool and dipped a foot in to measure the temperature of the water. It was just the right amount of cool. She took a few steps backward, took a breath, then ran and sprang into the water. She broke its surface with a

Chapter Eleven

splash.

The ripples that Eldana had formed from breaking into the water were just beginning to settle when she re-emerged from the depths. She gasped and smiled with delight.

"Oh, Meko, a thank you is not enough for this." She said aloud.

Eldana whooped and dove back in. She took longer this time to re-emerge, and when she did, she was no more in search of air, as she was the first time. Her face was an emblem of glee and satisfaction. She waved her arms back and forth through the water, as she stayed afloat. Then she closed her eyes and let her thoughts drift. The past came back, like the water, into her mind and bringing Sinto's picture before her. She hated him now, yet, she could not help but remember the times she had caught him staring pityingly at her. She sighed, letting the peace of the water seep into her, to wash the ugly feelings away.

A sound woke Eldana with a start. For a moment she had fallen asleep right there in the water! Her eyes flew open to stare fully into the sun before she flinched and shut her eyes. She turned away from the sun and opened her eyes slowly.

She was about to turn, and go for her clothes when the sound came repeated; a thud. Quickly, she turned, just in time to see something, a creature lying a few meters away from her, at the foot of the ascent that led out of the chasm. The creature was huge, almost the size of a brown bear. Eldana's heart pounded.

What's that? She asked herself.

The creature had hairy gray skin, covering a well-muscled frame. Just then, it grunted, shook, and got to its feet.

Eldana was silent all the while, watching the creature stand to its towering height, and then it turned, and she saw its face, broad, and long, with teeth like an array of miniature tusks...

Orc!

The creature roared and jumped towards Eldana. Without thinking, Eldana raised a wave of water and smashed the orc back to the edge. The orc spluttered and wiped its huge hands on its face. But it charged again. This time, Eldana raised water out of the pond in the form of a tentacle, and hurled it at the advancing orc, almost at the same time, that she muttered a spell. The tentacle of water became solid ice in mid-air and speared through the orc. The impact was so heavy, it knocked the orc back to the band of land circling the pond.

Eldana watched the orc twitch, and gurgle as blood gushed from its mouth, then it stilled. Her heart was pounding fast.

What is an orc doing here? She asked herself, before panic caught at her. *The elves!*

Eldana scrambled out of the water and was about to reach for her clothes when a fist smashed into her from behind. Eldana tumbled to the ground. She heard laughter in a very gruff voice, and fear spread through her blood like cold water. She groaned and tried to stand to her feet. But a kick to her ribs sent her flying to the edge of the water. Eldana lay, struggling to breathe beyond the stinging pain in her lungs. A large hand clasped around her neck and raised her into the air. She opened her eyes a little and stared directly into the face of an orc. But it was not just one orc. There were three of them.

The orc gave her a toothy grin. "See?" It roared to the others. "She is still alive."

"And naked." One of the orcs said, laughing mischievously.

The orc holding Eldana gave her a lecherous glare, and she felt the dire urge to vomit.

All the while, Eldana had been staring at the orc, keeping it focused on her, while she pulled out the shard of ice she had used to impale the other orc with her mind.

She roared, hurling the shard of ice at the orc holding her with her mind, for it to pierce the back of his head, and out of his mouth. The orc's grip loosened, and Eldana fell to the ground.

The remaining orcs stared, stupefied, at their fellow as he crashed to the ground. If Eldana were hale, then this would be a window of opportunity that she would have utilized to finish off the orc hunting party, but sadly, she was not. Blood spilled from her mouth, and she could feel her strength waning. Fear gripped

Chapter Eleven

Eldana tightly, she choked with it. She did not have the strength to mutter a spell or manipulate any of the elements with her magic.

She saw the remaining two orcs turn and face her, their eyes filled with such malignancy. Tears dropped down the sides of her eyes.

No, she thought. *Please, No.*

The orcs began to approach.

In the last bid of defiance and desperation, Eldana screamed, and stretched her mind out, seeking to slam into the orcs. Suddenly, Eldana's mind was filled with foreign thoughts and images. They were so much, that they induced a feeling of giddiness. She retched and cried because the motion hurt badly. Her mind was piqued when she noticed that the thoughts and images were centerd on her. It was then that it dawned on her. She was in a foreign mind.

She looked up at the orcs and saw that they stood still, like inanimate objects. Eldana began to laugh, and then she lapsed into a fit of painful coughing. And then she cried. She tottered between elation, relief, and pain.

Eldana had just successfully become a telepath. She looked at the orcs, whose eyes were still trained on her, and she felt a spike in their thoughts. Their thoughts had just moved from one of malice and aggression to full-blown fear.

I'll show you fear, she thought.

She forced her mind to go deeper, throwing aside any consideration that Kochob had admonished that the telepath has. The thoughts became clearer, and then Eldana touched something else. It was like a minute incorporeal mass. The thoughts seemed to emanate from there into the larger space. Intuitively, Eldana knew that this was their essence, the very core of their minds. This was what controlled their bodily movements. She latched on to it with her mind and fed it new thoughts.

Eldana watched with a cold stare, as the orcs turned mechanically towards each other and began to claw and bite at themselves.

Eldana's eyes stayed on them, even as they ripped pieces of their flesh out, and sprayed blood everywhere. She watched until they fell to the ground, dead from exhaustion and the gravity of their wounds. Eldana sighed, and breathed softly, so she would not aggravate her broken ribs.

I have to get back, she told herself.

Slowly, she placed her hands on the floor, heaving, and wincing with the pain that the effort had caused. After so many trials, she was able to use her hands as support, to lift herself off the ground. The pain was too grievous to let her stand straight, so she walked to her clothes in a slouch with one hand free, and the other arm pressed gently to the side of her ribs that hurt.

With her free hand, she managed to put on her clothes, and then she trudged up and out of the chasm. The walk back to the elves' settlement was difficult, and she often stopped to catch her breath but she kept moving anyways. As she went on, she established telepathic communications with squirrels, birds, badgers, and any other animal she could connect with. Their minds were different from the orcs. They did not have coherent thoughts as the orc did. Their mind worked with sensations and impressions. So she impressed on them her desire for directions back to where the elves were and also asked them if there were any orcs ahead. The animals, though wary of her presence, sent back images of the forests, leading up to the elvish settlements. But none came back with any sense of more orcs in the forests. She moved on anyways.

It was not long afterwards that she came to the spot where she had met Meko earlier.

How quickly things change, Eldana wondered, instead of the usual tranquillity that had pervaded this part of the Ciroc, the princess's feelings were now tinged with what she had just experienced.

What was supposed to have been a quest for relief, as Meko had suggested, had turned out as something much worse. As Eldana went further into the familiar ground, her ears began to pick the clamor of steel, and shouting voices. And when she broke into the

Chapter Eleven

home clearing of the elves, she saw a sizeable band of orcs engaged in a battle with elves. Some of the orcs had fallen, but so had some of the elves. Eldana heard a loud maniacal roar and turned to see Hermon battling an especially large orc. Hermon had transformed, his eyes were black. Yet he had not gone full berserker (surely for fear of shortening his life span). In the commotion, Eldana was uncertain of which side was winning. But it seemed to her like the orcs were growing more aggressive with every passing moment.

Eldana limped forward, and just then saw an orc about to bludgeon an elf who he had succeeded in knocking to the ground. Immediately, she infiltrated the orc's mind and fed it a new instruction. The orc dropped its striking arm, and turning away from the fallen elf, walked towards one of its kind, and caved his head in with their club. But Eldana was far from done. She controlled the orc, and sent it ahead to smash the heads of its kin. One, two, three. But then the fourth one was not as unsuspecting as the other three. He dodged the blow of the orc Eldana controlled and sent his sword through the other orc's skull. Without wasting time, Eldana infiltrated his mind and continued using him to finish off his own.

Just then a voice spoke in her mind.

Eldana?

She recognized that voice. It was Kochob's. She could not see him, but she knew he was the one.

How many are they? She asked back.

About thirty or so, Kochob replied *we are trying to hold them off so Fraweyni can get the others to safety.*

How are you doing this? Kochob asked after a pause. *I can feel your mind. You are controlling them.*

You are a good teacher? Eldana replied knowing this was not the whole truth. Her training was paying off, or perhaps it was the situation she found herself in that brought her spiked her powers.

So you becoming better than me that quick? She heard him asking. Without trying to discuss this point in a middle of fighting, she tried to get real answers.

Do you know why they are here? She thought was more important. Kochob did not answer immediately but when he did, she felt a slight nauseating feeling in her stomach.

Chaos is spreading. Chaos is spreading really fast.

She put an answer aside for later and focused back on the fight. Eldana's orc was killed, and just before she could gain control of another mind, she heard a roar behind her. Years of training kicked in, and Eldana threw herself to the side. If she had stayed there a second longer, she would have been impaled. She groaned in pain and turned to face the orc, who looked at her with a spark in his eyes like she was an amusing prey. The orc had seen her from within the fray and had connected her actions, whatever it was, to the unusual behaviour a few of his kin was beginning to manifest. So, he snuck off into the cover of the woods and stole towards Eldana.

"I am Grib, son of Grab." He growled. "Orcs are impervious to magic. But if your magic worked on some of us, it will not work on me. You will die."

"This is not magic, you foul beast." Eldana cussed and stabbed into Grib's mind.

She was alarmed at the level of resistance she felt. Grib's mind was fortified, as if by a wall. He smiled knowingly at her.

"The sons of Grab do not lie. You shall surely die." He growled with excitement.

Just then, Eldana remembered what Kochob had said about protected minds. With all the strength in her, she raised a spike of earth from beside Grib. The quick movement of the earth beside him caused him to look. Intensifying the force of her mind, Eldana speared through his distracted defense. The last thing that flashed through his mind as he became hers was horror and regret. Eldana sent him stampeding back into the fight, and she watched as he immediately started lopping off heads. The orcs began to notice that they were not just fighting against the elves, but also themselves. Their numbers were beginning to dwindle with El-

Chapter Eleven

dana jumping from mind to mind when the body of the mind she controlled was struck down.

The orcs tried to beat a retreat, but the elves adroitly surrounded them, and soon not one orc was left standing. Eldana staggered, as she heard someone call her name from the group of elves standing over the fallen orcs. She thought it sounded like Siem. The orcs turned and caught sight of Eldana, her shirt soaked in blood. Eldana was suddenly overwhelmed by a wave of exhaustion. Every part of her body complained; her mind clouded. She began to feel the air constrict like walls were sprouting from all around her and coming together to hem her in. Darkness began to eat up her vision, before it swallowed her whole.

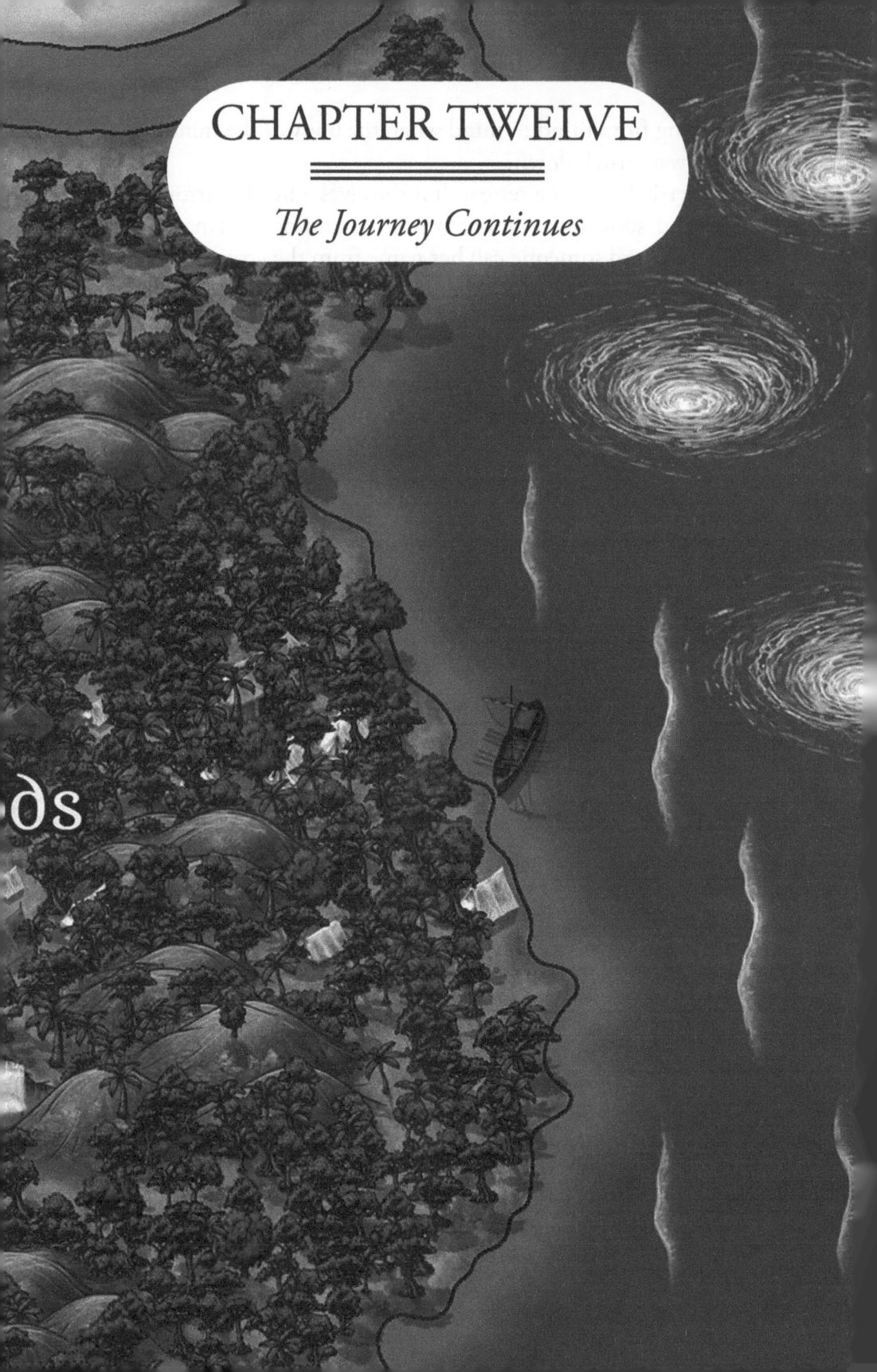

CHAPTER TWELVE

The Journey Continues

Chapter Twelve

It was dark when Eldana came to back to her senses. Her eyes opened, and she stared at the flat roof of the infirmary. She heard movement to her side and tried to move. Sharp pain spiked from her ribs, causing her to hiss.

"She's awake," somebody said.

Immediately, Siem was there at her side.

"Hey," she greeted, her eyes tearing with concern, and the hurt she felt for her friend. "How are you feeling?"

Eldana looked at Siem and smiled. "Well, I am not dead?" She replied. "Is everyone okay? Hermon?"

Siem nodded. "Everyone is okay. They are all here."

Just then, Hermon, D'rmas, and Mikko edged into her vision. They had smiles on their faces. D'rmas inclusive. Eldana could not help but wonder how odd the smile made him look. She had seen him laugh. And that was the only way he expressed his excitement. But this was new.

"Wow. I must be dead. D'rmas has a smile on his face." Eldana said, expressing her surprise.

D'rmas chuckled.

"The smile is not the only thing," Hermon said. "This piece of rock here has softened. And it all happened when Siem began to give him massages."

Eldana widened her eyes in surprise.

"Massages?" she asked looking at Siem. "How come I never knew of this!?"

Siem smiled.

"You were too busy with being of Balance and Chaos stuff." She replied.

"Ah." Eldana chuckled before a stab of pain ran up her side. "Ow."

Mikko came closer. "You may very well be the future of Toas, Eldana," he said. "There are talks, out there among the elves, that you controlled the minds of orcs. Is that true?"

"If I say yes, will you leave out any more questions you have, for now, Mikko?" Eldana asked.

"Mhmm," he replied. "I mean, of course."

"Yes," Eldana said.

"That I have never heard of," D'rmas said. "I have heard of and seen people who act out of control due to magic, but not this."

"One of the numerous quirks of being a being of Balance and Chaos," Hermon said.

"Even for a being of Balance and Chaos," D'rmas said, "this is enormous."

They could all feel it. Eldana was different from the other beings of Balance and Chaos they had heard in their stories, who went obediently to be slaughtered. She had more strength of will.

"Well, I think what is enormous at this point is us pestering Eldana with so much chatter. She needs some quiet so she can rest." Siem said.

Turning to Eldana, she told her:

"Meko sends her sympathies and a heartfelt apology at what befell you in the stream. He thinks it is his fault."

"No, it is not…" Eldana paused, and she furrowed her brows. "How did he know about the stream?"

"Kochob." Siem replied.

"Kochob?" Eldana questioned. She was not getting it. "But Kochob was not with me."

"You forget, Eldana, that he is a telepath," Hermon said.

Eldana groaned. "Of course." She said, remembering when he must have made mental contact with her during the fight. *I need to give more thought towards building walls around my mind*, Eldana thought. I cannot have Kochob snooping into my mind whenever he wants to, nor anyone else!

Just then, it occurred to Eldana to enquire about their hosts and how they were faring.

"How about the elves?" Eldana asked.

Siem sighed. "They sustained losses." She said. "About seven of their own were among the bodies lying in the field. The orcs were ferocious and strong, but we could have finished them without procuring this many casualties if magic had worked on them. Ev-

Chapter Twelve

ery spell we threw at them was impotent."

"I know," Eldana replied. "How is Fraweyni taking it?"

"Exactly as any mother would. She is in deep pain. Even the radiance that usually attends her has dulled." Siem replied.

Just then an idea dropped into Eldana's mind. "Our location and the location of the elves were supposed to be a secret," Eldana said.

"Yes, it was," Siem replied.

"Then how did the orcs get here?" Eldana asked.

Hermon, Mikko, and D'rmas exchanged looks. Eldana spotted them, and quickly got the sensation that there was something they were not telling her.

"What are you guys not telling me?" she asked warily.

"We should tell her," D'rmas told Siem.

"Tell me what?" Eldana asked. Nobody replied. "Tell me what, Siem?" Eldana asked again.

Siem looked at Eldana. "Uhm...one of the dead orcs reanimated," Siem said, ignoring her friend's question.

"What do you mean by reanimated?" Eldana asked, the look of puzzlement on her face.

"What Siem is trying to say", Mikko said, "is that one of the dead orcs came back to life."

"Okay. Is that even possible?" Eldana asked.

"It is," Siem and Mikko replied simultaneously.

Eldana gazed at them.

"I thought that kind of magic was forbidden?" Hermon questioned.

"I know of someone in particular who practices forbidden magic with impunity," Mikko said. "There are a few of them, but this magic, in particular, is nasty."

"How nasty?" Eldana asked.

"You'll see," Siem replied.

"What!" Eldana exclaimed astonishment splashed on her face. "You mean the orc is still there?"

"A living corpse. Not breathing, and bloody." D'rmas said.

"How long have I been out?" Eldana asked.

"I was about to say seven hours," D'rmas said.

Eldana's eyes widened with surprise. "Whoever is holding the hex on the orc is very strong and experienced in the forbidden arts. But the elves are beginning to fear that the orc is going to decompose. Already he is beginning to smell. The elves request your presence so whoever is behind the orc will pass across his message, and they can dispose of the body." Hermon said.

"But Fraweyni understands your current condition and is worried about your healing. She wants you to stay and get as much rest as you would like..." Siem said.

"I want to see," Eldana said after a while.

"But Eldana, you are not completely healed." Siem protested. "Meko could not complete your healing, because the effort might have killed you. What you need now is rest."

"I think I have had enough rest," Eldana said. "I should get the message the orc has for me. It could be very urgent. And you said it yourself. It wants me."

Siem saw the steel in Eldana's eyes and knew that she was resolved. There was no talking her out of it. "When you are ready." She told Eldana.

"Good," Eldana said. "Help me up."

Hermon rushed to her other side, while Siem took Eldana by the arm gently. Eldana winced and hissed as she sat up.

"Easy, easy." Siem soothed.

Eldana was still in her old clothes – encrusted with dried blood, torn to tatters at some places. However, Eldana was insistent on heading straight to see the orc. As she got to her feet, her eyes picked up the rows of beds that led from hers up to the infirmary's entrance. They were all filled with elves, all of whom had bandages all over their bodies.

"These are all the injured?" She asked.

"There is a few more outback," Hermon replied. "Those needed critical attention. Severed limbs, and the like."

Eldana nodded, as Hermon stepped closer, allowing Eldana's

Chapter Twelve

arm to rest on his shoulder.

Eldana's other arm was bandaged along her chest, so she could not lift it. Instead, Siem placed her hand gently on the arm to support Eldana as they walked.

As they came out of the infirmary, Eldana noticed that it was fully dark. There were globes of light in the air, but the lack of elven merriment that usually characterized the nights gave the atmosphere a touch of gravity. The elves Eldana, and her comrades passed, were of such dull countenances that Eldana could not help feeling sorry for them.

"I cannot imagine what it must feel like for them." She said. "Having to lose their own over and over again."

"If there is any race that has been so maltreated in the world," Mikko said, "it is the elves. Such glorious creatures. Mightier and stronger in every way, yet their undoing is their preference for peace."

"There is an old tale in our lore," D'rmas said. "A tale so old, I hear it spans from the very first hour. It tells that the first elves were warriors. The tale tells that they were so fearsome, and so unstoppable, that everywhere they went they seemed to leave a sea of blood behind. But then, the gods arranged a parley with them for fear that if allowed, the elves would kill off the rest of the other races."

"For some reason," Siem said, "If your tale were true, and not some figment of someone's imagination, I would like for the elves to revert to that nature. If only to remind the world that they are not to be trifled with."

"I wish they shared your sentiment," Hermon said. "I have been around them, and during conversations, all I hear are wishes to remain secluded, and to live peacefully from the rest of the world."

"I am Qeltifom," D'rmas said. "Battle is our destiny. It is in our blood. The only reason we are brought into this world. However, I tell you, that if the elves are to take to arms, nothing can stop them. I know this from personal experience."

Just then, Eldana's leg kicked against a loose piece of rock in the ground, and the pain in her ribs spiked. She hissed.

"Sorry," Siem said, signalling for Hermon to slow down. "Are you okay?"

Eldana nodded. "Have we not gotten to where the orc is, yet?"

"It is not too far now," Hermon replied. "It is at the clearing up ahead, and under constant watch."

"Are the elves trying to determine who is behind the hex?" Eldana asked.

"Kochob was about to try when we came for you," Siem replied.

As they broke into the clearing, Eldana saw a group of elves a few meters away standing around the body of a very large orc. The elves were rigid, their eyes fixated on the orc. Eldana got the feeling that if the orc so much as moved a finger, the elves would slice him to bits.

Meko espied Eldana approaching in the company of her friends, and whispered to her mother, "She is here."

Fraweyni looked up from where she sat, and a smile adorned her face. Even with all the sorrow hanging in the air, Fraweyni still shone. It was only when one looked into her eyes that they would be aware of the gravity of pain and loss swirling deep inside her.

Eldana saw Meko break out from the group of elves and walk towards her. Eldana put up a smile as Meko drew closer.

"How are you doing?" Meko asked.

"The pain is less severe than I remember, and I hear I have you to thank for that," Eldana replied.

"Oh, please," Meko said. "It was the least I could do, considering that it was my fault that…"

"Meko, Meko," Eldana called, interrupting her. "Please, look into my eyes."

Meko did.

"What happened to me was not your fault. And I do not need to read your mind to know that. I did have a good time at the pool though; the best I have had in a long while."

Chapter Twelve

"You do not mean that," Meko said, smiling.

"Of course. And thank the stars I woke up when I did! Who knows what those nasty orcs would have done while I slept?"

"I am glad you are alive though," Meko said seriously.

"I am glad you are alive, too," Eldana replied. "And I apologize for the kin you lost today."

"Thank you," Meko said. "I think I have held you long enough. My mother would very much like to see you. I hear you have beat Kochob as the strongest telepath, now."

Eldana smiled, "I think some things come to you when you have relaxed, and when danger springs on you suddenly."

"I expected you to get rest!" Fraweyni chided her when the company approached.

Eldana smiled. "I could not. Not while I heard tales of a living corpse."

"Ah, that," Fraweyni said. "There is not an ear that would not tingle at the mention of that. Whoever is behind this is tenacious as he is deeply rooted in the practice of forbidden magic. Reanimating a corpse is no small business."

"I am so sorry about the children you lost," Siem said. "We all are."

Fraweyni sighed. "I have been in this position often," the Elven Queen said sorrowfully. "But each time, the pain and the sorrow is fresh. Like I have never felt it before. But the elves are a strong people. We will survive this. We always do."

"Since you are here," Fraweyni continued, "We should get on with this so we can dispose of this body. No soul deserves such torture. Not even an orc that has slain my children."

Fraweyni got up, and walked towards the ring of elves, with Eldana and her comrades in tow.

"I hear Kochob has tried to determine the identity of the person behind the hex?" Eldana enquired.

"Yes. But the mental defenses are strong. Thousands of years strong. One thing is certain though, that whoever is behind it, is not a normal mage. He or she must be a master mage."

The elves surrounding the orc parted to create an entryway, as Fraweyni drew near. With her mind, she controlled a globe of light from the fringe of the security ring and drew it close, and over the orc.

The dead orc half slumped on a log.

Kochob was standing in front of the orc. He turned when he sensed people approaching. He gave Fraweyni a slight bow, then turned towards Eldana.

"He has been waiting for you." He said, gesturing towards the orc.

"It is about time," Eldana said. "Please take me closer." She said aloud to her friends.

"Are you sure about this, Eldana?" Hermon asked. "Anything could happen."

"Look at the orc, Hermon," Eldana instructed.

Hermon looked at the orc.

"Can you see how stiff his body is?" Eldana questioned.

The orc's muscles were still, and his limbs hung stiffly at awkward angles. His lips were parted and hung that way without even the slightest tremble.

"Rigor mortis." Siem said.

"I bet you he cannot get up from there. Not without difficulty." Eldana said.

"I agree," Siem said. "Plus we will be there with you, just in case."

"Thank you," Eldana said.

Eldana looked at Fraweyni, and their eyes met. Fraweyni gave her a nod of encouragement.

The globe of light hovering over the orc, illuminating his form and grotesque looks. His eyes had milked over. Suddenly there was a few popping, and cracking sounds coming from the orc. Eldana eyed it, and could not help feeling a wave of horror wash over her, as the orc's lips spread with difficulty into a smile.

"Hello, my girl." The orc said. "It is nice to see you again."

Eldana felt her heart lurch, and then all the hurt she had tried

Chapter Twelve

to suppress rose again. There was only one person who addressed her this way.

"Sinto?" Eldana asked. Her voice broke.

The orc smiled wider. "I cannot tell you how glad I am that you even still remember me." the Sinto/Orc said.

"How could I forget you?" Eldana asked. "You trained me, practically raised me, positioned yourself as my friend, and then tried to kill me. Is that something anyone should be forgetting too soon?"

"Ah, you must be annoyed about last time. And I am sorry about that. You see, the intention was to bring you in. But then things went out of hand, and I apologize for that."

"What do you want?" Eldana questioned, her voice cold and hard.

"For you to stop being selfish for once."

Eldana scoffed. "Me? Selfish? You call me not wanting to die in the hands of gods who rule Toas like they are rearing sheep, selfish? I thought you were smarter than this."

The orc was silent for more than two heartbeats, and then it spoke again.

"While you have been hiding in the safety of the Ciroc, Eldana. The rest of the world has been tearing itself to shreds. The entire kingdoms in Toas are snapping at each other's throats, and to think that you hold the key to long-lasting peace in your hands."

"If you are so concerned about peace, then why are you trying to capture me?" Eldana asked. "It is peace that I am after, too."

"Is that what you think?"

"I am after the peace that does not involve people getting raised for slaughter every 100 years! Beings of Balance and Chaos are living beings too. We deserve to live," Eldana hissed.

"Is that what these losers you have for friends have told you? Is that what they have gotten into your head?"

Eldana laughed.

"You never had friends, Sinto. I was the only friend you ever had. So, you do not know what it means. When you die, you will die sad, and lonely, and pitifully."

Suddenly the orc's voice changed to a very aggressive one.

"You foolish child!" the orc roared.

Eldana recoiled in shock.

"That is not Sinto." She said, comprehension dawning on her.

"Then who is it?" Hermon asked.

"Lord Taboon." Mikko said suddenly, his voice echoing through the clearing.

The orc grew silent and smiled.

"Ah, I see this is what you have come to, my boy." The orc said. "My Mikko, associating himself with outlaws, and fugitives." The orc hissed. "You are wasting your talent out here!"

"No." Mikko cried defiantly. "I am not."

The orc tsk tsk-ed. Its neck could hardly move.

"You have picked the losing side, boy," the Lord Taboon-Orc said. "As for you, Eldana. Know that you cannot run far enough. I'll have you sacrificed, and peace restored to Toas. By the gods, I will. Not even Sinto can stop me."

"What did you do to him?" Eldana asked.

The orc smiled.

"Ah, so you still care for him?" he taunted. "Well, your old teacher is still alive, but I suspected for a long while that his misbegotten affection for you was getting in the way of his job. His assistant is more eager to see that you are brought back, and the right thing is done. You and your friends seemed to have vanished from the face of the earth after you had left the Middle Kingdom. But I always suspected that Sinto had the means to find you. I was right. Tabeli had someone follow Sinto to where he went to get a locator spell, and when your location was revealed, Tabeli got the information and relayed it to me. And now, here we are!"

Eldana stared with rage at the orc. She wished badly that Lord Taboon was present so she could make him suffer in the worst way possible.

"As it stands", Lord Taboon continued, "there are only two paths open before you, in which you both die, but one for the

Chapter Twelve

greater good…"

"The greater good, being what?" Eldana questioned.

"You are sacrificed to Camin and Lowus, of course, and peace is restored to the world."

"You said there are two paths before her? Speak, vile sorcerer!" D'rmas demanded.

The orc smiled gruesomely. "A free warrior." He mused. "How I love your guts. You would make a nice experiment in my chambers. Maybe if your friend, Eldana, makes the wrong choice, I will get my wish with you."

Facing Eldana, Lord Taboon continued: "First, you surrender and come to us peacefully, and of your own will. There is a delegation waiting for you just within the outskirts of the Ciroc, who will escort you hospitably back."

"That is never happening," Siem said sternly.

The orc smiled again. "The second path", he continued, "is that you refuse, and we are forced to come to apprehend you. You know what that means, that those around you, whom you care about like your friends, and the elves who are harboring you will get hurt."

Eldana knew now how the orcs had come at the elves without their knowledge. They had help, the bumbling fools. Lord Taboon used them for his own desires.

"I do wish you pick the second choice though. I have never had an elf for my experiments. This would be a wonderful opportunity to have one!"

Suddenly the breeze around the clearing grew stronger until it howled. Branches creaked violently in protest; the leaves beat rapidly against themselves producing a loud swashing sound. It was like a storm was on them.

Eldana had someone shout behind her, and she turned to see Meko, holding, and shaking Fraweyni. Fraweyni's eyes glowed more than their usual golden. This was brighter. Like fire.

"Mother!" Meko shouted, trying to draw her mother's attention.

"I think we should leave," Kochob said, coming upon them.

"What is happening?" Siem asked.

"It is Fraweyni," Kochob said. "She has not been this way for a very long time."

"What is happening?" Hermon asked.

"She is annoyed, that is what is happening," Kochob said. "You should leave. Things could get much worse."

Just as Hermon and Siem helped Eldana turn around, the commotion slowed. Eldana looked to where Fraweyni sat and saw that the glow in her eyes was diminishing.

All the while, the orc had been watching with a smile on his face.

"What a wonderful display." Lord Taboon's voice boomed – but then his voice caught, and he began to choke.

Eldana sensed a burning psychic presence, going through the orc, and to the mind in control of the hex. Eldana turned with astonishment, realizing that the psychic presence was Fraweyni herself.

"Hear me, vile mage. My name is Fraweyni, Child of the First, Daughter of Tessa, Mother of the Elves."

The skin of the orc glowered like coals and then caught fire.

"You have slain enough of my children. And we are not vacating our natural home for anyone. Again, I warn you. Disturb us again, and you will find that the wrath of the elves is the nightmare you cannot wake from."

Lord Taboon began to laugh, even as the body of the orc was covered in flames. The smell of burning flesh pervaded the air. Eldana and her friends were forced to retreat as the flames increased in density.

"You are a dying race!" Lord Taboon shouted through the flames. "We will watch you go extinct. Hide in the Ciroc for now, but we will come for you. One day we…"

Lord Taboon's voice was cut off, as the fire burnt the orc's speech organs.

The fire lessened to reveal a charred black carcass. Eldana felt

Chapter Twelve

Fraweyni's psychic presence withdraw. Fraweyni shut her eyes and walked out of the clearing without a word.

Siem never knew Fraweyni could be anything other than her usual bright, and happy self. She always looked untouchable, resistant to anything that she did not want to affect her. She saw another side today and knew that she never wanted to be on the wrong side of Fraweyni's wrath.

"You did not have to see that," Meko said, as she walked towards the group.

"Oh please, we have seen worse," Hermon said.

"Hermon," Siem called. "She is not talking about the burnt orc."

"Ah," Hermon said, quietening as he came into the realization of what Meko meant.

"She very rarely gets that way." Meko continued. "If Lord Taboon values his life, and the joy in it, he should never come in contact with her. She bears grudges."

"This is one threat I pray Lord Taboon carries through," Mikko said. "The man should die already."

"Well, the elves are not ready to go into war just yet. Though with the kind of attacks we have received, and the losses we have taken, I do not know for how long that decision will continue to stand," Meko said.

"They know where we are now," Eldana said. "Something has to be done about that."

The entire group was silent. The next course of action hung in the air, haunting them. The time had come to leave the elves. Though no one had asked them to leave, yet they could not throw Lord Taboon's threat and the chances of another attack to the wind. A bigger company of orcs might mean more trouble than the elves ever anticipated. The orcs were like pawns, wondering wherever anyone with magic wanted them. They were the loosest race on Toas, with settlements spreading far and just about anywhere there was thick forest. They had no leader.

"Well," Meko interrupted their dark thoughts, "I should look at your injuries Eldana, and complete the healing process. You are no good to the fate of Toas like this."

"Thank you, Meko. For everything." Eldana smiled.

"Do not thank me yet," Meko replied. "We should head back to the infirmary."

Siem turned to Mikko and D'rmas. "Eldana's healing will not take time. And we must be away from here by tomorrow at dawn. While Hermon and I take her to the infirmary, you two should begin to saddle up."

"Aye, aye, mother." Mikko mocked.

Siem grimaced. Mikko laughed painfully, while D'rmas grunted. Then she turned and, still supporting Eldana, followed Meko's lead.

Eldana did not expect the healing process to be this painful. She was grateful that Meko had given her a slim piece of hard, burnished wood to bite on. Meko's eyes were shut, but they glowed red like coals. Her hands hovered over Eldana's limbs, and emitted a soft golden glow. Eldana felt like her insides were on fire. She could feel everything moving inside of her. Blood, bone, muscle, tissue. Everything screamed in pain, but she had to be awake to complete the healing process or she would sail away into the light. Siem held her comfortingly, while Hermon stood to one side, watching the process.

Gradually, Eldana's agitations began to drop as the pain she felt subsided. And then the glow on Meko's hands dissipated. She opened her eyes.

Eldana was heaving, and sweating profusely. She sat up, and let the piece of wood fall from her mouth.

"How do you feel?" Meko asked. "Any pain?"

"Are you kidding me?" Eldana asked, her eyes widening with excitement. "It hurt so bad, yes. But I feel like a whole new being right now."

Siem and Hermon's faces brightened at this, a small piece of good news on an otherwise dark day.

"Do I have the ability to heal?" Eldana asked Meko.

Chapter Twelve

"The being of Balance and Chaos can learn almost all the kind of magics available. That you do not know how to perform a magic skill is because you have not learned it. If you had the time, I would have taught you."

Eldana smiled and said:

"Perhaps, if all this blows over, and we are still alive, I would be free then, and have almost all the time to learn anything."

"Perhaps," Meko said. "You and your friends," she cast her eyes on Siem, and Hermon who nodded as their eyes met, "will always be welcome among the elves of Ciroc. I am sure my mother feels this way too."

Eldana, Siem, and Hermon conveyed their thanks at the honor.

"I should leave you all to get prepared for your departure," Meko said.

They bade him good night and then watched him walk out of the infirmary, and the friends were silent for a while until Hermon spoke.

"I cannot believe that we are finally getting back on the road." He said. His voice was low, as the prospect of continuing on their journey was daunting.

"Same here," Siem said after a while.

Hermon chuckled, "We have spent so much time here that I have forgotten what it feels like to be on the run, and sleeping out in the open. This place has almost become…"

"Home." Eldana completed. It had been almost five moons since they first intruded on the elves, she realized. "This place is a home."

Siem and Hermon looked at her and sighed. They were all saddened at having to leave the beauty and elegance of elf life. At the same time, they were apprehensive at facing the rest of Toas again. They did not know what it was going to be like, but they knew they would not meet it the same way they had left it.

"What time have you all decided to leave?" a voice said, interrupting their silence.

Eldana, Siem, and Hermon turned to see Fraweyni walking

towards them. She had a smile on her face, and the light seemed to have returned to her.

"We...Wh... Uhm..." Eldana stuttered.

"Meko told you we were leaving?" Siem asked.

"No," Fraweyni replied with a smile. "You just did."

Eldana, Siem, and Hermon laughed.

"Well, if it helps," Fraweyni said, "you did not entirely tell me everything. The other half I conjectured for myself. I have spent to long in this world, and I am about the wealthiest person alive when it comes to experience and knowledge. With what had just occurred, I knew you would be blaming yourselves and would want to leave immediately to prevent something like what happened today from happening again."

"Exactly," Eldana replied. "But we would not have left without telling you. We just did not know if it was feasible to approach you after..."

"Yes." Fraweyni said, nodding understandably, "After my temper. I am sorry you all had to see that. Call it a cup I had been storing for ages, now gone full."

"We understand," Siem said. "And I hope you understand why we must leave?"

"Yes, I do. But not for some of the reasons you have."

The three of them gave Fraweyni puzzled looks. She smiled.

"Let me put things succinctly. First, those orcs might have come here looking for you, Eldana, but it was not your fault that elves had to die for it. You heard the mage. It was always bound to happen. Elves have been killed in like manner in the past. So, leave the guilt from the reasons why you are leaving us. But, if you are leaving because the world is rapidly falling apart, and you need to fix it before it falls beyond repair, then I understand. Though Kochob argues that you, Eldana, are not fully trained, yet."

Eldana nodded, thanking the Elf Queen for her understanding. "What about you?" she asked.

"What about me?" Fraweyni enquired.

"Well, Kochob says I am not ready yet. But what do you think?"

Chapter Twelve

"I think, there is no time for any of us to get fully ready. The way the world is unravelling does not allow for that. We can only equip ourselves with what is necessary, and hope to gain more on our way to battle."

Eldana nodded respectfully. "Thank you," she told Fraweyni.

Fraweyni nodded, "There is someone though you have to meet before you can have a chance at restoring order and balance without dying."

"Who is that?" Eldana asked. "Another teacher?"

"Something like that. You will learn a few things from her. Things that may turn out to be fundamental to your victory."

"Where is she, and who?" Siem wondered.

"Well, as for where she is at Piece Island."

"Piece Island?!" They all chorused in unison.

"That is exactly what I said," Fraweyni said. "Piece Island."

"But that would warrant us exposing ourselves to the main roads and cities. And in doing that we risk capture." Siem protested.

"All that has been put into consideration, and that is why you all will be going by sea," Fraweyni said with calm authority.

"What an adventure," Eldana said drily.

"An adventure indeed," Fraweyni said.

"I do not think any of us have any experience steering a ship." Siem expressed.

Fraweyni smiled. "There will be no need for that." She said mysteriously. "The ship was a gift from a family of Technocons. They were helpful to us during our stay in Kleas."

The Technocons wanted peace and progress, Eldana understood. At times, they behaved like they were the father of all the races. It was easy to relate with the elves who were equally as peace-loving as the technocons.

"So you are saying, we would not need to steer her?" Hermon enquired.

"No. The ship steers itself. It seems to have a recollection of all locations in Toas. All you need to do is select your intended location and it takes you there. There are provisions though, for the ship to be controlled manually, too."

Eldana, Siem, and Hermon conveyed their gratitude and appreciation for everything to Fraweyni. Fraweyni merely smiled.

"I do hope this is not the end for all of us. It would be nice to have you, all of you, here again. Well, I have said enough. You all should get some rest. You have a long voyage ahead of you. And speaking of voyage, the ship is going to avoid ports and harbors along its routes. It would take you far out of the waters near Kleas. You will ride close to the Hinterlands... Beware of this place, as it is true to its name! Once you are out of the waters of the Hinterland, and the Technocon, Piece Island is before you."

The friends thanked her again before Eldana called to the Elf Queen one last time,

"Mother. I can call you that, right?"

Fraweyni stopped, her hand holding the infirmary's entrance flap open. Without turning, she smiled.

"You can call me anything you want, Eldana. If I have deserved that name, then I am the happier for it."

Eldana smiled.

"Okay. Mother, you did not tell me anything about who I am meeting at the Piece Island."

Fraweyni paused for moments before speaking, "The person you are going to meet is like yourself."

Eldana did not understand what Fraweyni had said immediately, but her eyes widened an instant later when comprehension dawned on her.

"Are you saying the person we are going to meet is a being of Balance and Chaos, like Eldana?" Siem asked She had a surprise all over her face. And it was not just her. All of them.

"Yes," Fraweyni replied.

"How?" Hermon asked.

"My question exactly," Eldana said. "How?"

Mikko and D'rmas stood at the periphery, no less interested in the answer to Hermon's question. The birds seemed to have

Chapter Twelve

stopped their singing, hanging overhead on tree branches, and the wind made the grass beneath them bend towards the mother of the elves to hear what she had to say.

"I do not think I am in the best position to answer that," Fraweyni replied. "However, I think that when you meet her, all questions you have will be answered. I should leave you now. We may meet again, just before you leave."

Bidding them a pleasant rest, Fraweyni walked off into the night, leaving the friends to stare helplessly at themselves.

At first light, Eldana, and Siem were already up and prepared. They had slept in a different place from the men and wondered if the men were up already or still sleeping where they were.

"How are you feeling?" Siem asked Eldana as they sat together on the bed. Siem still harbored concern for Eldana's well-being, especially after yesterday.

"Siem, I am fine. Really." Eldana replied.

Just then, they heard the snap of fingers in rapid succession just outside the tent. Eldana and Siem snapped to attention before they heard Meko's voice.

"It is me," the elf said. "Can I come in?"

"Yes, please," Siem said.

"I was not expecting you to be awake," Meko said as she came in. "Not with the stress you all went through yesterday."

"Well, we decided that the earlier we move on, the quicker we get all this over with," Siem said.

"I feel the same way too," Meko said. "If you are all set, we should be on our way. Kochob went over to the boys. He will be coming with them."

"This is goodbye to a comfortable bed, a roof over our head, safety, and proper food!" Eldana said.

Siem sighed, "Indeed."

"Perhaps," Meko said, "You should garner solace in the fact

that if we all survive this, we can be as comfortable as we want to be. If you find and end to this chaos thing, we might have a chance to live in peace forever."

The early morning air was cool and gentle, carrying the humble and silent demeanor of an infant child. The trees bowed gently, ruffling their leaves in response to each gust of wind. Where Eldana and Siem's footfalls constituted part of the symphony of early morning sounds, Meko's was noiseless. Like her feet were not touching the ground at all. Eldana and Siem followed Meko through a few clearings that contained a scattering of tents. If the elves were awake, they did not indicate. The entrance to the tents flapped, but other than that, revealed nothing else.

They took a turn, then ventured into the woods. They walked on in silence, boots squashing against shrubs wet from early morning dew.

"How long till we get there?" Eldana asked. She had not seen any of the men. They had probably set off before them to see the ship, letting their curiosity get the better of them.

It was not that she had grown tired from working, far from that. In fact, since her healing session with Meko, Eldana felt extraordinarily strong. Like some new pocket of health and vitality had been discovered inside of her. They walked for a few miles under a cloud of silence, until Eldana sought to dispel it.

"It is not too far away now," Meko said, and then a cunning smile grew on her face. "You know, if you both want, I could carry both of you in my arms, and run towards our destination."

Eldana and Siem shared a small laugh at the joke.

Soon, Siem detected a change in the atmosphere. A fresh gust of cold pervaded the air, spreading through it with calm. Eldana recognized the change of air as coming from a body of water nearby.

"I think we are close to the river." She spoke in a low voice to Siem.

In the next few seconds, Eldana's conjecture was proven right. They broke out of the trees, and into a riverbank. There was a fine

Chapter Twelve

line of light on the horizon, which was beginning to spread out into the rest of the sky. Not too far away from them, there was a small group, standing close to a ship in the anchor.

"Wow," Siem exclaimed.

The ship had been so unexpected that Eldana just stared wide-eyed. They did not need the light of the sun to reveal the sleek nature of the ship or the fact that it seemed to have a glow that was inherent in its timber planks.

"Is that it?" Eldana questioned after a short while of standing and gaping.

"Yes," Meko replied. "That is it."

"Do you have a name for it?" Siem asked.

"The family that gave it to us named the ship *Marta* as they built it. Though they also explained that the name was subject to the change of its owners. But we have not had cause to use it, and so it has remained without a name. Or, at least, our name."

"How is it that you were able to get something like this through to here?" Eldana asked as they finally began to move, following Meko's lead, and heading towards the group standing at the foot of the ship.

"Through the same way, it will take you out," Meko replied.

Eldana could not help but feel honored that the elves would gift them something as incredible as this. As they neared the ship, the outline of the people at its feet began to get clearer, and they could make out the forms of Kochob, Fraweyni, Hermon, Mikko, and D'rmas.

Hermon was the first to see them approach. With a huge grin on his face, he broke off from his group and walked up to meet Eldana and Siem.

"A good morning to you" Hermon greeted Meko, nodding. Siem thought she could see Hermon, and Meko's eye lingers on each other longer than necessary before

Hermon flicked his eyes towards them, and his smile widened. He rushed to Eldana and Siem and encircled them in a big embrace.

Eldana, and Siem's lips spread into huge pleasant smiles.

"Okay. I think that is enough." Eldana joked. "There is no need showing the entire world, how both our tiny bodies can make up almost one of yours." Hermon laughed.

"I do not think you should dally any longer," Meko advised. "The light of dawn is quickly upon us. You should be gone before it is fully dawn."

Siem caught that lingering eye contact again between her and Hermon, and then she thought:

Yes, I knew it was not just in my mind. Something is going on between these two!

Fraweyni was dressed in a long white gown with a fitting bodice that progressed into a large skirt that was split into many parts like very long petals. And as the sea wind blew, the parts thrashed and played together. It made Fraweyni look like a wildflower in the eye of the dawn. She smiled as Eldana, Siem, and Meko joined them.

"I trust you had a pleasant rest?" she asked.

"I do not think they had rest at all," Meko replied. "They were already wide awake when I got to them."

"Same with their friends here," Kochob said, "I walked in on them performing some male ritual or something."

Siem cocked her brow inquisitively at Hermon, who just frowned, and shrugged his shoulders.

"The time has come," Fraweyni said. "For you all to leave us. I know it, without a doubt, that you will be dearly missed here. You have been such wonderful friends. The word, allies, does not suffice in your case. And I still insist that should all this blow over, and any, or all of you, are willing to make a home of this place, they will always be welcome in the Ciroc. I would also want to thank you for showing my children that there is something for them to grasp on to in this world that has treated us so unfairly."

Eldana and her friends nodded respectfully.

"My lady." Mikko said, stepping out a little, "If I may be allowed to speak freely."

Chapter Twelve

"Why, Mikko, you can say whatever you wish. This is far from a tribunal." Fraweyni declared.

"Well, since we are all throwing thanks and gratitude around, I would also like to contribute mine. I want to say a big, and heartily thank you, that all you did when we intruded into your borders, albeit unknowingly, was sing us to stupor, instead of killing us on sight!"

The company erupted into mild laughter.

"Serious." Mikko continued. "Anyone in your position, having faced what you have faced would have terminated on sight. But you chose to delay your hand and enquire, and that there, shows you abound in wisdom, and thoughtfulness, and insight. Thank you, once again. You are a mother indeed."

Fraweyni nodded in appreciation while Kochob turned to Eldana.

"And to my student," he said, "who has now surpassed her teacher."

Eldana's eyes teared up. "Oh, please, Kochob. Do not make this harder than it already is." Eldana said.

Kochob walked closer. "I am proud of you." He told her. "And always will be."

He spread his arms open, and Eldana went in for a hug.

Meko clasped her hand on Hermon's wrist, and quickly pulled him away from the rest of the group. Siem watched them slyly.

"Were you going to leave without saying goodbye?" she asked, glaring at the tall Beserker staring him dead in the face.

Hermon's eyes roved about, unable to look Meko in the eye.

"I really wanted to," Siem heard him whisper. "But next time, when I complain about sharing a room with the other guys, my complaint should be taken seriously!"

"I wanted to come to see you in the middle of the night, but they were engaged in a wrestle of sorts, and they pulled me in as judge!"

"That is all you did last night?" Meko questioned. "That is no excuse."

"I know," Hermon said. "But if I had tried to slink away, or just leave, I would arouse suspicion, and then everyone else will follow."

"Why are you scared about that?" Meko asked.

"About what?"

"About people seeing us together, especially your friends."

"It is not that, exactly. It is just that I do not know how they are going to take it."

"Do you trust me?" Meko asked, stepping closer to him, and gazing into his eyes.

"Ye…Yes. I think I do. I mean, I do."

Meko shakes her head and smiled.

"Of all the Berserkers I have ever encountered, you Hermon, are the most juvenile."

"I am not a child." Hermon objected.

"I know. But you act like one. And if you had waited for me to finish my sentence before childishly objecting, I would have told you that you are also the strongest Berserker I know."

Hermon looked at her like he was doubtful of what she had just said. But then, he saw the seriousness on her face, and a large, slow grin spread across his face then he allowed himself to smile.

"You are enlivened by your passion to protect the ones you care about, and that is your strongest weapon. Stronger than the power that runs in you, or the curse that flows in your bloodline" Meko declared.

"I care about you," Hermon told her. His voice was low, almost as if he was not sure how Meko was going to take it.

"I know," she said and looked at him. "I know, and that is why you will do one thing for me."

"What is that?"

"You will go with your friends, protect them, lift your curse if you can. And then come back here. To me. Can you do that?"

Hermon looked into Meko's eyes. He had never thought beyond what would happen when Eldana found her another way to restore balance to the world, or what would happen if his curse

Chapter Twelve

were lifted. He never even thought of living past the chaos of this time. But standing at the riverbank, a few moments away from boarding a ship, and heading into uncertainty, he realized that his future was not as horrible as he had thought it was.

"Yes." He told her. "Yes, I will come back to you."

"Do not disappoint me." She said.

With amazing speed, Meko pulled him in and pressed her lips against his. Hermon felt blood rush to his cheeks, and then he gave in and kissed her in return. At that moment, they each matched each other in passion and fierceness.

Finally, they broke free of the kiss, and putting their foreheads together, and sighed.

"Go in peace, Hermon, son of Biniamin." Meko whispered.

Instantly, Hermon felt coolness bloom inside him. He felt it sluice away the fears and doubts in his mind, and fill him with clear-headed intent.

Meko placed her palm at his nape and stared him in the eye.

"Remember what I said," the elf told him.

Hermon nodded and then looking at her one more time, turned, and walked towards the ship.

Onboard the ship, Eldana, Siem, Hermon, Mikko, and D'rmas huddled at the side of the ship, waving goodbyes to Fraweyni, Kochob, and Meko below.

"Eldana," Fraweyni called.

"Yes, mother." She replied.

"The name of the person you seek is Shewit. You will find her, or she will find you," Fraweyni said. "But it is more likely that she will be the one to find you. Go in peace, all of you."

Immediately, there was a rush of wind that brushed through all of them on deck, infusing them with a refreshing determination, and leaving them stronger.

The ship began to crawl further into the sea. Slowly and slowly it moved away until the elves on the beach looked like miniature dolls. Then the ship picked up speed and accelerated away following the designated path that had been keyed into its command

The Journey Continues

unit before Eldana and her friends came on board.

CHAPTER THIRTEEN

Chaos in Chaos

Sinto sat in his chamber, a pensive look on his face. Sunlight slanted into his room from partly opened windows, bathing half of the room in light, and the other in half-shadow. He was still partly furious that somehow Lord Taboon had gotten wind of Eldana's location in the Ciroc. He had gone alone to prevent such a brash attack as the one that Lord Taboon had instigated. Up until this very moment, he was still at loss as to how it happened.

Sinto had rushed home from the King's palace that evening, Lord Taboon had come to the King with news that he had discerned Eldana's location, and searched his home and his person for monitoring charms.

Sinto had laughed in his heart when Lord Taboon made the declaration to Henok. And then that mirth had quickly turned to horror, which he hid perfectly well when Lord Taboon divulged Eldana's true location. Henok had asked Lord Taboon how many soldiers he would need to make the arrest, but Lord Taboon had declined the use of the soldiers, insisting that the kingdom did not have enough to spare and that the elves would just finish them off like chaff in a tray of sorghum. Arresting Eldana, they felt, would make them look strong again and capable, it would restore the morale of their men, and quell the rebellious Tonar. Ordinary humans were supposed to be under the druids, not at the same level as them! The uprising, they felt, must have been a result of the chaos that Eldana's escape had brought with it.

"What then, do you suggest?" Henok had asked. He was restless and wanted the meeting to be over.

"I would like for you to leave the girl's apprehension to me," Lord Taboon had said with a courteous bow.

"Fine." Henok had said immediately. Even before Sinto could voice his reservations.

Lord Taboon had looked him in the eye, as a knowing smile split his face...

But right now, he sat on his bed feeling like an utter failure. Yesterday, he had the sixth visit from Camin and Lowus in just

Chapter Thirteen

two weeks. Things were getting heated. And he knew that soon, if he did not do the necessary, he would be damned with the consequences.

He got up, wore a straight face, and headed out for the palace. The sky shone pink with the light of dusk. The streets that led up to the royal residence was a mockery of what it had been before now. It was manned throughout, every street and corner infested by soldiers of the kingdom. An attack from Tonar had only recently been repelled. The puny Tonarians had gained courage and sought to end any perceived form of dominion against them. The Middle Kingdom did not have much to show as a testament to the attack. Much of its infrastructure was still intact. The streets were still patrolled by a multitude of soldiers. However, they had still suffered some casualties among the soldiers. Enough to make them retreat to the inner gate and fortify it. The houses lining the streets gaped emptily with doors and windows ajar. Many of the people had escaped to the woods, seeking solace in any form at all.

In what must be a stroke of ill-luck that Sinto he met Lord Taboon at the gate to the royal court.

"Sinto!" Lord Taboon called.

What now, Sinto inwardly wailed. But he put on an impressive smile anyways.

"Hello, Lord Taboon." He greeted.

"I hear that you spent the better part of the day in your chambers. Hope you are well."

Like you care about my health, you slimy bastard, Sinto thought.

"Of course." Sinto replied, smiling, "I had a few pressing matters that required my full attention."

Lord Taboon nodded enthusiastically.

"Good," he said. "Because this entire wild goose chase with your student is about to end. And you, more than any other, should be fully involved in this. I learn that she possesses magic of astronomical proportions. Your expertise is needed."

Sinto nodded. "You know me enough, Lord Taboon, to know that I do not frown in the face of duty. The world can count on my ability to carry out that which is within my duties."

Lord Taboon smiled, and there was something about his smile that irked Sinto. It was something taunting, arrogantly boastful, and knowing. Like he knew something Sinto did not.

When Lord Taboon and Sinto walked into the throne room, they found Henok pacing across the elevated platform on which his throne sat. His robes, black, and glimmering, billowed against his body as he moved. His hair was ruffled and without the adornment of his crown. Henok espied Lord Taboon and Sinto approaching, and then he halted. He paced some more as they came up the stairs towards the platform, and then went back to his throne. He sat, and then began to shake his legs vigorously.

Lord Taboon and Sinto stood before him, like children awaiting a rightly deserved punishment.

"I do hope you both have come here bearing good tidings," Henok said.

Sinto harrumphed, about to tell Henok that after Lord Taboon's brash attempt no more news had been heard about Eldana, when Lord Taboon spoke.

"Indeed, my king."

Sinto flashed him a brief, puzzled look. Collecting himself immediately, he turned to face Henok, his face straight and calm.

Henok nodded. Then with a flick of his hand, he signalled for Lord Taboon to tell his good news.

"The girl is on the move," Lord Taboon said.

"How did you come about that information?" Sinto asked, despite himself.

Lord Taboon smiled. "A little trickery I performed when the orcs attacked the elf settlement in Ciroc."

Henok, knowing that Lord Taboon liked to boast of his accomplishments, nodded his permission for him to go into elaborate details.

Lord Taboon smiled indulgently, while Sinto was hating every moment of this meeting, especially with Lord Taboon by his side, but his hands were tied by no ordinary bonds.

Chapter Thirteen

"I got a little something from the Technocons. A miniature device that performs the same function as a tracking spell. A tracking spell would require I have a property of hers. But I do not have that. So, I improvised. I had one of the orcs, who I especially tasked to get close to Eldana, stick the device into her. Now I have gotten her location, and she is moving quickly. A few hours ago, she went past Kleas."

"Sinto." Henok called.

Sinto looked up, almost surprised at being included in the King and Lord Taboon's special banter.

"My king," Sinto replied.

"You were her teacher."

Sinto nodded.

"What do you think she is up to now?" Henok asked.

Suddenly, in a flash, an image of Camin and Lowus, appeared in his mind and disappeared just as quickly. Sinto knew what he had to do.

"She is a smart girl." He began, contemplation stealing into his face. "She cannot move on land, especially if it will require that she passes very close to the cities in our control. It is too close to the Middle Kingdom. We have eyes spread throughout the land, searching earnestly for her, and she knows that. My best and only guess is that she is going via water."

Henok sighed, and reclined into his seat, frowning in cogitation.

At the spur of the moment, Sinto received the spark of an idea that would, curry him a part of the king's favor, and at the same time, splash some mud on Lord Taboon's face.

"How quickly did you say she was travelling again, Lord Taboon?" He asked.

Henok re-emerged from his meditative state.

"Quickly," Lord Taboon replied. "Like she was on a horse."

"What is going on in that head of yours, Sinto?" Henok asked. "Spit it out already."

Sinto smiled and nodded. "She is not on land. As I said, she is a smart girl and will avoid traveling over land by any means. I will ask, my king, that you plant soldiers to route them from the water."

"Last I heard from General Meron," Henok said, "was that we do not have a fleet ready for a coordinated attack. So I do not know how we are going to go about that."

Quickly, Lord Taboon spoke, stealing the yet-to-be spoken words from Sinto's open mouth. He had sniffed out the game Sinto was playing and was pressed to get back on top. Already, Henok was beginning to lean away from him.

"We do not need to bother about risking the lives of the kingdom's soldiers, my king." He said.

Henok looked up at him.

"Are you proposing that we apprehend her using the same sources you used in your previous attempt?" he asked.

"That is exactly what I am proposing, my king," Lord Taboon said. "They were effective. Of course not in her apprehension. But if they had not gotten close enough to stick the tracker into her, we would not have this cord of hope that we have been graciously offered."

Henok cleared his throat and placed his fingers on his cheek as he went into thought.

"My king," Sinto called, "If I may."

"Go on," Henok said.

"Orcs are not a trustworthy force that one can work out a deal with. They are bound, just like the elves, by duty, love to themselves, and only to themselves. To put this succinctly, their words cannot be trusted as standard. If Eldana or any of her cohorts offer them a better deal than Lord Taboon offers them, whatever that is," Sinto flashed Lord Taboon a glance, and continued, 'they will be on you in the next moment, swords slashing at your throat."

"Hmm…" Henok said, musing. "Sinto does have a valid point. Right, Lord Taboon?"

"Yes. He most absolutely does." Lord Taboon replied with just the slightest sour note in his voice. "However, I have to give my king the assurance that these orcs will keep to the agreement we have."

Henok nodded.

"I do not know what the incentive in your agreement with the orcs is, and I do not care to know. However, you must answer a question, and answer this truthfully."

"Anything, my king," Lord Taboon said, bowing courteously.

"What Sinto said about the nature of the orcs, their tendency to renege on an agreement if the job offers them a better deal than the employer, is that true?"

Lord Taboon was uncomfortably silent for a moment.

Good strike, Sinto, he thought. *Very excellent strike.*

Sino's insides palpitated with exciting energy. Finally, he had succeeded in making Lord Taboon fall short of the king's accolade. He laughed raucously inside him. It was all he could do to keep himself from laughing out loud.

"Lord Taboon?" Henok asked. "Is there a problem?"

Lord Taboon startled as if he had just come out of a trance.

"No, my king," Lord Taboon replied. "There is none. Absolutely none."

"Then why can you not answer my question?"

"Yes, my king."

"Well then, which is it? Can the orcs be trusted?"

"I mean, yes, my king. What Sinto said about the orcs' frail, and distrustful allegiance to their employers is true."

"Hmmm," Henok said and pressed his lips into a hard line. "We cannot risk using them. This is of the utmost importance. What do you suggest we do?" Henok gazed at Sinto.

Yes! Sinto thought in a flush of pride. "I suggest, my king, that you send a squad or two of the warriors of the kingdom. The elite among them. Those you can trust to do what is needful, and to return with the girl, safe, and alive to finalise the ritual."

All of a sudden, a tinkling sound grew out of the silence. Lord Taboon cast his gaze upwards, to the source of the sound, and noticed that the palace chandelier was trembling. Henok turned to the sound of scraping beside him and found his crown jittering on its marbled armrest. He looked up to where Sinto and Lord Taboon stared, and they exchanged confused glares.

Within two heartbeats, they felt the vibration in the ground. It started like little tickling movements, and then began to grow, and increase, becoming violent, until the ground itself heaved and jumped. Sinto and Lord Taboon were flung to the ground, while Henok steadied himself, by gripping the armrests of his throne till his knuckles turned white. Veins bulged out of his neck, he clamped his teeth together till they were bared; all from the effort.

"Earthquake!" Sinto yelled.

The doors of the palace flew open, as the palace guards ran in, skipping skilfully, the cracks that were spreading through the ground.

All Lord Taboon heard was a metallic chink from above, and he rolled out of the way in time to avoid being crushed by the chandelier. There was a loud crash as the chandelier burst into a million particles of glass.

"Get the King to safety!" Sinto roared immediately.

The guards had barely scaled the pedestal to where the king sat on his throne when everywhere quietened abruptly. It was almost like it had been snuffed out, in one moment.

Henok's eyes were wide with horror. "It has come. The end of days is finally upon us." The King was saying. "Sinto, by my order, you have the elite warriors of the Middle Kingdom. Capture the girl and return her. I do not need to remind you how crucial this is."

Sinto nodded, as Henok faced Lord Taboon.

"You know what to do." He told him.

Lord Taboon smiled and nodded.

"Of course, my king." He said.

As Henok left the throne room accompanied by the palace guards, the enormity of the potential the quake held, brought his mind into the full glare of what he had to do. Not even his wrongfully developed affection for Eldana was going to stop him this

Chapter Thirteen

time. Not sacrificing Eldana, meant, without a doubt, that the world would end. And that was something he could not stand for. Never.

"Nice game," Lord Taboon said when the king had been successfully escorted to safety.

They were just outside the palace doors, at the platform before the stairs that was now riddled with cracks.

"I had no idea we were playing a game," Sinto said, giving Lord Taboon an innocent look.

Lord Taboon laughed, looked at Sinto like he was weighing him up, then laughed again. Sinto simply smiled and stared into the distance.

"True, true." He said finally. "There was no game at all. I am finally glad that you were able to see beyond your affections for the girl."

Sinto grunted and said, "I told you duty always comes first for me."

"Until now, I always doubted you when you said that," Lord Taboon said.

"Do you not think that there is a reason why I have remained the master teacher of the being of Balance and Chaos throughout time?"

Lord Taboon nodded his understanding. "I guess I was too bothered on seeing you take immediate action, I did not view things retrospectively."

"Well, while we stand there trying to get along, Eldana is speeding towards the unknown." Sinto pointed out.

"You do know that we have to work together for this to end quickly, right? Things have grown too contumacious for one person to handle."

"I thought that was what the whole point of this minute get-to-know-each-other was about?"

Lord Taboon laughed, "Well, off I go to go do my thing as the king mandated."

Sinto nodded his assent.

"I guess we will meet soon, then," Lord Taboon said.

"Soon." Sinto agreed, and leaped off the stairs, landing on a crouch at the very end. The runes on his robe were beginning to glow.

Time to save the world, Sinto thought.

CHAPTER FOURTEEN

Consequences

Consequences

The sea raged. Its waves rising in hilly turbulence. The ship was tossed about like a fallen branch, each wave protruding from the water like an appendage, and striking it with another waiting wave. The sky was carpeted with clouds of intense density. Thunder roared treacherously. Lightning crackled, splitting the air.

The turbulence had swept Eldana and her friends off their feet, leaving them clinging to the ship's starboard and port, to prevent from them being thrown overboard.

"I cannot control it!" Siem shouted through the din. "It is too strong."

The storm had come upon them like a thief. One moment, their day was going well. And then the next moment the sun, and the sky above was swallowed mercilessly by thick, ominous black clouds. Sooner than they had time to think about going closer to land, the sea began to broil under the command of the savage wind. Eldana had tried to dispel the storm, by defusing the concentration of the clouds. She strained against the strength of the storm until her strength waned. Mikko tried, as did Siem. But the storm was too strong. So far the journey had been smooth sailing up to this point, with the serenity of the sea laid out before them. It was frightening and shocking to the whole crew to see how something so peaceful and calm could turn into a raging, murderous storm the very next.

"Who is doing this?" Hermon cried.

"I do not know," Mikko replied. "But this is no magician's work. No one can be this strong."

The boat lurched violently to the side as a wave knocked against it. Just then, another wave rose from underneath the boat taking her high into the air. For a few instants, the hands of the people on board were the only body parts in contact with the ship as they scrabbled for railings and ropes. The rest of their bodies floated in the air, as the ship hurtled towards the surface of the sea. The impact of the crash knocked their bodies hard, back down against the deck violently.

Chapter Fourteen

Hermon's hands slipped off the starboard, and he began to slide across the deck. Quickly, Eldana reached out with one hand and manipulated the air to form an immobile cocoon around Hermon.

Hermon's motion stopped abruptly. Very gently, Eldana pulled herself across the floor while she winced in pain. Holding herself with one hand amidst the ship's tossing was beginning to hurt her muscles.

As Hermon neared the starboard, he reached out with both hands and grabbed the ledge. Eldana, whose fingers were beginning to slip, quickly put her now free hand back and sighed.

"Bring it on!!" D'rmas roared. There was a maniacal smile on his face like he wanted to face death and was not afraid to wrestle with it.

Eldana shut her eyes. And thought that she could hear voices in the wind. She strained her hearing, trying to pierce through the wind's howl and the sea's splashing.

She heard them again. This time clearer. There were two of them, speaking calmly. But Eldana could tell that the composure of calmness was just a charade. She could feel the riotous rage crackling under the voices, like a huge pit of rattlesnakes rattling at once.

"Girl." One of the voices called. "Open your eyes. Look at what you have done."

"Yes." Another voice said this one was soft, and lighter, belonging to a woman. "Look at what you have done!"

Eldana did not need an introduction, whether formal or informal, to bring to her knowledge the identity of the voices in the wind.

"Camin! Lowus!" she yelled into the storm.

Her friends flashed a concerned look at her but said nothing.

"So impetuous." Lowus scolded. "Look what that did to you. You fled your responsibility, without thinking. And for what? Your selfishness. You could not think of the consequences. Now, it stares back at you!"

Consequences

Eldana was the only one who could hear them. It was the first time this was happening to her, and with it came the consciousness of a practice that had lasted thousands of years. She had the memory of all the girls that had been sacrificed, and she intended to end it. They could find her if they wanted, but she had to be sacrificed as a show of all creations' subservience to their rule. Eldana did not buy into that.

"If you are not here to save, then I think you should be on your merry way back to the depth of the skies. I have the fate of the world to rectify," Eldana cried out into the face of the storm.

There was a chuckle, low like the grumble of thunder.

"You think you are trying to save the world?" Camin asked.

"Yes," Eldana answered defiantly. "What have you both done for this world, other than take the lives of innocent girls for your power craze? I am trying to do what both of you have never done!"

"You think you are saving the world? By running away from the one sacrifice you can make with your power to save it? What good has that done you so far? Or the world, most importantly?"

"I am doing something," Eldana growled.

"And yet the people you are trying to save are dying in large numbers. What better way is there to define selfishness and stupidity?" The spirit of the god-thing chided and jeered at her.

"You do not even know that what you are embarking on will work," Lowus said.

"I know it will," Eldana replied. "And my friends know it too."

"Your friends will die, just as you will, foolish girl," Camin said.

Almost as suddenly as it came, Eldana began to feel the wind lessen. The presence of Camin and Lowus disappeared with it. The sea that had only moments before churned, like there was a huge cauldron of fire underneath it, gyrated with gentle ripples. The ship rocked slowly with the ripples.

Siem, let her hand fall from the ledge of the starboard and sighed with relief. Relief, at the moment, was an emotion that all of them shared without question. The sea settled, and the ship was intact – a condition that owed to the spell of protection that the

Chapter Fourteen

elves had cast upon it – as well as its ability to chart its own course. Then it moved, gathering speed as it sailed. Siem crawled to where Eldana sat, as soon as she had collected herself.

"Hey, how are you doing?" she asked.

Eldana looked up at her.

"Fine." She replied. "You?"

"I have seen worse," Siem said.

Eldana gave her an inquisitive stare. "Are you sure about that?"

Siem chuckled. "No."

Still staring at Eldana, she asked: "What was that about?"

"What?" Eldana asked.

"You were talking to someone during the storm. I was scared. I had thought that you had been struck with madness, and wanted to rush to your side, to restrain you if it came to it. But if I had let my hands off the ship, I would have gone overboard."

Siem's hands were on her friend's shoulder as she looked Eldana over.

"I am grateful you did not," Eldana said. "Or I would have lost a friend to those arrogant gods."

Siem's eyes widened.

"You mean, they talk to you?" she asked. "Camin and Lowus?"

"Yes," Eldana said, nodding for emphasis.

"Who did you talk to?"

Eldana and Siem turned to find Mikko standing above them in the company of Hermon, and D'rmas.

"Please, Mikko", Siem pleaded, "I am not sure that now is the time."

"It is okay," Eldana said, placing a hand on her shoulder. "They should know. Their lives are on the line just as yours and mine are."

Eldana looked up at them all with a deep sigh before relating what she had heard. "During the storm, I was visited by the gods." She said.

Mikko's mouth parted.

"The gods?" D'rmas questioned. "You mean…"

"Camin and Lowus, yes," Eldana said.

"This is serious, Eldana." Hermon said. "Very serious."

"Yeah," Eldana said. "You do not get to be meat for the gods and escape their throats too easily."

D'rmas sighed.

"And I should say this. To all of you. Irrespective of how long we have known each other." Eldana looked intently at Hermon and Siem while saying this. "Camin and Lowus said that if I continued on this path, I would die, and so will the rest of you" she looked intently at Siem, and Hermon, "and you have both become like, parts of my own body, that I cannot lose. I have known you, D'rmas and Mikko, since the Middle Kingdom a few months ago, and you have stuck to this mission even to your peril. But now, I must say that I cannot have any of your blood on my hands."

"What are you saying, Eldana?" Hermon asked.

"I am saying," Eldana said letting her eyes go from one to the other, "that I have to do this alone. I cannot let any of you die for my sake. I am getting to the close of all of this. I can feel it deep in my bones."

The sound of Siem's laughter followed as soon as Eldana was done with her address. The sound of the laughter grew and grew until it became a guffaw. Siem heaved spasmodically, and placed a hand to her stomach, to soothe it from aching.

Eldana watched helplessly, and so did the rest of them. Although Hermon and Mikko did have the suspicion of amusement on their faces. Finally, after it had looked like she would never stop, Siem sighed audibly and looked at Eldana.

"How much of a fool can you be?" she asked her.

Eldana stared.

Siem turned to face the others. "D'rmas." She called. "Were you forced to come along with us?"

"Certainly not." He replied. "I came along at the promise of payment when my contract was complete. Even though I knew that this looked like a fool's cause and that I would likely not be getting any payment from it at all!"

Chapter Fourteen

At the mention of his not getting any payment, Hermon perked up.

"I cannot renege on my word, D'rmas." He said, earnestness and confidence creeping on to his face. "I am a berserker of the royal five. You will get your payment."

Mikko was so flushed with amusement, he could barely withhold his chuckle.

"Oh, serious and mighty, a man of his inexorable word. What D'rmas, our good friend here is trying to say is that he does not need a contract. He works with us now, as a friend. Do I reflect your thoughts, D'rmas?" Mikko looked at the Free Warrior.

D'rmas grunted in affirmation and nodded.

"See?" Mikko said.

"Ah," Hermon said, flushing with embarrassment.

"I did not know that," Siem said. "Are you seeing this, Eldana? He willingly chose to come along, even though he knew this was a fool's cause."

She turned to Mikko. "And did anyone force you, Mikko?" she asked.

Mikko wanted to tell her that he had come along with them because of her, and was still in it, well partly, because of her. But he shook his head in the negative instead.

Now is not the time, he thought.

Siem faced Eldana. "And this is after he had been taken by the elves for being with us."

She turned back. "I should ask Hermon." She said, "but that would also mean asking myself. Since we three have been together for such a long time."

Eldana had long since gotten the purpose of the lecture and was feeling embarrassed about what she had said.

Siem faced her finally. "None of us are children, Eldana. You did not twist our ears till we cried and force us to come with you. We chose this. Do you hear it? *We.*"

Siem and Eldana exchanged stares in silence until Eldana looked away. "Now, I do not want to hear another word from you about this. We have a being of Balance and Chaos to meet."

Eldana smiled awkwardly, her embarrassment clear on her face. "Come here," Siem said, widening her arms for an embrace.

Eldana walked into it and buried her face deep in Siem's shoulders. Hermon, touched by the show of fidelity, went in and encircled both of them in his wide arms.

Mikko was about to join in the group hug when D'rmas placed a restraining hand on his arm. Mikko faced him, and Hermon nodded in the negative. Mikko fell back in place beside D'rmas.

"Erm, guys," Mikko called, the tone of alarm creeping into his voice. "I think we are…"

The ship lurched violently, throwing everybody to the side. Even Eldana, Siem, and Hermon, who were tangled in a hug, were broken apart.

Eldana groaned as her shoulder ached from the impact of her fall. She flexed it as she sat up, and then asked:

"What was that? Another storm?"

"Right now, I do not know if I would prefer the storm to this," Siem said.

Eldana followed the direction of Siem's gaze, and then caught sight of the company of two ships heading with unbelievable speed towards them. A sudden spume of water burst from the calm sea's off their port bow.

"They're shooting cannonballs at us!" D'rmas observed, before running for the steering wheel.

"Do you know how to do that!?" Mikko cried in alarm.

"Fear not, Mikko. You will not be swimming today. Not yet."

"Do you know how to pilot a ship?" Eldana asked.

"A little." the Free Warrior gruffly shouted back.

The rest of the company looked at each other unanimously in surprise.

"You could, and you did not say anything?" Siem asked. "Even when we almost died?"

D'rmas turned back to them. "First, we did not die. Second, I am familiar with the rubrics of piloting a ship! I do not know how

Chapter Fourteen

to ride one professionally or steer efficiently out of a storm. But the occasion calls for desperate measures, and I am taking one."

He turned and drew back a lever a little off the bottom left of the wheel. The lever controlled the steering of the ship between a physical manning, and the basic manning of the ship, where the ship steered itself. There was a grumbling sound within the ship, the only mechanical and rugged sound from a vessel which was sleek and tall, with the head of a swan as its prow.

"Now, get yourselves busy," he said, as the ship lurched forward, beginning to pick up speed as they felt her slice through the waves.

Eldana, Siem, and Mikko turned towards the pursuing ships, and devoted their attention, in magic and strategy, to them. Mikko manipulated the water to try and parry the cannonballs from the air. With magic, raised an energy wall that should protect them from further damage. Siem went into attack mode and started to whisper magical power into her arrows. Though not as powerful over sea, demon arrows still could create damage. She decided to hit the bigger of the two boats. The arrow slit through the water like a knife through butter, but it never reached the destination. They had their own protection shield. Even the second or the third demon arrow never went through.

"They have powerful mages on board. I can tell you that." Siem was saying, more to herself than anyone.

While all of them were on the offensive, Hermon just paced the ship, helpless, and furious at having to do nothing.

Suddenly, Eldana felt a sharp spike of pain in her ribs. She screamed and fell to her side. Siem abandoned the attack before her and stooped.

"What is the matter?" Siem asked, concern flooding her face.

"I do not know." Eldana cried, turning, and clutching at her ribs. "I do not know."

Mikko turned. "What is the problem?" he asked, still using his hands to wave tentacles of water wildly in the air.

"Mikko!" Hermon cried, pointing forward.

Consequences

Mikko turned just in time to intercept a cannonball that was heading directly towards them. Mikko did not turn back anymore. He focused on the ships, who were now closer than before.

"D'rmas faster," Hermon yelled. "They are gaining on us!"

Siem looked out at the pursuing ships. She could spot both a company of battle-eager orcs on the decks, as well as a company of the elite warriors of the Middle.

"Not now." She moaned, turning to face Eldana who was still crying. "Where does it hurt?" she asked her.

"It burns. It burns." Eldana cried.

"Where?" Siem asked. "Tell me, Eldana. Try. I need to do something."

Just then, one of the cannonballs, slammed into the hull of a ship, smashing a gaping hole right through the hull.

"I do not know." Mikko said, fear beginning to creep into his voice, "just what these balls are made of, but they are trumping any protection spells!"

"Mikko, watch out," Hermon cried out again.

Mikko stared, rooted to the spot as a cannonball hurtled directly towards him.

Hermon dashed across the deck to him, and diving, pushed him out of the way of the incoming shot. The ball smashed a hole in the deck where Mikko had been standing.

The ship lurched forward, pushing Siem onto Eldana's body. D'rmas turned and found that the pursuing ships had caught up with them. The ships behind were faster and were closing in. From fifty feet away, they had inched closer to six feet behind them, almost touching...

"They are here! They are on us!" the Free Warrior warned.

The first orc that jumped on to the board got a dagger to his forehead. He fell backwards into the waves without even making a sound.

Siem looked at the influx of orcs and soldiers and knew this was one attack they were less likely to hold off.

"Mikko.!" She called, getting to her feet.

Chapter Fourteen

Mikko ran to her.

"The Princess! Take her away from here!" Siem cried out.

"To where?" Mikko asked.

"To Piece Island." Siem gasped as she fired one arrow into the throat of one boarding orc, then another, and another.

"That is going to be difficult. Extremely difficult. And we do not have the time for that nor can I jump that far."

An orc roared as it stepped on board.

"Do it. I will give you time. Just jump from horizon to horizon." Siem said.

Mikko nodded. Stooping, he hovered his hand over Eldana's writhing body and began to cast a spell. Siem stood in front, protecting Mikko and Eldana, and nocked another arrow.

"Come on!" She yelled at the orcs.

D'rmas was already engaged with a few of the Middle Kingdom warriors. They had come with the orcs and the ship was in disarray. They moved about, trading blows and evasive manoeuvres with alarming speed. An orc dashed towards where Siem stood, and she shot an arrow straight through his head and expertly notched another. While she attacked Siem changed into a living fireball and killed another orc by burning his flesh from his face.

Hermon began to scream in pain. Blood streamed down fresh cuts appearing over his body as he began to transform.

Suddenly, a mage in a dark hooded robe, and a staff in hand, jumped onto the ship and stood in front of him. Shouting words of forbidden magic, he slammed Hermon with a wave of energy. Hermon flew backward and crashed on the floor and screamed as his body began to shrink back to its normal size.

"Boy!" the man in the dark robe yelled. He climbed onboard and pulled down his hood. Lord Taboon stood with daring confidence on board Eldana's ship, a victorious smile on his face.

"Mikko! I see you, you ungrateful little bastard!" Lord Taboon snarled.

"Continue," Siem said to him, barely turning back. She whispered a strengthening spell on her arrow and sent it flying towards

Consequences

Lord Taboon. Just then, another man jumped in front of him, plucking the arrow from thin air.

Siem stared wide-eyed as Sinto stared back at her, pinching the arrow between his fingers. They came prepared.

"Where is she? The Princess!" Sinto demanded.

"You cannot have her," Siem said, standing over Eldana's form, and sheltering the mumbling, incanting Mikko.

"I do not see how you are going to ensure that," Sinto said.

"Look around you. You are grossly outnumbered." Lord Taboon said. "You are an excellent mage, Siem, but not even you can stand against two master mages, as well as our elite warriors of the Middle, and our orcish allies, too."

"Try me," Siem growled back, her eyes steely.

"You just have to hand the girl over." Lord Taboon said. "We have no wish to harm you."

Siem smiled. "Who said anything about you harming me?" she asked.

"I gave you a chance," Lord Taboon said.

Lord Taboon and Sinto sprinted forward at the same time. It was like they shared one mind.

"Now, Mikko, get her away!" Siem screamed and exploded in a ball of fire.

Mikko yelled and with all his energy disappeared with Eldana in a flash of light.

CHAPTER FIFTEEN

Shewit, the Life of the First

The Middle Kingdom

There was no one person more integral to the continuation of Toas existence than the being of Balance and Chaos. Since their birth of time, each being of Balance and Chaos had through their ultimate sacrifice ensured that the doors of chaos were kept firmly shut, so the legend goes.

But one thing most people did not know was that the birth of a being of Balance and Chaos was as much a thing of sorrow and pain as it was a thing of joy. Of course, the majority of the people in the cities that made up Toas would rejoice and jubilate. Their messiah, the means to their continued existence had just been brought into the world. They were once again safe. Their future was safe. But if they would pause and listen attentively, they would pick out the cries of pain and sorrow. They would know that the being of Balance and Chaos were not children plucked out of trees – indeed, that they belonged to parents, and had siblings, families...

It was with such pain that a peasant farmer and his wife gave out their newly born daughter. The people who would oversee the training of the girl stood outside their farmhouse, waiting, their faces devoid of any trace of emotion. The father's eyes were moist with tears. The mother held her baby and wept uncontrollably, as she stepped out of the house to meet the people who would take her away. But they were both helpless. Everyone that had visited them the night before had made them see that. Other families had let a child go for the good of the entire world. Why could they not do the same? To refuse their child to fulfil her destiny was to go against the whole world. They had no choice but to give in and do what was right. It had never happened like this before; beings of both Balance and Chaos were usually of royal blood, but when he found the mark of chaos on the child's body, the peasant knew it was only a matter of time.

Their leader, a strong stout man stepped out from the rest of the group.

"You put her to sleep using what I showed you?' the leader asked.

Chapter Fifteen

"Yes," the man replied.

"Good," the leader replied. "She should sleep peacefully throughout the length of the journey."

The father narrowed his eyes. An idea had just come to him; an idea that would assure him that his girl was going to be properly taken care of.

"What is your name, sir?" the father of the being of Balance and Chaos asked.

The leader of the group stared at the father for a while before he replied:

"Lull. My name is Lull."

The father stepped forward so he could stare Lull clearly in the eyes.

"Promise me," the man said. "as one man to another man, that you will take care of my daughter."

Lull sighed.

"We take care of all the being of Balance and Chaos," he replied. "We're employed for this very purpose, to see the growth and happiness of them. Why else do you think they live in the King's palace? They stay there to receive everything they could ever ask for. All the care they need, no matter how minute, we supply them. It is the small price we pay for their ultimate sacrifice."

The father and Lull stared into each other's eyes for some three seconds before they broke eye contact. The father went back to his wife's side to console her.

And then placing a firm supporting hand on her shoulder, he walked with her as she moved towards Lull. As she neared him, Lull rose both his hands a bit in the air. They stopped somewhere close to his chest, upturned, with the palms facing upward and the back of his hand facing downwards. And then the child's mother placed the baby in Lull's arms.

"Shewit," she told Lull.

"What?" Lull asked, looking puzzled.

The mother sniffed.

"I said Shewit," she repeated. "Her name, the name of the child is Shewit."

Lull stared at her, and the woman stared back. Lull could see the fire in her eyes, and he knew that this woman was ready to brave almost anything for her child.

'Fine," he replied. "Shewit is her name. The whole of Toas lies at your feet today for this sacrifice you have made for the kingdom. We will never forget you."

Such is the way of things, Lull thought; the way of necessity.

As the men drove away with their Shewit, it dawned heavily on the couple that they would not be seeing their daughter ever again.

The woman turned her face, buried it into her husband's chest, and cried. Her husband simply stared ahead, watching the company of horsemen as they carried on down the road, growing into tiny dots until they disappeared once and for all. He sighed and bent down to kiss the top of his wife's head. He did not tell her it was okay. Because in truth, it was not. He felt just as bad without the tears. Their only hope at having a semblance of peace was in each other.

Now the being of Balance and Chaos had come into the palace, everyone set making sure that everything was okay for her stay in the palace. She was their savior after all and deserved to be given all the adoration and the worship before the event that would shape the entire kingdom, and even that was years ahead from now.

The moment Lull brought Shewit into the palace, even before he had mentioned her name, Lady Adiam, the woman in charge of the child's housekeeping, sensed that this being of Balance and Chaos was going to be a different child. When she had whispered it to the other ladies in attendance:

"I've got a feeling this one is going to be different from the others."

"Why?" one of them asked. "Because it is Lull who carries her himself and not one of his men?"

Chapter Fifteen

Lady Adiam snorted. "You have not lived as long as I have," she said. "Or you would know the carrier of the child handles the babies only if collection is more difficult."

"You mean those whose parents refuse to give them up?"

"No," Adiam replied, rolling her eyes, "it's not that. In all my years as housemistress, I have never heard of parents who have refused their children the chance to be a hero of Toas. Usually, it is seen as a great honor. But some never wanted that for their child, those who are giving them up will be emotionally difficult. The carrier of the child intervenes for those. Somehow, his presence should make letting the child go, a little easier."

"Okay," the others agreed. "But why did you say this one is different?"

"She is not crying," Adiam replied shrewdly.

Just then, Lull explained to the king (who had been curious about the child's silence) that the baby had been given a sleeping drug to prevent her cries from getting to the parents and making an already difficult situation worse.

The ladies in attendance turned and giggled at Adiam. There was a more tangible reason as to why the baby had kept mum all the while. This was much better than her unjustifiable hunch that the child was different. But even then, Adiam felt it within her bones that the girl, soporifics or no, was different.

It did not take long for her hunch to become a reality. Everyone began to see the difference as Shewit grew. In retrospect, the beings of Balance and Chaos that had graced the court before had always been exuberantly joyful and playful girls. These behaviours stood to change as they grew older, but in their younger years, they would always constitute most of the noise in the palace, squealing and running about, taking their caretakers through a lot of trouble, while also reminding them the joy of what it felt to be young and free.

But not Shewit.

Shewit was quiet and reclusive, choosing to keep things to herself no matter how weighty than to confide in another soul. It was easier to get words out of her mouth during training, and that was either because the specific moves she wanted to make required spells, or her teachers had asked her a question. Her quietness made it difficult for her caretakers to give her fitting care. Lady Adiam three hundred years of age allowed her to see three other beings she had taken care of, each one expressing what they liked or disliked, moaning, laughing, or complaining – but not so with Shewit, who would move through her care passively.

Shewit was as unusual in the control of her powers as she was in her demeanor. Lull and the rest of the teachers noticed a special ability in the young being of Balance and Chaos: her ability to retain instructions, skills, and utilize them as if she had been practicing magic for eons.

This quality saw her advance through training quicker than the previous sacrifices, and this uncanny ability of hers to retain and internalize instructions was first noticed when Lull taught her how to control the element of air. In the past, it was usual for Lull to hit a temporary dead-end when it came to teaching the being of Balance and Chaos this particular skill. Controlling the elements was always very tricky.

Being elements of nature, they stood on their own and could be accessed both as a battle magic and an ordinary magic. Accessing the elements through ordinary magic was way less effective than when they were accessed under the guise of battle magic. And it was in teaching this balance, and the poise required to control the elements in the desired way that made it at first difficult. So, Lull had taken to introducing them to this skill first of all, then leaving it out, and taking the being of Balance and Chaos through a different skill. The motive being, that in the course of the little detour, the level of confusion would have subsided enough for him to hit back at the subject later. For ordinary magic was easier to tap into, such as making food, making beautiful glows on air, while battle magic came from strong emotions like anger and was harder to control. Most times, warriors leaned too much into battle magic to forgot how to make ordinary magic.

Chapter Fifteen

Shewit had walked into the training square, her demeanor as still and quiet as usual. Upon getting to Lull, she had bowed and said:

"Greetings, Lull."

"Greetings," Lull replied. "I take it you have had a splendid rest, yes?"

"Yes," she replied.

A few of Lull's men trained farther away to her left and right, in training grounds annexed to hers. Once in a while, she would hear the noise of magic being worked, and feel a slight thrill go through her body.

"For today's lesson," Lull started, "I would be teaching you how to control the element of air. Like we established during your theoretical teachings, there are generally two types of magic," he looked at Shewit, indicating that she complete his sentence.

"Ordinary and battle," Shewit replied.

"Good," Lull said, giving a satisfied nod. "And you also know that there are other groups of magic that exist, more special in forms than the general classifications, yes?"

"Yes," Shewit said.

"In what class of magic would you put the control of air?" Lull asked.

"Elemental or Nature magic."

"Good. Now, I want you to observe. The air in this room is free and soft, almost unnoticeable, and difficult to catch unless you are paying extra attention to detail. An ordinary magic-user can reduce the flow of air, or increase it. That's about the extent of control an ordinary magic-user has over nature magic. However, as the being of Balance and Chaos, or any other magician with access to battle magic, like me, we have the power to not only increase and decrease the flow but to shape the air, to weaponize it. You can control the air, for instance, into a club, a blade, depending on how good you are at precision. You can manipulate the air into shielding you from attacks. Some of us with access to battle magic use it as a shield, while sometimes you can also conjure a ball of energy to perform the same function. All that is needed here is your strength of will, imagination, and precision, and the elements are yours. When saying the spell, you have to feed your intent, the shape from your mind into it, and then you will have the shape of your desire.'

"Do you understand me?" he asked Shewit.

"Yes, Lull. I do."

"Now watch," he said.

Growing a little tense, Lull turned to the side and flayed his hands in the air. His movements were slow, deliberate. They would not be this way on a battlefield except if he was keen on dying. But here, he wanted Shewit to see his moves, every little thing that occurred before he made the magic work. He conjured the image he wanted in his mind, and then he spoke the magic words:

"*Nefas qetin!*"

At first, Shewit did not see anything, but then she noticed the rush of air increase around her, and then she saw it: a funnel of air hovering a little above Lull's palm, almost invisible but for the flurry of its movement.

"See?" Lull told her.

Shewit nodded, her eyes wide with amazement. Lull watched her, a little girl, hair and eyes black as the night, smiling for the first time. She looked diminutive for the kind of power she possessed, still, she seemed to love training.

"Now, you try," Lull said, releasing the funnel of air for it to dissipate at once.

Lull watched her get into position and began to prepare a comforting speech in his mind which he would use to placate the girl when she failed to shape the air around her. He already had the next lesson he would take her through to lessen the sting of her failure. Nothing had ever prepared him for what happened next.

Shewit had listened to everything that he had said, she had seen his moves, and more than that, she had seen through them as he worked the magic. She had felt the focus of his thoughts, and the way they had flowed with his moves, and how they had connected

Chapter Fifteen

with the spell and then formed the shape of his imagination. She understood that all she needed was the focus, and that had never been a problem for her.

Widening her legs so she could achieve a more stable stance, she flayed her hands in the air, just as Lull had done a moment before. She conjured up an image of what she wanted, she stayed on it, willed it to occupy most of her mind, to flow from her mind, through her, and into reality, and then she said the words:

"*Nefas qetin.*"

Nothing had happened at first. But that was just a second's delay as Shewit began to feel the rush of the air around her. Shewit continued to feed her intentions through the power of the spell until the shape was just as firm and sure as that which Lull had conjured. She turned to find Lull staring at the shape of air with an open mouth.

This was the first time since Lull picked up the career of training the beings of Balance and Chaos that one of them had successfully controlled air in their first ever try. Even the other mages who were training in the areas close by were drawn to the extraordinary feat and could only stare in wide-eyed wonder. Shewit saw the stares, the wonder in them, and she smiled. This was one of those rare moments when she did something other than preserving an air of utter seriousness.

From then on, Lull went all out in teaching the young being of Balance and Chaos the full extent of her powers. The faster she could learn meant the sooner she got to make the sacrifice.

But then, of course, Shewit fell in love.

He was a mage in the making, and a student apprenticed to one of the high mages in the School of Magic. Apprentices were not usually called upon to teach a being of Balance and Chaos unless, as in this case, the apprentice was exceptionally good at something. His name was Ermias, and with two years left to becoming a proper mage, he was already exceptionally good at Spell Studies. It was apparent that he had become more knowledgeable than his master mage, but appearances had to be kept for the sake of hierarchy. And so it was that when Shewit needed a spell master to help in her usage of the more formalized spells, Ermias was recommended as the best there was.

At first, Shewit had disliked him. He was too simple and rough in appearance. From his slim frame, his mop of curly brown hair, to his gentle demeanor, nothing about him radiated authority and expertise compared to the rest of her teachers. So she had started out being unresponsive, and even when she worked herself to give him a response, it was always cold. Normally, behaviors like this were to be reported to the headteacher – Lull. Shewit knew this and she expected it. However, to her surprise, Ermias kept coming back day after day, teaching her nonetheless; Lull had not come to her to complain about anything between the two of them. It only meant that Ermias had kept her little mannerisms to himself. Where others would have given up, Ermias still stuck to her, teaching her with the same fervour as though she were indeed interested in what he was teaching.

So she began to pay attention; too much attention perhaps, as she didn't even realize when she started to develop feelings for the man.

A relationship of this kind; a being of Balance and Chaos and her teacher, had never been heard before. And as such, it was easy for them to surmise that it would be frowned upon. They were able to keep in touch under the cover of spell lessons. Everything had gone so smoothly until Ermias made a special discovery one day during his studies.

"You seem to be in trouble," she said, studying him.

"Me?" Ermias said, looking at her, and then looking away immediately. "It is nothing," he replied, and as if forgetting that he had added it, attached a smile to convince her. "It is just a case of bad food. Nothing that cannot be fixed."

"You forget that I can read minds," Shewit said, her face grow-

Chapter Fifteen

ing serious. "Do not make me read the words out of you."

Ermias stared at her. He knew she was serious. Shewit never gave threats. She issued warnings which she would go ahead to take actions if the warnings were ignored. Also, for someone who kept a lot to herself, she disliked it when Ermias tried to do the same.

"Fine," Ermias said. "The problem is, is that I do not think you are ready for what I am about to tell you."

Shewit stared intently at him until he grew uneasy and said: "Okay, okay. I will say it."

He had gotten the message. Shewit was not flinching. She was never one to shy away from things no matter how extremely daunting they appeared to be.

"I was going through some ancient texts," Ermias began, "which revealed knowledge about certain spells while taking the reader on a trip down the history behind the spells. They were a bit confusing at first, and so, it took me more hours of intense study to finally understand them. In the end, I not only grasped the knowledge of very valuable spells. I also found a way for you to avoid offering your life."

He had finished the statement with a smile, but the stunned look on Shewit's face wiped it off. He knew he had done something awfully and regrettably wrong even before she asked the question.

"What do you mean by offering my life?" Shewit asked.

Ermias looked at her with an uneasy expression on his face and said:

"Take it easy, Shewit. Let me explain."

"What do you mean by offering my life, Ermias?" Shewit demanded, fixated.

Ermias began to stutter. He was caught between the suddenness of the realization that Shewit did not know the details of her role and trying to break the news to her – because obviously, she was meant to know but a lot later when she was ready to receive the message.

Frustrated and tired by Ermias's inability to give her a response, Shewit threw restraint to the wind and plunged into his mind. She saw it all: everything that Ermias knew and was trying to properly organize so he could tell her, what her role meant, and what her life meant to all the lands and kingdoms of Toas.

Ermias fell to the floor at the impact of Shewit's mind. Shewit did not know what to make of the discovery. She was furious. She was sad. But she was also scared.

"You knew this the entire time?" she said, turning to look at Ermias, fury glowing red on her face. "You knew all this time, and you pretended to love me!?"

Ermias tried to speak, but Shewit had choked him using her control of the air. Ermias opened his mouth and shut it as he searched for air. The only noise he could make as he stared pleadingly at Shewit was a croaking sound as his throat drew in nothing. Shewit stared at him, her lips trembled, and tears covered her eyes. And then, abruptly, she let go her of magical hold on him. Ermias rolled onto his side, gasping for air and coughing. Shewit flicked her eyes towards where he lay and began to sob.

"Shewit", he called, "I had no idea that you never knew this was the path your life was on. They probably would have told you in the future. Please, you have to believe me. That is why I took it upon myself to find a way out for you. A way in which you did not have to give your life for the peace of all, a way where we could be together. Please, look into my mind if you have to. Search my thoughts. You have my leave. You will see that I am not lying. I will never lie to you, Shewit." His lips trembled.

Shewit turned and stared at Ermias as she placed her palm to his face.

"Oh, Ermias," she cried, "I almost killed you. I cannot believe that I almost killed you!"

"It does not matter, Shewit," Ermias replied. "What matters is that you did not. You were infuriated, and I get that. I never knew that the being of Balance and Chaos made this sacrifice without the knowledge of what is involved."

Chapter Fifteen

They sat there, in silence, for minutes. Outside the room, the general notion was that the being of Balance and Chaos was getting prepared and better in her grasp of spells, and when she would emerge her vocabulary would be nothing short of incredible.

"I cannot believe that they have been training me so rigorously all this while just to offer me up like a sheep to the gods!" Shewit said breaking the silence.

Ermias changed his seating position.

"I had always thought when I familiarized myself with the being of Balance and Chaos and her destiny that it was odd that a group of select magically powerful and gifted children would give themselves up every hundred years when they still had so much to live for. But I had stifled the thought because I had thought that it was a thing of choice. I never knew that the sacrifice was an act of deceiving you," Ermias said, appalled.

"Now, I am beginning to understand all the deferential treatment I get in the palace. Sometimes the workers would look at me like I was a god, but disposable at the same time. They would go out of their way just to make me happy. And it irked me. The constant efforts, overacting, it was just too much, too glaring, and I did not like it. It all makes sense now. I am even sure Lull, who I have taken as a father knows about this."

"Do not be too sure," Ermias said.

"Oh, I am," Shewit replied hotly. "And I do not need to read his mind to know this. He cannot be the head trainer without being privy to this bit of knowledge."

All of a sudden, her countenance softened, and she turned to Ermias.

"I do not want to die, Ermias," she said. "Not like this. As you said, I have still got much to live for. *We* still have much to live for."

Ermias looked at her and smiled. The smile on his face was a welcome sight for Shewit, considering all the things that had just gone awry. But Ermias's smile was more than just a difference in the chain of bad events, it was a sign that there was hope.

"You know something, Ermias," Shewit said. "Spit it out. You know how I hate being baited."

"Fine, fine. Can we not have a go at playing a game of guessing?" Ermias asked himself.

Shewit chuckled, but sadly. "Someday," she said. "But not today."

Then Ermias told her about what he had surmised from his studies earlier before their encounter. Shewit listened aptly, and by the time Ermias was done, she felt hope. The path she had been walking all the while had only one end. But Ermias's theory charted a new course for not just her, but for both of them.

All they had to do now was plot an escape plan, and it had to be done quickly. Ermias had told her that the sacrifice was done when she was finally able to master the skill of giving and taking life. That was the last skill the being of Balance and Chaos needed to master, and it was the culmination of everything she had been learning since day one. It was already common knowledge that Shewit was a fast learner, and that she had advanced speedily through the training levels. At this rate, she would reach the day of the sacrifice very quickly. If she began to affect difficulty in comprehending her lessons so she could stall, her teachers would notice that something was strange. So, they decided on a prompt escape to any place that was out of the reach of the magicians. Ermias had told Shewit to leave the location to him. Shewit on the other hand was to focus on finding a way both of them could make a run for it.

And she found one.

The element of surprise was one of the oldest tactics in the book. Despite that, it never lost its efficiency. Keeping the teachers from knowing that she knew what was going to happen to her was a stroke of genius on both Shewit and Ermias's parts. And that was why when she slunk out during one of her habitual walks through the palace gardens, no one noticed until it was almost too late...

Lull had noticed that Shewit was late for her class, and was

Chapter Fifteen

surprised. It was highly unlike her to miss training. A visit to her chambers turned out fruitless. Lady Adiam had told him that Shewit was yet to return from her walk. It was not until one of the guards had told him that there had been an unusual working of magic at the gate that he realized what was going on.

Shewit was trying to escape. But he was confused as to why she wanted to.

Had she come to the knowledge of what awaited her at the fulfilment of her training regime? I should have told her but it was not time yet. The older man asked himself.

Lull did not have the time to link his thoughts together and settle on logical conclusions. The more time he spent doing that, the farther she got away. Mustering a squad of combat-trained mages, Lull went after Shewit as if his life depended on it.

Indeed, the future of all of Toas did.

Shewit wished that the horses would run faster. The plan had been simple, leave without being detected. But then they had come against unexpected resistance at the gate. One of the guards was being rather nasty. Shewit had worn a hood over her face to hide her features, and would have passed had the guard at the gate avoided harassing Ermias. It was something about a game they had played the night before, where Ermias had beaten the guard and won much as a result. But the guard was threatening to heap an accusation on him if he did not pay up, or worse, to stop them from going out. Ermias had cautioned her not to use her powers no matter what, and that if things became too difficult for both of them to maneuver, she should ditch him and leave. Ermias had insisted when he had instructed that she was all that mattered. But Shewit could not do that. So, she had intervened, and like Ermias warned, had attracted attention. Now, they had Lull and the rest of the teachers at their heels...

Shewit could not understand how Lull was catching up to

them so fast. She dug her spurs into the sides of her horse urging it to go faster. But this was also dangerous. The horses could not go on riding like this for too long or they would collapse from exhaustion. So Shewit turned and began to haul down trees to block the path and prevent Lull and his men from getting to them, or at least, getting to them in time.

She and Ermias exchanged looks, and they rode on. They were not going to lose each other. If they were fast enough, they would evade Lull and be free to be together and to live for the rest of their lives.

But all of a sudden, they crashed into an invisible wall and were plunged into the air. For moments, Shewit could not feel anything; even taking in breaths was difficult. Everything was dead silent, and then all of a sudden the world became alive again. She heard coughing to her side and turned to find Ermias on the ground. Their horses were nowhere to be found. They must have taken to their heels while she and Ermias were trying to get themselves on the ground.

"What just happened?" Ermias asked as he rose to his elbows.

Shewit could breathe better now and had opened her mouth to respond when someone else here provided the answer instead.

"*We* just happened."

The voice was too familiar that they knew whose it was before they even turned their faces. Lull, and a band of other mages stepped out of the trees to form a circle around them.

"Lull," Ermias uttered, sitting up.

Shewit just glared at him.

"One look at the both of you and it is easy to surmise whose idea this little escapade was," Lull said, staring hard at Shewit.

"But I'm curious," he continued. "Why now, Shewit? You've been in the palace all these years. You've been well taken care of. Everyone at the palace is at your beck and call, *yours*. You've never exhibited signs of erraticism until today. What was it?"

Shewit just stared back at him.

"Is it this puny apprentice?" Lull asked. "Did he somehow find

Chapter Fifteen

a way to wiggle into your mind? Perhaps mutter a few spells to put you under his control?"

"You very well know the answer to that, Lull," Shewit replied.

"If you had grown too familiar with the palace walls, and wanted to see beyond it, all you had to do was ask, and your wish would have been granted. We did not need to create all this drama."

Then he screwed up his face in a furious scowl.

"Unless," he said, "the being of Balance and Chaos got their hands on knowledge that is forbidden."

He stared at Ermias.

"Honestly, I must say, I did not know you had it in you," Lull growled. "Two years before being appointed a mage of the kingdom, and your skill is already widely sought. It must be frustrating for you, being so good, and still being relegated to the background. How you must hate your master taking all the credit for your accomplishments?"

Ermias stared silently at Lull. Lull, on the other hand, could see the fear already building in the young mage's eyes.

"So, you devised a means to place yourself as a true master, with the being of Balance and Chaos eating out of your hand. I must admit, that is genius on your part. A masterstroke. No one would have seen this coming."

"That is not true," Ermias protested.

"Enough, Lull," Shewit barked. "If you are here to take me back to the palace, you might as well have not come out at all. Because I am not going back."

Lull smiled. "Ah," he exclaimed. "He told you. And just what did the mage tell you?"

"That while you are lavishing me with care, you are fattening me up for slaughter," Shewit spat.

Lull chuckled. "And you think this power-hungry mage is telling you the entire truth? He is an apprentice, who had too much time, not more. The story is complex, Shewit. It is not only tapping into the power of Toas. This is what he told you, right?"

Shewit and Ermias stood there in shock. That was exactly what

Ermias found out. By tapping into the direct power of Toas she would have become a lot more powerful.

Lull read their emotional reaction correctly and kept going. "It is a lot more than that, my dear Shewit. Let me be your teacher and I show you." He smiled warmly.

"Well that, or I just find myself now," Shewit blurted and immediately stabbed her mind into Lull's.

The rest of the mages saw what was going on but did not react quickly enough. When they reacted, sending bolts of lightning streaking towards Shewit, she had already infiltrated Lull's mind.

Ermias rolled close to Shewit immediately and cast a shield spell.

"*Hasab totallus!*"

A sphere of energy materialized over them, encasing and shielding them off from the magic of the attacking mages. Lull gritted his teeth as he tried to fight off Shewit's presence in his mind. But she was the being of Balance and Chaos, and he could not do much against her. Not alone.

Ermias was no master of magic. He could conjure different magic with a vast assortment of spells, but seriously tired when it came to holding them up for a very long time; even now, when his life depended on it.

"Shewit!" he called. "You have to let him go. I do not know how much longer I can hold off the attacks."

Shewit still had her mind locked onto Lull's. And then she found something, so disturbing she could not understand if his mind was just hallucinating, or she saw the truth.

The moment made her weaker for a second. At that moment like bubbles of air bursting, the shield began to break. Shewit removed herself from Lull's mind to come to Ermias's aid, but not before he had been struck by a boulder of rock. The rock had been formed out of different stones levitated into the air, swirling round and round before finally fusing into one for the strike. All the mages were pouring the brunt of their magical strength on Shewit now. The motive was simple. Hit her with a massive as-

Chapter Fifteen

sault so that she spends all her strength on the defensive and when she tires out, it would be easy to bring her back to the palace.

Shewit risked a turn to look at Ermias on the ground beside her, bleeding from his mouth. She felt her heart break. "Do it," Ermias said, coughing as he spoke. "There is only one way you can set yourself free. Let go of everything, and draw your strength from the earth itself."

Shewit could feel the weight of the mages' assault pressing on her like a moving wall. She was forced down to her knees. She felt something touch her arm. It was Ermias. Tears began to drop from Shewit's eyes, if she was not defending from the mages' attacks, she could try to heal him.

"Let go," Ermias told her.

And she did. Seeing Ermias's life, about the only thing she had ever cared about in her life, slip away from her was the catalyst for all the powers she had kept within herself; all the doors she had chosen to leave locked and unexplored. The first lightning bolt hit her on her chest. All she felt was a blast of pain, and then she felt a massive surge of energy within her. It was not hers. The energy was old, stronger than anything she ever felt. She felt it envelop her, fill her to the very brim, and it was not even close to exhaustion yet.

Lull and the other mages stopped attacking for a second when Shewit began to glow like hot iron, only she did not glow red, she glowed bright yellow. Her eyeballs shone a radiant yellow, and her hair swam in the air as though they were alive.

"Attack!" Lull yelled. "Attack!"

The mages unleashed every magic they knew how to conjure to the extent of their strength and energy.

With one mighty scream, Shewit unleashed an arc of bright energy that radiated from her and washed through the mages, causing them to break and disintegrate. Done with her use of magic, the energy within her began to dissipate as she relinquished her connection to the earth. Then she turned and looked at Ermias's still body.

Shewit fell to her knees by his side and began to weep. He had given her the way out. She had finally let go and drawn her power from Toas itself, but Ermias was dead. Shewit placed her head on his chest and wept bitterly, wishing to all the world that there was a way she could bring him back. But short of dark magic, with its dubious untruthful results, she did not know of anything else that would be done.

She was free now. The only person she had ever loved was dead. This fuelled her anger until all she felt was hate for the world. A world that knew where she was headed yet had said nothing. They had contributed to her fattening process as if she was no more a living being as they were.

There was nothing for her to live for. She looked around her. All she saw was destruction and smoking heaps of ash. The Middle Kingdom would never leave her alone if she stayed within the vicinity. They would always come for her as far as she still had the title as the being of Balance and Chaos. She knew this for a certainty.

Shewit rose to her feet, her face turning into a mask of steel with tears still dripping from her eyes. She lifted Ermias's body into the air beside her. Then she closed her eyes. Conjuring in her mind the image of the place Ermias had charted for their retirement, she muttered a teleportation spell and vanished in a blinding flash of yellow light.

CHAPTER SIXTEEN

It was a lie

Piece Island

It Was A Lie

It is all a lie.

Eldana walked by the beach in slow steps. She exuded a thick aura of gloom. She tried to kick sand back into the waves lapping at the beach, but the patch of sand only went so far before falling back and re-joining its kin. The island was big enough on the side she walked on, spanning at least two kilometres. Some trees laid at the middle, an unspoken demarcation of the abode where she stayed and the other side. On the other side of the beach, the natives lived, people who her hostess did not have much to do with.

Eldana's eyes looked into the sea like she was searching for something. Her heart ached. It was two weeks since she heard what happened to her friends. Two weeks since she had found herself in a strange room, recuperating, and under the care of Shewit – the person she had come to Piece Island to see. And what she learned was beyond anything she ever expected.

Shewit was the only being of Balance and Chaos to escape the sacrifice apart from Eldana. She had absconded from her presumed destiny nine hundred years ago and had lived unobtrusively ever since; despite the enormity of her powers.

What Eldana heard from Shewit made her sick through every bone of her body. She could not comprehend the sheer craziness of it. Shewit, drew power from Toas, she was better at it than everyone else as a being of Balance and Chaos, that was her power. But she also drew power from every sacrificed being. Eldana did not understand at the beginning.

"But does that mean you are a god too? Eldana questioned her counterpart.

"God..well. Everything that we do not understand or is more superior to us is godlike, isn't it? What I saw back then, in the fight for my life with my beloved Ermias against Lull, was nothing else than the fact that *we are the gods*, Eldana."

Eldana was still puzzled.

She kept going." You see, Camin and Lowus are nothing else than Beings of Balance of chaos." Eldana couldn't believe her ears.

Chapter Sixteen

"They live for millennium because every time one of us is killed, they get the rest of the life expectancy of this being. In fact, every being of Balance and Chaos gets part of the life expectancy. As stronger one of us was, the more years in life you'll get. When we talk about the days of chaos, we only talk about the times many beings of Balance and Chaos existed and they fought about the country and more lifetime. "

"What happened to the rest of the beings of balance and chaos?" Eldana could already guess the answer.

"Well...they are all dead. It was a horrible fight but at the end, Camin and Lowus killed one by one. Till it was just them. The problem was, every 100 years another being is born. This being became another contester to their godlike status. So, they came up with a plan how to control them."

"The sacrifices," murmured Eldana while looking down on the ground.

"Exactly. It was a twofold win. One, the new beings of balance of chaos would never become a problem again, living in this fabricated heroic story that Camin and Lowus had created and two, they would make them the strongest fighters in Toas by letting them train with teachers from all parts of the country, just to kill them afterwards and drawing the most power out of their life."

"And because they do this for so long, no one knows what they look like anymore," she told Eldana.

Eldana just nodded in while looking to the ground. All seemed so surreal now. She still had unanswered questions.

"But what about the chaos? It is everywhere, even now. People die and go insane. That is not made up."

"That is the saddest part," Shewit answered her while looking at the wall. "You see, when people believe something, they will always find signs to prove it. It is a self-fulfilling prophecy. And Camin and Lowus support it by using their power..."

Eldana cried just a bit. "You mean to say, they kill them all..."

Shewit still looked at the wall. "Not all, but they support it, yeah! There, a volcano, here a bit of an earthquake, whispering lies

It Was A Lie

and deceiving messages around. People are easy. They don't need a lot to hate their neighbours.

It was just not real. Everything a lie, everything that she believed in, all a lie.

"Ah," she added. "Sinto, Lull, the carrier of the child, there are two…did you know that? Beings of Balance and Chaos..just not as strong. The mark of chaos is not complete on them. The mark just says how powerful you are. If it is fully developed, you have the power to plunge the world into chaos. They don't, so they do everything to adhere to the laws of Camin and Lowus to get their share of life expectancy. They have no chance, therefore just follow along. They always find a way to make a low level being of Balance and Chaos a carrier of a child, always." Shewit laughed bitterly.

Eldana just nodded. It made all sense now. An empty silence in her body numbed every emotion. She had the days to think through her whole life, all of it, just a lie. They did not talk about it again. Eldana was too much in shock about what really happened behind the curtains.

Shewit had proceeded to train and teach Eldana everything she knew. At first, Eldana had thrown herself fully into learning what Shewit had for her. She wanted to key into the special power so she could go rescue her friends, who she heard were under capture. That vigor soon declined into frustration, and then indifference. No matter how hard she tried, she did not get to learn the new power. Her mind was scattered.

One night, she had told Shewit that she felt she was ready enough and wanted to go after her friends.

"Your friends knew what they were getting into." Shewit had told her. "They were fully aware of the risks before getting into this quest with you. To leave now, you must have mastered your powers. Only then can you save your friends." The same calm fire that was in Shewit's eyes when they had first met was still there. The same awe when Shewit called her, "the flesh of my flesh."

Now, all she did was take occasional walks to the beach after

Chapter Sixteen

every lesson with Shewit. Somehow, the journey down to the seaside cushioned her mind, keeping it from falling totally apart. Sometimes, she sensed the presence of the Camin and Lowus afar off, unwilling to come closer.

Today, she sat close to the water, crossing her legs. The waves from the sea lapped at the under of her, but Eldana stared long and deep into the distance.

She missed her friends. So much. She shut her eyes, and with each breath delved deeper and deeper into her thoughts. Like in a dream, Eldana found pictures welling up into her mind. She did not know where it was, or how it appeared to her, but she looked on anyways. She was looking at a room, dark, but for shafts of light that came in through the little openings close to the roof. The roof itself was low, because just then a face came into the shaft of light, and its head was almost touching the roof.

Eldana gasped.

It was not just any face. It belonged to Hermon. Eldana almost screamed out to him. But she was frightened of shattering the vision. The little part of his face illumined by the shaft of light revealed the amount of suffering he had undergone. Eldana's heart burned for him. For Siem who she could not see. For Mikko and D'rmas. Tears slid down her face and dropped onto her lap.

Without warning, the scene changed. At first, Eldana had thought that the vision was over because for moments it was just darkness. Exactly as it was before she had seen this one. Then, suddenly she heard the sound of a voice, singing. The song was so soulful, its lyrics unintelligible because they were sung in another language. However, the voice and the language of singing had the halo of familiarity.

"Mother?" she whispered, the ghost of a smile on her face.

Eldana did not bother trying to cry out. She knew it would not help. Fraweyni would not hear her. Eldana had been surrounded by so much gloom and sourness lately that she felt choked. Unable to see past the murky darkness that enshrouded her. As she listened to Fraweyni's voice, losing herself into it, she began to feel a trickle of refreshment. Like cooling summer rain.

Suddenly, Eldana's eyes snapped open, and her mind was reinvigorated. There was purpose, there was intent, there was hope.

She got to her feet and stepped back from the edge of the water...

Thokk!

Just as an arrow stuck into the ground in front of her. Eldana turned alarmingly to her side. And saw a native of the island. A man, short, and thin. He nocked another arrow and shot. Eldana had to twist this time around to evade the shot. The man was good.

As the man reached for the quiver strapped to his hip, Eldana enclosed herself with a ball of air, and then knocked the man into the ground with air. She heard a shuffle behind her, and then turned to see a woman coming at her with an axe held high. Eldana took control of her mind, and ordered her to drop the axe, and return home. The level of hatred Eldana felt in the woman was enough to make her suck in air through her teeth and lean back in alarm. It was not the intensity of the hatred that baffled her most of all. It was the fact that the hatred was geared at her.

But why? Eldana asked herself. She had gone into the woman's mind too sharply and had come out almost in the same manner, and because of that had not had enough time to go through the woman's memories to determine the cause of the things she felt.

It occurred to Eldana that the man struggling at the beach floor was also a native.

There had to be a pattern here, she told herself.

She walked up to him and poked into his mind. She searched through his memories until she found what she was looking for. *Scheming heretics,* she thought when she was done with the man.

Sinto and Lord Taboon had spread propaganda concerning her through to the entire Toas. Using their skillfull tongues, they had subtly roused the people against her. And it did not require too much effort. The people were already weakened, and with already so much lost. They were battered by battles and natural

Chapter Sixteen

disasters. They could only overlook so much when they were fed information about the girl responsible for their plight. Information magically spread by birds singing atop the trees, or of winds whispering in the ears of people. She knew now that the natural disasters and the disastrous yields of crops, the nations battling nations and brother turning against brother were pretty much the gods throwing tantrums.

Eldana cast her eyes around the beach. Having made certain that no one else was present, she stood and walked hurriedly back to Shewit's. As she walked, she felt a psychic presence nudge at her mind.

One of the things Eldana had done during her stay with Shewit was to fortify her mental defenses. That way, she could keep intruders out of her head. But this presence nudged at her in a cryptic manner that she found familiar. She lowered her defenses, and she heard Shewit's voice.

Do not come back to the house, Shewit said. *Stay where you are, I am coming to get you.*

Eldana looked around. She had just left the beach. There were palm trees all around her, spaced equidistantly from each other. The surrounding did not offer a proper hiding spot. Eldana walked close to a palm tree and leaned on it. She stayed at a vantage point that offered her a wider sighting angle for any person coming into the beach.

Run towards the river, Shewit commanded.

Shortly after Shewit's instruction, Eldana heard the roar of a boat, growing louder by the moment. Eldana sprang from off the trunk of the palm tree and began to race towards the sea. Just then she spotted movement from the corner of her left eye. She turned to see a boat making its way towards her.

Hop in, Shewit said, having caught sight of Eldana's approaching figure.

Soon enough, Eldana saw the reason for the sudden trouble. Shewit had a company of boats, and ships on her tail. They were filled with roaring orcs, and Middle warriors, all on the ready.

It Was A Lie

Eldana even spotted a few boats that held what appeared to be the natives from the island, distinctive with their scanty dressing and the marks they made on their bodies. The sight of the pursuing company took Eldana down memory lane. This was exactly how she had lost her friends. But she brought herself back together instantly. This was no time to dally or fall into sulking, regret, or self-reprimanding. She increased her pace, and then manipulating the air around her, boosted herself up and onto Shewit's boat.

"Where did they come from?" Eldana asked, as soon as she came on board.

"The natives," Shewit said. "They called them in."

"Those damned people!" Eldana cussed. "I had to disarm two of them only moments ago. One was such a good shot with an arrow. He would have shot me."

Eldana heard a thud behind her and turned to see a spear sticking out from the boat.

"They are onto us," Eldana said. "Could you go any faster?"

Shewit chuckled. Teleporting would have been the easiest way out, but she could not teleport with Eldana. The gateway in the fabric of the universe could only be accessed one being of chaos and balance at a time, she knew. She had tried to go back for some others like her, but she had been unsuccessful, largely because of this.

"I did not have the time to stall just so I could pick the best boat. It was either get to you in haste or get to you in a really good boat. But if you are still bothered about the boat, then I can turn back, and get a good one?"

Eldana rolled her eyes and moved to the back of the boat.

"Keep your hands strong and firm." She told Shewit.

Shewit chuckled and tilted her head. Eldana stared into the ships giving chase, and she felt a surge of anger. For being separated from her friends. For her friends who were suffering such terrible, unknown tortures.

With one hand, Eldana caused a wave to erupt from the water, raising one of the ships high into the air, before dashing it down

Chapter Sixteen

on top of another.

"Are we just running, or do we have any place in mind?" Eldana turned, to ask Shewit.

"I have a place in mind," Shewit replied.

"Where?" Eldana nodded.

"We will just keep going forward," Shewit said.

Shewit kept the boat in place, while Eldana tossed, and slowed the boats as much as she could. Sometimes, she encountered counter magic from one of the boats. But ultimately, her will prevailed. If there were mages in the midst of the attacking ship, none of them were a match for a being of Balance and Chaos.

They had long since left Piece Island behind. And were speeding across the Ocean Wall. A smile was beginning to grow on Eldana's face. The gap between them and the pursuing ships had widened considerably. At the pace they were going, they would lose them entirely in an hour or two.

Suddenly, Eldana heard a grunt behind her. She turned. Shewit was standing, her hands gripping the boat's wheel, but Eldana noticed a weakness in her posture. A weakness that was growing rapidly and causing her to slouch.

"Are you okay, Shewit?" Eldana asked.

Shewit collapsed. She was dead before she even hit the floor. It was then that Eldana saw the shaft of an arrow, sticking out from Shewit's chest. it was an enchanted arrow from the presence Eldana felt around it. Her lips trembled when she saw a circle of blood was beginning to bloom from the point of entry. Eldana's lips began to tremble. Her eyes grew teary.

"No," she muttered. "No, no, no."

Just then a circle of space opened in the air before her. And something flew out of it, fast. Instinctively, Eldana rolled to the side, and with one guttural cry, sent a streak of flame into the portal. The portal vanished, and just at the same time, one of the ships behind her burst into flames. But Eldana was not there to see her latest score. She was by Shewit's body, crying, tears dropping on Shewit's still body, and mingling with the blood on her dress.

CHAPTER SEVENTEEN

One Last Time

Technocons

One Last Time

There were seven of them in a semicircle. Nobody moved. Swords drawn, faces grim.

She was here. The elite warriors of the Middle had her at last; the princess Eldana.

A vast expanse of vegetative land sentinelled by a small body of water, which separated it from the Mountains of Sinora at one side and spilled into the ocean at the other. The ships had not stopped after Shewit's death. Eldana never expected them to. She was the one they were after. On getting here, she had left Shewit's body and fled inland. But she was soon surrounded. Hemmed in by orcs, and soldiers. Lord Taboon, Sinto, and five other guards stood in front. This was a re-enactment of the fight in the clearing at Kleas. Only that this time, they came with far more manpower than they needed.

"Scared that I will beat you all to a pulp, huh?" she challenged.

Lord Taboon smiled.

"Impetuous girl." He said. "We are not taking any chances. Even if you do not have any more helpers."

"This is over, Eldana," Sinto said. There was impatience in his tone and stance.

"Yes," Eldana replied. "Yes, it is."

"Stop this, and give yourself over willingly. What you have done has been foolish, and selfish. And you know that. It does not have to end this way, but if I have to, I will fight you with everything I have."

Eldana smiled defiantly.

"You have done that before. All seven, or rather *the* seven of you. I would like to see you try again."

Lord Taboon and Sinto were well aware of the probability that Eldana's powers would have grown following the time succeeding their last fight.

"You do not have to go this way, Eldana," Sinto warned.

"I can go anyway I want, Sinto," Eldana said. "You of all people should know that. Because you had imbibed it in me."

Sinto smiled sadly. "I was wrong." He said.

Chapter Seventeen

"Enough of this, Eldana." Lord Taboon spit out. "The world is caving in on itself because of you. Hand yourself over peacefully."

Eldana laughed. "All lies!" She conjured a ball of flame, and then staring at Lord Taboon, tilted her head to the left, and smiled daringly.

Lord Taboon gave a grim smile of his own, and then clicked his fingers.

Suddenly, the men behind him broke ranks, and four figures were dragged out haphazardly and flung to the ground.

The ball of flame fizzled out. Eldana's eyes widened as she tried to make sense of the people kneeling before her.

They were all there. Looking battered, and spent, but they were there. Siem, Hermon, Mikko, and D'rmas.

Eldana gasped, and tears rolled from her eyes.

"Hand them over." She said, looking at Sinto. "Please."

"I cannot do that," Sinto said. "Only if you give yourself up."

"Do not do it! Eldana!" Siem yelled.

She got a boot to her mouth from Lord Taboon.

Eldana made one step forward, her fists bowled in anger. But Lord Taboon waved his finger at her, cautioning her to remain still.

"Their lives are in your hands. Whatever choice you make next is up to you," Lord Taboon said slowly.

Eldana stared at her friends. Their eyes were steely with resolve, but she felt the exact opposite. She was so helpless that all the vigor and strength housed in her moments ago, had evaporated.

"Just give up, Eldana," Sinto said soothingly.

Eldana shut her eyes. This was the end of it all. She knew that for certain. Many people had already been lost because of her. And she did not know how many more would die. She considered herself selfish enough to have let her friends go through all this pain for nothing. There was still something she could do to save their lives and the lives of everyone else remaining in the world. Maybe in 100 years the next one will stop this madness.

I can be selfless, just for this last time, she thought.

"Eldana, no," Hermon yelled as Eldana rose both her hands in surrender, and began to step forward...

Siem struggled against her bonds, glaring at Eldana.

"I am sorry," Eldana said. "But I cannot let any of you die for me."

Lord Taboon had a huge grin on his face, lopsided and revealing his browned teeth. Sinto breathed with relief. Suddenly, the air grew into a gale. Sinto cast his eyes up into the sky and saw storm clouds forming.

"Eldana..?" He warned.

"I am not doing anything," Eldana replied, her hands still up in the air.

Just then, a spear went through one of the men standing beside Lord Taboon. The spear was finely crafted from wood. Eldana found it strikingly familiar. Then, she stood taller, smiled, and put her hands down.

"What are you doing?" Lord Taboon asked, with the smile vanishing from his face.

"Showing you that I am not alone," Eldana replied.

Sinto cast his eyes around and was about to give orders to the men when a hail of spears dashed towards them. Sensing the whistling in the air, Eldana dove to the ground. Lord Taboon, Sinto, and the rest of the magical guard, the elite warriors of Middle Kingdom, dodged spears. The orcs, on the other hand, got hit by most of them.

From the surrounding green, there was a raucous cry as the elves of the Ciroc burst forth in their numbers. Within a minute, everything was chaos. Both in the skies and on the ground.

Meko slashed an orc in two and dashed to Eldana's side to help her cut the bonds restraining her friends.

"Old friend." Meko greeted, "Want some help?".

"How are you here?" Eldana asked. "All of you?"

"We decided it was time to change the world. You are our best shot at doing that, and so here we are."

Siem flicked her wrists as she got free of her bonds. Eldana

Chapter Seventeen

swooped her up in a hug.

"I missed you so much," Eldana told her.

"And you too," Siem replied.

"Erm, guys," Mikko called. "Excellent reunion, but we have a problem..."

Tabeli was heading their way with a company of orcs, warriors of the Middle, and Sandocs.

"Do you have any weapon for me?" Siem asked Eldana.

Eldana shrugged.

"Luckily, I do," Meko said, pulling out a bow and quiver full of demon arrows from thin air. She handed D'rmas a sword.

"Getting out of this one is going to be tough," D'rmas said. "Hermon should lead the charge against the orcs. They are no match for his fury. I will take the warriors of the Middle Kingdom, better to be killed by a warrior. Meko can handle the Sandocs."

"I am counting on that," Hermon said.

He knew what he had to do, and he did not care about what it cost any more. But before that, his eyes rested on Meko, who drew him in for a quick kiss. Hermon stood stunned afterwards before Meko tapped his back.

"Roar, my beast, roar," Meko whispered.

Whispering the ancient magical words, Hermon turned full berserker. His eyes were gleaming black orbs.

"Where is Mother?" Eldana asked Meko.

"She is up in the sky staving off Camin and Lowus' influence in the battle."

"Good," Mikko said. "Let us keep the gods out of this!"

"Don't call them gods," said Eldana with hate. "Call them Camin and Lowus," she spit out.

Mikko, confused about what to say just added an "OK" and went into battle.

With a yell from both sides, they crashed into each other. Hermon tore through the orcish fighters recklessly, sundering them limb by limb. He was a righteous incarnation of damage.

One Last Time

The battle raged on fiercely, and then by some forbidden magic of Lord Taboons, the slain soldiers began to rise again to rejoin and reswell the ranks of their enemy! Eldana stood still and watched helplessly as it seemed like the people fighting on her side were being overwhelmed. The sky was covered with menacing clouds. There were flashes of lightning from within, a testament to the war being waged within. Camin and Lowus had imposed themselves on Toas as gods and had remained that way because no one could challenge them, and through their exploitation were the only ones that provided peace to a kingdom that was plagued by chaos. However, they had remained unchallenged not because there was nobody to, but because there was no one interested in battling them. Today's battle proved that.

Fraweyni, daughter of Tessa, the first elf, was more than just an elf. The magic that radiated through her was of a time when the earth was still in its beginning form, before even Camin and Lowus ventured into the picture, drawn deep from the bowels of Toas as well. It was this ancient magic that she unleashed in battling the foreign gods. And would have long defeated them, if they were not still tethered to Toas by Eldana's inability to key into the magic reserved in the earth. Fraweyni believed in Eldana, but in the meantime, she focused her abilities on keeping Camin and Lowus occupied.

"Hello, girl." Eldana heard a voice say.

Quickly, she whipped around to face Lord Taboon. She heard footsteps behind her. She turned her face and spotted Sinto coming into place behind her. She smiled.

"So, this is it," she said.

"This is it," Sinto replied.

Eldana planned to infiltrate their minds. But she intended to distract them first. As she stretched out her hands to send gusts of wind towards them, she was knocked down by an energy wall. Eldana cried in pain as her sides pressed her into the earth. She flicked her eyes upwards and saw tendrils of black energy shooting forth from both Lord Taboon and Sinto's hands. Forbidden

Chapter Seventeen

magic. Eldana was assailed by despair. She had learned no defense against forbidden magic.

Eldana felt her strength waning. Like it was being sucked from her. Instinctively, she went into herself, digging up memories of the pleasant times she had once had. Times with her friends. The moments they had fought together. All the things they had been through. She thought of how privileged she was to have the friendship and support of the elves. And to see Shewit, before she was killed.

Just then, she heard Shewit's voice in her head. It was a memory.

"It is in you. The ability to draw energy from Toas and unleash chaos. You just have to surrender to it."

Eldana had not understood what Shewit had meant then. But she did now. She closed her eyes, and let herself go. She had been trying to draw from the well of power when all she had to do was dip into the well and be lost in it.

"Take me." She whispered, even as Lord Taboon's dark magic was all around her. Suddenly, something cracked inside her and opened. As a segment of her revealing itself; a segment that she had never known was there.

Eldana felt such a rush of energy that she screamed. A ball of radiant light exploded from her, throwing Lord Taboon and Sinto aside, and spreading through the entire land like a ripple.

Eldana lay there glowing like the sun. She was a conduit for the energy in the air. A giver and taker of life. She knew what she had to do – drawing from the depth of Toas.

With an ear-splitting shriek, the light drained from her, and back into the earth. It spread through the land like webs, growing, becoming larger, and swallowing the surrounding ground. And then suddenly, there was quiet. Eldana breathed. She felt weak. But she was still alive. Siem, Hermon, Mikko, D'rmas, and Meko rushed to her side.

"Eldana," Siem called. "Are you alright?"

Eldana gave a weak smile.

One Last Time

"Well done, child." Eldana heard a voice say. It sounded like Fraweyni's. But Eldana was not sure. She succumbed to her weakness and closed her eyes.

CHAPTER EIGHTEEN

Self-fulfilling Prophecy

Self-fulfilling Prophecy

Eldana, Siem, and Hermon had spent so much time running that they had forgotten what it felt like to live without having people on the lookout for them.

Immediately after the battle, Siem, Hermon, D'rmas, and Mikko, had lifted Eldana from off the ground and to a shelter that Fraweyni had caused to grow from the ground. There, Meko administered to her.

"Is she going to be okay?" Siem had asked, concern etched deeply on her face.

"Yes, I think so," Meko replied.

"You think so?" Hermon asked.

Meko looked up at him. "The kind of magic she has just worked has never been worked by anybody. Not even the being of Balance and Chaos that came before her. She just single-handedly blew out every enemy. And it's not just that."

"There's something else?" Siem asked.

"Yes. She is alive and the world is not crumbling to pieces."

"What're you saying?" Hermon asked.

"I'm saying that Eldana is not the cause of chaos in Toas. And if that comes to the people, there is no fear of gods anymore!"

"She told me not to call them like that. Gods. Rather Camin and Lowus" Mikko remembered.

Meko nodded.

"Everything will be different from now on, everything. Would you adhere to the rules if there was no appending chaos looming?" She left the rest to the thoughts of her listeners.

Sinto and Lord Taboon were nowhere to be found. Somehow, they had slinked off the battlefield. The orcs were a race whose love for battle was almost unbridled. Even after Lord Taboon, who had enlisted them, was gone from the battlefield; even when it was clear that theirs was a losing battle, they fought on. The Elvsoc faced them with strength and skill, decimating their numbers until the orcs were forced to flee for their lives.

Eldana woke back up in the shelter with all her friends surrounding her. She told them the stories she heard from Shewit,

Chapter Eighteen

crumbling their reality even more. The friends stared at each other in silence.

"What next" Siem tried to break the silence. "I am not sure," Eldana started "If you knew, everything is fabricated, would you stick to it? The chaos, the hundred-year cycles? Everything? I mean Camin and Lowus had killed so many just to keep their lie alive. What would you do if you figured that out?"

"I would go berserker." Hermon added, looking desperately around for a smile of his double pun. He could not find one. Just a serious answer from D'rmas.

"I would." He seemed to strike a nerve with this answer, everyone around him started to nod.

Fraweyni came to visit Eldana and found the group in deep thoughts in front of her.

"We go back to Ciroc."

"We've had enough interaction with the rest of the world." She added. "I need peace. The elves need peace. Our place is right where we started. In the forests of Ciroc."

"I will miss you," Eldana told her.

Fraweyni smiled.

"You and your friends are no strangers to the elves. For a fact, our songs will carry your names. You all are always welcome amongst us. Always."

"What happened to Camin and Lowus?" Eldana looked at Fraweyni trying to read what she was thinking. But this time, she did not let her in.

"Well, they vanished after your surge of power." It will be a lot harder to kill you now." Fraweyni smiled.

Eldana had a thousand more questions, but she left it there. There where gone, for now.

Hermon and Meko excused themselves from the rest of the company to go have a heart to heart about what they felt for each other. Siem had seen them leave and could not help the smile that appeared on her face. She had never expected that her friend would fall in love with an elf. And a very beautiful one at that.

Strong, and excellent.

They will make a good pair, Siem thought. Until the elves left, and Eldana and her friends found themselves back on a track to the Middle Kingdom.

"I could not believe that you would leave her, and come with us," Siem said looking at Hermon.

"You're talking to me?" Hermon asked.

"Of course, I'm talking to you," Siem replied. "Wasn't I staring at you?"

Hermon shifted in discomfort.

"I don't know who you're talking about," Hermon denied.

"Oh, please, Hermon," Eldana moaned. "Quit with the denial. It's not a bad thing if you're in love with an elf."

D'rmas and Mikko roared with laughter. Hermon's cheeks grew a bit red.

"But seriously," Eldana said. "I'm happy for you, for you both."

"You know," Mikko said, sitting up and a mischievous grin growing on his face, "I'm wondering what kind of babies the…"

"Mikko!" Eldana, Siem, and Hermon chorused.

The last time they had been to the Middle, they had run out of it with their hearts in their mouths. The King had just tried to apprehend Eldana. Lord Taboon had tried to capture Siem and Mikko, and Hermon had acquired D'rmas services through a brawl. As they went through the gates, they felt absurdly different.

The walls of the city were chipped in places. There were scorch marks on walls and buildings. Some of the buildings they had passed were in shambles. Some of them were undergoing repairs.

"A battle happened here," Eldana noticed.

"Yeah," D'rmas said. "Following the wave of destruction, I'll say that the battle had ranged well through these gates and into the inner sector. But some parts of the structures are still standing, so my verdict is that the enemy soldiers beat the kingdom into a retreat. The kingdom soldiers were fighting furiously in return. They had been beaten into the inner sector where they made their

Chapter Eighteen

last defense and succeeded in repelling the forces."

"Excellent analysis," Mikko chipped in as soon as D'rmas was done. "I should call you for a contribution to this text I plan on writing on war schemes and strategies."

D'rmas chuckled. "I'm always at your service, dear friend," he said.

"You know what?" Hermon asked all of a sudden.

"Techle," Eldana said.

"How did you know that was what was in my mind?' Hermon asked, looking surprised.

"You forget that our dear friend has become a telepath," Mikko replied.

"Come on, no," Eldana protested. "I did not need to read his mind. I was thinking about the same thing too. Techle helped us before we left here. Wow, it feels like years ago."

"Exactly," Siem said. "Perhaps after our intended tour of telling the people the truth, and our visit to the king, we'll go find him?"

"Well said," D'rmas replied. "There's no place I would rather spend the night."

The welcome that the group of friends received was unprecedented. As their caravan cruised through the streets, people began to pour out from the buildings to come meet them. Eldana was nothing short of surprised. She had not expected that the people of Middle Kingdom would accept her again, much less celebrate her. Not after she had abandoned her perceived duty at the time and run away; in the process releasing chaos into the world and exposing them to it. But here she was. Here they all were. Being called heroes. Their names took up most of the chants and songs that the people released. She did not understand it. The only explanation would be that the news is spreading like wildfire that there will be no more looming chaos every one-hundred years. Only two very old beings of Balance and Chaos that need to be fought. She had expected fear in the people, but everyone seemed released and happy.

Mikko whistled.

"I was not expecting this at all," he said.

"Same here," Siem said, as she looked across the crowd with wide eyes.

Their excitement was so lavish, that she could not help but have the funny thought that the people would not have enough excitement for themselves after this. The people dubbed Eldana and her friends the heroes and saviors of Toas.

"Do you hear that?" Hermon yelled so he could be heard above the roar of praise.

"What?" Eldana questioned.

"They are calling us heroes," Hermon replied.

"Are we not?" Eldana asked. "We just risked everything to make the whole of Toas better."

"We are even lucky we are getting a heroes' welcome," Siem said. "More often than not, good deeds go unappreciated."

"Aye." D'rmas agreed. "But I think I know why this one is this appreciated."

"Why?" Mikko asked.

"It is not just because you delivered the world from the maws of chaos, Eldana. I mean they are happy about that, sure… But it is not just that. That there," he pointed towards a man in the crowd, "is why most of them are happy."

Eldana, Siem, Hermon, and Mikko all looked in the direction D'rmas was pointing. And they saw him. There was no way you could miss a display of fire, even in a crowd like this. The man was holding a club, which he frequently set on fire, and after a few seconds proceeded to quench the fire.

"Meko was right," Hermon whispered.

The man caught their eyes and began to wave happily at them.

"Yeah, she was," Siem affirmed. "People are less obedient. There feel free again."

"How?" Eldana asked. "I do not understand."

"You did it, Eldana," Hermon said.

"Me?" she asked.

"Yes, you," he said. "You not only saved Toas from being torn

Chapter Eighteen

apart, but you also did more than that..."

"That is a good thing, right?" Eldana asked.

"That," D'rmas said, "only time will tell. For now, let us bask in this heroic welcome. We have deserved every bit of it."

"Well said, my friend," Mikko said. "Well said."

Eldana tried to step off the caravan, but Siem gripped her by the arm.

"What do you think you are doing?" Siem asked, giving Eldana a quizzical look.

"What does it look like I am doing? Joining the crowd of course," Eldana replied.

"Bad idea," Hermon chipped in.

"Look at the crowd, Eldana," Siem instructed. "Take a look at their level of excitement. I can very well tell you right now that this caravan is the only thing keeping us from being torn apart, and you want to leave its safety and deliver yourself into their hands?"

"But I thought they are celebrating us and our accomplishments?" Eldana asked.

"Of course they are, but the moment you get down there, everyone will want to touch you, the being of Balance and Chaos, the savior of the entirety of Toas, the liberator of the people, the one who made everyone free. Do you think you can handle it when all these hands are trying to touch you, to feel you, and cannot get enough?"

"Oh," Eldana said, her eyes widening in comprehension, "I see what you are saying."

"Please even staying at the edges are dangerous. Thankfully, none of them is wild enough to try to jump at us," Siem said.

Eldana laughed.

"There's also the fact where you do not want to miss out on the feast Techle has probably prepared for us," Hermon said.

"That's true," Eldana exclaimed. "There's no way he does not know we are in the Middle Kingdom already. It is just a day ride from here with Mikkos help."

"And if Techle is still the Techle we knew," Mikko said, "then you can only imagine what he has got brewing."

They all laughed.

"Let's just come out from this tour in one piece," Eldana said. "You know, just to make sure that everything is okay. And after all, now we have all the time in the world to enjoy the pleasures that Techle's tavern has to offer."

They all laughed and nodded their heads in unison, and turned to show their acknowledgment of the crowd's songs and chants, by waving, nodding, and smiling.

Henok sat in his chair, looking heavily morose. He had been this way since he had gotten a report that Lord Taboon and Sinto were nowhere to be found after their attack on the being of Balance and Chaos. Their bodies had not been found, so he still harbored the hope that they would return soon. With their absence, a new royal adviser could now present himself, hoping that now, the King could finally give him his ear.

Henok had gone from one of the most revered kings in Toas to one of the weakest within a very short time. He had not dealt with the stigma that dogged him from his loss to Tonar, a kingdom filled with humans, and now this. His most powerful magicians had been defeated by a band of friends, and elves. But this was not the most disconcerting news. The roar he could hear outside his palace. Oh, how his subjects hated him now...

Just a few minutes ago, a guard had come in to tell him that Eldana and her friends were in the kingdom. Henok had stared at the guard until the royal adviser had to dismiss him from the king's presence.

His people were giving Eldana and her friends, who remained nothing but a band of fugitives to Henok, a hero's welcome! Not only because she had single-handedly restored peace to the kingdom, but because in doing that she had given everyone the idea

Chapter Eighteen

that they can live a life in full freedom. Now, what power he still held as the king stood, by every indication, to be threatened. If it was not already.

The royal adviser, an elderly short man with a full, but neatly trimmed gray beard and a bald head, had been able to discern from the king's reactions what the problem was, and he had just the solution for it. His major problem was getting Henok to give him his listening ear. The royal adviser had always known since Henok's childhood that he was going to be occupying his position only as a figurehead for a very long time. In fact, till his death. He had been relegated to be background, unmentioned in the history books, unknown by the kingdom's poets. But this here was fate smiling down at him! He had never expected that a day would come when the magicians the king had taken to getting advice from would no longer be available! That day was here, and he was no slouch.

Even if the magicians were to suddenly and unexpectedly turn up, he would make sure that the king saw his worth as an adviser. He did not even mind being added to the magicians as a third person...

"My King," the adviser said softly, controlling his tone of voice so as not to sound anything but utterly subservient.

Henok looked at him, and then looked away.

The adviser swallowed. The king had not given him any indication to go on or to stop. He would take the silence to mean he could go on.

"Things may not look too bright at the moment, but you can make them be my lord," he stared at the king and continued. "It looks like your throne may have lost its power because it was not able to provide the peace which your ancestors have been providing before you..."

"If you intend to rub my failures in my face, you should know that you are succeeding, and that does not bode well for you," Henok told the adviser.

"I'm sorry, my king," the adviser replied hurriedly with a deep bow, "but that was never my intent. Not even the slightest bit. I intended to show you that though it may seem like you have been stripped of your powers and authority, it is not the case!"

"No one fears authority anymore," Henok said. "They can easily band together and challenge the throne. It is going to be easy for insurrections to rise among the people. How long before someone thinks he is better than the king on the throne and steps forward to challenge me?"

The royal adviser smiled inwardly. He had the perfect solution to that.

"My King?" he called, "Are these same people, not your people?" he asked.

Henok sat up a bit and looked more intently at the adviser.

"They are," he replied.

"And do they not reside within your walls and under your very own protection?"

"They do."

"They are subjects of yours, my king. And a few new magic tricks and a new hero are not going to stop that. They are still going to go back to their beds to sleep, counting on you for their protection. They will still move about, work, have lives, raise families, counting on you to watch their backs. You make the policies. You make the decrees. It is also your job as a king to act on foresight. And like you have rightly said, my king, you have seen this newfound power going to chaos."

Henok's face had gone from grave to a mask of brightness within seconds. The more he listened to the adviser talk, the more he understood what he had to do, and the clearer the plan in his head formed.

"What is your name?" he asked.

"Yoel," the adviser replied.

The king stared at him for a long while.

"Yoel," he called finally. "What do you suggest I should do?"

Yoel smiled and bowed. Inward, he felt a flush of satisfaction. "Call out for one-hundred years of war. Everyone for himself.

Chapter Eighteen

They want to be free? Show them what it means to be free, my king. Show them, that real freedom means chaos."

Everything had gone according to plan. Within a few minutes, he had warmed his way into the king's graces.

"I now know what I must do," Henok said.

The next day, the king stood imperiously on the portico to his palace and watched the gathering of people before him. They were all here to answer his summons. He watched the reactions on their faces as the guard beside him read out the new decree.

"No one can be trusted; We know that Camin and Lowus are trying to bring chaos everywhere. Therefore, we must always be on the lookout for the next enemy. Even within our own walls. From this day onwards, King Henok is calling a total war against every other race in Toas for the next hundred years. Until a new being of Balance and Chaos is born that can shift the balance in our favour. Until then, don't trust anyone, besides the guards of the Middle Kingdom. We will control every corner, so that you are safe," the guard read out loud.

But the people were not having any of it.

It did not take long for the crowd to turn into a riotous mob, shaking their angered fists at the king, and hurling all sorts of words. Henok simply watched with a calm demeanour as everything played out, and then when the first bolt of lightning came his way. He was not the greatest magician but growing up as a king had taught him important spells that made him strong. He quickly muttered one of them and formed a shield around him. But that was not the least of it. Whoever had just used his freedom, had given the right to the guards to intervene.

Without wasting time, Henok flicked his hand in the air, giving the order for the Warriors to quell the dispute. With their amazing speed, the warriors descended on the protesting mob with batons. The majority of the crowd took to their heels, throwing lightning bolts or fire carelessly into the air with the intent of warding off the warriors that were too fast to be seen. Without proper training, it was easy for the warriors to fight them off.

Self-fulfilling Prophecy

Henok stood and watched the crowd disperse and heaved with pride.

I am your king, he thought, *and I will always remain so.*

In the coming weeks, the streets resembled a war zone as people tried to fight back against the King's oppressive rule, but were being met with force. Anyone who so much as uttered a spell or was not obedient was apprehended by the warriors. But he did not stop there. Henok sent letters to every corner of Toas declaring war on everyone.

Smoke was rising from the kingdom. Chaos was far from over and war was looming on the horizon and at the moment, the Middle Kingdom was its home.

Mussie Haile

Final Note

Thank you for coming on this adventure with me. I hope that my words have brought you some excitement, joy; maybe even a thrill! This is my first published book, and I would love to hear your thoughts and comments on the exploits of Eldana, Siem, Hermon, Mikko and D'rmas. If you like, please consider leaving a review at the marketplace you bought this edition from!

Looking forward to sharing more tales with you~

Mussie Haile is a digital consultant turned fantasy writer with a love for a good twist. An avid traveller, Mussie can't help but snag a fantasy book off any shelf he passes, be it in English or German. Chaos Destiny is his first published novel, a creation to remind readers that imagination is the most powerful and fundamental tool mankind has to shape reality. He currently lives in Frankfurt with several other pieces in the works.

Lightning Source UK Ltd.
Milton Keynes UK
UKHW040658020621
384769UK00001B/2

9 783949 553011